King of Spades

The Gregg Press Western Fiction Series
Priscilla Oaks, Editor

King of Spades
Frederick Manfred

with a new introduction
by the author

Volume 4 of The Buckskin Man Tales

Gregg Press
A division of G. K. Hall & Co., Boston, 1980

With the exception of the Introduction, this is a complete photographic reprint of a work first published in New York by Trident Press in 1966. The trim size of the original hardcover edition was 5½ by 8¼ inches.

Text copyright © 1966 by Frederick Feikema Manfred.
Reprinted by arrangement with the author's agent.
Introduction copyright © 1980 by Frederick Feikema Manfred.

Frontmatter design by Barbara Anderson.

Printed on permanent/durable acid-free paper and bound in the United States of America.

Republished in 1980 by Gregg Press, A Division of G.K. Hall & Co., 70 Lincoln St., Boston, Massachusetts 02111.

First Printing, November, 1980

Library of Congress Cataloging in Publication Data
Manfred, Frederick Feikema, 1912-
King of spades.

(The Gregg Press Western fiction series)
Reprint of the ed. published by Trident Press, New York, which was issued as no. 4 of the author's The Buckskin man tales.
I. Title. II. Series: Gregg Press Western fiction series.
[PZ3.M313705Ki 1980] [PS3525.A52233] 813'.5'4
ISBN 0-8398-2592-7   79-26382

Introduction

I'VE OFTEN ASKED MYSELF: WHAT TWO PEOPLE ARE MOST APT TO make good friends, make true soul mates? What two individuals have basic natures that are in near-perfect correspondence with each other? What two human spheres come closest to overlapping? Is it husband and wife? Father and daughter? Mother and son? Father and son? Mother and daughter? Brother and sister? Twins, dissimilar and identical? Cousins? Grandparents and grandchildren? Where, in all those different relationships, is one most apt to find those two people who naturally and spontaneously understand each other at all times? Who discover and have true human bonding?

When I was a little boy, I remember asking my father and mother on our way over to visit a neighbor or a relative, "Do they have a little boy there I can play with? Who's like me?" When we went to a Fourth of July picnic, or attended church in another town, or if I was sent to a new country school, the first thing I did was to look around for a possible chum.

I wanted a confidant to whom I could tell all. I wanted to share all my secrets. I wanted a chum with whom I might do great things: explore the creek in our pasture, build an airplane, breed centaurs, read special books, win baseball games.

Later on, as I became older, as I grew up through puberty and young manhood, I began to look for that perfect friend in a girl. I hoped to find in her that perfect complementary mate, in which the man in me would love the woman in her, while the woman in me would love the man in her. And vice versa. By doubling our eyes we would quadruple our insights into The Darks and magnify our ecstasies into The Lights.

Of course, all too sadly over the years, I've come to doubt that I will ever be able to spell out the magic of a true human bonding, describe its origins and its workings, its fusings and its shapings. And I'm also afraid that no such thing as a true bonding has ever existed. It is probably impossible for any one person to know another person completely. We are all such very complicated flesh prisms, with our endless facets and sides, and whether it's love or friendship, we can light up only so many of each other's facets, those facets that our light falls on. The facets on the far side of another person's prism remain dark for us. Yet it is in the very nature of the human being that we continue to hope, to dream, to fantasize, that we will somehow light up all the facets of our chum-friend-love, and that our chum-friend-love's light will illuminate all our facets. If we are in love, we strive to light up the dark side of the moon of the other person. We truly hope, for a season, that we can reach a full understanding of each other.

Lacking that perfect friend, we sometimes settle for the next best thing. We cultivate a circle of friends. We need more than one friend to light up all our facets at one time or another. When a novelist uses someone he knows as a model for a character, he never really gets him or her down exactly as they are, but has to fill in the back side of the moon of that person with imaginative material taken from his general knowledge of human beings to create the fully rounded character.

The search for the perfect soul mate has been going on for a long long time. There are the quests of David and Jonathan, Paris and Helen, Achilles and Patrocles, Pericles and Aspasia, Tristan and Iseult, Lancelot and Guenevere, Romeo and Juliet, Aucassin and Nicollette, Abelard and Heloise, Frankie and Johnnie. The search for the perfect love is one of the dominant themes in all literature.

I've pursued this lovely problem in every one of my books, sometimes quite openly, sometimes indirectly. Taking just the five books in *The Buckskin Tales* we find, *among other things*, the following:

In *Conquering Horse* (1959; Gregg Press edition, 1980), the hero No Name is told by his mother's brother, Moon Dreamer (who was in love with his mother), that his vision, interpreted, contains two instructions: one, he must capture a white stallion, and two, he must kill his beloved father.

In *Lord Grizzly* (1954; Gregg Press edition, 1980), old Hugh Glass takes a liking to Jim and Fitz, mostly because they remind him of his own two boys back home in Pennsylvania. Further, Hugh Glass marries Bending Reed, an Indian woman, mostly because her heyoka or contrary behavior reminds him, subconsciously, of his former she-rip of a wife Maggie. And there is also his and the white race's addiction in wanting to touch strange skin, either to love it or destroy it, or both.

In *Scarlet Plume* (1964; Gregg Press edition, 1980), comely Judith Raveling, a woman from a white civilization, one of the first bloomer girls, falls in love with Scarlet Plume, a man from a Stone Age culture, a Yankton Dakota Sioux, when he tries to help return her to the white settlements. Scarlet Plume's uncle, Whitebone, has already forced himself upon her, and other Indian men have already ravished her, yet some powerful man-woman draw was at work between them. It was more than just the usual animal attraction between man and woman, more even than the white woman's fascination with colored skin. It was as if both suddenly found themselves caught up in an archetypal kind of bonding.

In *Riders of Judgment* (1957; Gregg Press edition, 1980), a dark tie exists between the cousins Cain, Harry, Dale, and Rosemary. There is also the counsel that a father had better kill his first-born son if he wants peace in his home. In cattle country times some strange ties were permitted. There weren't many women around and men were often gone for months at a time during cattle drives.

It was while I was looking for some material in the back files of the 1890 *Review* in Rock Rapids, Iowa, which I later used in the novel *Eden Prarie* (1968), that I came across the germ idea for *King of Spades* (1966; Gregg Press edition, 1980). In a local news column there was an item about a man of the town who wanted it to be known he'd spotted a fellow hanging around his home. He announced that he was taking measures to see that it was stopped. He said he'd also instructed his wife and young son to keep the doors locked.

Reading on through the files I found further references to the story. The man had bought a gun and said that the next time he caught the intruder hanging around his home he was going to shoot him.

Finally I came upon the news item telling about the murder. Some of the phrasing in the account was eye-catching: "He threatened to murder me unless I acknowledged I had been a bad woman"; "He repeatedly and publicly accused his wife of infidelity and charged her with relations with men, when nothing less than madness could imagine grounds for suspicion"; "Strong men could not gaze upon it without a thrill of horror!" "The ball entered her right breast just below the nipple"; "The monster emptied another chamber of the weapon."

It struck me, as I read all that, that the intruder was in the man's own home. The older the son became the more tormented the father became. The mother-wife was lavishing too much of her affection upon their son and not enough on him.

I had already explored, in part, the tie that existed between my father and a brother in the novel *This Is the Year* (1900; Gregg Press edition, 1979). And I knew that I would explore it further along with the tie that existed between my mother and myself in a later book. (Which I did in the rume *Green Earth* [1977].) I pretty much understood what had been going on in my own family with my father and mother and with my five brothers, but the bizarre murder-and-suicide that took place in Rock Rapids, Iowa, threw me back on my heels. What in God's name had gone on there back in that previous century?

I began to speculate as follows. In those days it was not unusual for a mature girl of 13 or 14 to get married. There were few women around in frontier towns, and the moment a girl was nubile she was subjected to pressure to get married. Let's suppose she had a baby boy at 14. By the time the boy was fully grown at 17 she would still be only 31. If she wore a long dress it would hide possible varicose veins on her legs and if she put on flour makeup she could pass for a woman of 24. If the young man let his beard grow he could pass for 23.

Suppose further that when the boy was seven, something climactic happened in the family, so that father, mother, and son were suddenly ejected into the world, with none of the three knowing where the other two had gone. Suppose still further that some ten years later mother and son ran into each other in some far Western city. More than likely, after all that time, they would not recognize each other. The boy would look like any other cowboy come to town to raise hijinks and the mother would resemble any other housewife window shopping along the boardwalk. Meeting on the streets of Cheyenne, would they be drawn towards each other in the ordinary natural man-and-woman way, or would they be drawn towards each other because of a one-time mother-baby tie? Would a subconscious kind of bonding be at work in them?

When I'd gotten that far in my speculations, I remembered that two other writers had been there, Sophocles and Shakespeare. What to do. I was sure that some critic somewhere would accuse me of arrogance to think that I could tackle the oedipal problem on equal grounds with them. And someone was bound to argue that I was ruining the genre of the Western by unnaturally thrusting a Freudian concept into it.

I had read Sophocles (in translation) a number of times and I had read Shakespeare many times. I had learned that Sophocles had actually borrowed the oedipal idea for his *Oedipus Rex* from Egypt. And I knew that Shakespeare had borrowed his idea for *Hamlet* from the Danes. In both instances the original germ had not come from the author's place. It came to me that I probably had more right to use the oedipal problem than did either Sophocles and Shakespeare. A love affair between mother and son was more apt to happen in our West than in either Sophocles' time or in Shakespeare's time. As was mentioned above, the women were few and far between. Also the frontier was in a continual turmoil as a new people tried to come to grips with a strange and sometimes hostile environment about which they knew little or nothing. And the few people going west were an outlandish lot. Anything was possible.

After pondering it all some more, and with a bow of apology to the ghosts of Sophocles and Shakespeare, I decided to go ahead. I'd add a new aspect to the story. In *Oedipus Rex* the father Laius is mistakenly killed by the son Oedipus offstage and we never get to see the father. In *Hamlet* the son Hamlet doesn't kill the father, the uncle does it for him, but we still get a glimpse of the father when Hamlet sees his father's ghost on the platform of the castle at Elsinore. In my novel I'd have the father Magnus King survive the attempt on his life and I'd let him come in on the scene at the end. I was curious to know what the father Magnus King would think about all this mother-son stuff. It might give still another sounding of that hoary old tabu, one that might be of value to help us understand the profound ties inside a nuclear family.

And, while I was at it, I'd try to deepen the problem so that at the end we wouldn't just ask what the father thought about all that unnatural affection, but we'd ask, what did the stallions think of it? For me the word "stallion" is a much richer word than the word "father." "When a son's blood is finally spilled, which mother weeps most? The stallions."

What helped drive the whole thing home, as I was writing the book, was the sudden appearance of the young maiden Erden Aldridge, whose Indian name was Blue Swallow, rising like a jinn from the end of my pen. She came all unbidden. She was not in the original plan for the book. But once I saw her, I knew she belonged. She helped set up the tragedy of the Ransom-Katherine tie. Erden was the girl Ransom should have married, not Katherine. Erden should have been his true love, his romantic ideal. And interestingly enough, with Erden coming in on the scene, she also helped tie the whole quintology, the Buckskin Man Tales, together. Carrying Ransom's baby, she disappears, going farther west.

By having the father Magnus King come in on the scene when Ransom is about to be hanged for shooting his wife Katherine, Ransom hears from his father that his wife was also his mother. It convinces Ransom all the more that life was not worth living. So he kicks the barrel out from under his feet and so hangs himself.

(The reader will notice that not once did I use the word "incest." That's because I didn't think "incest" to begin with. I was first of all interested in the problem of human bonding.)

And what did the stallion Magnus King think about all that mother-son bonding? That's the mystery I tried to unravel.

All through the writing of *King of Spades* it was as if I were possessed by a Better Writer, as if some kind of Holy Hand were guiding my hand. This was especially true after Erden appeared on the scene. Nights when I went to bed I couldn't wait until morning to find out more about what was happening.

Ransom and Erden. Every night I looked forward to breakfast and work.

Frederick Manfred
Roundwind
Luverne, Minnesota

To Alan C. Collins,
trusted friend

The Creator made the people—
come and see them.
                    —*Indian Prayer*

Program

of

The B U C K S K I N   M A N   Tales

Contents

PART ONE

When a son's blood is finally spilled, which mother weeps most? The old mother Europa? The new mother America? Katherine? Erden?

The first great miracle to appear on earth was the emergence of love in the mother lizard. And the first great bewilderment to appear on earth was the emergence of taboo: having learned of love from his mother, a son was not to return this love to his mother.

Caught in flesh and caught by flesh.

Even so, O Lord, how marvelous are all Thy fleshly works.

Magnus King

1

His mother was of good lineage. She was born in 1812 at the ancestral seat of the Worthingtons in Wessex, England. Her father the old earl lamented she wasn't a boy, but he loved her nonetheless as his firstborn and named her Henrietta after a favorite uncle.

The Worthington name went far back into hoary Anglo-Saxon times. It belonged to a family of Old Frisians known as the Wurthinga or the Woartelinga, meaning "root people" or "people of the root." The Wurthinga, who originally lived in Fryslân on the Continent, were once great sailors and shipwrights. The Wurthinga helped transport the Angles and Saxons and Jutes to England and in the end elected to settle with their tribal cousins in the new land.

Henrietta Worthington's childhood was a happy one. She was given all the advantages of being born into an English first family: the best private tutors, travel abroad, the best friends, leisure. She was loved by her mother and adored by her father. Because of her charm and sturdy intelligence, she became much more the favorite of her family than her younger brother George.

When she reached the age of eighteen, blond, sweetly mannered, attractive despite her rather large feet, her father the old earl announced that he had made plans to marry her to the son of a duke, a neighbor.

Then the trouble started.

Henrietta had fallen in love with another young man. Quietly, but with some show of force, she told her father that she did not much care for the neighbor's son, that she had already made up her mind she would marry an Alan King, a dark-haired lad living in Wiltshire.

"Pah! Who's this Alan King you speak of? An orphan. With no expectation."

"Alan can hardly help that, Father. His parents died during the plague."

"Too bad the plague didn't carry him off too."

"Mother approves of him."

"Pah! Your mother is a goose. With no sense in such matters."

"Father."

"Appears to me this Alan King of yours might have poor blood too. In more ways than one. Weak."

"Please, Father."

"No matter. I have already made the arrangements with our neighbor. It is too late for your Alan."

Alan King was far from weak. It was true Alan tended to be mild-mannered, but he could also be a winning man. One day Alan talked Henrietta into eloping with him. Her mother helped him arrange it.

The old earl was shocked, outraged, and immediately cut

Henrietta off without a cent. He announced that forthwith the title of earl as well as all the Worthington holdings would be handed down to her younger brother George. George was a wild one and up until then the old earl had always had misgivings about him.

A year later the old earl had a stroke and died, and George Worthington took over. Henrietta's mother died soon after.

Brother George issued orders that Henrietta should never again be allowed to set foot on a Worthington acre. George had his own reasons for hating Henrietta and her husband Alan King.

Not too much was known about Alan King, except that his father had once dug ditches and his mother had taken in washing. Even his given name, Alan, was of obscure origin.

Alan remembered his father talking about the better days when the Kings sat above the salt. There was the story, often told at family gatherings, that the name King had come from their once having had some kind of connection with the royal family. Another story often told was that the Kings had got their name from an ancestor who had played the part of the king in a village pageant. In any case, Alan's father, who sometimes wore a monocle, betrayed more than usual pride in the name King.

Alan was incensed when both Henrietta's father and her brother had cut her off because of him.

"We will go to America," Alan announced. "We will make our fortune there. Because I'll never give your drunken brother a chance to lord it over us. Gloat."

Henrietta was willing. She was of a mind to show her family they had made a mistake about her darling Alan.

Meantime the Honorable Elizabeth Dulcie, an aunt, assured Henrietta that should George die young and without issue, and there was a good chance he might as he was very reckless, she would take it upon herself to make sure that the earldom and the estate should pass on to any man child born to Henrietta.

A promoter named Newhall told Alan about a place in Iowa, America. It was a town called Weldon.

"For just a hundred pounds, or four hundred dollars American money, you can be settled up on eighty acres of land, with a house, yoke of oxen, horse, cow, twelve sheep, poultry, pig, wagon, plow, harrow, seed, and thirty weeks' provisions—enough to live on until you've raised a small crop."

Alan raised a dark brow. "This has been done?"

"Often. And if you happen to have a wife who doesn't get homesick, I can see no reason why, with ordinary luck, and blessed with patience and perseverance, you shouldn't prosper equal to your utmost expectation."

"It has been done then."

"You have the hundred pounds?"

"My wife can get it from her aunt."

"Take it and go. Because at Weldon you'll be living with the very pick and flower of British immigrants."

Alan and Henrietta went. Early in 1834.

Weldon turned out to be a rawboned place. There were, however, several British homes of some elegance some miles out in the country.

Alan and Henrietta built a house on a hill beside a stream.

They plowed and planted. They lived frugally. They sweated and dreamed through the summer months.

But the crop of wheat they reaped that first fall was so bad they couldn't sell it for hog feed. Luckily game was plentiful in the area and they managed to survive through Christmas.

They sold out for a pittance and in January moved to town.

Just in time. Magnus was born a week later, in 1835. Henrietta was in severe labor for three days, almost died. She was badly torn inside, and was never to have another child.

Alan King was known to have little or no knack with

either animals or farm machinery and when he looked for work the next spring he was laughed at. The people in Weldon felt that if a man couldn't make a go of it farming, under ideal conditions, he couldn't make a go of it at anything else either.

Nor could Alan get on with his new neighbors in America. He could not unbend from what he thought he had once represented in England. He persisted in wearing his Oxford hat and his bright linens and his fashionably cut weskit. Local Weldonites considered him to be a conceited ass and for final proof of it pointed to the monocle he wore on any and all state occasions.

Alan was good at cards. But when he tried to work up a little friendly game in either of the two saloons in town, the House of Commons or the House of Lords, the callow swells hooted him out of doors.

Particularly galling was the fact that many of the Britishers around Weldon had money to burn. They were in most cases second sons of titled English families who had been given a liberal remittance to go to America and to stay there. Some drove a four-in-hand, with a man winding the horn. All of them went fox hunting, and played polo, and called each other "a capital fellow," "a brick," "an honest chum." Bitterness ate into Alan.

At last Alan came to the point where he was flat broke. When he tried to raise yet another fiver at one of the saloons, as well as a snit of beer, the elegant drunks spoke of him over their cups as having a great amount of cheek.

Henrietta decided to swallow her Worthington pride, and took in washing. They lived as beggars in a one-room shanty on the south edge of Weldon. Because they had fallen so low from high estate they were all the more despised by the townspeople.

Somehow Henrietta managed it that at least her husband could put in a good appearance, and Alan continued to wear his Oxford hat and his bright linens and his fashionably cut weskit. The more bowed and bent she became, the more Alan strutted and paraded.

One of little Magnus' first memories had to do with how his father Alan, after fixing a monocle to his eye, would tell about the illustrious Kings back in the old country, about how someday they would yet give Uncle George Worthington his comeuppance.

Little Magnus was nine when his father Alan went duck hunting, alone. It had rained; Alan fell into a slough; it snowed. Alan was chilled to the marrow. In three days Alan King drowned in his own phlegm.

Henrietta wrote her aunt the Honorable Elizabeth Dulcie in England to tell of Alan's death. There was no reply.

Henrietta continued to take in washing. She refused several offers to run the households of the richer British around. Lowly as it might seem to take in washing, at least it gave her independence. Both she and Magnus lived for the day when certain blessed news should come from England.

Henrietta taught Magnus everything she knew about the Worthingtons. She instructed Magnus on how to behave as an earl, should that day ever come. She told Magnus where the ancestral seat was; where certain Worthington cousins lived, one family in Friston in Sussex and the other in Frizinghall in Yorkshire. On occasion she even had Magnus practice wearing a monocle, and how he should swing a cane, and how to doff his hat and bow to the ladies, all in the manner of his father Alan. The Worthington line as well as the King line was in his blood and he was to keep it up. "Always remember that you're truly one of the bloods of England."

One day the Weldon town bully bumped Magnus off the boardwalk.

Magnus understood instantly what was afoot. He drew himself up to his full boyish height. "Don't you know who I am?"

"Sure I knows who you are."

Magnus fixed an imaginary monocle to his right eye. "I'm the grandson of an earl and my name is King."

"You're the son of a loafer and your name is bull."

"Get off the sidewalk, you clumsy ox, and let me pass."

The bully beat him up.

When Magnus told his mother about it, she complimented him. "Now you begin to sound like my father, your grandfather the earl. A true king after all."

As time went on, Henrietta became more and more dispirited and lonely. Gradually she lost all pleasure in life. Even the times when young Magnus washed her feet, something he liked to do because he loved the slim length of her foot, meant little or nothing to her.

Magnus grew up to be a handsome fellow like his father: dark wavy hair, dark darting eyes, a long nose, full lips, a strong chin. From the Worthington side of the family he inherited double-jointed fingers. He could wrap his hand around the head of his walking stick like a monkey might grab hold of a knot.

Magnus had gone to deliver some laundry one day, when the postmaster spotted him and handed him a black-edged letter. The letter was from the Honorable Elizabeth Dulcie in England and it was addressed to his mother.

Magnus ran home with it all excited. At last the great news had come.

Henrietta read it; and collapsed at her ironing board.

"Mother!"

Henrietta stared at the calluses in the palms of her hands with low-dotted eyes.

"Mother?"

"Uncle George is dead."

"Oh." Pause. "Isn't that good?"

"The letter says Uncle George went through the whole estate before he passed on. He died a poor man. And without issue. There is nothing left. It is all gone."

"All of it?"

"All of it. Except the title."

"Ha. Without the fortune the title means nothing. Not in America anyway."

"I know."

Three days later Henrietta died in her sleep. Mercifully.

Magnus was just nineteen. Magnus had never worked a day in his life. Without his mother to support him Magnus was no better than a common tramp. Of no use to anyone. Excess baggage in America.

Luckily the mayor of Weldon was a decent fellow and took pity on Magnus. He knew there was some good in Magnus, that Magnus in his leisure time had read widely and well and could write presentable letters. He suggested Magnus become notary public as well as town correspondent for a Chicago newspaper.

Magnus gave it some thought, finally decided it was not for him.

Magnus had observed that the local doctor had more freedom than any other citizen in town. A doctor could be an agnostic, even a town knocker, and it was usually overlooked. A doctor was generally allowed his crank notions in return for his ability to heal rotted limbs and spoiled brains.

Magnus decided that if he had to work for a living it would be as a doctor.

Magnus sold what few possessions his mother had left him and was off for Chicago. He enrolled at Rush Medical College.

To his considerable surprise, Magnus discovered that learning came easy for him. He had a retentive memory, a graphic imagination, quick analytic ability. He outstripped everyone in his class.

Magnus soon became impatient with the slower minds around him. He even presumed to question his professors. His naturally imperious manner grated his classmates as well as the medical faculty.

Magnus saw that prescribing castor oil when constipated,

and cinnamon when loose, and calomel when in doubt was not true medicine, not even as Hippocrates had conceived it to be. He decided to investigate Indian medicine and country folklore remedies. He managed to get hold of a microscope and began his own exploring. In short, Magnus graduated from Rush with a reputation for being a brilliant malcontent.

At about the same time Magnus' love life underwent an abrupt change. Magnus had been totally devoted to his mother and as long as she had been alive had never dated a girl. Now suddenly he began to notice the girls, everywhere. It was as if he was out to make up for lost time. Let a body be wearing a dress and he was out to court it: waitresses, streetwalkers, older women, whores on the line. He even jumped the color line several times. His appetite was insatiable.

The last months at Rush it happened that Magnus had to change boardinghouses. He landed with an elderly spinster named Agnes Rodman. Miss Rodman had room for but one person and it was soon apparent that she expected the boarder to become a member of the family.

Miss Rodman was originally from England, and that Magnus liked. However, Miss Rodman had just reached the critical age, change of life, and she was as different in behavior and attitude from his own mother as a woman could possibly be.

Eventually Agnes Rodman would have been intolerable to live with if it hadn't been for her niece Katherine Rodman.

Katherine was an orphan. Her father was Miss Agnes' brother, and he and his wife had died in a pestilence. Aunt Agnes generally called her niece Kitty.

Kitty fooled one. Kitty looked seventeen but actually was thirteen. She was well developed physically, was precocious emotionally and mentally. Though shortish she had the long stride of the taller person. She had a large foot like Magnus' own mother, and curly light brown hair, and sensual lips cut hauntingly at the corners. Most arresting of all were her eyes. They were dissimilar, the left eye green and the right eye brown.

While Aunt Agnes prattled on her end of the table about such things as that horseback exercise was not proper for a girl, that a hot mustard bath was good for the hidden sin, that a pregnancy could help to terminate an insanity, that a marriage was one of the best tonics for the female psyche, Magnus and Kitty were exchanging warm looks at their end of the table.

Kitty had been a recent problem to her aunt. A nine-year-old boy named Dennis had been their previous boarder. Kitty had on occasion been left alone with Dennis. Dennis was shy. To get him to play with her, Kitty had enticed him with candy. Dennis loved jelly beans and finally became quite friendly. Soon Kitty took to hiding the jelly beans so he would have to reach across her body to get at them. Or look under her. Then she took to hiding the jelly beans on her person: inside her folded knee, in her clapped-shut armpit. She got him to explore her everywhere, until he explored that part of her where, tickling, it made her dizzy. Aunt Agnes caught them at it. Dennis was promptly shipped off to distant kin.

Aunt Agnes trusted Magnus on first sight. His quietly superior airs, the way he swung his walking stick, inspired respect.

Soon Aunt Agnes was busy spinning webs and fantasies around Magnus, mostly in behalf of Kitty, but also in part for herself. The thought went through Aunt Agnes' mind that in a few years, just as the young Dr. Magnus King should have established a fine practice in Chicago, Kitty would need a husband. Marrying Kitty off to Magnus would mend both sides of the fence at the same time—a girl who threatened to go wild would be safely harnessed in marriage, while she herself, Agnes Rodman, would for the rest of her natural life have free doctoring.

Aunt Agnes made up her mind that it wasn't going to be her fault if Kitty didn't make the perfect doctor's wife. Aunt Agnes got out several old doctor books and began to bend Kitty's ear knowingly about such matters as depraved appetites and prenatal impressions, about how tight lacing could be ruinous to the female innards, and the like.

Aunt Agnes also presumed to instruct Kitty on the nature of love. "At first one is attracted to the opposite sex because of animal passion, my dear. Plainly just that. Yet you must always bear in mind that out of this animal passion can rise a mighty and pure love, which is to the other what the delicate flower is to the unsightly tuber."

Aunt Agnes even told Kitty what her husband could expect of her in the way of submission, and how much of this she was to allow her husband. "Two or three indulgences a week may be looked upon as within the proper bounds of propriety."

The truth was Kitty was already miles ahead of Aunt Agnes.

The second week of Magnus' stay, on a Sunday, Kitty managed to sniffle convincingly enough so that Aunt Agnes permitted her to stay home from church. Magnus himself never went to church. Around eleven o'clock in the morning, with Aunt Agnes gone, Kitty knocked on Magnus' door to ask him if he didn't have some kind of cough syrup around for her cold. All Kitty had on was a wrapper.

Magnus did have something for her cold. He mixed together some brandy, honey, and the extract of horehound. He gave her several spoonfuls.

Magnus was terribly taken by Kitty. As he watched her lick her quaintly cut sensuous lips upon taking the cough medicine, he longed to kiss her. It came upon him suddenly that he had missed out on the whole business of a boy being in love with a girl, especially during puberty. What was more lovely to look upon, and to touch, than a just-budded girl of thirteen? Magnus began to regret his exploits with cheap women.

Kitty noted a small tintype on his desk. She leaned forward to have a look at it, and as she did so, she let slide a sidewise silverish look at him. Her green eye in particular smoked with it. She asked who the tintype was a picture of.

"My grandfather Worthington."

"He looks distinguished."

"He was. He was an earl."

"In England?"

"Yes."

She noted an emblem in one corner. "And this?"

"Our family coat of arms."

Kitty bent for a closer look, and so managed it that her wrapper parted, revealing a lovely apricot of a breast.

Magnus could not resist a touch. And while Aunt Agnes partook of the blessed sacrament, the Lord's Supper, in church, Magnus and Kitty partook of the blessed temptation, fornication, in bed.

Neither regretted it. Both fell immediately and deeply in love. The delicate flower of pure passion replaced all former philandering on his part and sneaky fun on her part.

She had no maidenhead. But Magnus was sure that no grown man had touched her there before. She had probably picked it apart herself.

Kitty told him she was in a family way the same day Magnus graduated from medical school. It was early spring. They were even more in love than ever. He had heard of an excellent opening in a new town on the frontier, Sioux City, in western Iowa, and felt he should make his start there, where he could begin with a clean slate on all counts. She agreed it would be a good place to go to, and suggested they elope.

Two days later, on a Sunday morning, they took the stage to Dubuque. From there they took the steamboat down the

Mississippi to St. Louis, then back up the Missouri to Sioux City.

The captain on the first boat married them. The year was 1856. Magnus was twenty-one; Kitty was thirteen.

They lived in a back room, behind his office on Main Street in Sioux City.

The first months they were as happy as a couple of sleek minks. He couldn't get enough of her. He had to be touching her all the time, nipping her Indian-dented lips, shaping her apricot breasts, stroking her long slim feet. They made love most every night.

He loved the scent of her. She'd found some puccoons growing wild on the prairies, and falling in love with them, decided she had to have their aroma around all year round. So she squeezed their orange blossoms until she got a drop of juice, then boiled their roots down to their essence, and made of the combination her personal perfume.

About the fourth month of her term she began to initiate the lovemaking. This inflamed Magnus all the more. That he should be having fleshly communion with her thirteen-year-old body at same time that he loved her as the mother of their coming child made for madness. A master passion took hold of him. It seemed to release him at last from the lethargy of his sad youth.

They were lying together in their back room after the noon meal. He was about to go out on call.

"Aunt Agnes would never approve of this." He kissed her on the nape of her neck. "Never, never." He suckled the lobe of her ear.

Kitty opened herself under him to hold him the more. "Why not?"

"Indulging your husband's base passions in the middle of your term . . . why, Kitten, you know that can be injurious to the child. Besides, it's a sin to enjoy it."

"Can it?"

Magnus went on imitating dear Aunt Agnes' manner. "I am minded of what your own dear mother told me. My sister-in-law. That it put the stamp of a passional nature in you. Yes, Kitty, you were a honeypot when you were already a year old."

Kitty laughed. She kissed him. "My husband. My dear daddy husband." She kissed him again. "I can't help it, dear daddy husband, but I never did think that tubers were unsightly."

"And I never did think that a mighty and a pure love was but a delicate flower." Magnus sighed luxuriously. "I like all of it. As well as the fruit of it."

They were desperately poor at first. In pay for his services they accepted chickens, cabbages, roasting ears of corn, pigs. They robbed prairie nests of part of their eggs for their breakfasts. They grubbed out wild onions to flavor their soups. Often they accepted the invitations of the nearby Yankton Indians to eat with them.

On Sunday they sometimes played a game.

Magnus would ask, "Lovey, what suit shall I wear today?"

"Oh, I don't know. Suit yourself."

"Ha. Shall it be the gray suit? Or shall it be the powder-blue suit? Or shall it be the tux? Or, perhaps, shall it be the black?"

"Oh, dear, what a dilemma."

"Yes."

"For a change, why don't you just make it the black?"

Laughing, with all the gesture of a prince standing before a kingly wardrobe that ran the length of a castle bedroom, Magnus would reach into the closet and take out the only suit he had, the black.

That summer little Sioux City became the jumping-off place for western expeditions to the Dakotas. Steamboats brought supplies up the Missouri to the wharves of their town, where they were transferred to mule-drawn wagons. Magnus and Kitty watched many a mule train head out on the new Military Road, toward Yankton, despite wallows of gumbo mud.

Also that summer great lunging stagecoaches began to roll in from the East, across the prairies from Fort Dodge, bringing new citizens, special supplies, and ever-fattening bags of mail.

By the end of July, Sioux City had a population of four hundred souls and more than ninety buildings. Articles of incorporation were drawn up. A man named Weare opened a bank. The first issues of the Sioux City *Eagle*, named after Chief War Eagle, rolled off the presses. Boardwalks appeared on both sides of the main thoroughfare. Finally Sioux City was named the county seat of Woodbury County.

No one ever talked much about the fact that wolves still made nightly forays into the residential sections of town, sometimes even chasing down Main Street; or that Smutty Bear and his Yankton bunch occasionally beat the war drum all night long, still vainly hoping to scare off the whites; or that winters could be bone-cracking cold, so that the Missouri froze over; or that great prairie pumas still prowled in the tan bluffs north of town, sometimes yowling their great agony calls all night long.

Magnus and Kitty became part of the establishment. The ladies, not knowing Kitty's true age, accepted her as one of their own. The hard-cash men about town, observing that Dr. Magnus had tight-lipped class about him, also accepted him as one of their own.

What finally won Kitty over to her new surroundings was not a white woman, but a Yankton Indian mother named Gooseberry June. It was the way Gooseberry June came to their back door, calling softly, "Gooseberries, gooseberries.

Eat very good now. Before the goose comes down and gobbles." .

That November, Kitty began to have difficulty. The baby was due in January.

"I can't seem to eat much, Magnus."

"Why not?"

"I don't have room for it."

Magnus comforted her. He bathed her feet with warm water just as he'd done for his mother Henrietta.

"And the child kicks so."

"Sure sign it's a true King."

"The least little kick and it's like he tears me all loose inside."

"Sure sign it's going to be a boy."

"If that's the way boys behave I want nothing but girls after this."

"Don't worry, Kitten. It's nature's way."

"Sometimes I wish I was just a kitten. Just a plain old alley cat."

When alone in his office, Magnus searched through his medical books to learn more about childbirth. He found all too little. And there was nothing about having them when too young.

Kitty meantime began to fall into deep silences.

"Your Aunt Agnes hasn't poisoned your mind now?" he asked, arching a brow at her.

"But it does hurt."

"It's natural that it should hurt. And good."

"I want what's unnatural then."

"Don't let's be childish."

"So now it's childish, is it, my daddy husband?"

Magnus shivered. He said, "God has a plan in all this."

"Ha."

"Pain actually can be a very good thing."

"How so?"

"Because it makes things worthwhile."

"Ha."

"The human race would go downhill if it weren't braced by pain now and then."

"Lucky you that you're a man and have only the fun of it."

"Woman, gladly would I take on the pain of it for you if I could."

"That I believe."

"Besides, this pain you feel is really a key which is slowly but surely opening the door to the sleeping mother in you. To that greater love of which only a woman is capable."

"Ha. How would you know?"

"I've watched mothers come to bloom in the lying-in wards in Chicago."

"There had better be some reward for all this."

Magnus reset his black bow tie. "The more pain the more love."

"Sweet talk by the daddy man."

"Look at the she-turtle. She lays her eggs in the warm sand with hardly any thought as to what she is doing. With the result she never returns to see her young."

"Lucky she."

"Yes, but she sings no songs." Magnus fixed Kitty with a judging look. "That girl Katherine Rodman I used to know, who was so bold and daring in love, where is she now?"

Kitty's eyes glittered for a moment with a flash of hate, then slid off to one side.

Magnus went on. "Nature demands a payment for all she gives."

"And here I thought all of us were trying to ward off trouble, pain, as much as we possibly could. Be happy."

"Every new beginning is always accompanied by a great chorus of anguish. Since the very emergence of time even."

"There ain't no justice then."

"Pain is one of the unavoidable conditions of existence."

"I hate God then, if that's the way He meant it to be."

Magnus kept calm. He was sure they had been right to marry. Many a Southern girl had borne children successfully at thirteen. Besides, he and Kitty were in love. That excused everything. Pain was the negative to the positive of love.

She cried out wildly in her sleep one night. She clawed her way into his arms.

Upon examination they found a considerable discharge of blood. He had to bite down on himself to keep up his professional air.

He helped her clean up. He gave her a sedative.

Later, he retired to the office side of the building and searched through his books once more.

Reading, brooding, he was suddenly struck by a thought. Julius Caesar had been brought into the world by way of a surgical operation through the walls of the abdomen and uterus. Aha. Why not remove their own child a couple of months early by surgery? That would relieve the child-mother of pressure. The danger of infection made it terribly risky, but if it wasn't done, both mother and child might die.

He had a casual talk with a pig farmer one day. He had observed that the body of a hog and the body of a human being were very much alike.

"Ever cut open a sow to save the young?"

"Once." The farmer, a heavy-bellied man, spat a little brown snake of tobacco juice to one side.

"What happened?"

"Saved 'em all. 'Twas the only thing to do."

"And the sow?"

"She got over it. Pigs like to lay in the mud and that healed her."

"Tell me about it."

"Wal, 'twarn't much, really. Not if you've spayed dogs. It's in the same place."

"Weren't you afraid of corruption afterward?"

"Sure. But I cut my fingernails good and washed my hands in lye-soap water good. 'Course I was neat about my cut. I washed the needle and thread in lye-soap water too. Then sewed it up neat and gentle. A tailor couldn't've done it better."

Magnus reset his bow tie to square it with his white collar. "By the Lord."

It got worse each night.

Once Kitty woke up screaming, her long fingernails at his eyes in the dark. "Magnus, I'm going to die! I'm tearing inside. I really am!"

He willed his fingers steady as he scratched a match alive and lit the lamp. He gave her a nerve pill. He held her child belly in his arms.

The child inside kicked, kicked.

He thought: "If there was only some way to just slip it out."

She asked for Gooseberry June. "I want her to be with me when the time comes."

Magnus thought this a good idea.

Gooseberry June came the very next day.

Finally on the sixth of December, early in the evening, a full month before term, the baby made up its mind to come out on its own.

Kitty screamed and screamed in regular pulsations. Her face turned the color of leached ashes. Her eyes rolled off cockeyed. Her head bent back until her light-brown hair lay over her heels.

Magnus went in and examined her. There was no longer any need to pretend she had anything to hide from him. The baby had moved down against the pelvis. But there was little or no dilation.

Her dissimilar eyes revealed different females. An old dark mother squirmed in final agony in her brown eye; a fuzzy-legged maiden danced a dance of picnics in her green eye.

Gooseberry June sat beside the bed. She soothed Kitty with moving broad brown hands. An ancient expression took hold in Gooseberry June's face.

Kitty shrieked. There was a gush of sudden cherry blood. Kitty fainted away.

Magnus snapped open his medical kit. Swiftly he laid out scalpel and curette. He got needle and thread ready. He had already boiled everything in lye water. He pared back his nails; scrubbed his hands thoroughly. He set white pans within reach to catch the blood. He set a bottle of rye handy. He soaped up Kitty's distended blue child belly and washed it gently.

Then, calling on his memory of medical-college days when he'd dissected a cadaver, he chose a certain spot on her belly, between her navel and her hairy pudendum, held her bouncing body steady a moment, and then, with a single swift sweep of his hand, touched the knife to her. Her belly parted like old silk giving way. Her uterus emerged like a swimmer popping to the surface after a deep dive.

Gooseberry June's brown face turned as pale as faded grass. "Akk! The father has done a thing against the gods!" Then Gooseberry June clapped hand to mouth and rushed outside. Gooseberry June ran erratically toward her tepee in the wooded ravine.

Again Magnus' hand swept across her belly. This time her uterus parted. It popped open like a ripe milkweed pod. A transparent sack of incredible sleekness came to view. Inside it slept a folded baby. The baby lay still a moment; then, as if on signal, in one joyous jerk, it straightened out for a good stretch.

Magnus nicked the transparent sack with his knife.

In an instant the baby's face was free and there was a sudden loud bawl.

"Ahh!"

Magnus separated child from mother; laid the child to one side; covered it partially with a silk blanket.

The child let go another loud bawl.

"Now to save the mother."

It had all happened so suddenly Kitty's belly still hadn't had time to bleed much. Magnus quick stitched up the uterus, tight, with stout line thread. He didn't bother to catch the trickle of blood gathering in the cavity where the child had lain. Instead he took hold of the edges of her abdomen and stitched them together, also tight. The incision formed a long funny puckered wound, like the wrinkled smile of a pumpkin jack-o'-lantern.

The baby gave yet another sudden bawl. It kicked, kicked.

Kitty awoke. "Is that the baby already?"

"Yes, my lovey."

"It's here then already?"

"Yes, my kitten."

"Is it the boy you wanted, my daddy husband?"

"Yes, my child."

Kitty sighed a great sigh. "It was all of a sudden so easy."

What Magnus didn't tell her was that in opening her uterus he was afraid he might have spayed her. Accidentally.

Well, no matter. It was probably for the best anyway. She was too small to have babies. She would be that way even after she became of age.

Mother and child did well.

Kitty was wildly, deliriously happy with her baby boy.

The baby was baptized Alan Rodman King, after Magnus' father and after her family name.

Within the year, Magnus saved up enough to build them a white clapboard cottage on the west end of town, well out in the open in a meadow of grass. For a path to their door Magnus cut a swath through the meadow.

Some of the neighbors wondered if it wasn't dangerous living that far out.

Kitty thought it was all right. What helped was that Gooseberry June had come back, after a time, to see the miracle of the Knife Child. When Gooseberry June saw that the Knife Child was favored by the gods after all, she and her band maintained close ties with the King family.

About the second year both Kitty and Magnus fell naturally into calling their boy Roddy. Kitty seemed to like Roddy better than Alan, and Magnus, to humor her, went along with it. They could always go back to calling the boy Alan after he had grown up.

The third year Kitty finally guessed it. That she was never going to have another baby. When she finally got Magnus to admit the possibility of it, a change came over her. The sweet minerals of youth slowly leached out of her. A resigned look settled in her eyes. At sixteen she already looked like she might be twenty-two.

The sparkle of fire slowly winked out a little in Magnus too. He knew they should have at least been glad they could make love without having to worry about another pregnancy. Both could now relax and let themselves go, be as wanton as they wished. But they weren't glad. The bloom was off, the petals had fallen, and too bad.

The cottage had only one bedroom. Roddy for the first few years slept in a cradle at the foot of their bed. When he outgrew the cradle, and was given a cot, he continued to sleep in the same room with them. Several times Magnus wondered out loud if they shouldn't add another bedroom for the boy. When Kitty didn't say one way or another, and Roddy piped up saying he didn't want to sleep anywhere else, it was left as it was.

When Roddy was four, Magnus became uneasily aware

that the boy might be hearing them while they made occasional love. The boy had an uncanny way of inventing
excuses for getting into bed with them just as Magnus was of
a mind to touch Kitty. The boy seemed to sense the exact
moment when his father was inclined to make love.

It made Kitty giggle when Roddy would call out, "Mom,
can I come over and warm up with you and Dad?" just as
Magnus' hand had slipped under her nightgown. And it
exasperated Magnus to note that Kitty seemed to respond
more to his lovemaking at such times.

Usually Kitty helped Magnus chide the boy, told Roddy
he was all right where he was.

The boy's sudden calling out usually cooled off Magnus'
ardor. He couldn't go on. And so nothing happened.

The next day Magnus went about his work feeling abused
and Kitty went about her duties pouting.

Once the boy awoke them by crawling in with them
without asking.

"Hey! What goes on here?" Magnus cried, sitting up.

"Nothing," Roddy said brightly. "I was just lonesome a
little. So I thought maybe Mom'd let me have some titty."

Magnus crackled all over, he was suddenly so mad.
"What!" In the moonlit bedroom Magnus was almost sure
he'd spotted a fleeting malicious look in the boy's eyes. "Get
out! Right now!"

"Dad."

"Get in your own bed. Right now. By the Lord!"

Kitty said, "He don't mean any harm."

"Roddy!" Magnus roared.

"All right, Dad."

The next day when alone with Kitty, Magnus asked, "Do
you still have milk for that boy?"

"A little."

"Remarkable."

"Sometimes I think the reason he wants to keep on is

because I didn't really have enough of a nipple for him when he was a baby. At thirteen it isn't big enough."

"Nonsense."

"Well, I think so."

"Does the boy seem to enjoy the suckling?"

"I guess so."

"Or is it that he is merely hungry?"

"Both."

"Hum."

When Roddy was five, he began to ask questions about their family, about the Kings and where they came from.

Kitty told him what she knew. For particulars about the Worthington family, Kitty sent him to Magnus.

Magnus was loath to talk much about it.

But Roddy pressed him with so many questions about Uncle George Worthington that Magnus at last got out the old family picture of Uncle George, and wound up hanging it in the sitting room. Finally, Magnus even showed Roddy how to fix a monocle to his right eye.

"Then we could be kings someday, couldn't we, Dad? When our ship comes in?"

"We are Kings."

"I mean not our name. I mean for real."

"And I mean that too."

Kitty interposed. "Daddy, now, no riddles. The boy is only a boy."

Magnus thought: "Yes. A boy. That time of life when you can still believe that your ship will come in someday."

Roddy started school at six.

By this time Roddy had the long nose and the liberal lips of his father, including even the long slope under the nose. Roddy had green eyes, with brown flecks in them, and his brown hair was sun-touched with gold over the brow.

When Kitty would no longer let him have occasional titty, Roddy took to suckling the corner of his pillow, inside his pillowcase. When Kitty pinned the pillowcase shut on each change of bedclothes, Roddy switched to sucking the silk trim of his blue blanket. When she teased him about it, he gave her a very hurt look, then in boy rage rushed outdoors.

But Roddy was always soon over his sulks. In an hour he would be back, whistling, green eyes aglow with some new private game, mountain man and Indians, riverboat captains and pirates, boyish explorings. A couple of times he came back with a spray of puccoons, along with an offer to wash her feet if she was tired and would like it.

During Roddy's seventh and eighth years, Magnus was off to the wars to help put down the rebellion. The two years put the boy even more in the mother's corner.

Roddy took to jumping off high places, a cutbank along the road, the riverbank above the Missouri, even the roof of their cottage.

Seeing this, Magnus made him a swing.

Roddy became very fond of the swing. Sometimes Roddy pumped himself so high in it, above the fulcrum of the tree limb to which the swing was attached, that the ropes fell slack at the end of each swing, and he came down with a jerk, almost breaking the rhythm.

One day Roddy made himself a sack swing. He'd seen a picture of one in his reading book. He filled a sack with straw, tied it to a hemp rope which in turn he looped over the elbow of a huge cottonwood. He used the limb of a nearby ash for the jumping-off place.

The first time off the ash limb was the biggest thing ever. He stood teetering on the limb, just barely managing to hold onto a tit corner of the sack with his little fist, eyes as big as magnifying glasses, knees shaky—when of a sudden, daring it, crying out, "Here goes nothing!" he leaped.

And just made it. He'd just barely got his knees clamped tight onto the butt of the sack. When he passed the earth below, grass stubble rasped a pair of holes into the seat of his pants. Gollies!

Magnus gradually became taciturn, distant. He scowled a lot. He kept his experiences, good or bad, happy or sad, to himself. His liberal lips gradually thinned. His temples hollowed. His dark eyes limned over with what looked like smoke. Sometimes he appeared to be looking out of a pair of fire-scarred window frames.

Kitty on her part began to slam things, the irons on the kitchen range, the tops to storage barrels, the doors of the house. The worst habit of all was the way she slammed the lids out in the privy. When Magnus complained she'd cracked one of the lids, she only shrugged, told him to go get a carpenter and fix it.

Kitty also more and more began to let Roddy have his own way, especially when Magnus wasn't around. When Roddy wanted to go swimming in the Missouri with the boys, she let him, even though she knew Magnus would be violently opposed to it, and even though she herself would live in terror until he returned safely.

At noon when Magnus was out on call, Roddy sometimes tried to slide into his father's armchair. Kitty thought this was going too far and always instantly ordered him to go sit in his own place. When Roddy persisted she at last had to threaten him.

One noon Magnus caught Roddy defying his mother. She had asked Roddy to get some radishes from the garden and he had flatly refused.

Kitty turned red. "Do you want a stinger in the face?"

"You wouldn't dare, Ma."

At that Magnus picked up his walking stick and snapped it once. "Well, by the Lord! Now you get!"

Roddy got.

Afterward, cooling off, Magnus said, "Son, your mother is your mother. Respect her. You hear?"

"You sometimes fight with her."

"Not as my mother I don't."

"Aw, heck, Dad."

"You hear?"

"Oh, all right."

A carpenter showed up one day and began hammering on the window frames.

Kitty went out to ask what was up.

The carpenter told her he'd been ordered by Magnus to put on some shutters.

Kitty told the carpenter to wait until she herself had talked to Magnus about it.

Magnus went into a rage that night when she told him she'd asked the carpenter to wait.

"But, Magnus, shutters will spoil the look of our little cottage."

"Right now I'm not so worried about the looks of our cottage. I'm more worried about your safety."

"My safety? Isn't it safe living out here any more?"

"Some night when I'm not around somebody's going to take a potshot at you sitting in a lighted window like that."

"A potshot?"

"Yes."

"But why me?"

"I don't know. But somebody will."

"Who?"

"Somebody."

"Gooseberry June and her friends?"

"I've heard about a fellow hanging around here."

"You have?"

"Slinking around. Trying to catch you undressing."

Kitty gasped. "Why, you better tell Herman Bell about this then. He's our night watchman."

"Herman Bell's too dumb to catch anybody. Specially this fellow."

Until then Kitty had sometimes been antagonistic just to be a little devilish about it, as a part of the usual bristling between man and wife. But now instead she began to worry about him.

Going to bed one night, Magnus took a newspaper and scattered its various pages over the floor, around their bed, around Roddy's bed.

"Whatever is that for?" Kitty asked.

"Try walking across them once."

"No."

Magnus turned to Roddy. "You try it."

Roddy did. The newspaper rustled noisily.

Magnus grimaced, satisfied. "A newspaper scattered on the floor is the best burglar alarm ever made."

The next morning, after Magnus left for work and Roddy left for school, Kitty went back to bed to mull things over.

As she lay amidst her pillows, looking idly at the ceiling, holding her breasts in her cupped hands, she was startled to see a black widow spider come raveling down the air from the ceiling, on a thread of its own making. The black widow spider was a big one; and, Kitty knew, a deadly one. Magnus had lost a patient to a black widow spider's bite only the past summer.

Kitty knew she should bounce up and get the fly swatter and kill it. Once in the house it was bound sometime or other to bite her, and if not her, someone else in the family. Magnus would know what to do right off if he got bit and so would be able to save himself. But not she herself. Or Roddy.

The black widow spider came leasing and releasing down,

until finally it was within a few feet of her. It was about the size of a black horse bean. The red mark on the underside of its abdomen had the shape of an hourglass.

The thought went through her mind that she should let it bite her. One venomous bite, and all problems would be solved.

Then another thought went through her. The black widow spider represented sin. It represented the sin of doing it at thirteen with her daddy husband. The sin had finally come back to haunt her and was descending to settle on her breast and kill her.

She watched it come laxing and relaxing down, farther and farther, to within a few inches of her. In another moment it would land exactly on the point of her left breast, right over her heart.

It swept to within an inch of her.

With a sudden cry, Kitty slid out from under it, slipping out of the bedsheets and landing on the floor.

The black widow spider, startled, hairy legs all ascramble, began climbing up the thread again, taking in the thread without a hitch as it rose.

Kitty quick got to her feet. She picked up two of Magnus' fat doctor books and caught the black widow spider between them, mashing it.

2

Magnus stepped off the boat onto the wiggly wharf. He had just arrived from Omaha downriver where he'd gone to order some medical supplies.

Automatically his hand checked to see if he still had his revolver with him. He did. It lay warm in his right-hand pocket.

He wondered what he'd find at home this time. He was

dead sure somebody'd been lurking around the house before he'd left on his trip. And now he was even more sure that a man was spying on Kitty, perhaps even right then larking around with Kitty inside the house while she thought Magnus safely out of town.

In his mind Magnus went over the men in town one by one, wondering which one it could be. Any one of them could be guilty. Even that sly Herman Bell.

"When will my ship come in?"

So he'd lost Kitty. It was more than obvious she no longer cared for him. Not even a snap. He was flat to her. The last time he'd drawn her impulsively, even convulsively, into his arms, she'd lain inert under his pressures and invasions, almost as if she disdained him even a feminine show of resistance.

Yet he knew she still cared for love itself. She had to. She was much too sensuous, even lascivious, to lose that. In the old days she'd never been able to get enough of coupling. Even at thirteen she'd already had more desire and passion in her than most women had at thirty.

Magnus hurried up the river road into town. There wasn't a wisp of wind out. It was as still as a block of ice on the streets.

He turned a corner and started down Main Street.

Herman Bell had lit the street lamps without a miss. The glass fronts of stores gleamed a shimmering silverish gray, one after the other.

Magnus saw his own reflection coming and going. His walk was crisp and courtly, stiffly upright, even a little dandified. His squared bow tie had the look of a black mustache somehow fallen under his chin.

His eyes startled him. Their reflection glowed back at him feverish, with wide glaring big pupils.

"This has got to stop." His voice echoed hoarsely down the empty street.

His eye fell on the gold lettering above his office door:

MAGNUS KING, M.D.
Physician and Surgeon

For a second he imagined he saw the letters M.D. as MAD.

"This has got to stop all right."

He entered the residential section, his heels cracking hollowly on the boardwalk. Most of the homes were dark. Night watchman Herman Bell was nowhere to be seen. Herman Bell was probably playing cards with the tramps in the jailhouse. He'd better be.

When Magnus reached the end of the boardwalk, his feet automatically found the path in the grass leading to his house.

His cottage was dark. With the shutters closed it was sometimes hard to tell whether anybody was up or not. He glanced over to see if Herman Bell's house was dark. It was.

Again, automatically, his hand slapped his coat pocket to see if his revolver was handy. It was.

A couple dozen more steps and he began to walk lightly, on his toes. There was no horse or buggy tied to the hitching post out front.

His footsteps fell soundlessly in the soft dust. Too bad it wasn't light out so he could check the dust for tracks. His breathing came quick and shallow. He got out his gun. He headed around to the back door. A surprised intruder was more likely to pop out of the back door than out of the front.

He paused. He listened intently, one foot up on the back stoop.

The Missouri murmured with a muted ruckle behind its fringe of trees. An Indian drum boomed solemnly aboriginal in Smutty Bear's camp. Crickets whirred under the fallen stalks in the garden.

Then, yes, there it was, a low murmur of voices somewhere.

He listened intently.

The voices came from inside the house. Aha! There really was someone with Kitty after all. "By the Lord!" He'd been right all along.

He gripped his revolver hard and tight. There would now be some ball blood spilled.

When he started to open the back door it creaked lightly. Lord. One more squeak like that and he'd never catch them in the act.

He lifted the door by the knob a little and then tried it. It worked. No creaking. Good. Silently he closed the door behind him.

Halfway across the kitchen, and around the table, he stopped again. Perfume in the house. The essence of puccoons. Her perfume.

And more murmuring.

He cocked his gun. A remorseless revolver would know what to do.

He tiptoed into the sitting room. He directed his hearing toward the bedroom.

The murmuring was gone. Instead he heard what he thought was the slow measured breathing of someone deep in sleep. There was also the sigh of a lighter sleeper. Damn. It was only Kitty and Roddy after all.

He backtracked a couple of steps; listened. There it was again, the murmuring. In the kitchen.

Teakettle?

Yes. It had to be the teakettle. Kitty must have thrown in a chunk of wood before she went to bed for the water to be boiling so long.

God damn.

Well, in the long run it really didn't make much difference. He was right in any case. Somebody else was kissing her better than he was. Made love better than he did.

He stood stiffly erect in the dark.

Steady measured breathing continued to come from their bedroom.

He slipped the revolver back into his pocket.

"When will I come into my own?"

He tiptoed to their bedroom. He felt around in his other pocket for a match. By the Lord. Out of lucifers. He'd have to undress in the dark.

He placed his clothes neatly in a chair. He made a special point of making the creases of his trousers meet neatly at the knee. The floor creaked under his stealthy moving.

Goose pimples came out on him as he stood naked in the dark. Surprisingly he found himself partially aroused.

He reached around behind the bedroom door, found his nightshirt hanging on its peg. Shivering, he slipped it on over his head.

He felt his way round Roddy's bed, found the foot of his own and Kitty's bed, tiptoed around to his side, opened the covers, settled on the edge of the bed and got ready to swing in. As he did so, his elbow touched someone.

Someone was sleeping in his place.

Cautiously he reached out, feeling for the form under the covers.

Roddy.

He was both relieved and enraged: relieved that it wasn't a man after all, enraged that it was Roddy.

Fumbling around, he found a match on the nightstand and lighted the lamp. A lemon glow gradually lighted up the bedroom. Their bed, then Roddy's bed, then the commode and dresser, came to view.

Kitty stirred, and rolled over to face him. "Daddy?"

"What the hell is Roddy doing in my bed?"

"Is that you, Magnus?"

"What the hell is my son doing in my bed?"

Kitty whispered up to him. "Roddy's had a hard day. So, shh, don't wake him."

"Don't wake him? Where the hell am I going to sleep then?"

"Shh. I felt so sorry for him."

"So sorry? Damnation, woman, don't you know I don't hold with sons sleeping with mothers?"

Kitty's sleepy lips drew back in partial snarl. "There's no harm done. He's only a baby."

"Damnation, woman, you know what my wishes are in this matter."

"Oh, come now, Magnus, dear, you're not really jealous of that little tassel of his now, are you? It's hardly there. Just a little johnny-nods."

"Keep this up and you'll someday have him spoiled for a woman his own age."

"I don't let him touch me. Just excepting maybe my feet."

"Damnation, woman, but that's just the point."

"Just about everybody lets their kids sleep with them when the old man is gone."

"Old man, is it?"

"You're always at me when I do something nice for the boy."

"Well?"

"Well, I'm getting fed up on it."

"Not when you do the right things for him."

"Maybe you've got a rotten mind, Magnus, dear."

"In my doctoring I've run into some damned strange things. And now I find that lightning has finally struck here in my own house."

"Are you suggesting—"

"Goddammit!" he roared, in sudden black passion. "Wake the boy up and chase him back to his own bed."

"You do it."

"I want you to do it. So that he'll know it's you who's ordering him out of our bed. You. Not me."

Roddy suddenly sat up out of the bedclothes. "Don't bother, Dad, I'll get up by myself. All this racket waking me up."

Magnus shivered. Check. So the boy had been awake all along. Had probably been awake those other times too. The boy knew. Father and mother had no secrets from him. That made it all the more devilish.

Magnus waited for Roddy to get settled in his own bed, then said, "Now there'll be no more of this, you hear?"

Silence.

"You hear?"

Silence.

"That's an order."

"This is not the army, Magnus," Kitty said. "The War between the States is over."

"It's still an order."

Silence from Roddy's bed.

Magnus blew out the lamp; dropped in bed; covered himself.

Kitty sighed as if she'd finally had the last straw.

Magnus worked his head deep into his pillow. The more he wriggled down the more he could still smell Roddy in the pillowcase.

Kitty drew away from Magnus, sleeping as far away from him as she could.

Magnus continued to work his head deep into his pillow.

"Besides," Kitty said in the dark, "Roddy and me slept between different sheets. Not that it really matters."

"That I believe."

"If you'd just feel around a little, you'd see."

Magnus lay stiff. A muscle just above his left kneecap began to quiver.

After a bit, Kitty gave him a light touch on the hip through the sheet. "You see."

"Aha! Now I know for sure it did concern you. After all."

"You must be insane."

"Very likely. But it still goes. And now you can shut up about the matter and go to sleep."

"I don't intend to shut up when you accuse me of something of which I'm not guilty. There has been no one. As the boy, yes, as even God is my witness."

"The boy is a boy. And God I don't believe in."

"Now I know for sure you're off your rocker."

"We will see." Magnus snapped the sheet tight under his chin. Deliberately he stiffened himself for sleep.

"What a fool I was not to listen to my aunt. Ohh!"

When will our ship come in?

3

Clear weather pushed out heavy weather.

Magnus awoke cheerful in the morning. He swung out of bed full of charge for the day.

He also found himself full of affection for Kitty and the boy. Weren't they all orphans together, himself included? Singletons? All the blood kin they had in America, in the world for that matter, was they themselves. Suppose something should happen to one of them, who would rush to their aid with help and love except they themselves?

Magnus shaved over the washbasin in the kitchen. Kitty made breakfast. Roddy set the table.

Not much was said. Roddy and Kitty seemed to be waiting for Magnus to begin.

Magnus deftly worked the straightedge over and around his chin. Crisp. Crisp. He took hold of his skin over his cheek near his nose and began coming down the side of his face. Crisp. Crisp. He had a fine edge on his straight razor that morning.

Kitty banged a stove lid.

Magnus ignored the banging. He cleaned his razor on a piece of newspaper and folded it away. "What are we having for the breaking of our fast this morning, Mother?"

"Same old thing."

"Sounds good to me."

Kitty threw him a surprised look.

Magnus washed his face with soft water and tar soap. He combed his hair until it shone like the glossy back of a crow.

Kitty removed a tray of fresh toast from the oven. With her knee she slammed shut the nickel oven door.

Magnus felt a sudden regret for all the terrible things he said the night before. He shivered. "Jesus."

"What?"

"Nothing."

"I thought you said something."

"No." Magnus took his place at the head of the table.

Roddy looked up from his plate. He studied his father's face with grave green eyes.

Magnus summoned up a smile. He winked at Roddy. "What's on tap for today, boy?"

"Nothing."

"What about school?"

"Teach is getting married."

"Oho. No school then, eh? That calls for something special. Let's make it a holiday, what do you say?"

A gleam of interest appeared in the boy's eyes.

"What would you really like to do today, boy? Really now?" Magnus cut off a corner of his toast, next cut off a piece of fried egg and placed it precisely on the corner of the toast, next cut off a slice of butter and placed it neatly on the piece of egg, then, in one motion, put the running little triple-decker in his mouth. Very good. Kitty was a great cook for all that. "Name it, Roddy, my man, and we'll do it."

"You promised me once to give me some pointers on how to shoot."

"How about a walk out along the new Military Road? See where the Argonauts head out these days."

Roddy was instantly aglow. "Say, Dad, I forgot to tell you.

Down by the Big Sioux there I found a good place for target practice. Under those giant cottonwoods."

"All right, boy, done. That's what we'll do."

Kitty poured Magnus some hot coffee. "Do you think that's wise for a boy so young?"

"Why not?" Magnus gave Kitty a large smile. "The boy had better learn to shoot right. At least out here. The frontier is just across the river, you know."

Roddy slid over on his father's side of things. "Didn't you hear our mountain lion out howling again last night, Ma?"

Kitty wasn't sure. "I hope you aren't leading the boy astray with all that talk about guns and such." She took a bite of egg yolk. It ran yellow off her fork. "I just don't like guns."

"You really are going to take the day off then today, Dad?"

"Of course. A promise is a promise."

Kitty shook her head. "I don't know. Any time your father wakes up with a smile on his face as big as a small wave on a lake I begin to worry."

Magnus took a last sip of coffee. He put up his napkin in its ring. "Can't a doctor spend a little time with his family just like anybody else?" Magnus then got to his feet and went around to Kitty's side of the table and placed his hands affectionately on her shoulders. It was like in the old days, almost.

But when Magnus leaned down to kiss her, Kitty ducked away and his kiss fell on her light-brown hair instead.

Magnus still smiled down at her. "Don't begrudge me those lovely Indian lips of yours now, doll. They're like cut rubies."

"Hmf."

Roddy got up from the table too. "C'mon, Dad, let's go."

Together the two men of the house went out back and got the guns from the lean-to, Magnus his pistol and Roddy the double-barreled shotgun.

They carefully wiped off the oil. They polished the wood stock on the shotgun to a shining rosy brown. They filled their pockets with a supply of shells.

They sauntered out the new Military Road going west. It crossed several dry coulees. In places iron wheels had cut the black earth deep enough to lay bare its clay flesh.

The road skirted the foot of the north bluffs on their right. High above them leafless trees pricked against the skies like crowds of stick figures.

On their left, meadows fell away in varying slopes between the road and the Missouri. The meadows lay sweet with the year's last clover balls. Bees moved like loops of syrup, slowly, from ball to ball. A tangle of wild roses, belled with hips the color of ripe apples, ringed a buffalo wallow.

Magnus and Roddy dipped through an ancient riverbed, and then suddenly were in among the giant cottonwoods.

The cottonwoods loomed immense, their tops like high-thrown flukes of sporting whales. Sunlight moved under them in varying puffs.

Sweet grass underfoot, cropped short by the buffalo, gleamed a deep green. The last flies of the year rose out of the grass for a wondering bite. Across the river purplish-green waves moved across a slough of ripgut grass.

Magnus selected a fallen cottonwood limb as the target. Its bark was mostly peeled off, leaving a bone-dry bole. It had numerous little knots which made for excellent bull's-eyes.

Roddy shot well. He aimed instinctively and on the rise. He more squeezed than pulled the trigger. He took the kick of the double-barreled shotgun through the back leg where it rested lightly on the ground.

"Son you have only one fault that I can see."

"What's that, Dad?" The two barrels of Roddy's gun gleamed iridescent blues and greens.

"It's the way you handle your gun between shots."

Roddy's lower lip showed pink for a moment.

"Son, there's one thing you must always remember. Always. And you must never forget it. Just a touch on the trigger, on purpose or accidentally, and off she goes."

"I wasn't pointing it at anybody."

"You twice had it pointed at me. With your finger still in the trigger guard. Once you even had it pointed at your own foot."

Roddy's green eyes darkened.

"It's all right. But watch it."

"Nnn."

Magnus thought he'd better counter what he'd said with something pleasant. "Maybe this fall you can enter the town turkey shoot."

At that Roddy brightened. "Boy, Dad, if they'll let me enter, I'll win us a great big fat turkey gobbler for Thanksgiving."

"Atta way to talk. Might as well be a man as not. While you're at it."

Magnus took his turn with the pistol. Standing a good twenty paces off, he hit dead center five times out of six. A silver dollar could have covered the bullet holes in and around the tiny knot in the log.

Roddy took pride in his father.

Magnus found a penny in his pocket. He flipped it into the air above them and with a single shot hit it on the way down.

Roddy spotted where the penny glanced off. He went over and got it. "It's bent double, Dad."

"Didn't I drill it plumb center?"

"You hit it dead center all right. But it didn't go through. Just bent it double."

"That's blunt-nosed bullets for you."

"When can I try the six-shooter, Dad?"

"In a couple of years maybe."

"Why wait that long?"

"A revolver is trickier than a shotgun. Because it's too handy. It can turn on you so much quicker than a shotgun."

"That's why when a man wants to commit suicide he always takes the revolver then."

Magnus winced. "Where'd you hear that fool notion?"

"Heard the kids at school talking about it."

"Good Lord." Magnus punched his heel into the green turf.

"Say, Dad, suppose you was to meet a real road agent in a saloon? And he was out to kill you? How'd you take care of him?"

"I suppose you heard about that in school too?"

"Yeh."

"Hum." Magnus touched a hand to his eye as if refixing a monocle in place. "Well, in the case of a vicious road agent, I'd aim with the eyes, never the gun. Gut-shoot him."

"Say, Dad, when are you going to give me a monocle like you got at home?"

"Never."

"Why not?"

"It doesn't fit in America."

"We're going back to England someday, ain't we?"

"No, boy, no, I guess we never will."

Roddy kicked loose a round skipping stone from the grass. He picked it up and fitted it expertly in his eye as though it were a monocle.

"Don't, son. I have nothing but bad memories about those things."

Roddy skimmed the stone away, off across the grass. "Sorry, Dad."

Magnus shook himself. "Well now, boy. You got any advice to give me? Turn and turn about, you know."

"No, I don't think so."

"Nothing? Nothing about how I hold the gun or something?"

"No."

"Not even the way I stand maybe?"

"Nope."

"Good. Then I can qualify for a pistol shoot."

"Boy, I can't wait for the day when I can shoot a pistol."

Magnus sat down on the bony cottonwood log, and got out his pipe and lighted up. In a moment the tranquil smell of tobacco smoke wafted around them.

Roddy checked to see if his double-barreled shotgun was empty, then placed it carefully on the other side of the log with the barrels aimed up and away from them. He settled on the cottonwood log beside his father.

Magnus sat musing on the scene, eyes lidded half-over, free hand hanging.

A halo of mist wavered over the spot where the Big Sioux pushed its green water into the tan waters of the Missouri.

A mosquito wisped across Magnus' line of vision, so close that for a second he thought it a whistling swan going by legs adangle.

"Say though, Dad."

"Yes."

"Can I give you a piece of advice about something else?"

"Fire away."

"Maybe I shouldn't though."

"Fire away."

Roddy gave Magnus a look of young force. "Don't always be so picky with Mom. There ain't nobody bothering her. Hanging around her. Really. Exceptin' just me, Dad. That's all."

"Son, I don't want to believe bad about your mother either."

"Hain't you got some kind of a pill you can take that'll help you get over them crazy ideas?"

"Son, the next time I'm in the office, I'll go take me a great big cow pill."

"Now you're joking."

"A little. But not really very much."

Roddy got out his jackknife. He opened both blades, the long one straight out and the short one halfway, and began throwing the knife expertly at the ground, making it land with one or the other of the two blades coming point down in the grass. The long blade counted ten points and the short one five.

Magnus watched Roddy's game of mumblety-peg with a smile. He mused aloud, more to himself than to the boy: "Life. Yes. First there's the time when you talk about your jackknife and how wonderful sharp it is. Then there's the time when you brag about your horse and how many women you've made. And then there's the time when you hobble down to the poolhall and brag about what a good crap you had that morning."

Roddy glanced up at him briefly, went on with his game of mumblety-peg.

A coneflower stood erect at the end of their log. Its rays had fallen, and what was left of the flower, the cone, resembled the dark heart of a chicken.

A giant stag beetle tried again and again to climb the bluff edge of a buffalo chip.

A rough whizzing was suddenly around the heads of the man and the boy, and then a green bottle fly lighted on the glossy toe of Magnus' boot. It sat a second, blinking its wings and making a quarter turn; then whisked off.

Magnus picked a wild clover. He smelled its purple head. He twirled it between his fingers. A little drop of its juice appeared at its severed end. Magnus caught the little drop with a fingertip and licked it. Wild. Like the taste of fresh hay to a horse.

There appeared to be no atmosphere at all. To breathe was to savor what seemed to be subtly commingled fumes of alcohol and wild clover. In fantasy fingertips went about touching the tan points of waiting maiden breasts.

Roddy announced the result of the game he had been playing. "I win. One hundred to eighty-five."

"When our ship comes in," Magnus murmured. "One day."

4

Magnus searched through the bottom drawer of his desk; at last found it. A bottle of rye.

"Such terrible dreams I've been having lately." Magnus shuddered. "And then that last little tyke coming in here, a little girl pregnant at twelve. . . . Lord, it's no wonder doctoring drives a man to kissing Black Betty." With a push of his thumb, he uncorked the bottle; then, with a glance at his framed diploma hanging on the wall above his rolltop desk, tossed off a snort. "I don't know how much more of this I can stand. Whew!"

There was a strong smell of carbolic acid in the place. A clock ticked on a bookstand. A cobweb as big as a hairnet hung across one of the green windowpanes.

"Horrible." He took another shot. He was glad that for once there were no patients out front waiting for him. "Yes, if it weren't for that venomous carbuncle the human brain, maybe a man could enjoy the simple sins of life a little."

A dray rattled by on the frozen streets outside. The horse clopped along with a lazy tumble of hoofs.

"Magnus, old boy, you're just like one of those swine in the gospel into whose mind the devil has entered. It's time for you to jump off the brink too."

His big gold repeater watch in his vest pocket ticked like a tardy heart. "Yet I just know there's got to be someone. Just got to be. He started coming around right after Roddy'd learned to walk."

He recalled the mad dream he'd had the night before. In that dream he'd got up to check the lock on the front door. He was sure he'd snapped it shut when they went to bed but he still heard the door banging. He found the door open. Shaking his head, he closed it carefully again. Firmly. He went back four times to make sure it really was locked. Each time he found it open again. The last time it finally stayed locked. He staggered back to bed. Just as he entered the bedroom he heard a noise on Kitty's side of the bed. He quick looked. Great snakes alive! It was the fellow. A young man of twenty or so. Slim. Green-eyed. Dark hair. Bearded. A mocking disobedient smile lay curling over his Indian lips. There was even something gleeful in the young man's manner, as if he'd just then successfully got away with something. Pulled something off. Then, like a smoke ring almost, the youth began to drift out through the open window. At the same time Kitty awoke with a look of deep satisfaction in her eyes. She too acted as if she'd pulled something off. She drew the bedcovers up over her bare bosom against Magnus. At that Magnus let go with a roar of rage. What a dream that'd been.

His eyes fastened on a brown gleam. It was where the late-afternoon sun shot reflected through the top of the bottle. Soft alcohol fumes wimmered from the open bottle and slowly commingled with the brisk smell of carbolic acid.

"Set a man on the edge of a precipice and in a few minutes he'll feel the draw of it. Down there is death, he thinks. An awful smashing of guts and bones. The next thing, he'll start to lean."

Sunlight struck a pair of dark hairs on his forefinger. It touched them just right, changed them to golden brown.

He tossed off another snort.

"I'll have nobody treading my hen."

Outside on the street a bullwhacker let go with a wonderful avalanche of profanity. The bullwhacker's whip popped with the great sound of a ten-gauge shotgun. In a moment oxen groaned, yokes creaked, wheels cracked.

"By the Lord, I just know there's got to be somebody." Magnus touched hand to eye. "There just has to be." Magnus picked up the bottle; downed what rye was left with a long suck; slammed the bottle down on his desk. "And I'm going to get it out of her even if I have to beat it out of her with a club. I just know she keeps comparing me in her mind with that other fellow. I can tell. Knowing he's better hung than me."

He shoved back in his armchair and got to his feet. He clapped on his black hat, locked up, and headed for home.

The sun had just rolled off the rim of the earth when he turned down his dusty path. A high scarf of nimbus cloud before his very eyes became an enormous flame. Pink-yellow dusk swept over the whole world.

Magnus stumbled as he stepped across the threshold of his house.

"Damn that kid anyway, always leaving his racket laying around. Right in the path."

Roddy looked up from where he was sitting reading *Robinson Crusoe*. He gave Magnus a surprised green look.

Kitty gave Magnus but one glance from where she was sitting crocheting, then retreated into the kitchen.

Magnus skimmed his hat onto the hall tree. "Lord!"

Roddy put his book aside and got to his feet. "Say, Dad, what's the idea?"

"What do you mean?"

"Blaming me for making you stumble."

"Didn't you?"

"There's nothing on the doorstep. Because right there's my racket. Standing in the corner where it belongs."

"So it is."

"You said yourself once, Dad, that the first thing you're

gonna do, when our ship comes in, is to have a porch light put in."

It pleased Magnus to see the boy face up to him like a man. He couldn't help but give him a grudging smile. "Well, boy, right you are. Dead right."

"I was gonna say." Roddy went over and closed the door. "After what we agreed by the giant cottonwoods."

"Right."

But Magnus resented the way Kitty had retreated into the kitchen. He left the boy and went in pursuit of her. He found her busy at the stove. "I suppose the other fellow never drinks."

Kitty reset the coffeepot to the front of the range with a bang.

"But instead gets his jollies sleeping with other men's wives."

"Roddy."

"What about him?"

"At least think of him." Kitty threw some wood into the range. "If you can't think of yourself."

Magnus stood very erect beside her. "Roddy's young. And'll outlive it. But maybe I won't."

"Why don't you go sit down?" She threw him a mixed look, partly sneering, partly wincing. "And we'll get some food into you."

"Maybe I'm not hungry."

"How about some coffee?"

He grabbed her arm, bent it back around under her shoulder.

"Don't." Her voice came pinched.

He bent her arm farther. "Woman, if you don't admit it, here and now, before God and my son, that you're a bad woman, bad! goddam you, I'll take a club to you."

"Magnus."

"Because I know all about you."

"Please."

"Because my nightmares tell me so. And nightmares never lie."

"Please, daddy husband."

"And goddammit, please quit calling me daddy husband."

"Magnus then."

Out of the corner of his eye Magnus caught sight of Roddy standing in the doorway. He turned for a better look.

The boy had gotten out his blue blanket and was sucking its silk border.

Magnus staggered, he was so shocked. Only moments before the boy had shown him a pair of tough horns. "Son, put away that goddam blanket! Shame on you. Tit time for you is long ago past."

Kitty gave her arm a hard quick jerk, and managed to break free of Magnus. She ran for the bedroom.

Magnus turned in a rage on his son. "Why don't you keep better watch on our house?"

Roddy dropped his blanket to the floor. "What for?"

"To catch the man that's been molesting your mother lately, of course."

"Dad, there ain't nobody botherin' her. Like I told you. Exceptin' just me."

"And when you catch this fellow, and I'm not home, I want you to run over and call Herman Bell the cop."

Silence.

"And don't you forget it either." .

Silence.

"Some men are devils and they've just got to be locked up for their own good. Let alone the women."

Kitty burst out of the bedroom with strides long and lunging for so short a woman. She came carrying a chamber pot and a looking glass. Her face was as white as the skin of a bled chicken. Her dissimilar eyes glowed with dissimilar fires. She stuck the chamber pot, and then the looking glass, into Magnus' face.

Magnus stared into the chamber pot, then into the looking glass.

"Magnus, in the name of our common humanity, who are you to point the finger?"

Magnus abruptly collapsed within. He reached for her. And missed. He kissed air instead of lips. He wept. "Help."

Roddy saw it all. And slowly Roddy's eyes took on a distant glint. It was the same look he'd had in his eyes when, some years before, on a Sunday afternoon, he had seen his father lying on his mother and struggling with her in the act of love.

An October frost came, and soon ripgut grass was rolling in alternate floods of tan and blood, and oak leaves made a brown buckskin noise, and gardens lay sunken.

5

Men were hurrying home to wife and supper. Twilight dusted down in floating flakes of rust. High shadows humped off the bluffs north of town.

Down the boardwalk came slim courtly Magnus: black hat, black bow tie, dark suit, black patent-leather shoes, immaculate white shirt.

Magnus kept looking from side to side. His black eyes were smoked over and his large liberal lips worked and curled and worked. A blue revolver lay gleaming in his hand.

He had three more houses to go before his house. The three houses were log-cabin affairs, one-story, roughly hewn, chinked with clay. In one cabin fatty beef could be heard frying over a fire. From another came the smell of singed onions. In the back yard of the third house a single white chicken, roosting in the lower branch of a bare maple, sat with eyes filmy, wings fluffed.

Magnus' heels hit the boardwalk with determined drumming sounds. The palm of his hand was dry. Where his finger touched the trigger of his revolver the skin prickled.

"Hey, Doc, what in the world are you up to?"

Magnus stiffened, and came to a stop. Slowly he turned. It was Herman Bell, night watchman. "Yes?"

Herman Bell was sitting on the front stoop of the middle cabin, picking his teeth. "My God, Doc, you look like you're about to plug somebody."

Magnus' trigger finger continued to prickle.

"If you're looking for rabbits, Doc, I can tell you where there's a couple. In my garden. They're finishing off what the frost missed."

Magnus' left nostril fluttered once.

Herman Bell had a red nubbed face. His eyes were black, hard, speculative. "There been a burglary uptown?"

"No."

Herman Bell's eyes steadied on the gun in Magnus' hand. "No?"

"No."

"Then maybe it's rats you're after?"

"No."

Herman Bell continued to pick his teeth. "Not that I worry about you, Doc."

"No."

"How's the wife and kid?"

"Fine."

"You sure got you a winner in that boy."

"Thanks."

"Chip off the old block."

"Hm."

Herman Bell threw away his toothpick. "You know, Doc, that missus of yours, she's some, she is. Ain't a pair of pants in town but what he don't begrudge you your pretty little Kitty. Man."

Magnus shuddered.

"A word to the wise, though, Doc. You better pet that pretty wife of yours a little or you'll lose you a good woman. I know doctors are awful busy, but—"

"Thanks!"

Herman Bell got to his feet. "You sure gave me a scare there though for a minute, Doc. I'd hate to have to arrest you, ha, ha. Any man that can pick a penny out of the air and drill it plumb center is too much for me to shoot it out with."

With an impatient gesture Magnus squared his bow tie under his chin.

"Why don't you try strychnine, Doc? If it's rats you're after?"

"I might do just that."

"Hum. Well, Doc, you know how it is. I was only inquirin'."

Magnus waited stiffly.

"Well, happy hunting. I'm off to light the street lamps." Herman Bell shook the wrinkles out of his pants, cocked his round hat at an acey-deucy angle, and headed for downtown.

After a moment Magnus broke out of his stance and went on.

A couple of steps from his house Magnus stopped. He checked the bullets in the cylinder of his revolver. He listened intently. Then he began searching the loose dust on either side of the path.

"Hi, Dad. Play some bad with you."

Magnus jerked erect. "Damn." What a devil of a time for the boy to show up. Just when he was about to catch them at it. Besides, it was already too dark to be playing badminton.

"Say, Dad, what're you doing with that gun?"

"Nothing."

A light went on in the back of the house, casting an orange glow over the fallen garden. Kitty was in the kitchen.

Magnus asked, "Mom got supper ready?"

Roddy eyed the gun in Magnus' hand with interest. "Is our puma back again?"

Magnus looked down at his gun; then stuffed it into his coat pocket.

Roddy hit his leg a slap with his racket. "The kids in school was telling about the Indians seeing some fresh panther tracks down by the stockyards."

Magnus flashed his teeth. "The animal I'm looking for the Indians call a two-legged."

"Oh." With a swift movement of his hand, Roddy swept back his wavy brush of sun-touched brown hair.

Magnus let down a trace. Slowly he settled on his heels and then beckoned for Roddy to come closer. Roddy came and Magnus put his arm around him. "Son?"

Roddy stood quietly inside his father's arm. He shot his father a single sidelong look, more at his father's lean cheek than at his livid eyes.

"Son?"

"Yes?"

"You know what I told you the other day?"

Roddy shot his father another look. "You mean about that man sneaking around here window-peeking?"

"Yes. What're you going to do when you catch him?"

"Quick run over and call Herman the cop."

"Right." Magnus gave Roddy a hard squeeze around the hips. "And if it should ever happen that he gets into the house and is actually attacking Mother, then what?"

"Grab the shotgun and let go with both barrels."

"Right." Magnus gave Roddy another quick hug. "Though you wanna be careful and not hit Mother."

" 'Course."

"You've got to do that now. No matter what. Remember."

"Don't worry."

Darkness fell as they talked. Soon lamps were blazing on all over town and men walking home were carrying lanterns.

"Son, when it comes to harming women, these bad men will stop at nothing."

"Are they like road agents, Dad?"

"More like wild animals."

A small fog, creeping in off the Missouri, slowly widened up the Floyd River and then spilled into Perry Creek. As it spread, the fog engulfed lighted windows and lanterns one by one, softening them from sharp sunstone to pale moonstone. The fog held thin and the scattered lamps and lanterns gleamed as if they were gems caught in flung gauze.

"Remember now. Shoot the minute you see your mother in any kind of danger. Even if it's your father. You hear?"

The pupils of Roddy's green eyes widened. Slowly he nodded.

"Because I always want you to remember that we men have got to protect our mothers. No matter what."

"Is there a real wild-animal man loose around in town here, Dad?"

"I suspect so."

"You know for sure, Dad?"

Magnus let go of Roddy and stood up. "Suppose I was the wild-animal man molesting your mother, what would you do? Really now."

Roddy lifted his racket to his shoulder and aimed it right between Magnus' eyes. "Boom!"

"Good. Now let's go in to supper and Mom."

But Roddy wasn't done with it. He shot a look at the pocket where Magnus had put the gun. "Really, Dad, what was you really looking for?"

"Come. Into the house with you."

"Dad?"

"That wild-animal man."

Roddy ran ahead to open the door for his father.

Magnus stomped his feet on the doormat to let Kitty know he was home.

"Need cat eyes to see in here," Roddy said.

"Your mother should have lit the lamp for us."

"She was probably too busy, Dad."

Magnus dug a match out of his pocket, stroked it alive on the sole of his shoe, and put it to a lamp on a side table. Instantly soft illumination bloomed inside the lamp chimney. Walnut chairs, two bookcases, a black leather sofa, the painted portrait of Uncle George Worthington came to view.

The surface of Uncle George's portrait was dry and cracked, and its brown frame had begun to part at the corners. Because of the buckling canvas, one of Uncle George's dark eyes had begun to look cockeyed like a baffled sportsman. Above the portrait hung the Worthington family coat of arms: barry of white and azure with Frisian stallion rampant on dexter chief.

Both Magnus and Roddy let their eyes linger on the portrait of Uncle George a moment, then Magnus skimmed his hat onto the hall tree.

They passed into the dining room.

A pull-down lamp spread a cone of soft gold light in the center of the room. Table was set. Gleaming silver neatly flanked three blue-edged plates on white linen. The reflection of the set table glowed in the mirror over the walnut sideboard. A maidenhair fern, hovering on a flower stand in front of the bay window, stirred a little as if it were a little green octopus floating lazily in midair.

Kitty came in carrying a platter of meat in one hand and a bowl of onions and potatoes in the other. Kitty set them both at the head of the table in front of Magnus' place. "Roddy, wash your hands."

"Aw, Ma, I—"

"And please put that racket away."

Roddy set his racket in a corner. He threw a look at his mother, then went off to wash up.

The moment the boy disappeared into the kitchen Magnus flashed Kitty a silverish look.

Kitty moved about with long vigorous strides. She had done up her light-brown hair in a high glossy roll. She had on a green apron over a yellow flowered dress. Her sensual lips were more than usually dented at the corners.

Magnus sat down in his armchair at the head of the table. He was careful to arrange his suit jacket so that the revolver in his pocket didn't bump against the arm of his chair.

Kitty placed a carving set beside his plate.

"Anybody leave a call today?" Magnus tucked his napkin in under his chin.

"Nobody."

"Nobody come at all?"

"Nobody."

Magnus grunted.

Kitty next brought out the silver tea service. She placed a cozy over the teapot. She checked the table carefully, to see if anything had been forgotten, and at last, with a sigh, sat down at her end.

The two waited for Roddy to come.

There was some splashing in the kitchen, then the sound of a tin washbowl being emptied, then the soft sounds of hair being licked over with a brush.

Magnus picked up the carving knife and fork. "Roddy!"

"Comin'."

Kitty wetted the fleshy part of her lower lip with the tip of her tongue. "Don't be so rough on the boy always."

Magnus let his carving knife and fork drop with a clatter. "Dammit, Kitty, please don't interfere with my methods of discipline."

"And whose discipline are we to use when you're out on call?"

"Mine. An extension of them. Surrogate."

"And if you should happen to die tomorrow?"

"Ah. Looking forward to that already, eh?"

"Maybe."

"You see!" Magnus' fingertips crouched on the white tablecloth.

"Ahk! Ahk!" Roddy warned from the door. "Here we go again." Roddy drew up his chair to the table. "I sure wish you two would quit fightin' once."

Magnus and Kitty threw each other a surprised look, then stared down at their plates.

Roddy bowed over his plate. "Lord Jesus, look down in mercy upon us, bless this food, forgive us our sins . . . and please for goshsakes make Dad and Mom quit fighting all the time, it's hard on my stomach, I can't eat sometimes. Amen."

Kitty's lips edged up at the corners.

Magnus picked up his carving knife and fork again and slowly began to vibrate.

Kitty gave her table yet another look. "Oh, dear. I forgot to set out the water after all. Roddy, would you please get it for me?"

"Yes'm." Roddy went to get them each a glass of water.

Magnus waited until Roddy had finished, all the while continuing to vibrate at his end of the table.

Roddy had just barely sat down again, when there were solid steps outside, then a rap at the back door.

Kitty groaned. "Oh no. It would have to be just as we're about to eat. Roddy, go see who it is, will you, please? And ask them if they can't come back in half an hour."

"But I'm hungry, Mom."

"Do it," Magnus ordered.

Before Roddy could get to his feet, the back door opened and Herman Bell's flat unemotional voice sang out in the kitchen. "Oh, Doc?"

"Yes?"

Herman Bell stepped into the doorway of the dining room. "Begging your pardon, Doc, but Ted Jakes wants me to pay you his respects and to say that his wife's about to pop with her sixth. I've got the horse and buggy waiting outside for you."

Magnus slapped down his carving knife and fork. "By the Lord!" Magnus jerked off his napkin, got to his feet.

"But, Magnus, I've just put the dinner on," Kitty protested. "Can't this Mrs. Jakes wait a little? A few minutes?"

Herman Bell held his head to one side. "Ted Jakes says his wife's already pretty far along. And you know how it is, a stitch in time saves nine."

Red spots appeared on Kitty's cheeks. "Och! that Jakes. He's as bad a worrier as his old granny of a father was. Always shaking hands with the devil before he's met him."

Herman Bell held his head to one side even farther. "Mrs. Jakes has always had 'em in a rush, Mrs. King. I know. I've delivered several myself."

Kitty got to her feet too. "Daddy, please, I don't want you to go without eating something."

"I'm really not hungry," Magnus said shortly.

"You're slowly turning to skin and bones."

Magnus turned to Roddy. "Get my bag."

Herman Bell said, "You didn't have it with you when you came home tonight, Doc."

Magnus clapped a hand to the pocket where he'd put his revolver. "So I didn't."

Kitty's eyes opened some. "That's the third time you've forgot your bag in the last week, Magnus."

"It's all right," Magnus said. "We can drive by the office and pick it up."

"What's the matter with you lately, Magnus?" Kitty touched Magnus lightly on the elbow. "You've become so forgetful."

Magnus brushed off her touch. "Nothing's the matter with me. Please don't interfere."

Herman Bell's head came up. "Don't worry, Mrs. King. Your husband's got a lot of things on his mind."

"I still don't like it."

"Mrs. King, we here in Sioux City, we're thankful Magnus ain't like the last doc we had. Old Doc Walker. Why, Old Doc Walker was sometimes so mean from overwork he made the cook whistle in the kitchen to make sure she wasn't eating raisins."

"Thanks."

"Don't mean no misrespect, Mrs. King. But out here in the sticks, where doctors come and go like tumbleweeds, we get some pretty funny pills, let me tell you. There ain't only one kind of feller nuttier than a doctor on the frontier, Mrs. King, and that's a printer."

"I'll keep the supper warm for you, Magnus."

"Don't bother. I'll grab a bite downtown. You never know about these things."

"Bye, Dad."

"Bye, Roddy."

A deep sigh welled up out of Kitty. "I still don't like it, Magnus. You've been acting so funny lately. I'm afraid."

"Pah!"

Roddy's eyes came up in a wondering query. "Say, Dad?"

"Yes?" Magnus turned in the doorway.

"On the way back, maybe if you was to come along real sneaky like, maybe you can catch that wild-animal man you was lookin' for. Window-peekin'."

Magnus grimaced fiercely. "Maybe."

Kitty's face opened. The look of a startled doe came into her eyes, glistening, transparent. "Magnus?" Her eyes widened so far their strange dissimilarity gleamed vividly clear, the left eye as though obscured with racing green smoke, the right eye a severe brown. "Daddy? A wild-animal man?"

Herman Bell suddenly became alert too. "Did you say window-peeper, boy?"

Roddy saw right away he had said the wrong thing. Roddy dropped his eyes. "Dad and me was just joshin' around before dinner is all."

"Window-peeper?" Kitty echoed. She placed a hand on Roddy's shoulder. "Here?"

Roddy suffered his mother a moment, then moved out of her reach. "I said we was just jokin' around about it."

But Kitty wouldn't let Roddy go. She leaned forward and stroked back his hair. "Tell me, handsome is as handsome does, did Daddy say there was a wild-animal man window-peeking?"

Magnus made another fierce face. His large lips opened just enough to show even white teeth. "Let's shake a leg, Herman. Lead the way."

6

Four inches of snow drifted down during the day. It gave the little town of Sioux City a ghostly look. It made spectral the Indian dead lashed to stick scaffolds pricking out on Morningside Heights. There was no wind.

Into the silence of pure white a pileated woodpecker occasionally broke and rebroke the air with its rolling clatter on a hollow cottonwood. The steamboat *St. Louis*, arriving for the last time that season, also let go with several shrill shattering blasts.

That evening, light lingered for a long time after the sun went down. Each chimney exhaled a slim white plume a straight thousand feet high. The voices of children playing in the snow suggested angels. People took a couple of steps, then stood and looked. Just looked.

Down the path in the snow came slim courtly Magnus again, wearing his usual black hat and a dark Chesterfield coat. He came swiftly, overshoes scuffing out little throws of loose phosphorescent snow to either side. His face was blenched and his eyeballs were slightly protruded. A revolver also flashed in his hand again.

He went around to the back of his house and bounded up the stoop and burst into the kitchen.

Kitty was getting supper ready. Light from a kerosene lamp glowed golden on the bright papered walls.

He started firing the moment he saw her. His first shot caught her along the hairline.

She screamed and ducked down.

His next shot caught her in the hand, nicking the flesh between thumb and forefinger.

She screamed again and tried to hide behind the woodbox.

His next shot exploded in the toe of her left green button shoe.

"Magnus!"

His next shot ripped her belt on the right side. The belt dropped to the floor.

She came up out of her crouch and ran for the bedroom, screaming as she went, "Daddy, please don't kill me! Please. I'll do anything you say. I'll admit anything you say. Oh, God, I'm being murdered! Help! Help!"

He glimpsed her silhouette against the lighted bed lamp and his next shot nicked her left breast. The ball sliced across just below the nipple. Blood spurted.

She dove under the bed. "Help, help! My husband is killing me! Oh, God, God!"

He sank to his knees and elbows and peered under the bed. He spotted the outline of her mouth moving against the yellow wallpaper. He fired. This time he caught the outer edge of her green eye.

In a flash she slithered out from under the bed on the other side and clawed up the wall all in one motion. "Roddy, Roddy! Can't you do something to stop your father? Oh, God!" Then she collapsed and tumbled backward onto the bed.

Magnus got to his feet and aimed directly at the center of her forehead. He pulled the trigger. The hammer snapped. There was no explosion.

He looked down at his gun. He flicked the cylinder open. The gun was empty.

He looked down at Kitty. She was leaking blood on all sides. "I told you, woman, that before God and my son, if you didn't admit you were a bad woman, bad! goddam you, I'd take a club to you. Well, you kept on being bad so I had to take a gun to you."

There was a click of a gun being cocked.

He turned.

Through the bedroom door, on the other side of the sitting room, he saw Roddy standing with his double-barrel shotgun in hand.

"You see!" Magnus cried. "My nightmares don't lie."

Roddy raised his shotgun and fired.

Magnus ducked back. A blast of pellets knocked his hat off. Magnus started to lose his balance. "Son! Hey, it's all right. It's only—"

The second blast caught Magnus as he fell on the bed. The pellets traversed the length of his body, ripping his Chesterfield coat to shreds, gouging lines across his face. He landed across Kitty's body.

Neighbors heard the shooting. They came running in the dark. Bodies hesitated a second on the front stoop and the back stoop both; then burst in.

There was blood all over the place: on the bed, on the wall above the bed, on the bedroom floor, in the hall, in the kitchen.

"In the name of God!"

More came running out of the night.

"Poor poor boy. Ahhh."

Herman Bell pushed in. "Son, my God, you didn't shoot your own mother, did you?"

Roddy stared back with scared green eyes. "Dad did."

"Who shot your dad?"

"I did."

"Call the doctor, somebody!" a voice cried. "Hurry, hurry!"

"But it's the doctor who's dead!" another voice cried.

"Maybe we should just call the Reverend," a third voice said.

Herman Bell's red nubbed face stiffened over. "No use in calling him."

"Why not?"

"I'm afraid they're both in hell by now. The Kings never went to church."

"What a terrible thing to say."

Gooseberry June came running in. She stared at the fallen bloody bodies. She clapped hand to mouth. Her black plum eyes rolled up in horror. "Ai-ai-ai!" Slowly she backed away. "What the Knife Child has done." She ran back to her encampment.

A pool-hall bum also had a look. "Well, so they have both went to their eternal roost, I see."

Undertaker McVicker appeared. With a single glance his old glittering vulture eyes took everything in. "What happened here?"

"I guess Magnus went nuts and shot his wife," Herman Bell said. "Then the boy shot his father."

"What'd Magnus want to do that for?"

"I think he thought she'd gone bad."

"Kitty?"

"Mac," Herman Bell said, "if you know of anything between the lids of the Bible that will meet this case, I wish you would name it. Because I don't."

"Yes," Mrs. Herman Bell cried. "I believe somebody ought to pray over this." She folded her fat arms over her rolling bosom.

Undertaker McVicker made an instant survey of the crowd, and decided that to offer a prayer was the thing to do. He folded his hands and bowed his head. "Great heavenly Father. What a fearful thing this is that we have been called upon here to witness. It's a thing upon which a strong man can hardly look without a thrill of horror." As his mouth moved, McVicker's gray whiskers glinted in the light of the kerosene lamp. "We have here a case of a man who, from all we have heard, accused his wife of infidelity, who charged her with improper relations with men, when the truth is, a man would've had to be mad to think such things about her. We all knew her personal and we can all state for a fact that that's a dirty flat lie. So I say personal it's a case of plain ordinary cool deliberate murder done in the heat of passion. May the arm of heavenly justice properly punish the dastardly assassin. Father, we commend the soul of the woman into your care. Father, look down in love upon this poor tortured innocent boy. We know he knew not what he did. Amen."

"But where is the boy?" billowy Mrs. Herman Bell cried.

Herman Bell looked around. "Gone."

All the while that the neighbors were milling about, Roddy was running across town.

"I'm a murderer. Just like my dad. I better skip the country."

Roddy caught the steamboat *St. Louis* just as the Missouri River was floating it away from the wharf. No one saw him climb aboard.

PART TWO

Ten years later. June, 1875.

Earl Ransom

1

Two bearded horsemen detoured around an outcropping of fire-gnawed rocks. Each man led a string of four gray mules. The mules stepped along under light packs.

Toothy mountains on the left slowly retracted into the gums of a soft red land. Wind-combed prairies on the right gradually faded off into the mist of oncoming night.

The two men had taken their time coming north out of Denver. The eight mules, grazing mostly on buffalo grass, were silky and high-spirited. The two horses, both tan mustangs, were spunky.

The man in the lead was Sam Slaymaker, sometime freighter and prospector. He was the older, and a powerful chunk of a man. He was inclined to be fleshy when in town in the winter, and rawboned when on the trail in the summer. His long curly hair was gray, as was his bushy mustache, while his chin whiskers were as black and as scraggly as the beard of a buffalo bull. He wore buckskins from head to foot and was armed with a blue .45. His brown bear eyes continually roved from side to side, ever on the alert, sometimes hard and brilliant when some sign caught his interest, sometimes twinkling and gentle when some merry memory crossed his mind.

The other man was Earl Ransom, sometime swamper and prospector. He was young, at first glance appearing to be somewhere in his middle twenties, and a handsome piece of a man. He was always slim, summer or winter. His cropped hair was black, as was his gambler's mustache and wavy beard. He too wore buckskins and was armed with a six-shooter. His green eyes drifted from one object to another, sometimes dreamily silverish when looking up at the white mountain peaks to the west, sometimes smoky when looking within.

The trail straightened. Shortly, still heading north, they topped a rise. Ahead and below, on a wide light-green plain, lay the new city of Cheyenne.

Cheyenne lay mostly on the other side of Crow Creek. There were no trees. New brick buildings along Main Street lay stark in the sun. On the north side a dozen or so ornate houses with stables in back gave the town a little tone. A railroad lay along the south side, and down the draw on either side of the tracks stood huts, tents, dugouts, shacks, all sorts of ramshackle structures. Plumes of blue smoke from the various chimneys rose straight up to a level of a hundred feet, then bent off toward the east, forming a little cloud deck. An engine puffing in the yards added its deep black plume to the little cloud.

Both men reined in their horses, the strings of mules sauntering up around them. Both men settled back in their saddles and had themselves a long and loving look at

Cheyenne. Even Sam Slaymaker's tan mustang shot its ears forward, listening intently.

Sam observed his horse's interest. "From the way old Colonel's perked up here, you'd think he was as hot for a whiskey as you and me."

Ransom grunted.

Sam turned in his saddle. "Ransom, that's enough black sull out of you now. You've had a dally on your tongue all the way out of Denver. What's up with you, boy?"

"Nothing."

"More bad dreams?"

"Some."

"They'll pass, son. I used to have 'em myself on the trail." Sam stroked his mustache. "A long slow drink of good red American whiskey, plus a night with a girl on the line, will fix that."

Ransom nibbled on his lower lip. The tips of his mustache wiggled.

"Take them mice out of your mouth, boy. And no use to say they ain't there. I see the tips of their tails hanging out."

Ransom allowed himself a little smile. He touched his hand to his right eye.

"There! You did it again."

"What?"

"Like you was fixing on a monocle."

"You're loco."

"Like you was one of them London swells at the Cactus Club staring the people down."

"Don't know what you're talking about."

Sam's brown pig eye drifted off. "I'd give a pretty penny to know where you was born, bub." Sam waggled his head. "I'll just bet you my bottom dollar you was once some Lord's bastard kid somewhere. At least."

A young sneer moved under Ransom's black mustache.

"But you don't seem to remember much about who you

was before I picked you up an orphan off the prairie, so I reckon there ain't no use in guessing."

"No, there ain't."

"You really can't remember if you was hit over the head or something? Indian massacre?"

"No."

"Something powerful awful must've happened to wipe out your memory at that age."

Ransom didn't like the drift of the talk and showed it.

"And that name of yours. Earl Ransom. It smells a little like it was made up."

"It was."

"What!" Sam Slaymaker looked around greatly astounded. "Here I've given you the front tit for ten years, and all the mush and milk you want for breakfast, and you've never told me?"

"Well, I'm telling you now."

"I gave you a home, boy, and you never told me all this time?"

"That's right."

Sam's brown eyes bored in. "If you made it up, what was your real name then?"

"I don't know."

"You don't know?"

"No. That's why I made it up."

"How come you made up just that pa'ticular name? Instead of some other'n, say like Jim Clark or Jack Slade?"

"I don't know. It just come to me."

"Out of the blue?"

"Out of the blue."

"Not from some little kind of rememberin'?"

"No."

Sam sat in silence for a time. At last he heaved a sigh. "Wellsomever, lad, it's all right. But you are full of surprises."

"Just never thought to tell you."

"Well, I should've known. Any time a kid tells you he can't remember who he is, yet kin give you a name for himself, he is bound to spring a surprise or two on you in time."

A long haunting whistle rose white from the puffing engine below in the yards.

"Well, that's milk long ago spilled and dried." Sam waggled his reins. "Colonel, old skate, hup up. It's time we headed in." Sam's countenance brightened as he looked down at the little town in the light-green valley. "There's a woman down there that I've got a hankering to play fork with. By the name of Kate. She's the madam at The Stinging Lizard and this time she's gonna play my game no matter what her excuse may be. Broken ass or no. They say no man yet has ever got his horse between her shafts. Well, I'm from Pike County and I don't take no for an answer. Whoopee!"

The two horses, and the mules behind, began to move down toward Cheyenne. Leathers squinched. Hoofs clopped softly in the thick grass.

Ransom swayed with the walk of his horse. A crinkle of a smile lit up his green eyes. "This Kate woman now, sounds like she's got you hooked."

"You bet. And like a hooked catfish, I'll be glad to flop on the riverbank with her. You can have all the other young pigs she's got on the line there. Even that thirteen-year-old. Me, I like 'em around twenty-five. Like my Kate."

"A well-broke mare then."

"Right. Kate tells me she don't like it. But I know better. With that long English foot of hers she can't help but like her men big and horny."

"You know a lot about such things, don't you, Sam?"

"And this time, boy, you're coming with. It's time you had your pistol polished. And I don't mean your six-shooter."

Ransom flushed over his brow.

"Ha. You can still turn red, I see."

Ransom slapped his horse on the neck with the reins. "Prince, hup-up."

"Boy, that first time can be a wonder. Oh my. I know. Mine was with a widow in old St. Loo. She warn't no green girl, man no. She was choice."

Ransom continued to show red over the cheeks.

"Oh, you'll know when you finally make it, boy. It's like when all the birds fly out of the straw pile."

Ransom couldn't help but laugh out loud at that.

"And you shouldn't feel ashamed of doing it with a girl on the line. Out in the wilds here a man can't be choosy. Tell you, boy. Many a fine family has had its start with only a whore and a wild-eyed jackass for foundation stock."

The mustangs, then the mules, began to canter. The fringes on the buckskin clothes of the men threshed a little.

A bird fluttered up underfoot. Prince had almost stepped on it.

Ransom caught a glimpse of a cozy nest woven neatly into a clump of silver sage, and in it four eggs, deep brown speckled, pullet size.

"Nighthawk," Ransom said. "Hen."

"Yeh," Sam grunted. "Now watch close. Watch."

One of the buff bird's white-marked wings abruptly hung limp. The bird fluttered along as though hurt. It cried whimperingly. The bird slowly veered off to the right.

Sam said, "In nature the female is a sly one."

"Can you blame her?"

"No. That's her job. To think of her young." Sam rose in his stirrups, studying the ground. "Now somewheres around here she's got her nest hid."

Ransom didn't tell Sam he'd already seen it.

Gradually the horses carried them away from the spot, and presently Sam, interest lagging, resettled his broad butt into his saddle.

The mother nighthawk continued to whimper and flutter off in a wide irregular slant to the right, at last vanished into a spread of wolfberries.

Sam fell into a self-study.

Ransom noticed occasional wild flowers: prairie smoke with dusty purple plumes, puccoons with little golden trumpets, wild roses with five little pink tongues.

A jackrabbit squirted out of a whisker of grass, began to lollop off ahead.

Sam hauled up his horse. "Get him, boy! He's your shot."

Ransom's six-shooter was already out and fired. The jackrabbit knuckled over at the top of its second bound, hit the ground long legs over, and fell dead.

"Good shot, boy. With that hogleg you're just about the best shot I ever did see."

"Keeps me broke practicin' though."

"You should worry so long as I pay the freight."

"I'd rather be an expert at something else. Even go to school somewhere."

Sam was aghast. "You take up larnin' at your age? When it's time you already had you a family started?"

"Or make a killing somewhere. Strike gold."

"You will, boy, you will. If we don't make our fortune hauling freight to the Black Hills with this span of rats, we'll make it panning gold. We'll find us some lone gulch somewhere, where the gold lays for the taking at the roots of the grass. Provided the U.S. Army don't keep us out of the Hills."

"Or maybe I should take to cards full time."

"No, that I'm agin. No."

"Well, that's the one thing I do like to do. Playing with chance."

"Anyways, fresh rabbit first." Sam slid off his horse, and walked over and got the rabbit. He tied its rear legs together with a whang jerked from his buckskin pants, then, remounting Colonel, hung the rabbit from his saddle. "We'll barbecue this while we water the horses in yon creek."

Ransom wished Sam was his true father.

Later, while the horses and mules drank their fill, and the rabbit was roasting over a fire of buffalo chips, Sam couldn't help but let go some more. Clapping the underbelly of his horse with a loud pop, he crowed, "Whoops! I'm eight foot tall, I am, and my home is where the women are horny and the men are up like bulls on two legs. Ya-hoo! My parlor is the Rocky Mountains, my footstool is all of Nebraska, and my privy is the Grand Canyon. Yessiree! I smell like a wolf with his sword out. I drink water out of the crick like a horse. Look out, you short-armed sons of bitches, I'm going to turn loose and sire me up a nation of wild-eyed buckskin bastards."

Again Ransom couldn't help but smile at Sam's talk.

2

Sam got them a room at the American House.

They bathed, slipped into new fancy tan leathers, combed their hair and beards, saw their guns ready for action.

Sam cukked like a cock. "Come over here by the window, boy, and see the ladies. So you'll know one when you see one." The sun was just setting. "Ah, there goes one now. Whoops! Ain't she a pretty-looking thing? Look, man. Look at her." Sam waved a long fat smoking cigar. "First a big bump, then two little bumps, and then the good Lord only knows what a wilderness of crimps and frills besides. And a hauling up of her dress here and there." Sam gave Ransom a dig in the ribs. "Just look at that power of a hairdo stacked up on top of her head there. And that bitty little hat, with its poor lost bird's tail dragging along, ain't that something?"

"Nnn."

"Somewhere inside all that footer there you'll find a neat little trick that makes the world go round. Ee-yow!" Sam chomped on his cigar and clapped his sides with the flat of his hands. "It's that that I want and it's that that I'm going to get."

Ransom smiled.

"Don't worry, boy. With your looks, the girls at The Stinging Lizard'll come cooing around you like doves after corn."

"Ha."

"Now listen to me, you. When you've finally decided which one you want, this is what you do. You sweet-talk her about some gold you've found. You know. Gold, gold!"

"We haven't found any yet."

Sam stomped around. "Dammit, boy, will you listen to me?"

"All right."

"Gold, gold! Do that and pretty soon your gal will lean toward you like a sore-eyed kitten to a basin of milk."

"What if I don't love her?"

"Pah! Love will go where it is sent."

Ransom's lower lip came out. It showed pink, full, almost like an extra tongue under his black gambler's mustache.

"And don't worry, boy. From what I heard that wagon master say, the one that rode with Custer all over the Black Hills, there's gold a-laying there between them slabs of rock as thick as cheese in a sandwich."

"There better be."

They went down through the lobby. The air was heavy with the odors of pipe tobacco, whiskey, new corduroys, sweated leathers. In the wide doorway they stepped around a fat man looking at a watch as big as a biscuit. Two blue soldiers, leaning against a porch post, stood as if put there to hold it up.

Clouds of brown moved down the street, going from west to east, as much dusk as dust. Sometimes starlight caught a floating mote just right and made it glint like gold, an infinitesimal atom of it. Oxen droppings gave off a pervasive stinging smell. Occasionally a fiber of horse dung stuck on the edge of a wet lip, sometimes went up the nostril like a lost bit of snuff. The sound of clopping horse hoofs, rattling wheels, irregular squealing dry axles filled the air. Mares bugled for lost colts, geldings for lost studhood, mules for lost ancestry. Over it all, like a floating net, up and down, loose and taut, rode the ceaseless veil of human talk.

A gallows reared against the fleshen sky on the west end of Main Street. A single humped question mark hung dangling between its wooden parentheses.

Ransom and Sam turned right. Their heels made low stumping sounds on the hollow boardwalk.

They passed a stagecoach office, a Chinese laundry, an opera house, a blacksmith shop, a gun shop.

The doors to all the stores were jammed with floaters: railhead tramps, buffalo hunters, trappers, bullwhackers, miners, old mountain men, cowboys, soldiers, Indians, half-breeds, gamblers, promoters, lawyers, gunmen. Everybody wore a weapon of some kind, gun, rifle, knife. There were continual surges of raw laughter and raw talk and raw song.

"A real Saturday-night town," Sam commented. "Wild and woolly and hard to curry."

"With never a Sunday to worry about," Ransom added. "Nor any excommunications."

"God sure must've raked out the bottom of hell to outfit this place."

"That he did."

"Denver is heaven compared to this."

"Now, yes. But twenty years ago, no."

"Was Denver really tough then?"

"It was. And in some ways worse. There was more money there. By a long ways. This is only a jump-off place." Sam smiled out of his massy gray beard. "But wait'll you see the town we'll build us in the Black Hills when the new gold stampede is really on."

"I can hardly wait."

"You are in a hurry, ain't y'u?"

"I aim to get rich quick. There's a lot of things I want to do before I die. I feel it in my bones that I'm meant for something big."

"There's plenty of time."

They strolled past the swank brick Cactus Club. Two English dandies were taking it easy in a big swing on the wide veranda. They were tippling wine and smoking long cigars. They looked upon the turmoil of the street with brow-raised hauteur.

Sam muttered. "There's got to be a lot of money around somewhere for them classy bastards to be here."

"They're mostly interested in ranching, I hear."

"Maybe."

They stepped into the Hub of Hell for a drink. Hurdy-gurdy girls, tinhorn gamblers, road agents, prospectors milled around inside the place like whirling swill in the bottom of a bucket.

The barkeep asked, "What'll it be, gents? Speak right up."

"Some good red American whiskey. Long ones," Sam said. "A ticket to hell for two."

A buckskin hunter standing down the bar watched Ransom take a reluctant sip of his drink at the same time that he saw Sam throw his down. The hunter smoked a corncob pipe. When Ransom took yet a second slow sip, the hunter removed his corncob and asked Ransom, "First time in town, bub?"

"This town, yes."

"Don't be afraid of it. It's as good a place as any to get your family jewels shined."

Sam lit up another long fat cigar. "That's what I say, boy. Let go of them brakes."

Ransom shook his head. "No. I'm afraid I'm already headed downhill when it comes to liquor."

The hunter closed his eyes upon his own thoughts.

Later, when no one was looking, Ransom quietly emptied what was left of his drink into Sam's glass.

They next pushed through the swing doors of The Golden Man. It was the hangout for three-card monte men, graying Civil War vets, and remittance men down on their uppers.

"What'll it be, pardner?" the barkeep asked.

"Some good red American whiskey."

"I better warn you we sell the worst whiskey in captivity."

"That's why we came. We like honest whiskey."

"Drinks for a couple of the boys who want to play their harps with a hammer."

Again Ransom sipped reluctantly while Sam drank up.

A blue soldier wearing a black hat stood across the turn of the bar from them. He sneered at Ransom. "A one and only wonder, I see."

Sam turned a serious beard on the soldier boy. "What was that?"

"Your sidekick here wouldn't slap at a botfly even if 'twas laying an egg in one of his balls, I suppose."

Sam whispered under a hand, "Watch it, soldier. Don't let the kid's looking like a greenhorn fool you. He's got a temper like a hot springs geyser. Just take a gander at his gun. See it all notched up like a corncob there?"

The soldier looked at the handle of Ransom's gun, then at Ransom's hand.

"By the way," Sam said, "is the Army gonna keep us out of the Black Hills?"

"I don't know."

Ransom poured what was left of his drink in the soldier's glass.

"Hey!"

Sam laughed.

The soldier cried, "Who said you could throw your swill into my glass?"

Again Sam laughed. "Consider it a compliment, friend."

They strolled out onto the moiling street again.

Eyes worked at winking away floating specks of dust.

"It's getting on," Sam said, "and my one-eyed Kate waits. Let's head in and see what she's got for us at her hog ranch."

"I'm not interested in a whore the first time."

Sam laughed Ransom down. "But you are the second time, eh?"

"Not ever." Ransom stepped over a steaming batch of fresh horse biscuits.

"Boy, where in tarnation did you ever get such an idee, hey?"

"I wish I knew myself. Because otherwise I've got as much of a hot for a woman as you have." Ransom let his heels hit the plank walk in a slow measured fall.

"You sound like you wanna get married bad."

"I do."

Sam chewed on the tips of his mustache. "Hum."

"Nights when I lay there aching like a great big sweet toothache."

Sam laughed. "The tooth that bites the hardest is the tooth that's out of sight, eh?"

A smile moved inside Ransom's black mustache.

"Then you ain't comin' with?"

"Oh, I'll come with all right."

"Ah. Now I got you in my sights. You're going to be one of them eye-fornicators the Good Book tells of."

"As a favor to you, is all."

"Ha. Come on."

They turned a corner and went up a side street. Except for light from occasional windows, the street was dark. The walk was a path in the dust. Heels hit muted.

Two cowboys bumped past. They were laughing about somebody having big ears. The one cowboy said, "Buzz was four years old before his ma could figure out if he was going to fly or walk." The other cowboy said, "Why, I remember those big ears of his. In a picture of him his ma once said, 'The one in the middle is Buzz.'"

On the side street the smell of horse dung was not quite so strong. Scent of sage rode on the steady breeze. There were gunshots west of town.

Two miners standing in a shadow traded memories. The one miner said, "You never know when you're going to hit it. Why, there was Simp Dickson. 'Member him? That short-armed nut? He was just out diggin' a grave for a stiff who'd gone under, and, by God, there he found it." The other miner said, "Yeh, and look what happened to Smokie. Tired of prospectin', he lay down in the shade of a tree to rest. When he went to get to his feet, the rock he used to brace himself on was almost solid gold."

Pink lights winked on the next corner. There was a sound of laughter, of singing, behind the pink lights.

"Somebody's having fun," Sam said.

"Is that it?"

"That's it, my boy, The Stinging Lizard. Yessiree."

The building with the pink windows was a two-story affair, new, and more mansion than saloon. Curtains and blinds were drawn tight across the bay windows, though vague illumination still seeped out along the sides. The place had a big veranda, with porch swings and rockers, and the front door was huge, of oak, and like the rest of the house stained brown.

Sam pushed in, Ransom following.

They found themselves in a red parlor, ornate, restful. A half-dozen women dressed only in pink wrappers mewed a greeting.

"Welcome to The Stinging Lizard, the cowboys' rest," an assured woman's voice said. "Well, well, if it ain't good old Sam Slaymaker. Sam!" The woman speaking sat across from the girls, on a red chaise longue, feet up on a red footstool.

"Kate! Hi, beauty. How's tricks these days?"

"Pretty well. Just come to town?"

"Yip. And this time I mean to skin that onion with you. The one you left me with last time."

"Now, Sam, you know I can't cry. That is, if you mean to bring me to tears."

Sam roared a short laugh. "You see, boy? What'd I tell

you? Nobody, but nobody, plays fork with her. Her tines are too sharp."

Ransom saw that Sam was right about Kate. Here was no alcoholic old harlot, but a handsome good-looking woman with hair the color of gold puccoons and the waist of a young girl. Ransom decided she wasn't much older than himself. The neat black patch over her left eye became her. It was stitched all around with gold thread and was held in place by a narrow black ribbon slipped around her head. It worked for her like a single big plum in an apple pie—it gave her appearance a tang.

Kate swung her feet off the footstool and stood up. Her purple velvet dress touched the floor, making her seem tall. A gold-plated watch with a long mesh chain hung glistening high on the left side of her bosom. Her single brown eye examined Ransom critically point for point. "And who's this handsome is as handsome does, Sam?"

"'Member me telling you about him the last time I was here? The little shaver I picked up wandering lost in the tall grass west of Omaha? Well, that's him, growed up."

"He's no boy."

"Of course he ain't."

"He's a grown man."

"A wildcat, in fact."

Kate ranged herself alongside Ransom. She admired Ransom's slim height. "Just how old are you, mister?"

"Your guess is as good as mine."

Kate threw Sam a look. "Don't he really know how old he is?"

"Ask him."

"Well?" Kate gave Ransom an arching smile.

Ransom roughed the end of his nose with a forefinger. "Well, I always say I feel I'm about twenty-five, and that's good enough for me."

"Lived out west all your life?"

"Not yet."

Kate laughed. "Ha." She placed a light hand on his arm. "What's your handle these days?"

Her touch made Ransom jump inside. Also, something about the aroma of her, her personal perfume, caught him in the chest. He managed a playful smile. "Well, now, ma'am, that'd be telling."

"I'll just call you Mr. Handsome."

"Sam generally calls me boy."

Sam didn't like it that Kate had put a hand on Ransom's arm. "The kid told me his name was Earl Ransom. When I saved him from the wolves."

Kate's brown eye turned warm. "Well, I wasn't too far off, was I? Handsome is as Ransom does."

Ransom smiled some more. "Handsome, no. Ransom, yes."

Sam ratched out his throat with a big growl. "Kate, you know what this fool greenhorn told me?"

"No."

"That he didn't want one of your sweet pigeons the first time."

Kate's brown eye thinned. "I don't catch."

"He said he'd rather get married first."

The sweet pigeons behind Kate emitted little mews of protest. They came up and began to flutter around Ransom. They too admired his easy slim frame. They shimmied inside their pink wrappers so that it seemed they had purplish wings.

Kate said, "I take it then he's never visited a cowpoke house before."

"No, he hain't."

A new light, risen, appeared in Kate's eye.

"Can you imagine it?" Sam cried, scornful.

Kate said, thoughtful, "Good for him."

"What?"

"I'm not always out to work a man, Sam."

"Well I'll be blowed by a nosefly."

Scent of her worked into Ransom. It was like a ghost hand cocking a gun in him.

"I don't see that thirteen-year-old pokie around," Sam said, looking at the girls. "She busy?"

"Why?"

"I thought maybe she'd be more the kid's speed."

"She up and married on me."

"Too bad." Sam gave his beard a tug. "By the way, just what are you chargin' for tricks these days?"

Kate eased Sam off with a warm smile. "The usual. But don't you want a shot of Wisdom River first? Warm up a little?"

"Some red American whiskey will suit me just fine at that."

Kate clapped her hands. "Tidbit? Man the bar."

The shortest girl there, well under five feet, as pert as a kewpie, moving with all the slimness of a nymph, got busy behind a mahogany bar at the far end of the sitting room.

"Hey, where's your old barkeep Horses?" Sam said.

"Horses I had to let go."

"How come?"

"Two of my girls got to fighting over him. Sulie and Rut. And I had to choose between them and him."

"Good for old Horses."

"Then too, he was always starting fights with the customers. Stud jealousy, I suspect. Because since I let him go, I've had no more brawls. Not one."

Sam nodded. "I suppose he's skipped the country?"

"No. He's joined the Army."

"The U.S. Army?"

"Yes. Here. Fort Russell outside town here."

"Naw!"

"In charge of the Army's mules."

"Naw!"

"Colonel Bullock says he's the best mule man they ever had."

Sam regarded her suspicious. "You talk to the Colonel much?"

"He has a pet here."

"It's not you?"

"It's Lava Black."

"That's better." Sam threw Ransom a glittering look. "Well, Sir Jesus Horatio Christ, you gonna join me in a drink?"

Ransom shook his head.

Sam threw up his hands. "You see, Kate, what did I tell you? I show him where to find the honeypot and this is what he does with it. I'm afeared I raised me a pisswillie. A missionary maybe even."

"Let him be, Sam. A bee gets drunk on honey soon enough." Kate gave Ransom another touch on the arm.

Nervous, Ransom touched his right hand to his right eye. "I'll take some sarsaparilla."

Kate clapped her small hands, once. "Tidbit, you heard the man."

The three of them sat together on a red hair sofa near the bar, Ransom on the right, Sam on the left, Kate in the middle, their feet resting on a thick green Brussels carpet. In a corner one of the girls began to dream on a Barbary organ, lightly, romantically.

Ransom's eyes kept going back to Kate. He sipped his sarsaparilla slowly. He fingered and rolled the tips of his gambler mustache.

Sam drank up his tumbler of red whiskey with a flourish and immediately ordered another. He gave Tidbit a gold piece. The sofa groaned under his stirring bulk.

Kate sat closer to Ransom than to Sam. Her eyes kept sliding off to examine Ransom covertly. She kept spiffing herself up a little, slyly, a touch to the hair, a wet fingertip to the brow.

Sam wasn't blind. "Kid, how do you do it?"

"I don't get you."

"Since her whorehouse burned down in Denver, I ain't never seen Kate so feisty."

Kate said, "Come, come, Sam, it was my cowboys' rest you meant, wasn't it now?"

"Hell, no. I meant your whorehouse."

"Shh, now."

"Kid, trying to get Kate to open up is sometimes like trying to open a river clam with a blade of grass."

"Why don't you try tickling with your blade of grass, Sam, instead of trying to force your way in," Kate said.

A flutter of laughter came from the hovering pigeons.

Sam drank up again and ordered a third red whiskey.

Ransom still sipped on his first drink. He smiled at everything Kate said. He sometimes smiled so deep the muscles over his cheekbones hurt.

Sam rolled his massive hairy head. "Aw, Kate, I'm plainly jealous of the kid, that I am. He's young and fresh, with everything still in front of him. But since you're too old for him anyway, and are more made for me, what do you say this time? Ready to skin that onion with me at last?"

Kate gave Sam a soft bland smile.

Sam set his red whiskey down on the arm of the hair sofa. "Aw, Kate, I favor you." Suddenly Sam put his cumbering bear arm around her and handled her like she might be a bundle of wheat. "I favor you." He hugged her so hard that a sound came from her chest like a suddenly closed concertina. "I've beat on your door, and pounded on it, and yet I've just never had me the right key to open your lock. By God, if you don't open up to me pretty soon, I'm gonna have to tromp your door down, Kate."

"Sam, please!"

"Kate, I favor you." Whiskey tears filmed Sam's bear eyes. "Kate, girl."

Kate managed to free an arm and then grabbed Sam's glass of whiskey before it spilled onto the floor. "Sam! You're letting your nose get out of joint now. Be careful." Kate still had a soft bland smile for Sam, but her voice had turned chilly.

Ransom couldn't see for a moment. Red blankets seemed to have dropped down across his eyes. He tried to remember that Sam was his father and uncle and brother all rolled into one.

Kate said, "Sam, you know that's impossible for me. You of all people know this."

Sam gave a little cry, and swallowed over his pride, and after a bit let her go.

"That's better." Kate winked at Tidbit. "Another round for the boys. On the house this time."

From the back of the house came some scuffling, then laughter. A moment later a door to the rear opened and a cowboy and one of the girls sauntered in. The cowboy had a leached-out look around the eyes and the girl, a Mexican, was flushed. The cowboy was still sweet on her, and he clung to her hand.

A firm look passed from Kate to the Mexican girl.

The girl immediately withdrew her hand.

The cowboy was hurt. "Aw, honey. . . ." He reached for her hand again.

Kate said crisply, "Jamie boy, it's turn and turn about here, you know. Unless you care to pay double."

Sam woke up. "Hey. Ain't that Little Coyote? The one I've heard so much about? Why, I've even heard tell of her on Pike's Peak."

"Could be, Sam."

"Gives you as purty a waddle across a sheet as any duck alive today."

Upon a hint from Kate, Little Coyote threw another discouraging look at her cowboy; then worked up a little house smile for Sam.

- The downcast cowboy left.

Sam threw a last sad look at Kate. "When all's said and done, it's really all one and the same thing, ain't it?" Sam got

up and went over and put his great arm around Little
Coyote. "C'mon, you little prairie wolf, let's you and I dig
us a den on the other side of the hill."

Kate smiled approvingly.

Sam waved the flat of his hand against Kate and disappeared into the rear of the house with Little Coyote.

Kate and Ransom exchanged smiles.

A moment later there was a thunderbolt of a knock on the
door.

"Horses!" Kate exclaimed, bounding to her feet. Her
carven Indian lips turned white.

Ransom came to his feet too. "Where? Who?" His right
hand fell naturally to the butt of his gun.

"Close the bar, Tidbit!" Kate hurried to the front door. She
moved with long almost leaping strides. "Hurry."

Tidbit pulled one handle, then another, and two sliding
doors came out of the wall and in the flick of an eye
completely hid the bar.

Two other girls, Hermie and Frankie, both braw and
strong, rushed to Kate's side. Their chins were suddenly
hard.

The rest of the girls quickly dashed into the rear of the
house.

Kate got her hands on the bar to the door all right, but
before she could slam it to, the big oak door swung inward
and brushed her aside as if she were a whisk broom.

"Horses! Oh you! Now, no rough stuff now."

A shaggy stud of a man, black hair pluming straight up,
heavy nose ridging high between black eyes, lunged around
to face her. He was dressed in Army blue. His black boots
looked more like hoofs than human footwear. "Luv!"

"Now, Horses, you just be civilized now. You hear me? No
roughhousing. Civilized."

"Kate, you know I can't be civetlike."

"Civilized, I said. Not civet cat." Kate moved back from
Horses a good half-dozen steps, imperious, single eye glitter-

ing darkly. The two braw girls flanked her. "You're drunk, Horses. Go home and sleep it off."

Ransom edged over in case Kate should need him.

"Horses, please now."

"Luv, I've missed you so." Horses had more of a neigh than a voice.

"You go home or I'll call the Colonel."

"Why, I ain't done nothin' yet, Kate."

"I know you."

Horses worked to get both his black eyes focused on Kate; finally managed it. "Luv, you know you promised me I could come once in a while."

"You're a liar."

Horses reared back. "Liar, you say?" Horses reflected. "Well, maybe I sometimes do lie. But, by God, nobody's ever caught me at it. Not yet, anyway. Nosiree. Not even the Colonel."

Kate had to laugh. "Horses, please now, go home."

"Luv."

"Look, dearie. The girl you like, Ivory, is with a friend just now. Come back later and I'll let you visit her a little. On the house."

Horses held his head to one side. "Kate, you know I think Ivory is perfectly beautiful, with the exception that her mouth is a little crooked. Which comes from reaching after all them high notes when her heart ain't in it."

Again Kate had to laugh. Sometimes the remarks that originated in his huge horse of a head could be as piercing as horse radish. If only he had a bit more horse sense. "And your other two admirers, Sulie and Rut, they're busy entertaining two other friends just now."

"Aw, shucks, Kate, I never did care for Sulie or Rut none."

"Well, I'm just telling you, is all."

"Luv." Horses made a sudden plunge for Kate.

Ransom took a quick step forward and tripped Horses.

Horses plowed nose first through a row of chairs on the far side of the sitting room. Four of the chairs tipped over.

Silence.

Horses lay like a big overturned boat, unmoving.

Kate had a smile for Ransom. "Thank you."

"Hope I didn't kill him."

"Horses? Never."

"Looks pretty quiet to me."

"Pah. He's been known to run down telegraph poles, and get up off the ground none the worse for it."

Sam came in. Alone. Subdued. His brown bear eyes looked around uneasy.

A high light sparked in Ransom's green eyes. He couldn't help but stick it into Sam a little. "Well, and how was the neat little trick that makes the world go roun'?"

"Shut up."

Kate acted surprised. "You didn't find it satisfactory?"

"It was as flat as mouse urine on a plate."

The light in Ransom's green eyes continued to shine derisive. "You didn't get to dig that den on the other side of the hill then?"

"She didn't even begin to take the boil out of my blood." Sam's beard twitched. "I still say, Kate, you was made for me, and someday you'll be mine."

"Sam."

Sam banged his chest with a fist. "By God, woman, Sam Slaymaker will even marry you, if that's your wish."

"Sam, Sam."

"I'm still making you the offer. And I'm baiting it with gold. Gold, you hear? Gold, gold!"

A groan came from behind the fallen chairs. Then came a single word. "Luv."

Sam hauled up short. "Hey, look who's here."

"Yes, dear old Horses has paid us a call."

"Luv."

"What's that he says?"

"Luv."

Sam thickened. "By God, who's he calling Luv?"

"Ivory."

"Oh. That's different."

"Luv."

Sam went over and gave Horses a kick in the butt. "Get up, you two-inch fool. Who you holding down on the floor there, the mayor's wife again?"

"The mayor's wife?" Kate said.

Sam let go with a wild horse laugh. "Oh, down on the Des Moines once, Horses made a woman get down on her back in the bottom of his boat before he would row her across. Horses ran a ferry there."

"Why, the dirty old fool."

"Yeh, Horses is quite a Horses all right." Again Sam gave Horses a kick in the butt. "Get up, you brain-broke stud you, or your life won't be worth a gooser."

Horses, groaning, finally managed to get up on all fours, then on all two. He threw back his black hair, adjusted his six-shooter, and glared at Kate. The brass buttons on his blue uniform glowed. "You know, luv, more and more you're turning out to be a mean old hag of a thing."

"Now, Horses, dearie."

"And your tongue's got to be about as dangerous as a barrage of arrows."

A thought came to Kate. "Horses, I wonder, me and the boys were about to sit down to a couple of hands. . . . You wouldn't want to . . . ah . . . ?"

Gambling fever instantly flashed in Horses' eyes. Horses rolled back on his heels. "Draw?" Horses made little crinching noises between his thumb and forefinger.

"Draw." Kate threw a look at Sam and Ransom. "You still want to sit down to a little game, boys?"

Sam went along with her little ploy. Sam pursed his lips in his beard. "Aw, Kate, you know how I hate to take Horses' money away from him. It's like taking it from a little kid."

"Ho ho!" Horses roared. "We'll see about that."

Gambling fever also awoke in Ransom. He had never been able to resist the fascination of the luck of the draw, and ever since his first game in Denver, when he and Sam had been cleaned out by a mustached slicker, had worked hard at becoming an expert at cards. He had even learned how to play his hunches well when he wasn't sure of his averages.

"Mr. Ransom?" Kate asked.

"Oh, I guess I'm game for a few hands."

"Good." Kate led the way to a gaming table. Her purple dress swished on each vigorous stride. "Anybody object if the house does the banking?"

Nobody did.

Kate sat at the head of the table, Ransom on her left, Sam across from her, Horses on her right. Each man bought ten dollars' worth of chips. A blue chip was worth a dollar, a red chip a half-dollar, a white chip two bits.

Kate said briskly, "Ten percent kitty for the house. OK?"

"Suits us."

"And house rules will be as follows: nothing higher than a two-bit ante and a four-bit raise. That all right?"

"Suits us."

"I don't want the game to get rough." Kate produced a fresh set of celluloid cards and fanned them out over the table. Each picked a card. Ransom came up with the two of hearts, Sam the king of spades, Horses with the ace of clubs, and Kate the ten of diamonds.

"Ha," Horses cried. "I'm high man with God's card."

Sam growled, "I never could figure out why them birds who invented cards ever put anything above a king. Ain't the king always the head of the guv'ment?"

Horses smiled the superior smile of a horse. "Why, Sam, it's because there's something higher than the human bein'. Higher even than a king human bein'. And that's God, of course. The one and all."

"Deal out," Sam said.

"Ante before you see a card, all."

Everybody tossed in a white chip.

"Jacks or better." Horses had big rough hands, but when it came to cards they weren't clumsy. He shuffled expertly, dealt out five each in five wheeling revolving motions.

"Kate? How many?"

"Pass." Kate threw her hand into the discard.

"Kid?"

Ransom fanned out his cards one by one. "Just one."

"Ha. Drawing to a straight or a full house, I see." Horses flipped down one card. "Sam?"

"Three."

"Ha. Got a pair, I see. Three it is for Sam."

Sam growled to himself.

Horses looked down either side of his high nose at his own hand. "And two for me."

Sam passed cigars. Horses took one, Ransom declined. Sam and Horses lit up.

Silence. Kate sat back, watchful. Ransom rested easy. Sam blew up a little whirlwind of smoke.

Horses shifted on his hams. "Kid? Openers?"

Ransom had them. He'd drawn an eight to a bobtail straight queen down. He tossed in a white chip. "I'll bet two bits."

"Sam?"

"Check."

Horses pursed big rubbery lips. "Raise you a quarter." He tossed in a red chip.

Ransom wondered. Had Horses peeled one off the bottom of the deck? "Raise you another." He tossed in a red chip.

"Sam?"

"I fold." Sam threw his hand into the discard too. He sat back on two legs.

"Kid?"

"Raise you." Ransom tossed in another red chip.

Horses pushed out his big heavy lips even farther. He

gave Ransom a horse-nose sneer. "No round-the-corner straights now."

"Call or shut up."

Horses' ears set out. "You've got an awful big blab for a feller with such a teedly little gizzard."

Sam dropped down on all four legs. "Easy, Horses."

"Why easy with him?"

"The kid's got a gizzard as big as a tub. Loaded with gravel."

Horses looked Ransom over, from head on down. "Where's he keep it then?"

"Lay off, Horses. I'm warning you. He don't like that kind of talk much. He can be a wolf on a horse."

Horses studied his fan of cards. "All right. Raise you four bits." Horses tossed in a red chip and a white chip.

"Raise you another half-dollar."

"Sweetenin' up the pot a little, huh, kid? Raise you the same."

"Raise."

"Raise."

"Raise."

Kate threw Ransom a wondering glance, then looked across at Sam.

Sam smiled. "He's all right, Kate. A real student of the picture cards."

Horses said, "I got a cinch hand, kid. You sure you ain't bettin' on a skipper?"

"Buck the tiger or shut up."

Horses' high nose came up some more. "Kid, I think you're pretty much of a bluff. With your big slick toe sticking out there a-tripping people."

Ransom closed his fan of cards. A smile opened his dark beard.

"You can save your smiles for the wimmen, kid."

Sam said, "Dammit all, Horses, watch it. For godsakes, man. The boy don't take much fooster."

Horses said, "You talk a lot, Sam."

Sam bristled. "You don't believe me?"

"No."

"By the Lord." Sam bellied out. "You one-inch fool you. You must have a buffalo chip for a brain if you don't see he's good grit."

Horses put down his cigar and stood up. "One inch it is now, ha?"

Kate said sharply, "Tap her light, boys, she's deep enough."

Horses glared down at Sam.

Sam sneered up at Horses.

Kate first glanced around to make sure her two girl guards Hermie and Frankie were handy, then said, "Boys, all this pawing and blowing has got to stop right now."

Just then the big door to the rear of the house opened partially and the voices of two girls bidding a couple of cowboys good night could be heard. Then the girls themselves entered, brushing down their pink shifts and bouncing up the back of their hairdos. One had a hatchet face and the other the face of a sheep.

Horses, seeing them, sat down with a thump. It was Sulie and Rut.

The two girls squealed when they spotted Horses. "Sweetie pie!" They skipped across the room and fell on Horses' neck and began to kiss him up and down his big nose and all over his big ears.

Horses bore up under it all with the lofty phlegm of a Shetland pony being petted by a passel of town kids.

It made Kate smile. She relaxed. "Now, now, girls, please. You can have him when we've finished our couple of hands."

The two girls kept up their cooing and kissing.

"Sulie! Rut! Please now."

Horses finally had enough too. "Sulie," he said, and he took the dark hatchet-faced one by the arm and flung her gently aside. "Rut," he said, and he took the blond sheep-faced one by the shoulder and flung her gently the other way. Both girls fell to the floor, skinny shanks exposed.

Ransom's smile deepened. Ransom thought it one of the funniest things he'd ever seen that great big ugly Horses should invite the affection of two old beat-up railroad whores. The more he thought about it the more he had to smile. Finally a wonderful peal of laughter broke from him.

Horses gave Ransom a steady look. "People in torn underwear hadn't oughter laugh at the dent in the neighbor's hat. 'Specially when it's a silk hat."

Sam threw what was left of his cigar into the fireplace. "A silk hat, is it?" And Sam began to laugh and laugh too.

Horses fixed big glistening eyes on Sam, first one, then the other. "I've shot my gun off in a crib before, you know."

Sulie and Rut, having collected their wits, scrambled up off the floor and went back to the attack. They went at it so hot and heavy that Horses tipped over backward, chair and all. Horses landed on his back, knees up, the clawing girls on top.

"Girls!" Kate cried. "Let's be a little civilized now."

Ransom and Sam continued to roar with laughter.

Sulie and Rut bumped foreheads as they dove down to kiss Horses. The bumping hurt, and they backed off to glare balefully at each other.

"I'm first," Sulie said, flat.

"You know you promised me him first the next time," Rut said, flat. "Because there ain't never enough of him left the second time the same day."

"I'm first anyways."

"Now I am mad. Because you promised."

"First."

Rut hauled off and hit Sulie one, bony fist on bony cheek. "Ow! Why, you. . . ." Sulie in turn hauled off and hit Rut one.

While the girls with their skinny arms and legs and unleavened breasts flailed and flapped at each other, Horses still lay on his back, knees up, a big wandering eye full of wonder on each side of his high nose.

Between cloudbursts of laughter, Sam managed to gasp, "You know, watching them two fight over Horses, it's like seeing two sparrows fight over a turd. By the Lord if it ain't now."

At that Horses came up off the floor, first on his hands and knees, then on his feet. He backed off exactly four paces. He glared down at Sam with red-dotted eyes. "Sam, the Army don't like that. Even if you was to smile along with it."

"Well?"

Horses stood with legs wide apart, right hand poised. "Instead of laughing like you is."

Sam continued to sit laughing beside the gaming table. "Horses, you think too much like a calf in a swamp. Too slow and hardly at all. We don't mean you no harm."

"You just named your day to pay up your 'rears."

"Oh, c'mon now, Horses, lay off."

"Close your valves, and draw."

Kate cried, "Boys, please now!"

Everybody scrambled out of range.

Ransom stationed himself at Sam's right.

Sam lifted his upper lip. "You must be plumb off your mental reservation, man. This ain't no shootin' matter yet."

"Get to your feet! You're about to make a trip alone."

Sam laughed, short. "I'm not getting up for nobody."

"Sam!" Kate warned. "He's in the Army now, you know. If something should happen to him, you know what the Army'll do to this house. They'll close us down tight."

Sam waved Kate down. "I know my Horses. There won't be any cathop here."

Little spasms worked in Horses' right hand. "Cathop or no cathop, calling a man what you just called me is plain low wrong. Even if you was to just plain smile with it."

"Horses, you're an old pard of my bosom. Sit down and resume the game."

Horses continued to eye Sam malignant. "I'm standing pat on what I says."

Sam folded his arms and leaned back.

"Draw."

Sam tried a wink on Horses. He smiled forgiving.

"Work in one more wink, Sam, and I drills a hole right in the middle of the eye that winks."

Sam turned to Ransom. "Boy, can't you say something that'll set his intellects to milling the other way?"

Ransom found his right hand poised.

"Draw," Horses said down to Sam. "You dirty mother-forker."

Sam shook his head.

"Then, Sam, it's time for the Army to speak up. The whole U.S. Army of these here United States." There was a whirl of a big hand and a loud pop.

A little cloud of dust puffed out of Sam's buckskin shirt, from the left shoulder. Sam's face turned pale. "Horses! Why, you're crazier than a woman's watch, man."

Horses shot Sam again, in the stomach. "This time then."

Red life began to gush out of Sam's belly. Slowly he crippled over at the waist; at last, face first, tilted forward like a landslide.

"Sam!" Kate caught Sam in her arms.

The girls screamed.

Kate grabbed a red goose pillow off the chaise longue and eased it under Sam's head. "Dear. Dear."

Sam ignored Kate. He turned his head and fixed his eyes on Ransom. "I thought you had a quick gun, boy."

Ransom chilled over.

Sam let go a bloody sigh. "Wellsomever, it's all right, boy." He lay guggling. "Guess I better get in my last will and testament. Pronto." Again he fixed his eyes on Ransom. "Boy, them span of rats is yours. I give 'em to you."

"Sam," Kate said.

Sam managed a white smile through his bushy gray mustache. "You might say that this was a case of two studs trying to get into the same collar at the same time."

Kate wept.

"Don't waste any salt on me, woman. In a minute I'll be dead enough to skin."

The girls of the house filed silently in. Like bewildered magpies they stood ringed around Sam, gagging and gawking.

A green fly appeared from nowhere and buzzed in and around them and with a final turn landed on the tip of Sam's nose.

Kate shooed it away.

Disturbed, the green fly buzzed straight for the nearest window, hit the blind with a light thud, then came buzzing back. Once again it landed on Sam's nose.

"Shoo."

Sam whispered, "That fly is right, Kate. Leave it alone. Because I'm dead." And with a jerk Sam was dead.

Kate snapped a fingertip at the green fly.

The green fly again headed for the window; hit the blind with a light thud. This time it stayed put.

Gun still in hand, Horses stepped up. He circled Kate's waist with his left arm and hauled her to his feet. "All right, luv, now that we've got rid of him, let's spill some tallow."

"Horses!"

There was a click of a gun.

Horses turned, gun still leveled.

Ransom fired.

Suddenly Horses had three red eyes. He staggered backward.

The second bullet caught Horses as he was falling. The bullet cut his blue uniform up the front as neatly as if a running shears had done it. At the last second, kicking, Horses slewed around and landed across Sam's body. Blood spurted over the green Brussels carpet. Crimson rivuleted down the red goose pillow under Sam's head.

"Mr. Ransom!" Kate cried, a hand to her mouth.

"Horses!" Sulie and Rut gasped.

The green fly came for another look. It landed on Horses' forehead, then itched over to examine Horses' new red eye.

Ransom holstered his .45 and turned to go.

Kate quick caught his elbow. "Don't."

Ransom shivered at her touch. His green eyes glittered down at her. "Don't you think it's high time I skip the country?"

"Wait." Kate clutched at him. "Where were you and Sam staying?" Her single dark eye was sharp, imperious.

"The American House."

"In whose name were you registered?"

"Sam's."

"What room?"

"Twenty-one."

Kate quickly kneeled and rifled Sam's pockets. She came up with Sam's room key. "Hermie, scoot over to the American House and get all of Mr. Ransom's things." Kate tossed Hermie the heavy key. "All, you hear? You'll know them from Sam's. And don't get caught. Be sure, now."

Muscular Hermie shrugged herself into a coat and, whirling, was off in a limber manly trot.

"What's all this?" Ransom demanded.

"Just you stick around." Kate caught him by the elbow again, fiercely. "Don't you go, d'hear? Your whole life may depend on it."

Again Ransom shivered at her touch.

The green fly backed off from Horses' third red eye, flew up and circled Ransom's head four times, then shot for the window blind. It hit with a thwack, and this time fell to the floor, on its back.

Kate skimmed over and with a pouncing toe squashed it. "I just hate flies. Especially them loud green ones."

Sulie and Rut wept over Horses. But even as they wept, their hands pawed his clothes, each down a side. Sulie came up with a silver dollar and an old toad-stabber; Rut came up with a lucky penny and a straight razor.

Kate saw their gleanings. "The great big cheapskate. That's the Army for you. Thinking a blue uniform can get them in here for a lot of free fun." Kate pointed a regal arm. "Girls, get back to your cribs. I'll handle it from here."

Sulie and Rut, still spilling tears, mementos in hand, retreated to the back of the house.

Again Ransom made a move to leave.

"Please don't go." Kate touched her black eye patch to reassure herself it was still in place.

"I feel terrible."

"Please."

"Terrible."

Kate let her hand come to rest on Ransom's wrist, softly. "I know. And Lord knows, so do I. But don't go. Or you'll be in awful trouble. I know the Army. And worse, I know Colonel Bullock. Just leave everything to me."

Tears came into Ransom's eyes. The silver-limned tears made the red room gleam crimson. The black patch over Kate's eye resembled a dark cavern.

Hermie burst in, whistling. She carried a bundle.

Kate immediately bolted the door after Hermie. "You got his duds then?"

"I did."

"All of them?"

"All."

"Leave any sign?"

"None."

"Anybody see you?"

Hermie whistled with an eloquent lift of heavy dark brows.

"What happened?"

"I met a customer in the hallway upstairs."

"What I mean is, did anybody see you get his things?"

"Not one."

Kate took the bundle. "Mr. Ransom, you come with me."
Ransom touched a hand to his right eye. "I better not."

"Come."

"No."

"Don't be balky." Kate again took him by the elbow, and
gently but firmly drew him toward the door leading to the
back of the house. "Now, Mr. Ransom, if you don't please
hurry, I'll just have to take you by the ear."

Ransom threw a last look back at Sam. "Don't you want
me to help you with him?"

"Hermie and I will take care of everything. Hurry now."

Even as Kate spoke, somebody was at the front door, and
when the bolt held, the somebody began to pound on it.

"The Army must have a spy in here." Kate picked up a
faintly luminous night lamp. She turned it up. "Hurry."

Ransom let himself be pulled down a corridor, then up a
back stairs, finally into a corner room upstairs.

The room couldn't be true: gold wallpaper, canopied four-
poster, settee, two lounging chairs, dresser, full-length mirror, thick blue rug, gold-trimmed chamber pot, hanging
lamps with silver reflectors, bookcase full of books. There
were four windows, all muffled with curtains and blinds.
Ransom had never in his life seen such elegance.

"My bedroom," Kate said. She simpered. "It's where I live
and have my being." Then she added, "Our bedroom." She
set the night lamp on a low table beside the four-poster. She
lit one of the hanging lamps with a match. Light in the room
became a mellow orange.

Ransom's green eyes opened.

Kate gave him a veiled smile. "It's all right. It's only for
now. Until the Army finishes its investigation."

"I don't get it."

"Why, you handsome goose you, don't you understand?
You had to shoot Horses in self-defense. While protecting
your wife."

"Wife?"

"Yes. You're my husband for now."

"What?"

"Yes."

"Hold on. If I'm your husband don't you think they'll wonder what I'm doing up here? Instead of answering the door?"

"Because you were hit on the head. Grazed by a flying bullet."

"Lord!" Ransom remembered Sam saying once that in a tight a woman had more sand than a man.

"Down on the bed with you." Kate dug a razor out of Ransom's bundle. "I know just where to nick you. That little vein on your forehead there, where it runs down into your eyebrow."

"No."

Kate gave Ransom a hard push back; and down Ransom went on the four-poster.

Before he could cross his brows, a few drops of blood were already beginning to trickle down his cheek.

"Now you stay put and don't move. Or you'll have my silk bedspread all spotted. It'll quit bleeding soon enough." Kate slipped a small silk pillow under his head. "If you'll lie perfectly still until I come back, everything'll turn out hunky-dory." Kate bustled about, emptying his bundle onto the rug and then distributing the contents into various drawers and closets. "And when I bring the Colonel up, I want you to pretend you're still a little stunned. And don't you say a word. Not one word. You hear?" And with that Kate swished out and was gone.

After lying still awhile, Ransom reloaded his gun.

A last drop of blood stopped on his Adam's apple.

The aroma of scented woman wafted up out of the pillow he lay on. Sleeping on grass had never been like this.

The drying blood on his cheek began to draw up the skin under it.

"Runs a cowboys' rest home, yet don't take part herself."

Ransom crossed his legs, boots squinching a little where the one lay over the other.

"Maybe she's still in love with somebody and is saving it for him."

Girlish squeals came from below. A gruff voice barked. A door slammed. Then a second door shut. Again the heavy masculine voice barked.

Footsteps sounded on the back stairs. A moment later there was a knock outside the bedroom door.

Kate poked her head in. "We got company, dearie." She winked her one eye.

Ransom peered past his gambler's mustache. "Send 'em in."

Kate opened the door wide. "There he is, Colonel."

A portly man dressed in a blue uniform walked in. A thick island of hair grew at the back of his head, the longer strands of which were worn swept up over the top of the head. He carried a broad black hat clapped to his heart. Behind him came three blue soldiers, young men, and then limber Hermie.

Colonel Bullock stopped at the foot of the four-poster. Pompously he stared down at Ransom. "Is this the man?" he demanded, more of Hermie than of Kate.

"I can't say that he ain't," Hermie said.

Kate looked from the Colonel to Ransom. "Let me introduce you. Colonel Bullock, this is my husband, Earl Ransom."

"Now that's what I call pure cock and bull."

Kate bent over Ransom. "How do you feel now, love?"

"Tolerable."

With her lips Kate sought out Ransom's lips under his black mustache and gave him a fulsome kiss.

The kiss jolted Ransom.

Colonel Bullock continued to glare down at Ransom. "Young man, I can have you arrested, you know. Out here the Army is the only law, you know."

Chills shot up Ransom's back.

"Horses was the best mule man the Army ever had."

"That's what Sam always said."

"Then why did you gun him down?"

"Why, he killed Sam, sir. In cold blood." Ransom sat up in bed. "Then he took to pawing . . . the missus here. So I had to butt him out, Colonel. He'd got over onto my range."

Kate tried to signal Ransom to shut up.

Colonel Bullock's nose came up a little. "When did you marry . . . the missus here?"

"Is that question an order?"

Kate quick intervened. "We got married quite some time ago."

Colonel Bullock continued to glare down at Ransom with gray Army eyes. "Where?"

"On one of my trips," Kate said.

"Why can't the pup answer for himself?"

"He's far from being a pup, Colonel."

"Well, I suppose an old bitch like you would know about such things."

"Colonel Bullock!"

"I'll bet a brass cannon against a fart that this greenhorn of yours laying in bed here ain't never gored his critter yet."

"He just might surprise you."

"I've heard of fuzzfaces marrying what looked like their own hairy mothers out in the sticks. But now I can actually say I've seen such a case with my own eyes."

Kate stood as white as a sheet. "You might guess again, Colonel, as to who is the oldest between us two."

The Colonel at last swung his ponderous gray manner on Kate. He towered over her. "Kate, you're a liar."

Ransom flipped himself all in one motion up off the bed. His hand dropped to his gun.

The Colonel's hand jumped to his saber. His three men touched their guns.

"Wait wait wait!" Kate whispered hoarsely.

"Kate, where's the marriage license?"

"Why, Colonel, you wouldn't think I'd keep it here, do you? In this place?"

"Kate, really now, since when did this tender johnny take up living with you here?"

"He's just now arrived from Denver."

"Where was Sam staying, kid?"

Again Kate stepped in. "The American House."

"Jack, go check the hotel register. And check Sam's room. On the double."

After Jack left, Colonel Bullock drew his saber partway out of its scabbard, cursed loudly, once, then with a clang shot the saber home again. "Kate, if that hotel room is clean, I'll let you off. And him. This once. But if it ain't, this place is closed. And the pup gets shot. At dawn."

Kate had her own set of conditions. "For you and your roughnecks this place is already off limits. Forever."

Jack the soldier was back in a jiffy.

The Colonel turned on hard heels. "Well, Jack?"

"As slick and clean as a weasel's tongue, sir. No sign of him having been there."

"What did the manager say?"

"Said he wasn't around when Sam registered, sir. He let me look at the register and there was just Sam's name in it."

"Nobody saw this pretty fuzzface there then?"

"Not even the bellhop. The place is in worse shape than a Chugwater stampede, sir."

Kate relaxed. "Well, Colonel?"

Colonel Bullock let down too. "All right, Kate, if your Mr. Quicknuts here is your husband, he has the right to defend your home. So he is clear, I guess."

"Thanks." Kate strode to the door and held it open. "Gentlemen, if you please."

The Colonel shooed his three soldiers out ahead of him. As he passed into the hall, he gave Hermie a swift wink.

Hermie's face remained expressionless.

Ransom caught the wink.

Kate closed the door.

Ransom said, "Ah . . . wife, can we be alone for a minute?"

Kate brightened. "Of course, love. Hermie?"

Hermie, whistling, left the room.

Kate stepped hesitantly toward Ransom. "Yes?" In the soft lamplight her gold hair had light-brown shadows. The black eye patch especially became her in the gentle light.

Ransom was in an opulent bedroom with a lovely woman. He couldn't quite look her in the eye. "Miss Katherine . . . ah . . . are you sure of Hermie?"

"Why?" The bright look faded out of Kate's face.

"I saw the Colonel wink at Hermie just as he left."

Kate's lone eye opened wide. "So that's it!" Her hands flicked once against her thighs. "That bitch! Excuse me."

"That's all right."

"So. So. I might've known she'd be two-faced. That sometimes happens when a girl plays it both ways."

Ransom gave Kate a puzzled look.

Kate put a hand to her cheek. "Oh dear. How my tongue does run on. Well, it's still true. When business is slow and the girls get lonesome, Hermie sometimes plays the lover."

Ransom continued to look puzzled.

"You handsome goose you, didn't you catch on to that with that name of hers? Hermie? It stands for hermaphrodite."

Ransom's brows came up.

"I should never have let her in the house. Though I have to say that since she's come the girls have been more contented. There hasn't even been the hint of a cathop. It's all been one happy family."

Ransom sat down on the edge of the four-poster. His stomach didn't feel right.

"Hermies are sometimes quite handy. They can't father children. Yet they keep the girls quiet."

"Lord."

"Well, I'm not going to chase her out. Not yet. I have too much use for her. Meanwhile, even if she is the spy, we'll keep up the pretense of being married. At least until this blows over." Kate gave him a sweet smile. "That we'll manage, won't we?"

Ransom fell silent.

"I don't mean we should sleep in the same. . . ." Kate paused. "Well, maybe we should at that. And let Hermie have her peeps through the peephole. Hum." Kate snapped her fingers. "Mr. Ransom . . . er, Ransom, dear, we can always play at bundling. Sleep between separate sheets. Not that it really matters."

Ransom turned red. Slowly he shook his head.

"What is it, dearie?"

"No."

"What, no?"

"If I have to sleep up here, I'm sleeping on the floor. In my suggans there." Ransom pointed to his bedroll.

"But, Ransom, dear—"

"That's it, Miss Katherine. More than that and you can all go to hell."

3

Four days later, sitting in their bedroom, both Ransom and Miss Katherine overheard Rut say to Sulie out in the hall, "Well, if it was me, I'd never let my husband sleep on the floor. By his lonesome. I declare! If married I was, married I'd be, and in bed all proper with my own cockaroo. Yessiree. And I'd make certain sure he was happy up on his roost and blowing his bugle."

Miss Katherine stirred in her chair. She was looking out at the world through the east window. "Drat that Hermie."

Ransom sat staring out of the north window. In the falling twilight outside, the long swooping plains of Wyoming were slowly turning to rust.

"She has used the peephole."

Ransom crossed his legs. His thoughts were jumping about like sunfish caught in a boiling spring.

"Unless you want to take your chances with the Colonel's notion of mercy."

Ransom wanted to bed with Katherine all right. But he was afraid. Taking that first jump off the tree limb onto the sack swing, from a great height, was always a true sweet terror. To know what it meant to be a man with a maid, to know a woman belly intimate, was to know at last what lay beyond the mountain. But.

With a sigh Miss Katherine got up and lighted the night lamp. Then she came rustling slowly toward him. "I don't mean you any harm, Ransom. Believe me. You mustn't be afraid of me. The white sheet between us shall remain white."

Ransom touched his hand to his right eye.

"Was Sam really telling the truth?"

"About what?"

"That you're really still a twig not bent?"

Ransom's cheeks turned a maiden red.

She smiled. "There's always a first time for everything, yes. And if, as Sam said, you wish to save those first sweets for marriage, I shan't spoil that for you. I'll admire you for it instead. Oh, I may wonder a little. Yes. As any woman would. But I have no claim on you. So, so far as I am concerned, I shall help you keep yourself pure and untouched until you find that right one."

His eyes sweat.

"So you needn't worry that I shall tempt you. I am all the more the one, really, to help you keep yourself as you are." Another sigh broke from her, and a melancholy grimace drew down the corners of her sensual Indian-cut lips. "All the more me. Oh God yes."

Ransom shot her a look. He spotted in her expression the settlings of what must have been an awful time in the long ago. "Then you ain't never really done it either?"

She pointed to the black patch over her eye. "You've noticed this, of course."

He nodded.

"I lost it in defense of my person."

"I see."

"It doesn't become me, does it?"

"I wouldn't say that."

"Do you mind it much?"

"I like it on you."

She smiled, inward. "You'll do. Already you know how to bend a little to please a woman."

He couldn't resist knowing more. "How did it happen?"

"Someday maybe I'll tell you."

"A man with a gun?"

She stared down at him. "Someday I'll tell you. But not now."

"In a way it makes you look even prettier."

"Ah, you." Lamplight emphasized the light-brown shadows in the gold of her hair. A mischievous look quirked the corners of her mouth. "Tell me. Don't you really know what it means to be a king on the mountain with a woman?"

Ransom flashed green eyes at her.

"Surely you've seen a stallion have his way with a mare? How his head droops afterward?" She spoke with a touch of breathlessness.

Again Ransom turned a deep red. "Now you're just being nosy." Yet he thrilled to her pressing questions.

"A couple of seconds ago you were the nosy one, weren't

you, asking how"—she pointed to her black patch—"how did it happen?"

"Well, I guess I was."

"So?"

"Someday maybe I'll tell you."

Delight showed in her eye. "You'll do, my dear, you'll do." She reached a hand, gently, to touch him on his buckskin sleeve. A livid spark jumped between them. "And I can see you know at least one kind of playing. With words."

"Some things are too personal."

"I know."

"Better left alone. Like a skunk in his hole. A skunk looks tame enough to pet. But you better not try it."

Katherine laughed. "True enough."

They spoke in low tones. The sound of female laughter, of someone tinkling a piano below, came to them in washing irregular waves. Horsemen clopped by outdoors. There was a shooting on the other side of town.

His arm where the spark had jumped between them was hot all the way up to his neck. Ransom wished with all his heart she were someone else. The sweet woman smell of her gave him an edge so hard it hurt on every throb. If only she weren't a madam. To feel drawn toward a woman like Miss Kate was like licking a lump of sugar tinctured with alum.

"Mam, how come this kind of life?"

Her eye half lidded over.

"Well, it does seem odd to me. You yourself don't with the men. Yet here you are, making a living managing other girls who do."

"We all have to make a living, don't we?"

"The bridle still don't fit the horse somehow."

She picked at a thread in her purple dress.

"I notice you always wear purple. Never pink or red like the other girls do."

"A king's right."

"A queen's, you mean."

A shadow moved into her eye. "Yes, a queen's, of course."

He saw the darkling look in her eye, wondered about it, stored it in his memory. "Why don't you try some other line of work?"

"I've thought about it."

"Managing a store or something. A millinery."

"I've thought about it."

"There must be a reason."

"There is." She gave him a bitterish look.

"Revenge?"

"Maybe."

"Because of losing that eye?"

"Maybe."

"That's not good."

She touched her black eye patch. "Wait until you have to wear one of these."

"Sounds like you're on the prod. And that's looking for extra trouble."

She picked, picked at the thread in the seam of her purple dress.

"Just how did you get into this? I mean, how did it start?"

"Do you really want to know?"

"Yes. As long as we're going to play at husband and wife, yes."

After a silence, slowly, very reluctantly, she told a little about it. "It was in Denver. I saw a notice in the paper asking for a cook. At a boardinghouse. I needed the work so I took it. It didn't take me long to figure out it was hardly a boardinghouse. It was the hours. You know. Well, I felt sorry for the girls. The mood I was in after losing my eye and all. So I stayed. The wages were tops. The old madam told me I could do business on the side if I wanted to. I told her I couldn't. Just couldn't."

"You'd be drinking from the bottle with two straws if you did, huh?"

"Never thought of it that way before, but, yes, that's right."

"Then what happened?"

"The madam died. And the girls voted for me to take over."

Ransom waited.

"But I'm not sorry."

"You're not?"

"No. Because, Ransom, my dear, I am rich today."

Ransom gave her a sourish look.

"You don't approve?"

"You live your life and I'll live mine."

She threw him a sudden mixed look, partly sneering, partly wincing. "Each to his sheet, is that it?"

"I guess so."

"Well, maybe we both should hold the thought."

A trio of horsemen galloped up in the dark. There was the sound of raillery and rowdy pushing as the cowboys tied up at a hitching rack. There followed a knocking on the front door. In a moment high-pitched girlish greetings mingled with heavy male laughter.

Ransom couldn't resist asking it. "What was your family name?"

"My new husband is full of questions."

"Or were you an orphan too like me and never knew your last name?"

She nodded.

"An orphan?"

"Yes."

"Raised by strangers?"

"Mostly."

"No one to love you? Because you belonged to no one?"

"No one."

"Like me."

"Like you."

Ransom found himself wanting to pull her down into his lap. "Well, then after this terrible thing happened to you, you didn't take a last name like me?"

She smiled, indrawn. "I'm known as just plain Kate to some. And Miss Katherine to specials."

"You'd prefer to remain a riddle?"

She quivered beside him. Then she burned her single dark eye into his. "The Army considers us married. So I must know something. For sure. And I ask you again. Are you truly innocent of women? Come to a head with me."

Ransom flashed her a youth's tortured look.

She reached down to touch him again. This time there was no spark, only tender warmth as her fingers settled on his arm. "I'd be the last person on earth to start you off on a downward path." She laughed to herself. "Or on an upward path. I wouldn't want that on my conscience. I admire you for wanting to save yourself for your one true love."

He thought this over a moment. "Then you have?"

She withdrew her hand. "Yes." She paused. "And now I've probably lost you." She paused again. "Haven't I?" A smile twitched at the corners of her eyes. "I am mightily taken with you, Ransom. And I'm mightily tempted to lie with you."

"Don't."

"Come again?"

"I mean . . . don't take your hand away." He took hold of her hand and placed it on his buckskin sleeve. Then, shivering, he quickly pushed it away.

The smile on her face deepened and it drew the corners of her mouth back into knotted dimples in her cheek. The inner edges of her lips resembled taut rose petals. "Don't worry. I understand. That extra pillow on my bed shall remain un-touched. And your johnny-nods shall continue to have his

sweet innocence." She turned away. "There is work to do."
And abruptly she left the room, purple dress whispering.

He sat alone. He looked down at his hands. His lower lip
was doubled and dark and his green eyes were clotted with
torment.

If she could only have been a young girl. Untouched.

Some man, some lover somewhere, had once been there
with her. Sweet words had once been whispered and kisses
had been given. She had received and given flesh with
another. The darling inner tissues of her had been made ripe
with another man's bubbling bulb of flesh.

"Who am I? Where am I?"

He jumped up and began to pace back and forth. With
every step the fringes on his buckskins threshed as with the
sound of maple seeds shaken in a light breeze.

"I want her."

He clenched his fists. His eyes glowed like a puma's.

"Who am I to cast the first stone?"

He gripped the back of his chair so fiercely the top of it
shattered in his hands.

"That first jump onto that sack swing."

He strode to the window and looked out into the night.

"If you miss that sack, it's your neck. And if not your neck,
for sure your butt. Skinned. But if you latch onto it, what a
ride up on that other side!"

Hermie brought Ransom supper on a tray: crisp fried
potatoes, onions boiled in milk, a square of broiled beef-
steak, two slices of bread with wild honey, dried-apple pie,
and a pot of tea.

Hermie had a fuzz-lip sneer for him. "I hope you appreciates them onions boiled in milk, sir."

"Ah, there's only one milk cow then in all of Cheyenne, I
take it?"

Hermie squared her wide shoulders. "Well!"

"You sound a little like you might be jealous."

"You know an awful lot to be so innocent, is all I got to say."

Ransom hunched a shoulder against her.

Hermie left.

The moment the door closed, Sam Slaymaker began to talk in the back of Ransom's head.

"Well, boy, I see you've joined the outlaws for good."

Ransom stared down at the banquet in front of him.

"Killed yourself a man in a whorehouse."

Ransom suddenly didn't feel hungry.

"Got you a brand on your soul that every sheriff in the country can read. Even by moonlight."

Ransom sucked on his lower lip, even bit on it a little.

"The kind of brand that'll never come off. Or grow over."

The rich smell of the food began to gag him.

"Better skip the country, boy. Before you get in too deep with this Kate woman."

All of a sudden Ransom took the tray and dumped all of the food into the gold-trimmed chamber pot under the four-poster.

"Something about her just don't set right, does it, boy?"

Ransom lay down on the four-poster and crossed his legs.

"Ain't she a juicy piece though? Mmm-hmm. I told you it'd be fun if you could get her to skin an onion with you."

Ransom covered his face with a pillow. His crossed legs were a comfort to each other.

"How she can smile. Man, man."

Ransom whispered, "My God in heaven, how did I ever wind up in here anyway?"

An hour later Katherine came back. She carried a long package. "Guess what I have here for you."

"I wouldn't know." He still lay on the bed with his legs warmly crossed.

"Guess." Her purple dress rustled as she came toward him.

"Oh, a box of shells. To kill more Horses with."

"Ransom."

"Or a new pick and shovel. Along with a pan and a gold-dust bag."

She paused. "You really mean that last, don't you?"

"As soon as this mess clears up, I'm off for the Black Hills to find me a gold mine."

"Why?"

"I'm in a hurry to get somewhere. Be rich and independent. Do something big."

"Many a poor duffer has already come back from the Hills flat broke."

"Not me."

Katherine couldn't help but smile. "Well. . . ." She placed the long box beside him. "Open it."

With some reluctance he sat up and opened the box. He drew out a complete set of new clothes. "Holy bulls."

"Like it?"

"I don't know what to say."

"It's for you."

"But why for me?"

"Like it?"

"You shouldn't've done it. It's too good for me."

"Handsome is what Ransom wears."

"Where'd you get this fancy city suit way out here? A rich man's black like this?"

"A new clothier in town."

"But why for me?"

"Your wedding suit." Quickly she added, "In case anybody asks."

He had to admit he liked the black suit.

"Put it on," she urged.

"Now?"

"Now."

"I'd better not."

"Listen. Take it."

"No."

"Take it. Listen. Consider it pay for stepping in like you did when Horses went loco."

"Well. . . ."

"Please."

"All right. It's about time I had a fancy suit like this. But remember, I'm going to pay you for it, now that Sam's left me his span of mules."

"Don't be silly."

He brushed the suit with a loving hand. "But I do thank you for picking it out for me."

"Will you put it on for me? Just once?"

"Sure."

"Good." A lickerous gleam entered her eye. "I'll be back in a jiffy."

By the time she returned he had made the complete change: black suit, white silk shirt, high choker collar, gold cuff links, new black socks, drawers, new black patent-leather shoes.

She was taken aback by the transformation. "You really are a handsome man."

"Cut it out."

"When I finally turn you loose on the streets of Cheyenne, you're going to be rough competition for the rest of the men."

"I said, cut it out."

She abruptly turned pensive. "Tell me something."

"Shoot."

"Have you ever lost someone you most wanted to keep?"

"Well . . . Sam, of course."

"Oh, yes. Sam."

"And you?"

"I wouldn't even dare to begin to tell you."

"It was that bad?"

"It was."

Ransom placed a gentle hand on her shoulder. "I'm sorry to hear it. Maybe someday you'll find another to take his place."

"Never. There was only one like him."

"Is that the one who had to do with . . . ?"

"My lost eye? Yes."

He gave her shoulder a warm squeeze. "What was he like? Maybe I can help you find him."

"He's dead. At least so I think. Dead." Her whole face wrinkled over with an old anguish.

He was moved.

She turned woodenly from him.

"Katherine."

A tear appeared along the bottom edge of her black eye patch.

"Godsakes, Katherine."

Abruptly she left the room. Her footsteps slowly faded away down the hall.

"Poor woman. She takes it pretty hard."

He undressed and hung his new clothes in the corner closet. He stroked each piece, the coat, vest, trousers, silk shirt, neatly into place. "I'll make sure to pay for them when I sell Sam's mules."

Naked, he stretched to his full height, up on his toes, chest out. "Ahh!" His biceps came up like risen dough and his thighs rippled like taut lariats.

He caught sight of himself in Katherine's full-length mirror. He saw where his johnny-nods hung dreaming in its thicket of curly black hair. It resembled almost exactly his nose in the middle of his beard.

On an impulse he decided to go to bed naked, as he'd sometimes done on warm nights out on the prairie.

He blew out the night lamp. And, crawling into his suggans on the floor, was sound asleep in a minute.

After a while, body warming in sleep, an arm, then a leg, tossed the thick horse blanket aside. He lay exposed.

He dreamed he was swimming. He was paddling for all he was worth to get to shore. On the shore stood Sam Slaymaker. Sam was calling to him with warm encouraging words. Behind Ransom stretched a vast body of water. How he'd come to be in the water in the first place he couldn't figure out. When his knee hit gravel, Sam had a hand up for him. Sam led him to a crackling fire. Sam fed him venison and coffee. By the time his clothes were dry, Ransom found he'd outgrown them and Sam had to cut him a new suit out of deerskin. In making them Sam hadn't allowed enough room for his crotch. So Sam had to recut his buckskin pants. Then Ransom woke up.

He lay musing and breathing for a while.

Poor Sam shot and killed.

Sam had loved him with a true-blue heart. Sam had loved him up when he'd felt down. Sam had scolded him when he'd felt antsy.

Goddam that Horses.

But Sam had been mostly wrong about Miss Katherine though. All that talk of hers about bundling, and keeping the white sheet between them, meant only one thing: she wanted a man, bad.

Fantasies of what he'd do with Miss Katherine someday drifted through his mind. He would stroke her shadowed gold hair. He would cup her breasts. He would hug her to him, warm and close and hard.

Again he dreamed he was swimming. This time it was under water.

He nosed into some dark water where the seaweeds

stood thick. He swam with powerful stroking arms. The seaweeds kept trailing across his face.

He swam harder. Yet for all his stroking he just couldn't seem to make headway. It was as if his body had sent down some kind of root.

He looked down. Yes. His body had sent down a root. It was his phallus. It'd grown to be as big as an elephant's trunk, and where it'd been sucking at the bottom it had rooted in.

He was tied down. While he was swimming, his root had somehow anchored deep in the mud. Also, every little while, some goldfish, four of them along with a papa goldfish the size of a thumb, played around the root.

All of a sudden his root swelled up. And it began to burn deliciously. Deliciously. It was so delicious he had the feeling his phallus was going to back up on itself and turn around and swallow him complete. The end of it would be that he would disappear into the mud bottom.

"Wake up, wake up!" a doctor cried. "It's going to get you. Hurry. Before it's too late."

He bumbled out loud. "I am hurrying."

"Darling," a woman's voice said. "Darling, I know it's dreadful of me to be so forward. But the thought of your sweet boy innocence, oh dear God, it drives me wild to think that someone else should have it first."

"I'm hurrying, Doc."

"Also, the Army has let me know that they know you're only bunking in my bedroom and not sleeping with me as man and wife. So they're coming to get you tomorrow morning."

"Mum?"

"You're awake, aren't you?"

"Mam?"

"Darling, the sound of your voice drives me mad. I hear red when you talk. Lonely and red."

It had to be a dream.

"It's been so long, so long since I've done it. And I always loved it so. Even with that other. And even with shy little Dennis."

A dream.

"And I know I'm breaking my own rule. Because I once swore on my own soul that I'd never do it again until I'd found him. But, oh God, it's been so long."

It had to be a dream. In dream it would be all right. In dream one couldn't help it.

"But seeing you I now know I'll never find him. You're even better, darling."

He fought to stay as asleep as possible. "Mussent wake up." He struggled to stay down. "Or it ain't a dream."

"All those years denying it. Keeping myself pure for the day when I might find him again."

He found himself floating. And he let himself go on floating.

"We'll start over. A sweet little nest somewhere in the West. Make a new start."

A face nuzzled his beard. Full soft lips found his lips. Hair trailed across his nose. The fishes played.

"Darling, you are awake, aren't you?"

"Mum?"

"My husband. My dear daddy husband."

"Mam?"

A woman smiled in his ear. "Dear old Aunt Agnes might not approve." The fishes played. "But we don't care, do we?"

"Who?"

"I can't help it, sweet, but I never did think tubers were unsightly."

He suffered his lips to be parted and the tip of a tongue touched the tip of his tongue.

"Come, wake up, darling. Nnnh? Under that black patch I'm really a honeypot, you know. The stamp of a passional nature is set deep in me."

Again the tip of a tongue found him. Then the last of what

he'd hoped was a dream was gone, and he found himself being hugged by a wonderful woman. Naked. Now. A rush of red from a new spring swept through him.

Suddenly he threw his arms around her, and hugged her hard in turn, and kissed her compulsively.

With his fingertips he touched all of her. He felt the tender skin of her and the supple flesh of her, and under them the surprisingly hard female hipbones of her.

One of his hands found her softest hair. With a ripped cry he turned her over on her back and moved up on his knees and entered and possessed her. He was mad to have a woman at last.

"At last, at last, to be doing it doing it. After so many years."

"Nnn."

"My husband."

"Kathering."

"My King."

"Now. Now. Now. Now. Now."

She heard red in the sound of his voice.

He smelled puccoons in the loose strands of her hair.

4

Later in the night he carried her to the four-poster bed and crept in beside her.

She murmured sleepily. He murmured sleepily. And before they were comfortably settled between the sheets, he was upon her again.

"Come."

"Husband."

He'd swum his river finally. And once across he couldn't get enough of it.

As he dozed off he promised himself to look into why it

was that something about her scent always set off a trigger in him.

It wasn't just that she smelled of puccoons. It was more than that. It was as if he knew already beforehand that he'd smell the puccoons on her. Somehow he'd been there before, in some other kind of life if that was possible, before he'd been born into this life, with the edges of the being-there-before resembling the vaporings of a horizon on a hot summer day.

Vaguely he was aware of footsteps going away from their door.

He fell asleep.

After that the Army left them alone.

An unlabeled bottle of perfume always stood on her dressing table.

One day he saw her touch a drop of it to her ears.

He went over and stood behind her. There it was. That special Katherine scent. The one that always set him off.

He picked up the bottle. It was half-full of something that looked like light beer. "What's this?"

"A perfume I make."

"What from?"

"Puccoons."

"So that's why I always smell them on you." He uncapped the bottle and took a good whiff. "Mmm. Let me give you a word of advice."

"Yes?"

"See to it that you never run out of this and then you'll never lose me."

She laughed. "Maybe it's more the perfume you love than me."

"Just don't you ever run out of it. That's all I've got to say."

"You like it that much?"

"It's the key to you."

She told him how she made the perfume, from the squeez-
ings of puccoon blossoms and the dregs of boiled puccoon
roots.

The next day he took a stroll out on the prairie. Look as he
might, he couldn't find any puccoons.

He remembered then that on that first ride into Cheyenne
with Sam he had seen some growing off to one side of the
trail.

He saddled his tan mustang Prince and went to look for
them.

He found them. The stalk and the leaves were still green,
but the topmost flowers were edged with a withered brown.
Only a few of the lower trumpet blossoms, much smaller,
still had the true golden-orange color.

He picked them all. He also dug out several roots.

He carried them home to Katherine.

She was touched. She bit her lips to keep tears from
starting.

"They are the right kind, ain't they?"

"Yes."

"I just didn't want you ever to run out of it."

"I won't."

She was gone uptown much of the day. She came home
just before supper, tired, shadows under her eyes, face
gaunt.

"Where you been, my lady?"

"Let's have a bite first. Then I'll tell you."

She had on new black button shoes. She reached down to
rub them over the toes. After a moment she took them off.

"Your new shoes are too tight for you, eh? I bet you'd like
to soak your feet in warm water awhile, wouldn't you? And
have me rub them down?"

She drew in a sucking breath. "Why, Ransom, how nice of
you to notice."

"I'll wash them for you if you want me to."

"No-o. But it's nice of you to think of it."

After supper, sitting on his lap in their bedroom, she told him. "We're moving tomorrow."

He stirred under her like an uneasy horse. "What?"

"What would you say if I told you I've given The Stinging Lizard away?"

"You gave it away? To who?"

She blew her nose with a scented kerchief. "Well, to Hermie."

"Why her?"

"She's about the only one who'll know how to keep things running. For the other girls' good."

"The house too?"

"All of it." She turned in his arms. She sought his lips in his beard and kissed him. "I was practically given it free in the first place. So I decided I should give it free to somebody else in turn. So, I gave it to Hermie. I signed the papers today."

"Good riddance, I say."

"You're glad?"

"Where are we going to move to now?"

"You are glad. Good." She sighed, relieved. "Well, I rented an upstairs floor on the north side of town. In a nice brick house. We can move our bedroom stuff over tomorrow."

He shook his head. "Let's start fresh. With everything new. Bed and all."

"Earl Ransom, why, I can't do that!"

"Why not? Let's wipe the slate clean all around."

"Ransom." She looked around at the four-poster bed and the love seat and the vanity and the rugs and the curtains and the movable closets. "Why, Ransom, dear, these came all the way from Chicago. Why, it took me years to find and order them. And I've come to love them." She hardened a little. "What have you got against them?"

He pursed his lips under his gambler's mustache. "Nothing."

"Darling, these things . . . why, they're me! They've come to mean home to me." Her brown eye beseeched him to understand. "There's nothing wrong with them. Nobody's ever been . . . nobody's ever seen them except you and me. And Hermie."

"Yeh."

"They are fresh with us."

"Nnn."

"But they are. I just got them."

A silverish gleam danced in his green eyes.

"You're jealous."

"A little."

At that she suddenly seemed pleased with him. She kissed him. "Did you really mean that about washing my feet?"

"Of course."

"You darling."

He got up with her still in his arms, placed her on the settee, went over and got a pan of warm water and a cake of white soap.

She laughed like a young girl. "You foolish boy you." She drew up her skirt modestly around her knees and took off her stockings. Her toes wiggled in anticipation.

He took first one foot, then the other, and set them in the water. He soaped them thoroughly. He rubbed them. He ran his fingers in and out between her toes.

She laughed and giggled. She laughed involuntarily every time his thumb happened to stroke the sole of her foot. "Don't tickle so much."

"What long toes you have, lady."

"Don't you like them?"

"Now I see why you walk the way you do." He stroked her big toe in particular. "Leverage. It gives you that extra little jump in your walk."

"You're tickling again. Ha ha. Ho ho. He he."

"You know, my lady, it's like it was meant to be by God

Himself that I came to Cheyenne. So that I could wash your feet for you. Like the draw of an ace to fill out a straight in an important game."

She leaned down and kissed his nose. "We're perfectly matched. You've got a long nose and I've got a long big toe."

He spotted a shadow under her bright manner. He wondered what sad memory of another time was crossing her mind. It probably had to do with that other fellow. He was instantly jealous of that memory. He gave her feet a rough massage.

"I like that," she said in a low voice.

He loved her voice when she spoke low and husky.

He decided to swallow away any regret he had that he hadn't been the first with her. "It's like I say. Yessiree. Any time you want to put your shoes under my bed, why, go right ahead, I won't stop you."

She had to laugh in spite of herself. "Ransom." She leaned forward to kiss his brow. In so doing one of her feet slipped on the bottom of the white pan and water sloshed onto Ransom's buckskins over the thigh.

"Hold 'er, neut," Ransom cried.

"Now look at what I've done."

"It's nothing."

They laughed together, forgetting the shadow.

She kissed him. He returned the kiss. Lips became tender with lips. Soon a hammer beat on an anvil.

Life upstairs in the brick house was hardly different from life at The Stinging Lizard. The bedroom furnishings were exactly the same.

Ransom liked to take short rides on Prince out over the countryside.

Sometimes Katherine came along. She was a good horsebacker and rode Sam's mustang Colonel. They cantered east and had a picnic in Pine Bluffs. They rode north to see the aftereffects of a cloudburst on Lodge Pole Creek. They galloped west to see the sights of Granite Canyon.

Katherine was always radiant after the rides. The shrew's wrinkles at the corners of her lips vanished. There were times when she looked like a younger sister of Ransom's.

She did the giddy things of a just nubile girl. She fluttered about in their bedroom, trying on new skirts and blouses, trying out various hairdos, trying out different perfumes and sachets.

She also did tender things for him. She made him mush and milk for breakfast, which he loved. She trimmed his beard. She taught him how to knot his tie neat and square.

Ransom rode alone one day out to Lone Tree Creek south of town. The sky was high. There appeared to be no atmosphere at all. To breathe was to taste what seemed to be the fumes of fermenting barley.

He found a single cottonwood and got off and lay down in its shade. He kicked off his boots and drew his sombrero down over his nose.

Prince cropped curly buffalo grass nearby. A vulture hung in the dry air above.

Within his closed eyelids Ransom watched a floating mote become a wriggling maggot. It drifted down and down. He kept it from sinking out of sight with a toss of his eyes, up; then once again watched it sink until it was almost out of sight.

He napped. Soft sleep. Silence.

All too soon Prince nosed him with his rubbery nose, pushing his sombrero to one side.

"Nnn."

Prince blew a masty breath over Ransom's face.

"What's the matter, chum?"

Prince blew his nostrils with a wet flutter.

"Oh, you want some water. Pretty soon, chum." Ransom replaced his sombrero, again dozed off.

Prince went back to grazing.

When Ransom next awoke it was to dazzling crystals in his eyelashes. He had cried in his sleep.

Vaguely he recalled a piece of the dream he'd had. It was something about a grass lizard who refused to sting him and who wept tears over him in the ancient manner of the Yankton Sioux.

He savored a memory of the last time he'd made love to Katherine. She was always modest at first. But after a while, once begun, she became almost an animal in her ardor.

He loved that madness in her. In that respect he matched her exactly. Once in the saddle, he must ride, in excess, and if possible, forever. So that finally it was always Katherine who had to haul in on the reins. "Ransom! Dear, dear. Don't you think we ought to stay a little civilized? A little?"

He sat up, cocked his hat at a racy angle, squinted around at the sights.

Prince grazed nearby. The vulture still hung on nothing. Only the cottonwood's perfect single shadow had moved.

Ransom spotted a wild clover growing between his spread legs. He picked it. He smelled its purple ball. He played with it between his fingers. A syrupy drop of juice formed at its severed end. He touched a fingertip to it and tasted it. Sweet. Like good hay might taste to a horse.

He flicked a red ant off his shirt front. He pulled on his boots and got to his feet. He stretched, full length, and groaned in satisfaction.

He found Prince a waterhole in the nearly dry bed of Lone Tree Creek.

While Prince sipped at leisure, he had himself some target practice. He made several quick practice draws; then, tossing a silver dollar in the air, fired five times. Each shot caught the silver dollar and flipped it farther on, so that it resembled the flight of a dipping silverfinch. The silver dollar came to rest a hundred paces away.

Ransom went over and picked it up. "Dead center, Dad. And bent double." He dropped it into his pocket.

He spotted a coneflower a dozen steps away. Its single dark heart hung to one side, giving him a perfect silhouette to shoot at. With his sixth and last bullet he exploded its head.

Almost on the shot, something clicked in his head, very loud, making him blink.

He'd lived this moment before. This he knew for certain. It wasn't quite the same as that other time in that other life, not quite so shimmering and wondrous. Also, the coneflower he'd just shot still had its rays; the other coneflower in that other time had already shed them. But otherwise it was almost the same.

Nausea smoked in his belly. Sudden sweat beaded out all over him.

"Will I ever find out who I am?"

Loneliness like the scent of flowers wavering in and out of smelling range made it hard for him to breathe. Sudden need for that warm home he had found in Katherine yeasted up in him like a craving for a drug.

He swung aboard Prince and headed for home. He spurred Prince until the mustang, shocked, broke into a rattling puffing gallop.

It was dusk when he put up Prince at the livery barn. It was dark when he burst into their upstairs rooms.

Katherine was at the stove, back turned to him. She was safe.

He let out a great breath.

Katherine looked over her shoulder. "Ransom! Whatever have you been up to?"

"Nothing."

"You look like you've just seen the devil himself."

"Maybe I have."

Katherine laid aside the ladle she'd been using to stir the soup with. "What happened?" She came over and put her arms around him, her one eye squared in concern.

"Nothing." It was good to be holding her again. "Slept out in the sun a little too long." He managed a smile. The little smile gave his large lips a twisted-rope look. "And I guess I all of a sudden got a little lonesome for you. Like one leg getting lonesome for the other."

"Dear."

"You know something? I think I better go find me a job. Something to do. I've got too much time on my hands."

"I've thought of that."

"And we should get married. If not before a minister, at least before a justice of the peace."

"Do you want to?"

"I have to. Didn't I keep myself just for you until I found you?"

"We're probably married common law already, you know."

"I want it legal. For keeps."

"All right."

"And I want children. A son. To start off a new line with. And by new I mean new. I don't know who I am or where I come from. So with me and my son we start fresh. With a clean slate. No sad pasts. Only happy futures ahead."

A sudden grimace wrinkled her face, part sneering, part wincing.

"That's what it means to live out West. You know? That's what Sam used to say."

The odd look passed on and slowly her face smoothed over.

"Don't you want babies with me?"

"Oh, Ransom. Oh God yes, how I'd love to have babies with you."

He heaved a great sigh, then hugged her hard, for one moment pure in heart.

She coughed inside his tight hug. "You're sure you want to get married legal?"

"Of course. What else?"

"All right."

"What's the matter? You sound like you're not sure you want to marry me."

She was crying. "You're too noble for me."

"Oh come now, Katherine, cut it out, you know that's ridiculous."

"But you are."

Then that sweet devil desire returned, and stooping quickly, he pushed his nose through the lacy white frill of her blouse, down between her breasts.

"Ransom, cut that out."

"They're always so soft. Like fresh bread every day. What do you do to keep them like that, reheat and butter 'em every morning?"

"Ransom."

"And why must you always go putting a fence around them? Like they might be a couple of stacks of slough hay somewheres to be kept safe from a herd of wild buffaloes?"

"Ransom."

"Well, if you won't let me have my hay"—he abruptly let her go and with a sly smile picked up the soup ladle—"let me at least have a couple of onions boiled in milk."

"I'm not sure I like that, Mr. Earl Ransom."

They laughed together.

She served him soup, meat, potatoes, onions, a dried-apple pie, a pot of tea.

He ate heartily. There was about him the air of a hungry wild animal.

He talked a blue streak. He talked about his days with Sam Slaymaker: near drownings, buffalo stampedes, gunfights, prospecting for gold on Pike's Peak, blizzards on the Nebraska prairies, near massacres at the hands of the Sioux, barroom brawls in Denver. He rattled on and on. He couldn't seem to stop.

She eyed him, wonderingly.

He helped her wipe dishes, still talking.

She listened, vaguely hearing a boy's voice behind the man's voice.

He helped her tidy up the kitchen, still talking.

Finally she reached up and tweaked him playfully by the ear. "Ransom, what makes you so talkative all of a sudden? Hey?"

"What?"

"Ha ha. You haven't got yourself another girl, have you? That I don't know about?"

"What?" he cried. His green eyes rolled a high white. "What?"

She let go of his ear. "I'm sorry. Skip it. I didn't say it."

His brow and cheek blanched to the color of a turnip.

"Forgive me, dear. I was only teasing."

"You," he said, choking. "You."

"Really. I'm sorry."

"You better be."

"Well, I said I was."

He stared great green eyes at her.

"Ransom!"

Of a sudden he reached down and picked her up and stiff-legged carried her into the bedroom. He landed her on their four-poster and lay down beside her.

"Ransom!"

He continued to give her great green eyes.

The night lamp was on. The room was full of gold glints and gold shadows. Her tumbled hair resembled a throw of gold coins.

"There's one thing I never did get about you, lady. About how you'll never let me kiss your bare breasts. Nose 'em a little."

"My God."

"I can play with your feet bare, but not them."

She closed her eyes to crinkled slits.

"And another thing, while I'm at it . . . how come you never let me see you bare naked? We shouldn't have any shame in front of each other any more, should we, as man and wife?"

She closed her lips to a line of whitened flesh.

"Pussy?"

"I can't. No. No."

He began to unbutton her dress.

She fought him, clawing fingernails, kicking toes.

Laughing, in part malicious, in part impish, he ripped her clothes off, from head to toe, until she lay lovely and exposed before him. "Now look at you. What was wrong that you'd never let me see you as God made you? You're beautiful. You wouldn't deny your own true husband that, now would you?"

She cried aloud, then with both her hands, flutteringly, tried to cover her breasts and her belly at the same time. She crossed her legs tight.

"Pussy, do me a favor?"

"What."

"Please let me see under that eye patch. I want to see what it's like."

"No, no."

"Why not?"

"Because."

"It's not your fault you have it. And if it is a fault, it's the one thing that makes you perfect."

"Perfect? Oh, God, you're tearing me all to pieces talking like that."

He reached to remove the eye patch anyway. He managed to lift one corner of it to catch a glimpse of a single teardrop glistening in a quivering cup of flesh before she could push his hand away.

In fighting him off she exposed her middle.

He saw something. "What's this?"

"Nothing."

A large scar, exactly like the wrinkled smile of a pumpkin jack-o'-lantern, lay across her little mound of a belly.

"Is this what you didn't want me to see, for godsakes?"

She turned her face away from him.

"Why, pet, it's only an operation scar. Why, on you, it's a kind of beauty mark even. Like a birthmark almost, you might say."

She covered her face with both her hands. Sobs shook her.

"What was it, a gallstone operation?"

"Mmm."

"You're lucky to be alive then." He leaned down and kissed the scar. "It makes you that much the more precious."

She groaned as if she were about to die.

He looked upon her. A rush of compassion for her as well as an impulse to hurt her came together in him. The two emotions were like the alternate troublings of two rivers at a confluence. "Katherine."

She rolled her head back and forth in a frenzy of torment.

He stripped off his clothes, blew out the night lamp. With a surgelike motion he took her in his arms.

She lay inert for a long time, no matter what he did to arouse her.

At last the impulse to hurt her, to be the cruel topdog to her abject underdog, won out. He roughed her up, brutal.

Then she responded, stirring a little, until, more and more, she became as actively savage as he.

Soon velvet wings, open, began to fly.

They lay musing together in the dark.

The windows were open. A soft summer night's breeze trailed threads of invisible gossamer across their faces.

The clock on the mantelpiece tocked irregularly, as if it

might have heart trouble. Crickets sawed under the loveseat. Outside a lone horsebacker came clopping down the street on a tired pinto.

"Ransom?"

"Umm?"

"You're funny."

"Mmm."

"A silly boy."

"Nnn."

"You don't like it when I don't let you see me naked. Yet when it comes right down to it, you're no different."

"Prove it."

She laughed softly in the dark. "Why did you blow out the night lamp?"

"Well. . . ."

"And pull up the quilts to our chins?"

"The night air is chilly."

Suddenly the sound of wild galloping came to them.

They lay listening to it.

The galloping came on louder.

"Hey," Ransom said, rousing.

It was a half-dozen horses. In a moment the horses thundered by on the street below.

One of the horsemen was crying something. It was repeated again and again.

Ransom jumped out of bed and ran to the window.

"Ransom, for heaven's sake, what're you doing, leaning out all naked like that? The neighbors will see you."

"Shh." Ransom turned his head to hear the better.

The horsemen had gone on about a block before Ransom finally made it out.

"Gold! Gold! In the Black Hills. They've found the real mother lode at last!"

PART THREE

Earl Ransom

1

Ransom struck out for the Black Hills alone.

At the southern edge of the Hills he came upon occasional gold hunters who'd gone belly up. They were hungry, ragged, lousy, bitter. The new strike still wasn't the true mother lode and for many it had turned out to be a trap.

Near Shirttail Canyon early one morning, Ransom came upon a man who really was busted. The prospector rode a bony mule without a saddle and had no other possessions but the torn dirty clothes he had on and a six-shooter stuck in his belt. His boots were shot, bare toes showing through. His black beard was long and mangy.

Both men drew up their mounts at about the same time. Both men checked each other's guns, and then looked each other over point for point, Ransom with wondering eye, the other with derisive eye.

Ransom let both hands come carefully to rest on the horn of his saddle. "Howdy, stranger."

The stranger's look of derision deepened as he eyed Ransom's fancy buckskin clothes and his tan mustang Prince and the chestnut packhorse behind laden with tools and supplies. "Howdy."

"Where you headed?"

"Can you lend me fifty dollars, handsome?" The stranger scratched himself vigorously. "Then I just might tell you."

"I just broke camp." Ransom blew some road dust off his sleeves. "Or I'd offer you some coffee."

"You wouldn't care to cool your saddle?"

Ransom tipped back his sombrero. "I mean to make Custer yet tonight."

"Ha. Another fool jackass."

"Hey. How so?"

"Thinking people can run through the Hills and go picking up gold just for the taking."

"What's wrong with using a spade?"

"Like hogs let loose eating ground nuts off the grass." A big louse emerged on the surface of the stranger's black beard and began to fight its way through various tangles.

Ransom's nostrils edged open a little.

"Crazy people on a wild stampede for fool's gold."

"That your story?"

"I hate to admit it. But, it's true." The stranger scratched and scratched. "I've got the I-quit-fits. For me, it just didn't pan out. I sunk five hundred dollars into this expedition and, by God, I never took a color." The stranger gave Ransom another careful study. "You really can't lend me a fifty spot? Because I'm strapped."

"How far is it to Custer?"

"Fifteen miles of pure up and down."

Ransom stared up at the high shoulders of the canyon, at

the thick stands of lofty ponderosa down the steep sides, at the tender ferns growing underfoot. "Any water?"

"None to speak of."

"Any Indians?"

"None so far."

"What happened to that new boom camp up north?"

"Color petered out."

"Hard luck."

"Worse yet, General Crook's chasin' everybody out."

"Where'd he come from?"

"Orders from Washington, D.C. He says the Hills is still off limits for us. And will be for at least another year. It's according to an old treaty we signed with the Sioux. The whole of the Hills still belongs to them and they're being balky about selling so much as a square inch of it."

"That's a helluva thing."

"I know I'm not going to stay and tough it out any longer." Pause. "You hain't got a smile of whiskey on you?"

"Not a drop."

"I couldn't badge some bacon off you? I can make the other two meals out of water."

Ransom reached down into a saddlebag behind him and came up with a strip of jerky. He tossed it across to the man. As it passed by, the mule made a sudden snap at it; missed.

The man began to gnaw at the jerky ravenously. "When I get back to old Cheyenne, I mean to order me a meal of oysters, eggs, beef, and a stalk of celery. But this'll have to do for now."

"Think you can make it?"

"I have to. I can't let my wife down back in Omaha. Not with a thunderhead of debt hanging over her. Well, hup-up, old skate, maybe we'll find us some wet grass yet. On the back trail home." And with that the raggy prospector rode off into the shadows, going south.

Ransom thought of his Katherine back in Cheyenne. At

least she didn't have any debts to face. In fact, it was the other way around. Katherine was too rich.

Ransom remembered the promise Katherine had extracted from him when he'd left, that he was to let her know the minute he'd struck it rich, so that she could follow him with all her household goods. "Then we can have it wonderful," she'd said, "in our sweet little nest far out in the West."

Two hours later, just as Ransom was about to climb a hogback, he spotted a blue color darker than the blue of the sky. First black hats appeared under the pines along the skyline, then blue uniforms, then gray horses. It was an Army patrol out looking for stray prospectors.

Ransom was off his horse in a whip. Quickly he led Prince and the packhorse into a thicket of lodgepole pines. He threw an arm around each horse's neck and with his hands muffled their rubbery lips. Luckily the two horses were too tired to be unruly, and stood patient and still.

"Sooner or later," Ransom muttered to himself, "the Sioux are gonna have to get out anyway. And I mean to be the first in to make the big strike."

The patrol halted on the crest. While they blew their horses, an officer carefully surveyed the canyon with a glass. Once Ransom was almost sure the officer had spotted him. The officer's glass swiveled back suddenly and seemed to fix on Ransom's hideout in the thicket. Silver reflection gleamed momentarily on the glass like a flash of gunfire.

"Damn, but I don't want to go back after coming this far."

Ransom checked his packhorse to see if any of the metal might be gleaming in the sunlight, the new spade, or the pickax and pan. There was nothing glinting that he could see.

His heart clopped in his ears.

The officer at last put his glass away. He raised his arm curtly. And then the patrol was off, galloping along the top of the hogback, going southwest toward the Cheyenne trail.

"Now, if I don't run into them mad Sioux, I'll make it." Ransom led his two horses out of the thicket. "And I'm sure not going to stop in Custer now." He checked the one-man diamond-hitch on the packhorse to see if all was secure. "I'll go around it to the west. Cross over on high ground."

More and more pinnacles and peaks of rock emerged out of the green mantle of the forest. Stunted pines no higher than Indian corn passed under the belly of his mustang. Ransom rode over weathered granite passes as slick as river ice. On the right, far ahead, he spotted the highest point in the Black Hills, a bald crag of gleaming granite.

The canyons deepened. Most were dry. Heated bark exuded clouds of pine perfume. Even the raw rock had a singular aroma.

Occasional Indian graves hung like clots of moss in the trees. The bodies were invariably wrapped in green blankets. Offerings in memory lay in the grass underfoot.

Ransom came upon an awesome ravine, long, deep, a stream trickling down the middle of its green bottom.

"I better take it. It leads straight north. Besides, it's time to irrigate the horses."

He slid off Prince. He checked the diamond-hitch on the packhorse. Then, peering down and picking out a route, he carefully led them down. They inched along narrow ledges. They passed under teetering boulders. They slid between massy trunks of ponderosa pine. They circled through mazes of half-fallen trees. They plowed across powdery rotten trunks. Occasional rattling rockfalls splashed to either side of them.

"One slip and our name'll be mud."

Magpies, dippling their long tails and flashing white, clattered angrily at them.

The head of the stream began exactly where they hit the

bottom of the ravine. A spring poured quietly out of a wall of green turf. It ran as if someone had only just then punched a hole in the green wall.

The packhorse stepped up and drank sidewise at the falling jet of water.

Prince waited. Prince had taken a fancy to drinking out of Ransom's sombrero.

Ransom, thirsty himself, had to laugh at Prince's delicacy in waiting. "All right, you win." Ransom filled his hat and held it out for Prince.

Prince drank in his usual graceful sipping manner.

"Don't know what'll become of you should they ever gun me down."

Prince drank the hat dry, down to the last drop, then nudged Ransom for more.

Ransom obliged him.

When Prince had finally filled his belly to almost double its size, Ransom helped himself to a hatful.

The two horses had gone to grazing lustily, and Ransom was about to sit down on a rock and have himself some jerky, when he became aware of another presence.

A dozen paces away, in deep brush, stood a prospector. He had on a big black floppy hat, a red flannel shirt, a black vest and pants. His leather belt and boots were badly scuffed. He'd half drawn his gun. He was an old man.

It was too late to go for his own gun, so Ransom decided to bluff it through, easy. "Hi there, Old-timer. I see the Army sweep missed you too."

The old prospector's red-streaked eyes oscillated. His cheeks swelled in and out like a turkey gobbler's.

"Find any colors?"

The old prospector rolled his head from side to side, all the while looking at Ransom and his horses exactly like a mad bull.

Ransom stayed cool. A smile wriggled in his black mustache. "We're just passing through. We don't mean to run you off your claim."

The old prospector lifted his gun an inch.

"C'mon, Old-timer, pour your coffee in a saucer and let it cool."

The old prospector chewed with a gobbling sound.

Ransom eased his feet apart. "Got yourself a prospect hole and won't let anybody else in, eh?"

The old prospector raised his gun another inch, almost free of its holster, the tip of the gun sight flashing.

"No need to snap your gun, friend. I don't intend to hang around. I've got my own idee about where the mother lode is." Ransom quietly scratched his belly through his buckskin shirt.

The old prospector's mad grizzly face finally parted in the middle. "No funny tricks now, sonny. You moughtn't fare so well with a feller what warn't brought up gentleman-like."

"Them's high words, friend."

"You better board that horse again, pilgrim. And dust. Before I decide to take him for myself."

"What's the matter, did the blue ducks take yours?"

"No." All of a sudden the old prospector began to break. "No, the Army didn't get 'em. 'Twas a goddam panther."

"Cat? In the Hills?"

The old prospector let his gun fall back into its holster and sat down with a thud on a rock. "The Hills are full of cats." His head sank between his shoulders.

"I'll have to be more careful from now on."

"Had me a fine mare with a stud colt. Bays, the both of 'em. Best friends I ever had." The old prospector wept. "It happened t'while I went to set out my location marks. Left the mare and colt behind. Tied the colt to a tree, thinking the mare would stick close. Well, a panther came along. The mare broke away, of course. I can't blame her for that. And when I come back, all I found of the colt was that over there." The old prospector pointed behind his back without glancing around.

Ransom looked. Not forty steps away lay a colt's fuzzy head, tail, and feet. Green flies buzzed around the remains as thick as swarming bees. "Lord."

The old prospector wept unashamedly. "I'm as brimful of bawl as a egg is of meat."

"Too bad."

"I ain't had an hour's sleep in four weeks, thinking on where my darling went, waiting for her to come back."

"Your darling?"

"My mare."

"That's awful."

"Yep, that's what comes of concluding to make a shortcut to wealth."

Ransom sat down on a rock across from him.

"Yep, when I came out here a couple of months ago, I felt like I'd at last dealt myself a royal flush in the game of life. That the whole world was my jackpot."

"The mare never did come back?"

"No, she didn't." The old prospector wiped his tears on his sleeve. "The panther probably got her too." Hate flashed out of his black beard. "But, by God, I got my revenge. I got the panther what got the colt. Hrr!" The old prospector's eyes blazed yellow for a moment. "I waited patient for a week and finally nailed him. He came back for the rest of the colt."

"Good for you."

"Yep." Then the old prospector's head sagged again. "But after killin' and eatin' the panther, I been dreamin' of cats every night. For a fack." The old prospector heaved a beard-ruffling sigh. "You hain't got some barbwire juice on you?"

"I don't drink."

"Just my darn luck." The old prospector scratched himself. "Yep, goddam, here I am, three hundred miles from a lemon."

"You said something about location marks. You did find some colors then?"

At that the old prospector turned shifty. "Well-l . . . you know . . . you set out stakes along a likely gulch."

"But there are colors through here then?"

"Well-l . . . some ways off from here there is."

Ransom worked his nostrils once.

"Could be the real mother lode is still farther north."

"That's what I heard."

"That where you headed?"

"Likely."

"Plenty of gulches up there all right."

Ransom fixed him with steady eyes. "This gulch of yours, what's it like?"

"What do you want to know for?"

"To get an idea how wide and how deep a gulch should be before you find gold in it."

"Well, mine's wider'n a horse can jump. Though a hen might be able to fly across."

"And it's deep enough for gold to start showing?"

"No doubt about it."

Ransom stood up. "Thanks."

"You're on your way then?"

Ransom nodded.

"Now I will be lonesome." The old prospector got out a dirt-specked quid of tobacco and bit off a corner. "Goddam, I almost wisht the Army had'f found me."

Ransom climbed aboard his horse. He dug out a strip of jerky and threw it down to the old prospector. "Need anything else? I can't spare you much."

"Naw. On your way."

"So long, Old-timer."

Ransom had proceeded down the blue gloom of the canyon some fifty yards, when the old prospector yelled after him, "Don't peach on me now."

"I never saw you."

"If anybody asks after me, say you know me all right, but that you'll be damned if you'll tell 'em when or where you last saw me."

"I never saw you."

Ransom pushed northward.

Hogbacks lay across his course like a series of quarter-moons with the horns up. A couple of hours later the crests began to curve the other way with the horns down.

"It's like working your way through a bunch of ringworms one inside the other."

There was little or no water. Prince and the packhorse sweat. Luckily some of the draws were deep with lush wet grass.

One high slough was black with ripe huckleberries. Ransom filled up on them.

At dusk he shot a blacktail drinking from a wriggling stream. "Mule deer," he murmured to himself. "Sometimes they're pretty dry and stringy." But this was a young doe, fat, and he had himself dripping venison broiled over a low fire. He jerked the rest of the meat and hung it up to dry.

While the horses grazed, he panned the little stream. A little mica shone in it. That was all.

During the night a storm passed to the south of them. A great wind brushed across the tops of the trees. The deep ponderosa pines moaned. He felt lonesome for Katherine and her bed back in Cheyenne. "If only she hadn't made all that money the way she did."

The wind gusted ferociously at times across the higher crests. He nuzzled deeper into his woolen suggans. "Never heard the wind get up and howl so."

The wind died down after a time.

He slept soundly under the great dreaming pines.

Daylight came as usual. He had fresh rabbit for breakfast.

By the time the sun speared down into his gulch, he'd packed his gear and was ahorse.

He worked his way along sinuous canyons. He climbed wave after wave of pinnacle and mountain. His course was wormlike. The farther he penetrated the heart of the Black Hills, the more mysterious and dark and brooding it became.

"Good place for a murder."

The gnarly rock took on strange shapes: a warning granite finger, a forbidding granite turret, a looming granite fortress. One of the bare granite ridges even resembled an enormous sleeping lizard half-buried in mud.

He loved it all. He was lonesome, but that only made it that much the better. He had never felt so alert, so alive, in his life. His eyes picked up the smallest detail. His ears caught the call of magpies a mile off.

Occasionally Prince stopped to nibble a bit of moss off the side of a tree. Or nipped off a juniper bud. Or cropped a few leaves of buckbrush. Or tested the leaf of a white birch. The packhorse meanwhile, having a fondness for rose hips, often nosed through wild rosebushes looking for them.

He stumbled upon some animal carvings on a red wall facing the sun: deer, puma, bear, geese. One was of a huge reptile, some dozen feet long, with a terrifyingly long tongue. There were also several sunbursts and other geometric figures. The carvings were Indian and ancient.

Ransom puzzled over the petroglyphs. He tried to imagine the kind of people who might have made them. He contemplated them until they became dancing sunspots in his brain. His eyes lidded over.

In the evening he came upon another long deep gulch. Dreary patches of burned-over dead pine covered the upper slopes.

He descended into its gloom. He spotted several holes resembling the raw broken mouths of lizards dug into the sides of the gulch.

Presently he came upon a half-dozen deserted shanties

beside a fast-running stream. Wagon parts, shovels, picks, pans, and other camp debris lay around in the grass as if a tornado had ripped through the tight valley.

"Some joker done this out of pure cussedness."

Ransom spotted a board nailed to a tree. Someone had carved an inscription on it with a jackknife. Ransom rode over for a look. Peering down from his horse, he slowly made it out.

WAS ORDERED OUT BY CAPT. POLLOCK.
CAPT. POLLOCK IS A DAMN SHIT ASS

Ransom had to smile to himself.

He spotted other prospect digs into the slopes farther down.

"No use sticking around here. The Army is sure to keep checking this place."

He looked up toward the head of the long gulch.

"Think I'll go up this stream a ways. If the boys found gold float here, it's bound to have washed down from above."

He let the horses have a drink. Then, in the falling dusk, he crossed over on an abandoned beaver dam and ascended the gulch.

He found the head of the stream just as it became dark. A lively spring poured out of the roots of a giant ponderosa pine. He unburdened the horses of all the gear and staked them out for the night. He had a cold supper of dried jerky, hardtack, dried prunes, and cool mountain-spring water.

He rolled out his suggans on a thick bed of pine needles and old moss. For the first time since he left Cheyenne, he undressed. He gave himself a brisk hand bath in the spring, changed to another set of red flannel underwear, and with a happy sigh of anticipation crept into his suggans. When he looked up he found that a vast hoarfrost had come out over the skies.

He missed Katherine again and her lipping kisses.

"Got to strike it big now. So she can give her bad money away to some charity somewhere."

He nuzzled his head back and forth on his leather saddle. "Sure miss her. More than I ever missed old Sam."

A branch cracked behind him.

Automatically his hands checked to see if his six-shooter and Winchester were ready.

"Can't be a cat. Because if it was the horses would've already been in the suggans with me. More than likely a deer."

The spring murmured sweetly.

"Never saw such a blizzard of stars before. We must be pretty high up."

Breathing the crisp night air was like drinking pure sweet alcohol.

"The whole West is my nut to crack and I'm going to bust her wide open. Right here in the Hills."

He went to sleep thinking about how he would kiss away the tiny wrinkles in the corners of Katherine's eyes. She would like that.

2

He awoke about light. The horses were safe. There were no cat tracks about. Good.

He built a fire and made himself some hot coffee and fried some bacon and venison and warmed the last few biscuits Katherine had sent along with him. The sun broke over the Hills and touched his face just as he was finishing the last of his breakfast. In the clear morning light he could make out, beyond the last peaks, the prairies of the far Dakotas.

He watered his horses, gave them a good brisk rubdown, and staked them out to some new tender grass.

He studied the spot carefully. At that point the gulch wasn't too deep, with rock walls but a dozen feet high. Winds had knocked off some of the tree tips, and here and there had pushed over a few of the older ponderosa.

"No blossom rock that I can see. But then you never can tell."

He saw where a small yellow pine had been torn out by the roots a couple of rods above his campsite. It was at the base of the wall. The little pine was dying so he went over and got it and threw it next to his gear. Later he would chop it up for fuel.

He next carefully checked the raw earth from which the little pine had been torn. He scratched through it with trailing fingers.

"No glance rock here."

He was about to turn away, when there bloomed in him the feeling that a pair of eyes was watching everything he was doing.

He drew as he wheeled.

Nobody. All he could see were four horse eyes busy looking for the best grass.

He studied every pine branch, every shadow, every boulder, with intent care. Still nobody.

He kicked through a patch of grayish-green wolfberry. Nothing.

He stepped carefully through a thick patch of glittering green-leaved shrubs. The shrubs clung close to a slope of loose dirt. He had the feeling that something else besides leaves waited glittering in the shrubs. Nothing.

At last, shrugging, he gave up the search. There probably was nobody watching him after all. He turned to the business at hand.

He panned upstream a ways. Where the stream purled over a natural riffle, he scooped up the loose sand caught behind the riffle along with some water and began swishing it around and around in his flat pan, all the while allowing some of the sand and the water to slosh over the sides. He flicked out the bigger pebbles with a finger. He washed and spilled it all down to a last few grains. Nothing. Not even so much as a flyspeck of a color.

He panned downstream. No colors.

He panned down the stream until well out of sight of his camp. Still nothing.

He surveyed the gulch with measuring eyes, up and down, and on both sides.

"There may not be any gold here, but it sure would make a swell spot for a cabin and a garden. Make even a great place for a little town. Water. Trees. Grand view."

It was straight-up noon when he trudged back to camp. The sky held clear. The ground was warm with sun. The pines stank sweetly of sticky rosin. His nose worked overtime in the midst of all the fresh forest smells.

He got out his ax and reached down to pick up the little yellow pine.

The little pine wasn't there. Gone.

He turned warily on his boot heels, a hand to his gun.

Nobody.

His eyes next sought the place in the wall from which the little pine had been torn out.

That spot was gone too.

Quietly he stepped over. "By the Lord, I even worked it with my fingers for gold." He knelt and examined the wall very carefully.

Ah. The hole had been carefully filled in, first with dirt and then with fresh sod. The sod was exactly like the sod around, except where the edges showed beneath what appeared to be a casual sprinkling of pine needles.

His spine began to tingle. Again he drew as he wheeled.

And again nobody. Nothing.

"I'll be damned. Now I know for sure there's somebody watching me. Besides the Almighty."

He stood slightly crouched at the knees. He sent his ears

out all around. Yet all he heard was the steady cropping sound of the grazing horses.

"What the hell kind of spooky place is this?"

He took a long slow sniff, intent on catching any odd smell.

There was only the new aroma of fresh horse dung.

"Sam would say I was being notional again."

The mystic Hills shimmered in sunshine and silence. The far-off prairies of the Dakotas wimmered a misty blue sea.

He reholstered his gun. Slowly he sat down beside what was left of his morning fire. "The biggest mystery is where that little pine tree went. And why."

He picked up a stick and poked around in the ashes. He found a few live coals.

"Why wouldn't they let me burn it? That I don't get atall."

He threw on a few leftover twigs. When flames spurted up and took hold, he added more wood. Soon he had a good fire going.

He got out a small iron pot and had himself boiled jerky spiced with fresh wood sorrel. The sour juice of the sorrel always brought out the true taste of venison.

"Meat's real meat, if you know how to fix it."

He put everything neatly away. He got to his feet and stretched.

"Dammit, and why should anybody want to hide that hole in the wall? Unless'n there was something to hide?"

He gave it all another run through his mind. Then, swearing "By God," he grabbed his spade and went to work. He first skimmed off the sod, then dug deep into the friable rock-studded wall.

He'd thrown out a dozen spadefuls, when his eye caught glitter in a curdle of dirt.

He knelt. He picked up the curdle and broke it gently in his hand. So. Well. There it was. At least a half-dozen bright-yellow bits of something the size of flakes of pepper. He got out his jackknife, edged the jackknife on the sole of his boot, wiped it clean on his buckskin trousers, then cut into one of the yellow flakes. Soft. Next he bit into it. It gave. Finally he tasted it. By God. "Gold."

He stared down at the yellow flakes awhile.

"Not a lot of it. But there it is. And somebody didn't want me to find it. There's probably still more and better higher up."

He spent the rest of the afternoon digging out his prospect hole. There was always a flake or two of gold in each spadeful. But never more.

He forgot about the eyes watching him.

It was midnight, he'd been asleep several hours, when of a sudden he awoke to the vague gray light of a half-moon high overhead. He awoke without stirring. Only his eyelids parted.

There they were. The eyes. And not a dream either.

It was a young girl. The pupils of the young girl's eyes were as glossy black as freshly hardened tar. They glittered. Her hair also was black, and was plaited Indian-fashion, a fat braid behind each ear. A doeskin dress glinting with green beadwork hung to her knees. She wore leather leggings and moccasins. Her breasts had just begun to form.

He stared at the girl without moving a muscle.

The thought flashed through his mind that for all her buckskin garb and long black braids she wasn't Indian. Her cheeks were dusky, yes, but not dusky enough.

He had heard of white children being stolen by Indians to replace lost children. She was probably one of those.

Then the dusky girl did a strange thing. She slowly leaned down until her face came to within a few inches of his. Her breath wisped on his beard. She seemed to be examining him minutely, beard and mustache, nose and lips, cheeks and forehead.

Her breath on his beard tickled him a little. The smell of her was the smell of wild ferns and sage.

Of a sudden she wept large tears. One of them, glistening in the weak moonlight, fell big and wet on his upper lip. Salty.

Of a sudden he made a grab for her; and caught her by the elbow.

The low shrill scream of a caught fawn broke from her. "Got you."

She jerked to break free. She almost made it.

He rose sitting to hold her the better. "Not so fast, my little wildcat."

She squirmed, rolled, twisted. Abrupt undulations like that of an inchworm in agony rippled through her.

"Snaky. Like she ain't got any bones."

He wrestled her, trying to get a solid hold on her. He couldn't quite manage it. He became aware of her wonderfully supple waist, her firmly muscled seat, her slim resilient neck. "She's as slippery as a greased mink, by God." He caught her around the neck from the rear with his left hand. He squeezed, powerfully. "I don't mean to hurt you, little one, but by the Lord I do aim to tame you." Finally his fingertips found the right spot and, suddenly, she was quiet.

"Let's have a look at you."

Picking up a stick with his free hand, he reached over and stirred up the embers of the fire and then threw on a piece of fat. In an instant both he and the girl were bathed in a warm crackling glow.

"Just what's the idea, coming into my camp like this sneaky-like, hey?"

He kept a tight pinch around her neck to keep her in control. She was as helpless in his grip as a pullet in the mouth of a fox.

"Speak up."

Her body hung slack, and the fall of it was abject.

"I'm not going to hurt you, child. But I do mean to find out what this is all about."

Something in the way her eyes drifted off told him she

couldn't understand him. She had been raised Indian all right.

Firelight played on her face. The forlorn look of the caught animal gentled her eyes. Her eyes were not as dark as he'd first thought. The dot was black enough but it was ringed by a light gray. He pulled her forward a little and with some little delicacy looked down her neckline.

"Yep, skin's white inside."

She was full of sudden squirmings again. And once more she almost broke free. A large neck tendon slipped out from under his thumb.

He regrabbed her, hard, and then had her firmly in hand again. "Still full of fight, eh? With still nothing to say." He cocked his head, considering her. "Sure wish the hell I could get you to talk."

She whimpered in his pinching grip.

He leaned into her face, eyes hard. "Talk? American?"

She tried to duck away in his hand; couldn't. The smell of her was still wonderful: crushed ferns and brushed silver sage. Like a female wolf puppy.

"Pretty little wild thing." He smiled at her. "Well, I guess there ain't no use'n holding onto you any longer." He paused. "Though I suppose you'll go running off to your Sioux ma now and tell her all about it, won't you? Because I know all about you pigheaded Sioux not wanting the white man on your holy ground."

She spoke. "Paha Sapa." She managed to squeeze it out through his pinching fingers.

"By the Lord. She may not know American but she does know when I'm talking holy talk."

"Paha Sapa!"

He studied her.

"Paha Sapa!"

"You sure you don't know any white talk?"

"Paha Sapa!"

"Let's try it once." He leaned gently close to her and spoke winningly. "Ma-ma? Pa-pa?"

She stared at where his lips moved in his beard.

"Ma-ma? Pa-pa?"

At last, very slowly, a vague recognition of something stirred in her eyes.

"Mum-mum? Milk?" He watched her. "Papa spank? Hanh?"

More vague recognition appeared in her eyes.

"Kind of silly of me to be talking baby talk to an almost grown girl. But, by the Lord, I've got to know." His leg had begun to fall asleep under her weight. "No, no, no. Papa spank?"

At last a wondering, a marvelous distant look opened the dark pupils of her eyes.

He pointed first at himself, then across at the prospect hole he'd dug into the wall. "No, no, no?"

She caught on. She tried to nod in his grip.

"She does know a little white. It's weak in her, yes, but it's there." He pointed at himself. "Bad, bad?"

Again she tried to nod.

"Aha. That explains it. She knows there's gold around here. And was only trying to keep me away from it." He played pinches into her neck. He began to like the feel of her. "It ties in with what I heard at Fort Laramie. That every once in a while the Sioux will come in with a handful of gold nuggets to do some trading. But won't tell where they found them."

She observed him intently, trying to understand what he was saying.

The fat he'd thrown into the fire was almost out.

"Well, like I say, there's no use'n holding onto you any longer." He let her go. "Nothing I hate more than to see a wild bird caught in a cage."

She sprang up and away. She gave him a wild glittering

look. Then she bounded across into the glittering green
shrubs he'd noticed earlier; and was gone.

"So she was looking out at me from them."

An instant later, the fat-fed flame fell down. He was back
in the vague gray light of the half-moon.

It took him a while to find the same warm spot in his
suggans. He let his tongue run over his lip. There was still a
little left of her salty tear. Also, it seemed to him, strangely,
that the very questions he'd asked her, "Ma-ma? Pa-pa?"
and "Mum-mum? Milk?" had awakened, almost, some memories of his own childhood, going back to a time before Sam
Slaymaker had picked him up wandering alone on the
prairies. Almost.

Stars multiplied in his eyelashes. "That's one cinch that's
pulled up tight and painful."

The next morning he had a lonely breakfast of venison and
coffee.

He moved about soberly thoughtful. "I'd give a pretty
penny to know where my wild girl holes up at night."

He cleaned up around camp. "And I'll bet a horse she lives
alone too. She's the kind that don't need to live with anybody. Indian or white."

He curried the two horses, watered them, and staked them
out to new grazing ground.

"Well, I'm not going to look for her nest. Like a grouse
she'll have it too well hid." A smile crinkled through his
black beard. "No, I'll just keep looking for gold and that'll
fetch her out. Sooner or later." He shouldered pickax and
shovel and picked up his pan and started upstream. "Pretty
little thing. Smelled just like a pretty little wolf puppy."

He walked slowly upstream, panning as he went. The
weather was a miracle. Cool at that height. Clear. The air
was scented with the smell of sun-warmed pine needles and
cracking rock.

He found a few colors. It was still nothing to get excited about.

He went about his work as if no one were watching him. Yet he knew that somewhere, following him, those gray-ring eyes of hers were peering at him from secret places. She would move through the shadows of the pine forest like some bird of the night.

"Wait'll I tell Katherine about this. A wild girl living alone in the Black Hills. She won't believe it."

Near the top of the gulch the colors came a little thicker. Also the flakes were coarser.

"Kate'll probably be a mite jealous."

He climbed onto a small plateau. He stopped for a look.

He could see for miles in all directions. He was standing on top of the sun almost and could look down at it all. He'd felt this way once before. Something about squatting very high up and getting ready to jump. Like that first time with Katherine.

"You know, Wild Girl kept saying 'Paha Sapa.' That couldn't be her name. Indians usually don't like to give their names. More'n likely she was trying to tell me something about this gulch. Or the Black Hills."

He took several whacks at various crumbling outcrops of rocks with his pickax. The granite broke up easily.

He'd taken a half-dozen cracks at one of the larger mica-flaked outcroppings, when someone suddenly grabbed hold of one of the points of his pickax, just at the top of his swing. The someone had grabbed so hard and jerked so sharply that he almost fell down. His hat flipped off onto the grass.

He let go of the pickax; recovered; whirled; drew.

It was Wild Girl. Pointing at the ground. Outraged. "Paha Sapa!"

He put his gun away. "By God, I knew you'd show up again."

Wild Girl held the pickax behind her as if she meant to

keep it. She shook her head, stamped her foot. "Wakantanka!"

A smile opened his beard. "What you mean is, Pa-pa
spank."

She paused; drew back. A frown, at first only puzzled,
then deepening, ringed the dusky smooth skin between her
brows. And again, vaguely, a wondering, a marvelous distant
look of recognition opened her gray eyes.

He waited. He thought her even more comely in the sun.
She still had on her beaded doeskin dress, and her hair was
still done up in two braids. There was a beauty spot of red
on each cheek and a line of vermilion ran down the part in
her black hair. She was of that age where her cheeks were
just beginning to fill out.

She let the pickax fall to earth.

To help her remember, he rolled up his sleeve to show her
the white skin of his arm.

"Sanyan?"

He lifted his leather shirt to show her his white lean belly.

The expression in her eyes changed, from one of wondering to one of hate. The black dot of her eyes enlarged, her
dogteeth showed. The next moment a knife glittered in her
small hand.

Again he made a sudden grab for her; and caught her by
the elbow of the knife hand. "Oh no you don't." He twisted
her arm around behind her, up, hard, until she let go of the
knife with a yelp of pain.

Even in her awkward bind she kept jerking and wriggling.
Every time she moved she hurt herself, like a she-wolf
caught in an ever-tightening bear trap.

He slipped his other arm around her waist and drew her
body tight against his. He lost his footing and they both fell
down in the grass. The turf beneath was as resilient as the
fleshy rump of a horse. The sweet wild smell of her and of
the lush grass was keen in his nostrils. Even more quickening

was the feel of her supple body, just nubile, where her breast flattened against his arm and where her firm buttocks rippled against his belly. He was instantly aroused, hardened to the game. Sudden desire, delicious, snaked through his belly. It raced through him like brandy in the blood. The thought ran through him, a regret, that it wouldn't be the first time for him, while it would be for her. Innocence should be for the innocent. A wandering Adam for a wilderness Eve. With gold as their Devil in Eden.

"Sanyan!" Of a sudden her arm was free. She undulated so swiftly and with such a powerful humpneck motion, he almost lost her. She slithered ahead under him. She clawed in the grass for the fallen knife.

He lunged. He caught her by the back of the neck just in time and pinched for all he was worth. A snarl opened his black beard. He thought of biting her.

She became limp under him.

He lay on her. Again desire swelled in him. It lifted up like a wild lily, fully open, the petals turned back as far as they would go. He pressed down on her until he thought he'd either break or burst. She lay under him like an imprisoned grouse.

He let go of her neck. She didn't move. He caught a hint, the vaguest suggestion, of the coy woman in the way she lay supine.

He turned her over gently. He looked at her through a quivering gauntlet of tumescent anthers.

She lay looking up at him wonderingly.

"Fly, little girl, fly. Before I hurt you."

She looked past him at the blue skies above.

He trembled to ravish her.

Once more large tears appeared in her eyes.

He blinked. He couldn't understand the large tears. At the same time he was pleased to see them. They were more than just tears of weakness or compassion. They were tears one sometimes saw at a benediction.

"Fly!"

Her free hand came up and wondering touched his beard.

Impulsively his trembling hand slid under her buckskin dress. She was naked under it. Her flesh had the resilient fullness of tongues. He stroked her once over the belly. He watched his brown hand move over her very white skin.

She quivered under his touch.

He felt compassion for her; withdrew his hand.

Her face softened.

With a fingertip he touched her right brow, then her left brow. He touched her right shoulder tip, and, lifting himself, touched her left shoulder tip. He touched the point of her right hip, then her left. He touched her right ankle, then her left.

A smile, wondering, opened her lips.

He kissed her nose tip. He kissed her eyes, first the right, then the left.

She closed her eyes. The smile grew.

He traced a fingertip, lightly brushing, over each dark brow. He ran a fingertip down the length of her nose.

The smile awakened dimples in her rose-brown cheeks.

He kissed the left pink edge of her lips, then the right edge. He kissed the saucy double-u of her upper lip, then the faint cleft of her full nether lip.

Her eyes moved under her closed lids like kitties stirring under blankets.

He kissed her nether lip again, suckled it a little a moment. He let his tongue glide along the wet inner edges of her lips.

Shock of pleasure tightened and lifted her neck muscles.

He did it again.

Her tongue tip emerged fleetingly.

He waited.

Her tongue didn't quite touch his again. Her eyes volved and revolved under their lids.

He touched her lips with his tongue again.

She raised a little brown hand against him.

He hung over her, admiring her. He couldn't help but make comparisons. When Katherine looked angry, or tired, or sad, wrinkles appeared at the corners of her lips and around her one good eye. Katherine showed age at times. When Wild Girl looked angry, or sad, or tired, there was only youth's firm skin. No wrinkles. When Katherine smiled, deep, the corners of her mouth sometimes drew back into knotted wrinkles. When Wild Girl smiled, deep, her lips drew back into baby dimples. How old was Katherine, really, if Wild Girl was, say, fourteen? Or was it that Katherine looked old for her age? It hurt him to think of how Katherine's beauty couldn't hold a candle to Wild Girl's beauty. Katherine's skin was slightly parched no matter how much makeup she put on, even a little stringy. Wild Girl's skin was welling and full.

Wild Girl moved under him.

He caught a whiff of her out of the open neck of her doeskin dress. Again it was of wild ferns lightly pressed, of silver sage caressed with strong brown fingertips. It made a man think of galloping. Of gathering up mares. The alluring smell of puccoons was as nothing compared to it. The greening scent of the wild fern and the holy aroma of silver sage had it all over the puccoon.

Wild Girl's eyes fluttered open.

He saw the awakening in them. In Katherine the same look was one of plain lust.

He touched, stroked, brushed Wild Girl's doeskin dress. So supple did the leather dress make her feel, it was as if she had on two skins, the one over the other.

Once more, impulsively, with a boy's groan at being restrained too long, his hand stole under her dress. He touched, brushed, cupped her plum breasts. He moved a peaceful hand between her breasts up to her throat. He played at choking her. He kissed the pink edges of her open mouth.

She swelled against him.

He slipped an arm under her. With his free hand he touched her softest hair, where it was barely tufted and cleft. Again the differences. Where Katherine had a love's entrance as easy as swimming, Wild Girl had a knot as intricate as a new bud on a wild rose.

Wild Girl quivered.

The quivering set him off. With a slow boyish surge, he loosened his gunbelt and opened his clothes and rose over her. He divided her. He possessed her. Tightness made the throat and tongue rhue aloud.

She received him with a maiden child's cry. The precious vessel of her loving received him.

A high hot sun broke in on their inner drifting. Both stirred, the one above and the one beneath. Both turned their heads at the same time. They gazed at each other.

She was the first to smile. It was a smile full of wonderful awakened affection.

Ransom returned the smile. Wild Girl was the one meant for him all right, the one he'd originally intended to save himself for. He'd been right back then to want to save himself until he'd met the right one. Sam had been wrong.

Wild Girl's smile deepened, widened, full of giving.

While poor Katherine was not for him. She was wrong for him.

Wild Girl pushed her slim brown fingers into Ransom's beard, and laughed.

It was crazy to think the Army might be able to keep the white man out of the Black Hills. Where gold, money, was involved the white man was worse than a hog. As even he himself was. So eventually Katherine was bound to follow him to the Hills. And it was equally crazy to think that Katherine might fall in love with someone else. The fact she had kept all men at arm's length until he'd come along was proof of that.

Wild Girl gave his beard a tug, and laughed some more.

Hope that Katherine would die somehow? Get killed on the way over by Indians? Road agents? Horrible thought. Because he still loved Katherine too. Different. But there. Besides, he was tied to her. He had lived with her, had shared selves with her, had dreamed dreams of a future happy time with her.

Wild Girl lifted her hips under him. She was surprisingly strong. She was one of those who could bear a man all day. The taut nubile bundle of her in his arms was an Eden delight.

He withdrew. Modestly he closed his clothes. He stretched out on the grass beside her.

She sat up. She paused. She moved privately beside him. Then she said with gleeful pride in her voice, "Poge we."

After a moment he understood. She'd bled a little. She'd been a virgin all right. "Damn that Sam."

She covered herself. She got to her feet. Her brown face was all smiles for him. She held a finger to her mouth, gesturing that she would be back in a moment. She picked up her knife and was gone.

He lay back in the grass. He smelled again her natural wild perfume of ferns and sage. Mingled in with it was the wonderful scent of fresh girlish flesh.

She was back. She touched him on the shoulder. There was on her face the look of a woman who'd discreetly arranged things.

His gullet twisted in him. What would Katherine think?

"Uwa."

He tried to smile. "No savvy."

Wild Girl gestured for him to get up and follow her. "Uwa."

"You've got something to show me?"

She cocked her head a little, smiling; again gestured for him to get up and follow her.

"All right." With an agile roll he came to his feet. "Coming." He buckled on his gunbelt and clapped on his sombrero. He stashed his tools off to one side. "Let's see what you got in mind. I trust you."

She led him back down the gulch, past the several spots where he'd panned for gold. Her slim hips swung bewitchingly girlish ahead of him. He couldn't get over it that he'd possessed them. He loved her. Exhilaration opened his eyes to a high wide green.

She turned up a short side gully.

"Seems to know where she's going."

Some fifty feet into the gully she stopped beside a wall of what looked like crumbling milkstone. She pointed. "Mazaskazi."

He looked at the whitish rock wall; looked at her; looked at the wall. The white wall was about as large as a storefront. It was as bare as a tooth.

"Mazaskazi." Then, to make it perfectly clear what she meant, she reached down to her right legging and from a little side pocket drew out something. She held it out to him.

He stared. A locket lay flashing in the palm of her small brown hand.

"Mazaskazi."

He took it dumbly. "A gold locket. She really was white once then." A tiny lip showed along one edge of the locket. With his thumbnail he pried the locket open.

He found a twist of brown hair, and under it a curly-lettered inscription. Gently he lifted the twist of hair, the better to read the inscription.

Erden Aldridge

He stared at her. "So that's your name. Erden Aldridge."

She gave him a puzzled look. She had expected him to be very pleased that it was mazaskazi she was showing him.

"Erden Aldridge. I'll be goddamned."

She continued to look at him puzzled. Finally, frowning,

she took the gold locket from him, and first pointing at it, she then pointed at the wall of whitish rock. "Mazaskazi."

"She's trying to tell. . . ." He stared first at the locket, then at the wall. "It can't be." He went over and broke off a small piece of rock from the crumbling wall about the size of a big potato. "But, that's just what it is. Float quartz." A fresh gleaming piece of yellow metal the size of a watermelon seed stuck out of the rock. Yes. He broke off more of the rock wall. More pieces of yellow metal gleamed to view. There were pieces the size of birdshot, pieces the size of watermelon seeds, pieces the size of chicken hearts.

"Mazaskazi?"

He took one of the small pieces of the yellow metal and with a stone in hand pounded it flat on a rock. It was too malleable to be copper.

"Mazaskazi?"

Gold. Nuggets of gold. He stared and stared. He picked up several more rocks from the foot of the white wall, big and small, broke them on each other. More seeds and more hearts of gold popped to view. By the Lord. His eyes flicked back and forth across the wall of milky quartz. His green eyes glittered. Here was a vein of gold God only knew how deep. Enough gold to run a nation. A true mother lode at last.

"Mazaskazi? Sha?"

"Gold? I'll say." He stared at her. "Wild Girl, Erden, do you know what? We're rich. Rich!"

She folded her hands flat together under her chin.

"Gold! Gold! Just think." He leaped up off the ground and cracked his heels together for joy. "I can't believe it. Just can't believe it. But, goddammit, it's true. Boy, wait'll I show Katherine."

"Kazanyan?"

The sad way she spoke sobered him.

"Kazanyan?" she repeated.

Oh yes. Lord. What a picklement he was in now. He could

never show this to Katherine. Once Katherine saw this he'd never be able to break away from her. If breaking away was what he wanted.

Erden, watching his face, frowned with him. What was the trouble?

He let the raw gold fall to earth. This mother lode belonged to the wild girl Erden. She was giving it to him. They had made love together and now she took him for her man. Also, little Erden was Indian raised, and as such wouldn't want the white man to know about the gold. Erden would never let him use the gold as white-man wealth. She'd only shown it to him to share a secret with him. It was her thought that the two of them would know about the bonanza together and would go on living in the Hills forever and no man would be the wiser. He sat down on a fallen boulder of milky quartz.

She stood quietly before him.

He plucked a solitary spear of grass, bit off the end of it, ran the point of it between his two front teeth. Seeds caught in his mouth. He spat them out.

She took a step toward him. She quirked her head, trying to understand his mood.

"Wild Girl, it's time you and I understood each other. And to do that, you and I've got to go back to school. Me to learn your Sioux, you to learn my American."

She cocked her head the other way, still trying to understand him.

He took her by the arm and sat her on his knee. He drew her warmly close, an arm around her bird-slim waist.

Her gray eyes held intent on his eyes.

He touched the center of her bosom with the thumb of his right hand and spoke her name. "Erden Aldridge." He said it again, meaning "you," by the way he lightly pushed into her a little. "Er-den Ald-ridge." Then with the same thumb extended he touched his own breastbone. "Earl Ransom."

"Anawin?"

He thought a moment. He picked up a gold nugget and held it up. "Mazaskazi?"

She nodded brightly at that.

He pointed to himself. "Ransom?"

She caught on. She smiled a vivid white smile. Instantly she pointed to herself with her thumb and said, "Ica Psin-psin-cadan."

"Psin-psin-cadan?"

She looked around for something to explain the name. She thought to herself a moment. Then she took her two hands and made them flutter about like swallows fleeting by, and imitated perfectly their whistling and crying sound. "Psin. Psin. Weeb. Weeb."

"A swallow. Sure. Psin-psin-cadan."

"Toya." Again she looked about for something to explain what she meant. She spotted a blue flower a few steps away. She leaped off his lap, pointed to it, and returned. "Toya."

"Blue. Toya. Sure. Blue Swallow. My pretty little Blue Swallow. Or, like the Indian says it, Swallow Blue."

Her brown face flashed a smile of triumph.

"Blue Swallow. A wonderful name for you. Just right."

She sat down on his knee again.

"Paha Sapa?" he asked. He had to know what she'd meant by that.

She pointed around at the rocks and the pines and the grass, at everything in sight but the sky.

"You mean the Black Hills. Now I begin to catch. Sure." His face flashed a smile of triumph.

They pointed things out to each other, calling off the names, each in their own language: a pine, a tree, a blade of grass, a rock, a wolfberry bush. They named everything in sight. They laughed together about the way both stumbled over the other's strange words for things.

He took the locket and showed her where her name had been engraved upon it. He pointed his thumb at her bosom again and pronounced her white name, slowly.

At last she tried it. "Err-dann Alt-ritch."

He had to laugh. "That's enough for today."

He looked over at where the sun was sinking behind them, falling toward the high ridge where they'd first met. He made the sign for eating, passing the tips of his fingers in a curve downward past his mouth four times, and then for sleeping, inclining his head to the right while holding both hands under it in a line. "Eat. Sleep."

She understood instantly.

"Good. She knows the old-time sign language. All those days Sam spent teaching it to me won't go to waste after all."

She jumped off his knee and signaled she had something else to show him and for him to come along. Her lips were quirked at the corners with the smile of one who had a special secret to tell.

He followed her, wondering.

She led the way back to the main gulch; turned down it. Some hundred yards below where his horses were staked out, on the left, she walked toward a pinnacle of granite standing apart from the wall of the gulch. She stepped around it; and vanished.

"Hey." He hurried to catch up.

A cave opened behind the pinnacle.

"Erden?"

Then he saw her. She was standing just inside the cave, in shadow, smiling, a modest hand to her mouth. The single pinnacle served as a perfect screen.

He stepped into the cave beside her. A gentle wind, coming out of the deep back of the cave, breathed over them. The gentle wind felt cool in contrast to the warm air outside.

His eyes adjusted to the semidarkness. Gradually he made out the articles of an Indian home: a willow backrest facing a circle of hearthstones in the center of the cave, various storage parfleches set in a row to one side, dried beef hanging from icicles of crystalline. The floor was covered with several bearskins. The back of the cave, where it became a natural tunnel, was curtained off with a huge piece of buckskin. Off to one side, out of the draft, opened another and smaller room. Its floor was laid with woven sweetgrass on which were spread buffalo-skin sleeping robes.

Ransom was amazed at the lovely wonder of it all. "Just enough draft to keep it cool and carry out the smoke. With a cozy little bedroom off to one side. This beats all, this does."

Erden gave him the smile of the child who'd successfully come up with a truly great surprise.

"A real hideout. There ain't a road agent on earth but what he wouldn't give a pretty penny to know about this." He gave the rock wall in the bedroom a closer look. "And all of it probably peppered with gold." He flashed a big smile. "Need some hard cash, Ransom, old man? All right. Chip a piece of your house and have it weighed at the bank. And, at the same time, give yourself that much the more elbow room in it." Slowly he shook his head at the wonder of it all.

She touched him on the arm, again gesturing for him to follow her.

He laughed. "Lead on, my Swallow. After this I'm ready for anything."

She led him back to the horses. She pulled up the picket pin of the docile packhorse and motioned to him to do the same with Prince's.

She took them down to a bend in the gulch below her cave. A draw led off from the point of the bend, going up into a dense stand of ponderosa. The draw narrowed into a dark defile, then into an awful redstone chasm some thousand feet deep and only a dozen yards wide. The gloom was suddenly deep and profound. They went a short ways, when of a sudden the red chasm opened onto a small glade. The floor of the glade was carpeted with lush buffalo grass and veils of daisies. In the falling sun the light-green grass and the yellow daisies seemed to grow out of a thick mat of blue shadows. A small trickling stream ran down the center of the glade. The red stone and the dark-green pines and the autumn-touched quaking aspen gave the little glen the aspect of such glory as to make Ransom's eyes widen high and green.

"By the Lord," Ransom whispered. "A perfect little park. All we need to do is build us a little pole fence across the pass here and we've got our horses safe. Even a panther'd have to be careful how he went in after a horse here." He gave Erden a great smile. "Girl, this is just like finding the Garden of Eden. The one Adam and Eve lost."

The horses neighed with pleasure when they were freed. The horses cropped a few test bites, then threw up their tails and ran around and around in their new grass heaven.

Erden laughed with delight at the frolicking horses. She made the sign to show that the horses had sunrise in their hearts. Ransom replied with the sign of yes. And together Ransom and Erden fixed a temporary pole gate across the pass into the pasture.

They next went back to his campsite and collected his gear, as well as his tools stashed above, and brought it all into her cave.

She got out another willow backrest specially for him and faced it to the hearth. She gestured for him to take his ease on it.

Smiling, he tossed his sombrero to one side and let himself down and lay back.

She pulled off his boots. She got cool water in a Sioux pot, and kneeling, and placing his feet in a basin in her lap, washed his feet, and rubbed his ankles, and soothed his calves.

"A king never had it better."

She got kindling and firewood. Brushing away the ashes in the hearth until she found live embers, she soon had a little fire going.

He glowed as he watched her.

By the time the sun had sunk, she had a pot of soup and meat for him.

He ate ravenously.

After she had dampered the fire with a handful of ashes, she sprinkled the warm ashes with wisps of sweetgrass. Soon the cave and the little bedroom off to one side were filled with a sweetish smoking aroma.

They went to bed early, naked.

They slept sweetly together on a dark buffalo robe. He lay with his body curled around her. He did not touch her, though occasionally upon a deep breath her child-naked back brushed against his boy-naked belly.

He reveled in the incense coming from the hearth and in the smell of dried sweetgrass rising from the woven mat beneath them.

He couldn't get over the sudden wonder of it all. It was almost a dream. Whatever it was, truth, dream, or parts of both, he wasn't going to spoil it with lust.

Early-morning sunlight struck into their hideout and woke them. They opened their eyes. At about the same time they turned their heads and smiled upon each other.

He formed an incomplete circle with his thumb and forefinger and holding it horizontal to the left, raised it a little. "Morning."

"Hanhanna."

They smiled some more, each delighting in the sleepy appearance of the other.

Ransom found his hand sliding under the warm robe and reaching for her bare shoulder.

She appeared not to see it and before his hand could touch her, she was up and out of bed.

"Erden."

She stretched deliciously in the cool air, rising to her toes at the end of a deep yawn, her young breasts flattening a little along the edges.

"Erden?"

Even as he spoke she skipped outside naked. He heard her bare feet padding on the path a moment; then silence.

He rose on one elbow. "What the heck? Running outside stark nun naked?"

A few minutes later she came back, dripping water, cheeks a dark rose-brown, eyes merry. She saw his questioning eyes, and said, "Oihduzaza hanhanna." With her hand she made the sign for the morning bath.

"So that's what you were up to."

He loved her wet body. In the shadowy light of the cave he saw again how white her bell-like belly was. Her face, neck, hands were like those of a lighter-skinned Indian, but the rest of her as pale as shimmering egg peel.

He loved the lithe form of her, especially her hips which had only just begun to swell with coming womanhood. She was almost too perfect to touch. He regretted having once touched her at the same time that he longed to touch her again.

He thought to himself: "And then, there's Katherine."

Erden turned. A questioning look opened her face.

Quickly he made the sign for eating.

She quirked her gray-ringed eyes at him. She'd caught on that he'd just then remembered someone else. She smiled, and with a wink forgave him, and motioned for him to stay abed while she got him something to eat. She put on her buckskins and skipped into the larger room.

"The sweet little rascal," he thought, stroking his beard, "she ain't so dumb."

They had breakfast of roast venison and sliced pemmican and thimbleberries washed down with clear spring water.

When he'd finished eating, he held his hand level against his heart and swung it briskly out and to the right. "Good."

She nodded. "Was-te."

He lay back on his willow rest, bare toes to the fire.

She put the parfleches away.

He brooded on the problem of what to do about Katherine. He wondered what Katherine might be doing at the moment.

Erden tidied up the cave.

After a while, musing on the fire, he got to wondering about the various Sioux words Erden had used the day before. Using sign language, he had her interpret them while she did her housework. "Paha Sapa" not only meant "the Black Hills" but also "that place where a dark jealous spirit full of great vengeance guarded many forbidden secrets." "Wakantanka" meant "the Spirit of All Spirits." "Sanyan" meant "whitewash." "Poge we" meant "nosebleed" or "you have broken my maidenhead." "Uwa" meant "come." "Mazaskazi" meant literally "yellow silver." "Sha" meant "scarlet," "very wonderful." "Kazanyan" meant "parting." "Anawin" meant "to tell what is not true."

They talked in liquid gestures. Both were quick to catch the other's thought.

He made out that she did not remember anything about white parents. Her first memory of life was of riding a spotted pony very fast in moonlight. She had good Indian parents at first. They loved her dearly. She lived very happy with them for at least six winters that she could recall. Then the hated white man with his blue breeches and his terrible wagon guns came and wiped out her village. She herself had been wounded. She showed him a white bubble of a scar in her armpit. Somehow she had been overlooked by the bayoneting white man. Afterward she had crept, then run, to the safety of certain tribal cousins of her foster parents. Several winters passed. Her new parents had little to eat. They soon let her know she was not welcome. Besides, her skin turned white when she did not run naked in the sun as she had when a little girl. She became more and more unhappy living with them. On one of their trips to the Black Hills to get lodgepoles, and to treat themselves to thimbleberries, she jumped camp and fled into the higher Hills. She knew her second parents would not follow her because of their fear of the mad spirits in the Black Hills. They believed that the mad spirits deliberately sought to terrify man and beast with their vindictive lightnings and their terrible rumblings and their black snouts of whirling winds. She herself wasn't too afraid of the spirits and their mad behavior. Soon she found the cave off the gulch and then the high little park. The place of the gold she knew about from her first Indian father's description. It had not taken her long to learn to live alone, and like it. She'd felt terribly lonesome at first, yes, but soon the pines and the bushes and the streams and the flying two-leggeds and the preying four-leggeds got used to her, and she got used to them, and then they became friends.

That spring, several months before Ransom came along, some white prospectors had stumbled upon her, and she'd almost been caught. But she was too swift, too wary, for them and their bullets. A few days later she managed to stampede their horses with a scaring robe. Later still she'd scared the daylights out of the grizzly prospectors themselves by yowling the Indian death cry and following it up by starting a small avalanche into their camp. The prospectors left in a rush, cursing and muttering about a "banshee." She had to smile as she told about it.

Then Ransom had come along.

She had to know about him too.

He told her some things about himself, about his adventures with Sam Slaymaker, about his attempts at mining, about his tries at driving mules.

She had tears in her gray eyes when he finished signing that his early memory was wiped out and that like her he too was an orphan. The two of them were heart kin.

He didn't tell her about Katherine.

She asked him by sign if he'd ever eaten the white man's "snow in summer."

It took him a moment to understand what she meant.

Then it came to him. Ice cream. He told her, yes, he had, and that someday when they should go to the great place of many wooden lodges at Cheyenne he would get her a whole parfleche full.

"When?"

"Soon. Perhaps before the snow flies."

That afternoon they checked the horses in the little park pasture. The horses were fine. The horses pricked up their heads and came trotting over to the pole fence and nuzzled them both. Ransom ran his hand over their backs for sores and found none. Sam would have been pleased with his grooming.

Ransom wanted to see the mother lode of gold again. Erden frowned at the thought, but went along anyway. To her it was not a treasure to gloat over.

He was struck again by the richness of the milky quartz and couldn't help but fill a pocket with a handful of nuggets the size of rose hips.

She frowned at that too.

He dreamed ahead to that great day when, after he'd mined it himself or had sold it outright, he would be a wealthy man. He swore he'd build himself a great mansion in one of the little parks around. Katherine would adore him for it.

Erden touched him on the elbow.

He jumped. And then groaned as if struck in the belly by an arrow.

She touched him again. "Uwa."

He made up his mind to push all thought of Katherine to one side and concentrate on Erden.

She signaled that she had yet another secret place to show him.

"All right, little Swallow Blue, lead on."

They climbed a small hogback to the northeast; filed past thrusting fingers of shining granite; dropped into a canyon with flared sides. The walls of the canyon were brilliant crimson sandstone and studded with patches of blue spruce. Then, going up a side ravine, they descended into yet another little perfect park. Here too the meadow was lush with wonderful grasses, and instead of daisies it was veiled over with myriads of nodding sunflowers.

Ransom's eye fell on some red deer grazing nearby. A big buck cropped alone off to one side of the herd.

Erden put a finger to her lips. She threw a soft look back at Ransom, and then, seemingly out only for a stroll, casually headed toward the deer. She paused now and again to lift the sunburst head of a sunflower. She had the appearance of a red doe out grazing.

The big buck lifted his head. Ransom could see him savor the scent of her, drawing in long slow breaths through slightly flared nostrils. Apparently the head buck didn't mind what his nose found for he went back to grazing.

Erden waded quietly through the grass, continuing to lift the head of first this sunflower, then that, until she was well amidst the red deer. She stopped. She lifted yet another sunflower. Then, easy, casually, she stroked the back of the nearest fawn. The mother's head came up out of the grass. She too sniffed of the Erden smell on the air, then, satisfied it was well, went back to grazing. After a moment Erden touched the mother.

Ransom couldn't move.

A crow came fluttering out of a stand of quaking aspen, its wings flashing an iridescent purple and a warm welcome in its caw-caw. It lighted on Erden's shoulder.

Erden turned her head, easy, and cawed a warm welcome in reply.

The crow and Erden exchanged kisses.

A tear jumped glistening down Ransom's beard.

The crow sat on Erden's buckskin shoulder this way, that way. The crow's feathers were exactly as black as Erden's braids.

The crow and Erden talked together. The crow spoke a parrot-like Sioux; Erden spoke a liquid Sioux.

Presently the crow lifted off Erden's shoulder and dipped over to the back of the head buck. Except for a slight shiver of hide over the back, the buck hardly noticed. The crow found something to peck at in the fur over the buck's shoulder. The buck kept on grazing.

The crow looked around, bright, perky; saw something in a far pine. It flew over, dropping a falling arrow of bird-splash on the way, and then vanished into the dark forest.

Almost on the crow's last caw and flap of wing, a male bobolink spurted up out of the grass at Ransom's feet. The bobolink fluttered up in joy, not fear. It sang. It whistled its pleasure. It was as fat as a butterball. It somersaulted. Buff hindneck and white shoulders alternated with fat black belly and curt black tail. It tumbled and tumbled in midair, each tumble a little higher than the one before. It sang short quick bursts of liquid sound. It sang that the fat two-legged was very happy they'd come to visit him. It rose. The little meadow rang with its catchy airs. The little meadow widened as the bobolink rose higher and higher and as its melodious notes swelled and swelled in power.

Ransom and Erden stood rapt.

Of a sudden the bobolink speared straight up and its song became a frenzy of pure purling euphoria.

Ransom gasped.

"Sha," Erden whispered.

Up. Up. A form flashing off into delicious hysteria.

"By the Lord, Robert's going to explode."

"Wakan."

Up above the tree tips up above the mountain tops.

And then the bobolink was gone. There wasn't even a single drifting afterimage mote in the eye. Only lingering, very slowly fading, echoes. Eloquent gurglings receding to liquid purlings receding to little tinklings receding to tiny pink notes.

"Angel heaven."

"Comes-through-the-Cloud."

A pair of blue swallows fleeted in. They'd spotted Erden from their mud nest up on a sandstone ledge. They flew directly toward her, and as they neared her they flipped iridescent wings at her black hair, and then rose and dove and swalved around her. They swept up all the flies. They too were at home with her. They were careful not to fly too near Ransom and showed him nothing but sharply forked tails.

Erden began strolling again, touching this flower, that flower, with the two blue swallows forming a swift aureole about her head. She touched the tip of a blade of bluejoint grass. She touched a quaking aspen at the edge of the glade. She touched a spruce, a pine, a chance rare oak, an ash, an alder, a dogwood. She touched them as if they were the dolls of childhood. A sound came from her as of an inward murmuring.

"No wonder she's named after a bird," Ransom mused.

Presently Erden beckoned for Ransom to join her. She'd found something.

He went over, eyes grave with love.

"Kanta."

Wild plums. The plums hung in the midst of arrowhead leaves like big drops of scarlet blood. "Ripe."

She took up the corners of her fringed deerskin skirt and held them above her hips. She motioned for him to pick the plums and fill her skirt. Sunlight shone on her white nubile thighs. The small triangle of her dusky pubic fuzz seemed more a thing of innocence than entrance to a primal womb.

He concentrated on picking the ripe plums. When his eyes did shy off a little, he made an effort to look up at the swealing swallows.

Ransom picked plums until her buckskin skirt sagged with their weight.

She motioned for him to take his sombrero and fill it with

some scarlet bullberries from a nearby whitish thorny bush.

He filled it heaping.

They trudged back to the cave, she naked from the waist down, he bareheaded.

It was all a dream, pure. If he could only hold his breath, forever, it would forever stay that way. He found himself thinking of Erden at last as truly a blue swallow, something to be looked at and adored but never caged.

While she made supper, he fell into a study that quivered with holy green little lightnings. His thoughts sparkled more than drifted. He had fallen into the loving lap of a savage angel. Pray that he might not lose her by some foolish word or act on his part. He'd already taken her, mingled fleshes with her, but more and more that taking and that mingling seemed of another time and done by another man.

They went to bed together as brother and sister.

A couple of weeks went by.

Green aspens turned gold. Prickles of frost caught at running water. Turtledoves sang late autumnal laments.

Ransom went through the days as though he'd smelled too many wild roses. He knew he should be staking out his claim. He knew he should be going back to tell Katherine about his great strike. But he couldn't get himself to do it.

Moods, suppers, sleeps drifted by.

Erden got him to bathe every morning in the little brook, cold or not. They bathed unashamed together. The aroma of wild ferns and silver sage never left her. Her smell, like Katherine's, became a part of his flesh: Erden's pure wild, Katherine's tinctured with manufacture.

While Ransom learned to talk more Sioux, Erden refused to learn more American.

"Why not, my little two-legged?"

"It is not at home with my tongue."

"Someday you may want to live with the white again."

Erden shook her head. "I have found my true home. I wish for no other."

"Perhaps your children will wish to speak white."

"The mother carries the tongue. Therefore the children will speak Dakota."

"Do you not wish to please your husband?"

"You keep the beard. I keep the tongue."

Inevitably he continued to make comparisons. Erden's skin was as satiny as the petal of a sundrop; Katherine's was as set as the leaf of a milkweed. Erden's eyes were gray-ringed and trusting and bird-wise; Katherine's one eye was brown and full of private shadows and citified. Erden's hair, taken out of braids, rippled like a filly's flowing mane; Katherine's hair, a rust-shadowy gold, hung stiffish like a bell mare's tail. Erden flowed, toes light through the day; Katherine strode, strong-muscled through the day.

He loved them both, worshiping Erden and lusting after Katherine.

When he tried to come to some kind of thought as to what he should do about Erden, his mind shied off into fantasy.

He made it a point not to touch Erden, or reach for her, even though they slept together. It became a religion with him.

Nightmares came to him. By the time he realized what they were, they already had him in the grip of something taking place. It was already too late. Later, when he finally came out of them, he couldn't for the life of him remember what they were about.

His bad dreams troubled Erden. Several times he'd flailed out at enemies in his sleep and she'd had to tame his arms. "An evil spirit has entered your open mouth," she said. "It has gone to live in your heart. Come, my husband, you must take the purification bath."

That Indian wild he wasn't. "No, the morning bath in chilly water is sufficient."

She held his bearded head against her bare bosom. She whispered in the dark, "Yet it is the evil spirit of a bad witch who has entered your heart. You must prepare for the purification hut."

"No."

"I would help you prepare it but the woman must not touch the purification hut."

"No."

After fright's sweat had dried, and his heart went back to beating normal, he withdrew from her taming touches.

Sometimes he slept. Sometimes he didn't.

"Come, sleep well, my husband."

He shuddered.

"What, has the evil witch come again?"

God, God, if only he'd waited. As he'd wanted to.

One morning, after a bath in the brook, where they chased and splashed each other shrilling through stiff webs of frost, hilarious with the joy of being tinglingly alive so early in the dawn, he caught up with her, grabbing a braid just as they reentered their cave. She didn't resist; instead with a shy little ducking motion cuddled against him.

"A hawk has at last caught you, Little Swallow."

"What have I done that my husband no longer looks for acorns?"

"What is this you say?"

"The wild squirrels still hunt for acorns in the forest."

His breath caught in his beard.

"My foster father and mother sported on their sleeping robe together many winter nights. Now that I am a maiden and you are a brave, must it be forbidden us?"

Then he understood why it was she had been so willing and ready the first time.

"When I was a child it was explained to me that this sport was only for the grownups, and not for children. That someday after my nose had bled it would also be granted me."

He trembled.

"Husband?"

He picked her up. Convulsively, yet with an effort at tenderness, he carried her to their sleeping room and placed her upon their robe bed.

Drops of water still dappled her rose-brown cheeks. One glistening jewel stood trembling on the very point of her nose, reflecting her paired gray eyes. As she lay in his arms, she stirred, and a clear drop slid off her near nipple and ran over the curve of her plum breast. As it ran the drop collected other drops, and after a moment, hitting her slim arm where it lay tight against her body, it riveleted onto his arm. The little pouring of drops was warm.

Lightly he stroked her belly. Her skin was still catchy with moisture.

"Husband."

"Swallow."

She raised a round knee and moved it coyly from side to side. "Husband?"

Two women called him husband.

"Bearded one?"

His hand moved. He had not willed the moving of it. The hand trembled between her plum breasts. The hand stole tenderly up to her slender neck and again played at choking her. Then the hand moved up to her hair and touched her braids.

A sliding smile widened her lips.

He'd often seen such a smile on Katherine's lips. It did not become Erden.

The edges of Erden's lips parted with a wisping sound.

"Yes?" He remembered what Katherine had taught him about a woman, how to kiss her behind the ears and over the closed eyes with the lips hardly touching, and behind the point of the chin with a quick darting tongue tip, and along the patch of tan around the nipple of the breast with nipping lips, and finally in the soft depression in the V of the collarbone kissing in rhythm with the beat of the heart. This he could never do with Erden.

Another whisper parted her lips. "Husband?"

"Yes?" He recalled his ritual of touches with Erden the first time. It'd been a good thing to do. So with a fingertip he again touched her right brow and then her left, and touched the point of her nose, displacing the glistening jewel drop, and touched the point of her chin, and touched the point of her right shoulder and then her left, and ticked her right hip where the point of the bone whitened her white skin and then her left, and dropped a fingertip on her right kneecap and then her left, and tapped her right ankle bone and then her left, and took hold of her right big toe and gave it a pull, and then her left.

She quivered with delight. "That sport my Dakota father and mother did not have on the sleeping robe."

The drops of water on her skin shrank before his very eyes. He watched one of them on her cheek diminish to a bead of dew, then close to nothing.

She moved her body to find his hand.

He savored the musky smell of buffalo rising out of the robe beneath them.

Again she undulated her body to find his hand.

He caught sight of his tumble of silken phallus. He remembered that when he'd been with Katherine there had been such an edge of lust for her that he thought he would break before she could give him enough of herself. Here with Erden it was pure.

Erden became impatient. She was gentle about it but she was firm. "Husband?"

"Swallow."

She took hold of his hand and placed it where she wished it to be.

His middle fingers fell upon a wound, freshly cut. He

remembered when the knot of her had been as intricate as a rosebud.

A ripple began in her neck, moved down her body, ended with a comb of motion under his hand.

His tumble of flesh swelled. Silken skin began to shine.

"Husband?"

Of a sudden a bobolink began to sing in his head. Good. It must not be as with the ram, a brutal driving. Birds had it better. Especially the tinkling bobolinks.

She placed her hand on his hand and pressed down.

A fingertip broke through.

An undulation, as delicate as the sidewise sliding of an eye, touched the tip of his finger. "Husband."

He held. He turned his head. Could this be woman? He had to know.

Of a sudden both her eyes wept. Big yellow tears. Her face became a torment of joy and hunger.

He leaned to kiss her closed eyes. The taste of salt burst on his tongue.

"Wan-sum?"

His bobolink speared straight up and its song became a frenzy of sweet desire. It was still pure. As he'd always wanted it.

He moved, and she moved, and there was a sweet sliding of flesh within flesh, and of a sudden there were many bobolinks tumbling about everywhere, and flights of spirits were caroling above tree tips. A routed yearning flowering over.

His eyes parted. Beneath him lay a woman ennobled. She too had heard and seen the bobolinks. Sha.

"Wakan."

His eyes opened further.

The aspect of the mother had also awakened in her face. Suffering. Understanding. Forgiveness. He remembered having seen it once before, on the face of a female wolf at the moment of giving birth to puppies. Beautiful.

Something snapped in his head. It snapped loud enough to make him blink. Yes. He'd lived this moment before too. Besides the female wolf, some other mother somewhere had also looked exactly like this. But when or where he couldn't remember.

After breakfast, Erden spoke of their son to come.

Ransom had popped a ripe plum into his mouth and on the word "son" almost gagged. Words of another time sparked a dazzling green in his head: "And I want children. A son. To start off a new line with. And by new I mean new. I don't know who I am or where I came from. So with me and my son we start fresh."

"Was it a bad plum, my husband?"

He swallowed the fruit, pit and all. "It was."

Erden handed him a bladder of spring water. "A drink will help it down."

He drank. He wiped his lips with the back of his hand. He thought: "What a holy terror I turned out to be. No-good tramp. First took on a retired whore for a wife. Then practically raped a pure wild girl. What if I have a son by both of them?"

Erden studied him. "Husband?"

He couldn't look her in the eye. "And here I've killed men for less."

"Come." She tugged at his leather sleeve. "Come."

Numbly he followed her. Both love and belly made him go.

Several miles down the canyon they came upon the beaver dam he remembered seeing the first time he came up the canyon. It was a wide place and the beaver dam had backed up water and mud into a meadow. Frost had turned all the quaking aspen and white birch into veils of shivering gold. Bushes were lemon-tipped.

She led him directly to a thicket of wild roses on the far

side. She reached into the thorny branches and came up with a handful of wrinkled scarlet hips. She gave him a few, ate some herself.

He savored them. Their taste was like that of dried apples.

"Meat relish." Again she made a basket out of her skirt held up at the waist.

They picked until they had a couple of quarts of them. Bits of wrinkled red skin caught in their teeth.

He couldn't resist a quick look for colors in the stream splaying out over the wet meadow. And he did it despite her frowning. He poured sand from one hand to the other. There were colors all right. Plenty. Sometimes so many his hand became heavy with them. He found several nuggets the size of cow-pumpkin seeds.

"Husband?"

He stood up. His eyes roved speculative. "Sure. Everything washing down from above gets caught here behind this beaver dam. The meadow's probably loaded with gold. Another place for me to stake out." He nodded. "I'll placer-mine this. And I'll use a crusher on that rotting quartz above." He waggled his head from side to side. "Lord, Lord. Right now I'm probably the richest man on earth."

She nudged him with an elbow. "There is meat," she whispered low. "Shh."

His eyes moved.

There it was. A young doe. Not with kid either.

He waited a second to fix it all in place, then drew and fired. He dropped it.

They returned to their cave happily burdened with food.

As he skinned out the doe, knife swift, hands and wrists bloody, he said to himself, "Before the snow catches you in here, you'd better gallop back to Cheyenne and let Katherine know. Break it all off clean."

He cut them steaks for the day.

"And instead I'll become a man of the country." He cut flesh deftly. "Marry me this wild one."

He hung up jerky to cure.

"Someday I'll take Erden into town. Dress her up. Build her a big brick house and give her servants and a carriage."

Ransom was the hunter and provider. Erden was the nest-maker and counselor.

From the meat he brought in and the hips she picked, Erden made several parfleches of pemmican. She caught small fish in the stream, suckers, chub, dace, and after cleaning them, hung them up to be smoked. She dried bullberries. Soon their cave had the smell of a country grocery store.

Ransom kept deferring his trip back to Cheyenne, and instead filled the days with sorties in all directions.

Several times he spoke of going over and having a look at the principal peak in the Black Hills.

Erden forbade him to go. She was emphatic. "The great Hill of Thunder is the Forbidden Hill. Wakantanka is much offended when buckskin two-leggeds ascend it. He is known to have struck down those who have tried this."

He was half-inclined to believe her.

"There is a place near the Forbidden Hill where white smoke puffs out of the ground. It is the place where a certain Great White Giant once defied the gods. He looked for gold. He was struck down and thrown under the grass and rocks."

"This is a true thing?"

"The white smoke is the breathing of the Great White Giant buried beneath."

"It is difficult for a white one to believe this, Little Swallow."

"Often unnatural noises are heard. These are the moans of the Great White Giant when the rocks press upon him in punishment for entering our country."

The whites were trespassers all right. Greedy.

"Sometimes the gods feel sorry for him and they let him

up. His tracks have been seen in the snow. They are as long as a good man's arm. He staggers about." Erden's gray eyes glowed. "When it appears that the Great White Giant will run away, the gods once again hurl him under the grass and rocks."

"How is it that Little Swallow chooses to live in such an evil country?"

Her eyes opened wide. "The gods have love in their hearts for Psin-psin-cadan. This they have shown."

He fell silent.

She looked about the cave and their rich store of provender. "They have provided her with a home and with food. They have also provided her"—she looked down demure—"with a noble husband."

Noble? He squirmed. Katherine had once used the same word.

To vary their diet, he decided to go after some fat squirrels he'd spotted in a grove of red pine below the beaver dam.

"Does my husband go?"

"Blue Swallow, I have a great fondness for squirrel soup."

"You will see the Forbidden Hill?"

He stiffened. "You doubt the word of your husband?"

"It is good. Go."

"You do not wish to go?"

"It is time to air the bedding."

He examined her point for point. Was she with child? "I will be back by sundown."

"Turn and go."

He saw to his gun and shells, slipped a strip of jerky in a pocket, clapped on his sombrero, and was off.

A hundred steps below the beaver dam with its wide meadow he spotted fresh boot tracks in the sand along the stream. There were also places where pans of sand had been newly scooped out of the bottom of the stream. Someone had only yesterday been panning the stream.

"By the Lord! So the Army hasn't been able to keep them out after all. And I hain't got around to setting out my claim stakes yet."

He forgot all about the squirrel soup.

He hurried back to the beaver dam. With his knife he cut off five stakes, cut his name into each of them, measured off three hundred feet along the gulch from rim to rim just above the beaver dam, and with a rock drove a stake down on each corner and then one in the center of the meadow.

He also hurried to set out stake claims around his white-quartz find higher in the Hills.

His thoughts were in a boil. The moment the Black Hills became United States property, he was a rich man and could put on tails. But, at the same time, the moment the prospectors came streaming in, it would be the end of Erden's paradise.

He said nothing to Erden about the fresh boot tracks.

But Erden sensed something. She mocked him with a child-bride's smile. "I have the pot. Where are the fat squirrels?"

"I did not see them."

A white man's lie.

The next day, very chilly, while both were sunning themselves in the door of their cave, they heard the sound of a great whistling high in the Hills.

Erden's gray eyes became dots of troubled darkness. She turned pale. "Ai. Ai. Wakantanka is greatly offended. What have we done?"

A few minutes later yet another majestic wail rose high over the Hills. Presently the vast wall split up into myriads of echoes, and gradually faded away.

"Quickly. We must take the purification bath," she cried. "The man in his hut and the woman in the stream."

Ransom didn't move. He wasn't about to let himself be stampeded by something he was sure he could explain if given a little time.

"Hurry. Or we shall be struck down."

He sat his ground.

"Hurry, my husband."

He thought the idea of a bath all right. "I will wash in the stream in the usual way," he said. He shivered, thinking of the ice-coated water. "I will purify my skin with many hands of rough sand."

She clapped a hand to her mouth at his blasphemy, then hurried off to take her bath.

His eyes narrowed as he watched her fly about. He combed his black beard with his fingers. A rush of compassion for her as well as an impulse to hurt her came together in him.

A few days later he managed to get away again. He immediately checked his claim stakes around the meadow just above the beaver dam.

The stakes were gone. Even the holes in which the stakes had been driven home were gone.

He stared. It couldn't be true.

Yet, look as he might, there wasn't a sign anywhere that he or anyone else had ever passed through the spot. Even the strange fresh boot tracks he'd found earlier in the sand were gone.

He couldn't cipher it. There had been no rain to erase them.

Then the thought shot through his mind that Erden was the only one who could have erased all sign so thoroughly. She had been Indian trained.

"The little dickens. She really don't want me to have that gold."

He stared some more. "Well, we'll see about that."

Grimly he whittled himself new stakes, cut his name on them, hammered them home.

He next checked his white-quartz claim. Damn. The stakes there were gone too. These he also replaced.

He said nothing about what he'd found when he returned to their cave.

Three days later he casually announced he was going to make another try for the fat squirrels.

When he checked his stakes they were gone again. Both claims.

"I'll be goddamned. When in hell did she do it? I've been with her every blessed second day and night." He clawed at his black beard. "Unless she puts me to sleep with some kind of Indian herb in my meat and then does it." He scratched some more. "You know, I wouldn't put it past her. She's a stubborn little thing." Cool smoke coiled in his green eyes. "I'm gonna have to watch her closer."

He once more put down stakes to his two claims.

And he watched her.

She didn't put anything unusual in his food that he could see. Nor did he sleep any deeper than usual. Nor did she behave as if she were secretly scheming against him.

Ransom awoke one morning to a great silence. The air flowing through the cave had turned warm overnight. It was as though someone had lit a stove in the back of the cave. There was even a smell as of wood burning.

He sat up with a start. So did Erden. Their sleeping robe slid to their laps. The warm air was pleasant on their naked backs.

"Something funny out there."

"Wa."

He made the sign that he didn't understand.

"Wapa."

"It is snowing?"

She nodded.

"Snowing? And our ventilation in here suddenly turns warm?"

Another nod.

Snowing? Instantly other thoughts milled in him a mile a minute. What if they became snowbound? Mmm. That would take care of his going back to Cheyenne, wouldn't it, and having to tell Katherine? At least for a while. Snowbound. Locked in the Hills for the winter. Well. Well. So. If that came about, good. Maybe that would also take care of those disappearing claim stakes. A couple of feet of snow and they'd be buried too deep to find. A smile awoke in his belly and moved up and finally emerged on his lips.

There was a new smile on Erden's lips too.

Naked, barefoot, both got up and went to the door of their cave for a look.

They couldn't see across to the other wall of the gulch. Snow was falling in flakes so huge they resembled floating crackers. A white and clotted silence was rapidly filling all the canyons in the Hills.

A fat snowflake floated sideways. It wavered, dipped, sailed. At last it struck Ransom's ear. It melted almost instantly, making a collapsing sound.

"A three-day snow, I betcha."

"Icamna."

"Wow. Wait'll the wind gets behind this stuff. What a real old-fashioned snowstorm that'll make."

He noted that the snow melted in midair where it fell in the wind from the cave. "Sure is funny our cave should suddenly turn so warm in winter." The smile on his lips grew as he watched the snow come down. "This is gonna be the best yet. Snow heaven."

Erden stood slim and apart from him.

"Swallow." He slipped his hand around her naked waist and then around her belled bottom. "Come."

But she would have none of it. With a laugh and a skip, barefoot, she was out into the falling snow.

"Hey!" he cried. "At least put on some clothes, you idiot."

In an instant her dark braids and hair were white. All he could see of her was the diaphanous dancing outline of her naked body. Even her triangular patch of pubic hair soon whited over.

"Erden!"

She put on a little show for him on the path down to the stream. She danced a grass dance in the snow. Then, laughing, she mimicked a frolicsome fawn. Then, gravely, she put on she was a mother grouse shamming a broken wing.

"Come back here. That ain't rain, you little fool." He shivered, thinking how cold it must feel on her skin.

What she did next utterly dumfounded him. She went beyond play. She lay down in the snow. Leisurely. Then she stretched her arms above her head and slowly and luxuriously became lost in herself, in vagary, in sweetest self-joy. Flakes caught in the fuzz of her armpits. Snow caught in the short hairs over her belly.

"My God in heaven."

She rolled from side to side as if she were bathing in a pond. She laved her face and arms and shoulders and breasts with handfuls of loose white fluff. She covered herself as though with sand on a river bar, heaping it up over herself. At last only the point of her nose and the nipples of her breasts and the nails of her big toes were visible.

"Even if she does take baths in the winter, this is going too far." He hugged himself to keep warm. Shivering, he snuggled naked within his own armclasp. His manhood shrank to nubbins.

She lay very still under the snow.

"She'll turn into an icicle."

Snowflakes, huge and wafer-like, continued to dazzle down. First the tips of her toes, then the points of her small breasts, then even the point of her nose went under.

That was enough. He ran out to get her.

To his surprise the snow underfoot wasn't cold at all. It wasn't warm, but it wasn't cold either. It was like running in cool massy cottonwood fluff. And where a few of the big snowflakes melted on his skin it even felt hot. Delicious. No wonder she was dazed over it.

He stood above her. He called her name. "Blue Swallow?"

Little openings, paired, appeared in the snow. It was where her eyelashes parted. Pure gray eyes stared up at him out of pure white snow.

In a gush of affection, he fell beside her in the snow. His hand sought her body under the tender white blanket. The two of them hugged each other for the wonder of it all. Deliriums of white joy suffused them. In the white snow their bodies became as slick as chilled grass.

A few kisses. Then to his surprise he found himself wanting to hurt her again. He found himself wanting to bite her, crack her in his arms, crush her beneath him, thump her powerfully. Somehow he managed to resist the brutish impulses.

"Eagle."

"Swallow."

Her body sought his hand again as before. Even in the snow her quiver was warm to his touch.

He couldn't hold back then. His pendant of flesh rose. Snow melted on its red comb. He went in. He became very rough with her.

"Ahh," she cried, "the war eagle pecks his hen."

He thought: "But this is wrong. This ruins our snow heaven."

"Sometimes my foster father treaded upon my foster mother in a like manner in their sport. He was like the pecking eagle with my foster mother. Then it was she trilled for joy on the grass."

Ransom began to punish Erden.

"Akk! Husband! On the white grass it is even better."

He thought: "Thank God I'm not married legal to Katherine."

Snow lovers.

Snow fell heavy for two days and two nights. Then a great wind rose. The wind blew and blew for another two days. When it was over, the gulch was almost level full.

They were truly locked in at last. It would be months before they could travel in the Hills. Or before anybody else could move into the Hills. They were safe for a time.

They tumbled into winter housekeeping as peaceful as two pups in a basket.

There was plenty to do. She mended their leather clothes and made new ones. Preparing for the coming baby, she made a cradleboard and fashioned little leather shirts and pantlegs and moccasins. She made all their meals. She kept the cave as clean as barked pine. Meanwhile he kept the entrance to the cave free of snow. He made them both a pair of snowshoes out of ash branches and buckskin strings. He cared for their two horses in their park pasture, sometimes bringing them sweet cottonwood branches as a treat. He shot an occasional red deer or an antelope, and skinned and fleshed them out. He brought in such firewood as was needed for the cooking fire. He cleaned his gun meticulously. He honed his knife on a deer hoof until it cut fuzz.

He loved her neat ways. He thanked his lucky stars she wasn't buggy like some people were out in the wilds. He couldn't abide people who tolerated lice.

As the winter deepened into January, then February, her face and hands slowly turned light, and she almost looked white again even in her buckskin garb.

The returning white in her skin made Ransom happy. He swore again to himself that someday soon he would take his Erden, his little Blue Swallow, to some big city in the East and show her off.

Her belly swelled slowly with child. Already he loved the

little pear growing in her. He longed to see it. He longed for the time when the little pink eyelids would flutter apart and the little pink mouth would open in a bawl.

Just so he hadn't made Katherine with child that last time they made love together in Cheyenne.

He had helped Erden clean up after breakfast, and had stepped outside to slip on his snowshoes on his way to look after the horses, when he heard the great whistling high in the Hills again. It was March and cracking cold outside, very still, and the sound of it prickled in his nose. The whistling began as though at first a giant were blowing low over an empty bottle, and then gradually the whooing deepened, and then the giant seemed to shift his lips to a bottle with a larger opening. The giant held the big note for a long full minute. A few seconds of silence followed. Then the giant played back and forth on the two bottles for a while, and then, very slowly, the whooing fell away and died.

Ransom turned, to find Erden standing directly behind him, a pale hand to paler lips. Her wide gray eyes looked above and beyond him toward the granite peaks.

"Do not worry, Little Swallow. Your husband is with you."

Slowly her head began to shake under her hand. The shaking moved her body. Her hand was clapped so tight over her mouth that where the fingertips pressed into her cheek the skin slowly turned bluish white.

"Erden?"

She spoke in suddenly aged accents. "Ai! The gods are weeping. It is because the Great White Giant has escaped. The gods foresee much destruction. A great shaking will level Forbidden Hill and all the other hills. Oh-oh-oh-oh."

"Come now, my Swallow Blue, it—"

Immediately there the great whistling was again, and this time a multitude of whistlings, piercing cries, and all coming out of the needle peaks to the south. The great shrieking hurt the ears. Even their cave began to howl.

Ransom stiffened. Great spooks were aprowl then in the Hills. Erden's earth spirits really were there. And they had gone crazy. Ransom could feel his beard bristling out over his cheeks.

Erden tottered.

Ransom drew his gun; saw how ridiculous that was; re-holstered his gun.

Erden fell flat on her face in the snow.

The otherworldly screeches continued for another long minute; then, abruptly, broke off. Echoes succeeded echoes, and only slowly faded, until at last they too fell away.

"Swallow?"

She didn't move.

When he went to pick her up, she weighed as one dead. He carried her inside. He wrapped her in their sleeping robe. He comforted her in his arms. He chafed her wrists. He rubbed her ankles. He stroked her swollen belly gently. He kissed her cheeks.

"Swallow?"

No answer.

He wrapped her in yet another fur robe and lighted a roaring fire in their already warm cave and then once again took her close in his arms.

"Swallow?"

It was a week before a little of the old-time fluid motion returned to her limbs. Sparkles never did return to her gray eyes.

3

Two weeks later, a chinook passed over the land, and spring came in, and all too soon the snow melted away. It all went out of the Hills with a rush. Every gulch and every canyon roared with brown crashing meltwater.

Ransom checked his claims. He found the stakes at the

white-quartz claim still in place. But the stakes around the meadow above the beaver dam were gone. Again. Only this time they were replaced by another set with someone else's initials on them, T. B.

A smell of burning pine knots and frying bad bacon came wafting out of the trees below. Looking, Ransom spotted a plume of smoke rising from behind the beaver dam.

Ransom checked his gun; then stepped onto the dam.

A man in very ragged black trousers and red shirt was sitting on his heels and was just then spearing up a piece of bacon from a sizzling pan. The man wore a gun on his hip.

"What the hell you doing here, mister?" Ransom called down.

The man's head whirled and looked up. His eyes were light, almost moon eyes. He had a rusty beard. "I'm sinking a shaft here." He pointed to a hole he'd dug into the near wall.

"Didn't you see my stakes? With my name cut into 'em? Earl Ransom?"

The man's light eyes turned shifty for a second. "I didn't see any stakes."

"Well, this is my ground and I warn you to get off. I'm chief here."

The man carefully set his sizzling pan to one side of the fire and slowly stood up. "The hell it is and the hell I will." The man's right hand opened a little.

"Don't do it."

"Well, I ain't getting out."

"The hell you ain't. And while I don't aim to shoot yet another man, I will if I have to." Ransom found himself cool and easy. It pleased him.

"So that's the way it is."

"Yes." Ransom set his feet a little wider apart. "Tell you what I'm going to do. I'm going to put down a new set of stakes. Where I had 'em before. Because this is mine. I've been here all winter guarding 'em."

The man said nothing.

"And I'll be back tomorrow. If I find you at work here again, I'll stuff you dead into your own prospect hole."

Pause.

"You hear me?"

"Anybody stake out below you yet?"

"You don't see stakes around, do you?"

"No, I don't."

"Then it's yours."

"Well." Pause. "I was just asking to make sure. I don't mean to raise a trouble." Pause. "I'd just as soon be neighborly, I guess. A man alone ain't gonna have much of a chance here a week from now."

"Why in a week?"

"Friend, they're coming out of Cheyenne like starved cattle making a beeline for a fresh stack of hay."

God in heaven. The dream was done. The idyll with Erden was over. "What's the matter with the U.S. Army?"

"The Army has decided to play hands off now. The guv'ment's about to sign a treaty with the red devils and turn all of the Hills over to the whites. First come first served."

By the Lord. All too soon his green canyon would be a dusty roaring encampment. He'd seen it happen before in the Rockies above Denver. Men and mules would come driving up, one after another, and drive Erden and him and their bobolinks out, even their whistling granite gods. The cursed thirst of gold.

"Partner, I guess I don't have to tell you that there is considerable sand here." The interloper moved nearer Ransom. "We better be ready to guard it."

"I know."

"Where you holing out?"

"Up the gulch a ways."

"You better camp down here with me. So we can take turns guarding it."

"I suppose so."

"We better file our claims the minute some kind of guv'ment comes in."

Ransom nodded. Well. It was all over with. Done. Gone. Because right behind the hordes of wild-eyed prospectors would come Katherine and all her fancy household goods.

The interloper held out his hand. "Well, Earl, my name's Troy Barb." Again the man's moon eyes turned shifty for a second. "It's a deal then?"

"Call me Ransom."

"Ransom? Ransom it is then." Troy Barb still held out his hand. "It's a deal then?"

Ransom shook hands with some reluctance. At least the fellow would act as a sort of a stopper for a while and that would give him that much more time to figure out what to do with Erden.

"Me, I can't wait until they've built up Deadwood. Hain't got enough clothes left on me to dress a China doll with."

"Deadwood?"

"Yes." Troy Barb pointed up at the gulch rims where long ago a forest fire had flashed across the country. "Got to name it after something everybody'll recognize."

"Might as well."

"As a name it ain't nothing special. But it'll hold."

"Where did you put my stakes?"

"I burnt 'em. For my cook fire."

Ransom nodded. "Fair enough. I'll cut your name off your stakes here and put my own in place of it. And you make yourself some new ones for your claim below the dam here. That clear?"

"It'll have to do."

Ransom examined Troy Barb critically. It was obvious the man's red shirt was lousy.

"When will you move down and join me?" Troy Barb asked.

"Quite a population you got there already, I see."

"Can't find any red ants to take care of 'em."

"I can't stand lice."

"Too bad."

"Boil 'em out."

"I've done that. They're back the next day."

"Then shave yourself bald. Between your legs too."

Troy Barb gave his rusty beard a tug. "Ain't got a razor."

"Got any blue ointment?"

"Out here? Nary a dab."

"I'll give you a week to get rid of them graybacks. Because, me, I hate lice so much I'm just liable to take a shot at 'em." Ransom turned his back on the man and with his skinning knife began cutting his own name on the first of the Troy Barb five claim stakes.

After a moment Troy Barb called up. "Don't forget, Ransom, that the lice that bite the hardest are the ones that are out of sight."

Both Ransom and Erden sat in gloom the next several days. They didn't speak.

The weather turned sultry. Grass jumped. Opening yellow-green buds veiled the quaking aspen. Tender green came out on the birch.

Late one afternoon a comber of cold air shoved across the land. It boosted up the warm air. Enormous thunderheads built up. The thunderheads teetered on gray granite peaks. The thunderheads and the Hills took on the look of massive building blocks delicately piled one on top of the other.

Ransom, sitting on a rock beneath a big pine, watched the deepening storm come toward them. Erden watched from the doorway of their cave.

Soon rain began to thresh through the pines at the head of the gulch.

"The thunderbirds gather, my husband," Erden called. "Come into your lodge."

The black bottoms of the clouds continued to lower toward them. Taut ropes of black mist rushed down the gulch. It darkened terribly around them.

"Husband, do not dare the gods." Erden held her belly in the palms of her hands. "Come inside."

"Shh."

Almost on the sound of his shhing, a dazzling shaft of blue light stabbed into the top of the big pine. Equally dazzling was the blast of sound. There was a further click, and then a razoring stream of blue light raced up and down the red trunk of the big pine, going both ways at the same time, and a blow hurled Ransom from his rock, and pitched him a dozen feet down the slope, and tumbled him stunned to the grass.

Erden ran out a few steps; clapped hand to mouth and bethought herself; ran back to the safety of the cave. "Aii!" Again she ran out a few steps; clapped hand to mouth and bethought herself; ran back.

Ransom lay flat out. He knew just enough to know he was almost dead.

Erden stood shrilling in the cave entrance.

Rain wlapped all around them. It hit like a falls. And lightning hit again, across the gulch, dazzling, booming.

Erden fell silent.

Cold wet coursing through his beard roused Ransom. His eyes opened. Rain was falling into his nose and mouth. His chest gathered itself up for a mighty cough, and did cough, and he sat up.

Lightning cracked farther down the gulch.

He rolled over onto his knees. He found himself to be stiff, like a piece of very dry leather. He got to his feet. Rain came down in such heavy ropes it almost knocked him down. He put out a hand to a tree to hold himself up.

Lightning again knettered a dozen rods away. Instinctively he jerked back his hand.

He stood bent, taking in deep breaths as fast as he could. His head cleared a little. He turned. Then, numbly, he lurched into a wobbling run for the cave. And made it.

He more fell than slumped onto their sleeping robes. He lay puffing. His head buzzed like a hive full of angry bees.

When his head had cleared some, he called, "Erden?"

No answer.

"Swallow?"

No answer.

"That's funny." He labored for breath. "Hope to God she didn't spook on me now." He rolled his eyes around to find himself. "She does have a mortal fear of her gods."

He lay puffing for a while.

"Well, guess we better see what the damages are."

He sat up and began to feel himself all over. A side-bolt of lightning had struck him on the cheekbone, just under the eye, burning off a patch of beard as slick and clean as if shaved off. The stream of dazzling fluid had then passed through the length of him and had gone out at the ball of his foot. It had burst a hole through the sole of his boot as clean and as round as though made by a bullet. Wonderingly, shaking his head, he took off his boot and sock and found a blood blister the size of a coneflower.

Later he went out to examine the big pine. The main bolt of lightning had cut a deep groove in its red bark from the top of the pine down into its roots.

Darkness began to drift in.

He stood in the path and called Erden. He called her again and again. All he heard was echoes.

"She spooked, all right. The poor dear darling."

He sat down on a rock. He still puffed. The buzzing in his head continued angry.

"Erden?"

Already he missed her terribly.

"She knew. That it's all going to hell up here. The poor poor dear."

His punctured cheek and blistered foot hurt like the blazes.

It became very black out. An after-storm cloud deck hid the stars.

Finally he got to his feet and trudged back into their cave. His stomach felt like a walnut. He looked at their bed of robes on the floor, finally crept into it, going to bed without eating.

"Bet she don't come back in the morning either."

The wind in the cave whooed gently. Little side eddies now and then drifted into the bedroom.

"Probably just as well. With all the damned miners coming in. She'd have gone wild with them stampeding up through the gulch here. Just crazy wild. Because now not even one of her avalanches will stop 'em."

Rock masses cracked above him in the roof of the cave.

"Swallow." Pause. "Swallow Blue."

He awoke hungry. He couldn't remember falling asleep. He fried himself some venison, drank a little from the stream outside, made his bed as he remembered Erden doing. Then, checking his gun and bullets, he went looking for her.

He first made a cast around their cave entrance. He found nothing, not a single footprint, not even disturbed grass or brush.

He wondered if she could have gone out through the passage in back, behind the curtain in their cave. That ever-flowing current of air had to come from somewhere.

He took a pine knot from her supply, lit it, and stepped behind the curtain into a big raw hole. The raw passage narrowed into darkness ahead of him. He got down on hands and knees and carefully examined the dust on the floor. No tracks. There were too many rocks she could have stepped on. He pushed in. Sharp stones hurt his kneecaps through his buckskin trousers. The cave wind breathed over and around him. The passage narrowed. He scrunched ahead until his shoulders caught on the sides. Here the wind pushed at him, making a strange gurgling noise.

Looking ahead with the wavering light of his pine knot, burning rosin almost choking him, he saw that in another dozen or so feet the passage narrowed to almost the size of a post hole. Not even a child could have crawled through it.

He backed out of the tunnel, threw the flaming pine knot in the hearth, brushed himself off.

"Beats me where she could've gone to."

He next made a cast farther out from the cave entrance, taking in the wall on the other side of the gulch as well as the rim above the cave. Still no sign.

"Poor little Swallow."

He next checked the horses in their hidden Eden, thinking she might have taken one of them. He found both horses cropping peacefully.

"Of course she wouldn't take one of my horses. It wouldn't be like her."

He next checked his white-quartz claim. No sign of her there either. And his claim stakes were still in place.

"She really was in an awful rush to get away."

By nightfall he was exhausted, haggard.

"It was too good to last. Especially after what I done."

When he lay down on their robe bed again on the fourth night, it came to him where she'd probably gone.

She had often talked about the Big Horns. Her foster Indian parents had often spoken of them. They'd told of the Old Ones living there, up near the timberline, an old people who weren't related to any of the Indians around. The Old Ones were a dying people, they'd said, and many of their cave homes were already empty.

Yes. That's probably where Erden had gone to. The Big Horns. It would be quite a long ways for her to go alone on foot, across miles of barren alkali flats, but if Erden had decided that that's where she would go, make herself a new home in one of the old abandoned caves, that's where she would go. And she'd make it all right. In fact, if it came to sheer survival, she'd be more apt to make it bare-handed, and pregnant, than he would with gun, and hard-bellied. Erden was as wild and as tough as the land itself.

The musky buffalo sleeping robe beneath him was still sweet with the aroma of wild ferns and sage. Her perfume.

He remembered their kissing in the snow. Lord. He remembered their bobolink nights. God. He remembered placing his hand on her belly and feeling their child threshing in it. Wakantanka.

He wept large single tears. "Swallow." How the heart hurt. "Blue Swallow."

Three days later, when he went down to make camp with his partner Troy Barb, he was astounded to find that five new log cabins had been built just below Troy Barb's claim. Troy Barb himself had built a crude lean-to onto his prospect hole.

Troy Barb had wild moon eyes for him. "Where the hell you been all this time, hey?" Troy Barb hopped about. "I ain't slept night nor day since you left, guarding our claims." He had gun in hand. He was in a fume of a rage. "Hey?"

Ransom ground his teeth together. "I got hit by lightning."

"It's enough to make a man holler like a bay steer, so mad I am." Pause. "You what?"

Ransom pointed to the burn on his cheekbone, then showed Troy Barb the sole of his boot.

"I'll be goddamned. That's different."

"I've only just now come to."

Troy Barb stared at Ransom's singed cheek. "That's a helluva note. You all right?"

"I've been off my feed a little. But I'm on the gain now."

"Well, all right for you."

Ransom waved a hand upstream. "Look. Why don't we go snucks on both our holdings here at the beaver dam? Even-steven."

"You mean it?" Troy Barb cast a greedy look at Ransom's holding above the dam. "Partners?"

"Sure. I won't be able to hold it alone either."

Troy Barb stared at Ransom a stunned moment; then began to leap about for joy. "Oh boy! Oh man! Oh glory be! Now my wife can be a lady and my children can get an education!"

Ransom grudged him a tight smile.

Troy Barb's shout of happiness brought the five new miners out of their cabins. They stood in dirty pants and ripped shirts, staring, wondering what all the commotion was about.

Ransom shook his head at what he saw behind and above the new cabins. The prospectors had denuded the surrounding hills for logs, for both their buildings and their firewood. Erden would weep to see it.

"See here," the miner nearest them growled, "what're you shaking your head for? We're in here every bit as legal as you are."

"I suppose you are."

"We can all bust a bull's-eye too, you know."

"I take it you're the he-coon of this new bunch?"

"Sure am."

"Shut off your worry machine. You're here now and there ain't much anybody can do about it."

Troy Barb put in, "We don't plan to bother you none so long as you don't bother us none."

Ransom stepped closer. "Look, it's all going to be good pickin's here." Ransom liked the miner's hard-nosed stance. "Maybe we can work out something."

Troy Barb stepped closer too. "That's what I say. Why don't we all set up like we was a town already? Make us a few rules?"

The hard-nosed miner tipped back his black hat. A dart-eyed scowl worked in his black beard. "Yeh, now that we've all panned gold here, I suppose all our hearts are big." He gave Ransom a close look as he lit his pipe. "You say your name is Earl Ransom?"

"Right."

"And you say your name is Troy Barb?"

"Right."

"Good enough. Me, I don't mind giving myself a name either. These days my handle is Bill Smith."

Ransom had to laugh.

The other four miners broke down then too, and smiled.

Soon all were friends. They stepped up and formed a casual ring around a raw pine stump. Smiling a little self-consciously, they all shook hands. After a bit all but Ransom were blowing tobacco smoke three ways.

Ransom put up a foot on the raw stump. "I take it then we all know we're all still living legally out of bounds here. That the law don't reach this far."

Bill Smith put up a foot too. "That don't make a particle of difference to me. Don't we come from law-abiding homes? All of us? So any rules we make are bound to be good."

Troy Barb said, "If we set it up right, fair and square, and elect us a mayor and a constable and a justice of the peace, why, when the regular U.S. guv'ment comes in, they'll take us as they find us. What else can they do?"

"Right."

Troy Barb went on. "Well, then, first off, like I said before, I say we name her Deadwood."

Bill Smith caught his nose between thumb and forefinger and gave it a good pull. "Deadwood?"

"Got anything again' it?"

"No." Pause. "Deadwood. Well."

"Well?"

"Kind of a funny name. Like it might be the end of the line or something."

"So what? I like it."

"Deadwood. Well, it'll do for the time being."

Deadwood it was then.

Later in the day, Ransom went to get his horses. It didn't surprise him too much to find that a fresh landslide had buried the entrance to Erden's cave, or that his gear lay neatly piled on the rock under the lightning tree.

He glanced up at where the landslide had started. A dark wet spot a few feet above showed where a big rock had been pried loose. It had hit exactly right, triggering an avalanche of loose earth with little sand or rock.

Erden had decided to close the record.

He checked the dirt for color. Nothing. Not a trace.

It was just as well. So long as no one found gold in the dirt the cave was safe. Hidden.

A month later Deadwood as a city was a fact. Three miles long, a hundred feet wide, Deadwood followed the gulch in all its tortuous length, beginning well above where the old beaver dam lay and going all the way down to where Ransom had first come upon an abandoned camp. A dugway was cut over the hogback to connect it with the trail to Cheyenne.

First came scattered prospectors, who, like Ransom, had holed up in the Hills during the winter. Then came the first stragglers of spring from Cheyenne. Next came a couple hundred miners from the Montana diggings. After that the gold hunters came in from everywhere, floods of them: from the jumping-off points first—Sioux City, Sidney, Bismarck— and then from all over America—New York, Boston, Phila-delphia—even from England and Germany. They came mostly broke, with few supplies. They came on horseback and on foot. Some were educated, men of promise, even men with their careers well started, who wanted one more lark out in the wilds before settling down: lawyers, teachers, professors, doctors. Some were tradesmen: merchants, clerks, druggists. Some were common laborers: factory hands, farm hired men, draymen. Some were drifters. Chinamen launderers came too. The old miners did the best digging; the rest struck out blindly.

Tents, huts, cabins, houses, stores, saloons, opera houses, hotels popped up everywhere. Was there a boulder too big to move, or a stump too tough to extract, Main Street and its side alleys just went around it. Some pines were left standing for no reason at all. Some miserable hovels had boardwalks; some fancy houses had mud paths. On the least whimsy, gophering for gold sometimes took place on Main Street itself.

At high noon Main Street lay in garish eye-blinding sunlight; at midnight it was as dark as a cave. A dozen steps ventured after dark sometimes led to disaster. Often there wasn't enough starlight to illuminate the eye of a cat. Lanterns cost a fortune.

Deadwood resembled a new prairie-dog town. What had once been a lovely dell was now suddenly a dusty hell of uprooted earth. Each hole had its frenetic digger with dirty claws. Gay chatter as well as yipping complaints flew from mound to mound. Snakes in the grass were accepted. Dawn came up with everybody yipping and digging, and dusk went down with everybody yipping and digging.

To supply this welter of humanity, various freighting companies soon had huge bull trains on the rail, carrying clothes, food, shelter, powder, mining tools. The freight trains were sometimes so long they couldn't turn around on the narrow main street, but had to go out beyond city limits to make the maneuver.

Stagecoaches ran from Cheyenne on regular time schedules. That brought in the spongers. Gamblers, wearing fine linen and broadcloth fresh from the tailor, soon were strolling down Main Street with all the air of men who had nothing on their hands but magnificent leisure. The gamblers, speaking quietly from behind poker smiles, lived by the philosophy that a poor loser was worse than a horse thief. Girls on the line, wearing dingy old fascinators, soon were strolling down Main Street too, with all the air of ladies who had nothing on their minds but clothes and gossip. The girls, lollygagging in the doorways of their cribs, lived by the faith that the making in private of lovely vulgar sounds was the be all and the end all of life.

Next to come on the stagecoach were the bankers and their opposites the road agents. Free-spending blood, already bored, rode with them.

A single preacher came last. He fit in like a turkey in a saddle.

In some respects Deadwood was born old.

When panning no longer paid off, the gold hunters tried rocking. When rocking no longer paid off, they tried placer mining. And all too soon a good share of the gulch was played out.

Some nearly starved to death. To survive, they had to cadge gold dust from the more lucky. They ate rancid sowbelly, they drank on the house when they could, and they dreamed the dreams of the improvident. Some whittled their lives away as they sat on logs along Main Street.

Rumors of new strikes came along almost every hour. Every so often the rumors caught, and like capricious crows on a wire, dusty dreamers took flight in one direction or another, higher up the gulch, or lower down, or across the hogbacks into unexplored draws and canyons.

Many a broke adventurer offered to muck for Ransom.

Ransom and his partner Troy Barb declined the offers. Ransom and Troy Barb worked their claims at the beaver dam just enough to pay their way. They were getting a hundred dollars to the pan and could afford to take it easy. Both were waiting for a rich mining speculator to come along and buy them out, a man with enough money to mine the ore with proper equipment.

Ransom was careful to register his white-quartz claim in his name only. Every so often he went up to check to see if his stakes were still in place. He kept his eye peeled for sign that someone might have stumbled upon it.

While up there, he also kept his eye peeled for Erden. But he never saw any new sign of her.

4

One noon late in June, right after dinner, some miners higher up the gulch spotted a plume of dust coming down the main dugway. The miners hallooed to those below and soon Ransom and Troy Barb were alerted.

"It's too early for the Cheyenne run," Troy Barb said as he leaned back on his spade. "That ain't due till about dusk."

Ransom nodded. He wasn't too anxious to look.

Troy Barb climbed up on a rock. He shaded his moon eyes with a hand. "Tain't the treasure coach either. Though 'tis a Concord. Because I see yellow spokes flashing."

Ransom set his spade to one side and sat down. He looked down at the brittle yellow calluses in the palms of his hands. The hands were no longer the hands of a card shark. Nor for that matter the hands of a gunslinger.

"The jehu handling the ribbons is sure pouring it on. Them stylish black flyers is coming on like the wind." Troy Barb laughed. "Probably one of them cock-up drivers who likes to give his passengers. . . . Oops!" Troy Barb grunted in sympathy. "What a jolt that was."

Ransom waited.

"There'll be no lady in a rig going that fast."

"Let's hope not."

Troy Barb stared down at Ransom. "You don't seem to have much time for wimmen, do you?"

The swift tattoo of fleet hoofs and the sound of rapidly clicking wheels came to them. In a moment six black horses galloped into view, followed by a red stagecoach lurching along on leather thoroughbraces.

"Well, we'll know in a minute."

Ransom got to his feet and deliberately began to dig in earnest. He worked himself around until he had his back turned to the road.

All too soon the galloping black horses, the clicking coach, and an exploding cloud of dust whirled by.

"There was a woman in there!" Troy Barb exclaimed. "I was wrong. Some rich dame. All alone."

Ransom dug harder.

Troy Barb pushed back his black hat. He scratched his wild hair with a single finger. "Well, well. Now Deadwood can say she's a big city. She's got herself a snooty rich woman."

Two days later, the same red coach with its spanking yellow wheels came back up the dugway.

Ransom was alone in his log cabin. He was sitting dull-eyed on the edge of his bunk. The bunk was a rickety affair, three boards placed across two sawhorses.

"Ransom?" a clear woman's voice called. "Ransom?"

The voice jarred him. It chilled him all the way down to his tailbone. He stared at the walls, noting idly that the pine logs were freckled with rosin.

"Ransom?" There were the familiar quick springing steps, followed by a knock. "Ransom?"

Ransom stared at where a tin of fermented dough hung above a sheet-iron stove. Above it the ceiling was decorated over with old newspapers.

"Ransom?" The log door opened with a loud creak. "Ah,

there you are, my handsome is as handsome does." Pause. "Why, Ransom, darling, haven't you got a hello for me?"

He ran his hand over his bearded face. The burn over his cheek had healed and his beard had pretty well grown back.

"Is this all the greeting I get?"

"Hello."

"Ransom. This is a dreadful way to greet your own dear wife. Why!"

Ransom slowly swung around to have a look at Katherine. "What're you doing here?"

Katherine stood in flowing purple in the doorway: hasped purple crinoline skirt over voluminous flouncings of underskirts, long purple gloves, a cunning curved purple hat. "Why, what do you mean, what am I doing here?"

"Why didn't you wait until I sent for you?"

"Why, Ransom, my husband, I've come to live with you at the scene of your greatest triumph."

"Deadwood is no place for a lady. It's a regular pigyard."

"Ransom, I came because I was determined to live with my husband wherever he was, come what might."

"You should've waited until I'd made it really big." The black patch over her left eye he now saw as a disfigurement.

"Really big? Why, Ransom, they tell me downtown you're potentially the richest man here." She stepped toward him. "Besides, even if you hadn't made it really big, as you say, I would have followed you." She stopped beside him and stooped to kiss him.

He turned his face away. "Don't. I'm dirty. Maybe even lousy."

"Well! So this is all the greeting I get after coming all this way. Through cloudbursts and wild Indians and dangerous road agents."

"Well, like I said, I didn't send for you." Her puccoon perfume caught him in the chest. He remembered all the hothouse smells of her.

"What's the matter with you, Ransom? Where's that fancy

boy of mine, who used to pick me a posy of wild flowers before breakfast every morning?"

He looked her in the eye. "Katherine, are you going to have a baby?"

"What?"

"Are you going to have a baby?"

"No, I'm not, worse luck."

His eyes shied off. He hated it that he couldn't keep looking her in the eye. At the same time he knew that she knew he couldn't.

"Ah, so you've gone and found yourself another girl, have you?" She stood arms akimbo beside him. "Some young slip of a thing? Cooing and billing? And not a brain in her pretty little head and going to have a baby?"

A nervous twitch tugged at his lips. He fought it away. What he needed now was a real poker face.

"Haven't you?"

Ransom just barely managed to keep his face straight.

"There is another woman then, isn't there? There has to be."

"Quit ropin' at me with all them silly questions."

"Earl Ransom!" She gasped, and backed off a step. "And after all I went through to get here. And after even getting us a house downtown."

"You—got—us—a—house—downtown? Already?"

"Yes. I bought that new green house a half-block off Main Street there. On the turnoff to Mt. Moriah. Across the stream. It's the only one in town with a water closet."

Ransom fought off a shudder.

"Our household goods will be arriving from Cheyenne any hour now."

Ransom touched his right eye with thumb and forefinger.

"You'll help me when they arrive, won't you, Ransom, dear? So we can set up housekeeping right away?" A tear gathered in the corner of her dark-brown eye. "It was always

my dream that we would at last have that sweet little nest
far out in the West." She sucked a deep breath. "Oh, Ransom, my darling, you still love me, don't you? Because if you
don't, my darling, I shall go mad with grief." She fell on his
neck and sought out his lips in his black beard and began to
kiss him passionately.

All the hardness he'd built up against her collapsed. A
weird impulse to smile twisted his lips.

"Please, Ransom, darling, do please kiss me. Like you used
to. You don't know how I've lived for this moment. Oh,
Ransom, I've had such an unhappy life, that if you don't kiss
me now, after all that, why. . . ."

He found himself turning, and at last, with wibbling lips,
kissing her.

He half-expected to hear the granite peaks whistling
again.

The green house set back from Main Street was lovely.
Ransom helped Katherine move in, furniture, furnishings,
trunks of clothes. He helped her roll out her expensive
Persian rugs. He supervised the movers when they set up the
four-poster in the big bedroom upstairs.

The house was quiet. Main Street was far enough away
for its usual hubbub to be muted. The little stream flowing
at the foot of the house purled just loud enough to give life a
murmurous tone. Occasional footsteps on the wooden bridge
made it homey.

Katherine persuaded him to clean up, so with a bar of
soap he took his first bath in a tub in months.

Katherine also got him to dress up for their first dinner
together since Cheyenne, in the black suit she'd once bought
him. She herself wore a young bride's white.

"And please, darling, don't come to the table wearing your
gun. For once."

"If you say so."

When he entered the dining room, she had the food on the table, steaming and savory, potatoes, gravy, meat, cabbage, dried-apple pie, set around a flower centerpiece.

Courteously he helped her into her chair, then went around and sat at the head of the table.

"You like it?"

He nodded.

"It's what I always dreamed of."

All too familiarly his hand picked up the linen napkin and unfolded it across his lap. "It's hard for me to believe."

She smiled tiny wrinkles around her one eye. "'Tis for me too."

He looked down at his plate.

"Will you ask the blessing, Ransom?"

He swallowed a loud click inside his high white collar. Pray? Finally he managed to shake his head.

She still had a smile. "There'll soon be a preacher here. Then we can be married legal like you always wanted."

There was already a preacher of sorts in town. She apparently hadn't heard about him.

"Even if we are already married common law."

"I see."

"I'm so glad you still want to." She spoke sideways to herself. "I should've known better than to let you go by yourself and live alone here so long. Bachelors out in the wilds always fall into bad habits. Get peculiar notions about things. Antisocial. They want a woman all right, but not all night."

Of all people Madam Kate ought to know. The thought left a bitter trace in his mind.

She lifted the bowl of potatoes with both hands and passed it to him. "Why don't you begin, dear."

The potatoes were done to a fare-thee-well. So was the gravy and the meat and the cabbage. And so was the sweet dried-apple pie. It was good to eat a town meal again.

All through dinner she kept up a bright patter of talk. She refused to notice his noncommittal air, that all was not well between them. Though every now and then she couldn't resist more bemused sideways remarks. "My, what a handsome man that stagecoach driver was." She pecked at her potatoes. "Once he called me a young lady." She poked at her meat. "I was most grateful to be called that, what with all that dust." She picked at her pie. "From where he was sitting up there on the boot, my skin probably did look young at that."

Ransom touched a hand to his right eye. Already about to be a father of a child by one woman, here he was now in a spot where he still might very well become a father of a child by a second woman. It was time he ran off to some other set of far dark hills.

She even had a box of cigars for him. Remembering how Sam had liked them, Ransom lit up. He blew out a plume of smoke.

"Now you just go over there and set in your easy chair, husband darling. By the bay window there. Where you can see the people go by."

"I'd rather watch the stream go by."

"Suit yourself." She watched him settle down in the big leather chair, watched him put his feet up on the footstool. "With that cigar, you look so . . . so dignified. Like a town father almost. Or a senator even."

Where was Erden? Right at that moment?

Katherine kept talking pleasantly all through washing dishes. She was as game as hornets.

After a while the cigar began to taste foul and Ransom chucked it into the brass spittoon beside him.

And all too soon it was time to go to bed.

She locked the front and back doors. She drew the blind to the bay window. She blew out all the big lamps. She picked up the small night lamp and headed for the stairs.

Ransom sat on, silent as a coyote at noon.

She paused on the bottom stairs. "Coming, dearie?"

"I . . . I think I'll sleep down here on the sofa."

"Why, Ransom, husband, we are going to sleep together, aren't we? We don't want to go through that again, do we?"

"I'll sleep down here."

She refused to see it except in a certain way. "Such a shy fellow you are. Like some rusty old bachelor." She breathed heavily. "Oh, please come, Ransom. We are man and wife now, aren't we? And it's been such a long time since we've made love. I've saved myself all this time for you. Oh, my darling, please."

The familiar winning tone of her voice reached into him so that he found himself once again turning a little in her direction.

She stepped behind him. She leaned down and kissed him on top of the nose. "Darling," she breathed. The front of her white dress opened.

The puccoon perfume of her poured over him. It tore him all up. "Katherine."

"Everything's all right, darling. Come away to bed. I can't wait to hold you in my arms." She touched her lips to his ear. "Don't deny your wife."

"Can't we first get acquainted a little?"

"First? You are deep, my husband."

He closed his eyes.

With a coy gesture of indulgence she placed the night lamp on the smoking stand beside him. She sat herself in his lap with a winsome flounce. She ran her fingers through his beard and gave several little tigerish tugs. She nuzzled him. She suckled the lobe of his ear. She lipped his lips. "Don't you ever say anything ever, darling?"

There was even some puccoon perfume in the stitched black patch over her left eye. He tried rough wit. "My bellows don't work so good with you sitting on them."

She liked that. She teased him with the tip of her tongue.

He let his lips and teeth be opened. He groaned. He could feel himself awaken under her. His flesh was willing.

She loosened his tie and collar. She ran a hand inside his clothes, stroking his skin, pressing her small palm around and over his shoulder muscles. "Darling. The thought of your sweet boy innocence . . . the thought that someone else's enjoyed it besides me, oh God, that drives me wild."

His arms were of a mood to betray him. They slipped around her. They pressed her close.

"Talk to me," she whispered hoarsely. "Talk to me. I do so love the sound of your voice. I hear red when you talk. The kind of red that drives me mad."

His fingertips found supple flesh under her necklace. He felt himself sliding.

"It's been so long."

Even as he was about to swing over her, it started again. That odd haunting business of knowing he'd lived that moment somewhere sometime before. And again it would not quite come clear. Though he was as sure of it being true as he was of the smell of her perfume.

She shifted in his lap. She loosened his trousers. There was in her gesture the hint that she might be helping a little boy.

The re-remembrance remained dreamlike. Something about being rooted and then cut off.

She fondled him.

He had to know. He gnashed his teeth to keep himself in hand. He found that to hold himself back was delicious, ecstatic. Ahh. It was touch and go. He could go either way. Ahh. If he could just hold himself back another moment, trembling, firm, quivering, he just might, finally and at last, penetrate the mystery of that not quite re-remembrance.

She fondled him.

It was wrong. There was Erden. But also because of something else. What was it? He trembled. He wavered.

She gave him a little tug of love.

It tipped him. The almost re-remembrance faded away.

"Love."

He cursed inwardly. Then, letting go, he hugged her hard. He drew back and taking hold of the top of her white dress with both hands, he tore open her bodice all the way to her waist. The sight of her half-fallen pear breasts and her slim waist was also an old half-remembered ache.

"What're you doing?" she squeaked.

"You have too many nice clothes as it is."

"Ransom!"

Carefully he tore the rest of her dress down to the hem. She looked like a halved white harvest apple. "You won't miss this dress."

She hated having her dress torn. Yet she took the tearing to mean he was crazy in love with her again. "Darling, you're mad." Quickly she covered her wrinkled scar with a hand.

"Mad I am, yes." He pushed her hand aside. He shoved his brushy face into her neck and between her breasts. He surged up, rose with her in his arms, placed her on the purple Persian rug and possessed her.

She took it all for true love.

He set himself against any other thought but the way of a man with a woman. Comb still bright and high, he next carried her upstairs, finished undressing her, finished undressing himself, took her yet again on their four-poster. If he was going to sin against Erden he might as well sin the whole hog.

She cried out from the midst of her rack of joy. "At last! At last! To be doing it again and again. Oh, Ransom, darling, I fear I have an unnatural appetite for it."

Through half-open eyes he saw that the throes made her a young girl again. The tiny netlike traces around her eyes were hard to find. Her sighs were those of a girl-child.

They were insatiable with each other. They seemed to be on top of each other all night long.

He went on a burst with her for a week.

5

Two months later. It was morning. They had just thrown back the quilts and were about to get up. Once again his eye fell on the scar on her stomach. It still fascinated him. The wrinkled smile of it was like the smile of an old woman with a secret to tell.

As before she tried to hide it with a covering hand.

He promptly pushed her hand aside.

"Please, Ransom."

"Sure is funny you ain't proud of that scar."

Her gold hair rustled in her pillow.

He gave her belly a light clap. "Lots of people used to die from gallstone operations. So you should be proud of it."

"Please don't stick your nose into something for which you may be sorry later on."

"What's the matter, chum? You got something to hide?"

She sat up blazing. "What do you mean?"

"Have you?"

"Listen, you." She quite deliberately placed her hand on her velvet wings. "I'll have you know that no child has ever passed these portals."

Ransom noted that for all her blazing manner her brown eye for one fleeting second couldn't quite hold up to him.

"I swear to God, Mr. Earl Ransom."

After a moment Ransom shied off himself. "I have to believe you."

"Well! I like that."

Then it was his turn to bristle. "Listen, puss, you were running The Stinging Lizard when we first met, you know."

Pause. "That hurt."

"All right. I believe you."

There came over her face again that familiar sudden grimace, part sneering, part wincing.

He leaned an elbow over her. With his finger he gently poked her near breast, then her chin, then the tiny crow's feet at her eyes.

His touches melted her. "Oh, Ransom, I do so love you."

He smoothed back her gold hair with his full hand.

"Though sometimes I think the way we act we're no better married than monkeys about the middle."

"Who am I?"

She blinked. "What did you say?"

"Skip it."

She studied him. The string to her eye patch had slipped a little from his stroking of her hair and she adjusted it.

"But I agree with you. It should mean more than just coupling in the dark."

She smiled, expecting advances. "How more, Ransom?"

He looked at the early morning sunshine glowing in the pine tree outside their bedroom window. "Oh, I don't know. Like a bobolink singing maybe."

"That's just what it means to me. Sweet birds sweetly singing."

He closed his eyes. He recalled Sam Slaymaker's remark. "Oh, you'll know when you finally make it, boy. It's like when all the birds fly out of the straw pile."

"Isn't it birds singing for you too when we're together?"

He couldn't get himself to say it wasn't.

"Isn't it?"

He let his smile linger for answer.

"You got to love me now darling. You've just got to."

He ran a fingertip up and down her long scar.

"You see"—she lisped the next words—"our baby should have the privilege of growing up with its own father."

His head came up.

"Because, you see, we are going to have a baby. You've probably noticed."

He stared big green eyes at her.

"What's the matter? Don't you want it?"

Silence.

"I thought you said you wanted sons?"

Silence.

She pushed his hand away from her scar. A pout darkened her face. But she couldn't quite look him in the eye.

In turn he pushed her hand aside and once more placed the flat of his hand on where she said she had his baby. The thought of a little acorn of his own flesh started there under the scar almost unhinged him. Lord. Now he was to be a father of children with two different women.

"Isn't it really birds singing for the both of us?"

He swore to himself inside. She couldn't have it. She couldn't. She had to get rid of it. Somehow. And if she didn't, by God, he'd drive the damned little nubbin out of her himself. Hard. Mean. If he had to.

"Aren't you happy about it?"

"I guess so."

"I thought you once told me you wanted a son? To start a new line off with?"

"I do."

"Well?"

He needed time to think. He masked his feelings as best he could. "Sure I wanted a son."

"Because if you don't want it, it's easily taken care of. With me it is anyway."

"It's fine. Fine. It's just that it's . . . kind of a shock to know . . . it's finally coming at last."

"Well, that's a lot better."

"Ahh . . . I suppose you would be the one to know how it could be easily taken care of. If need be."

Pause. "That hurt too."

"I'm sorry."

Abruptly Katherine got out of bed and began to slip into her clothes. "Time to make breakfast. For a hungry man."

He watched her. Erden didn't have wrinkles in the armpits. Nor creases under the thighs. It had to be that Katherine was one of those who couldn't help but look old for her
age. Because Katherine couldn't be that much older than he
was.

"Just you remember one thing though, my husband. I'm
not going to let you throw me on the scrap heap like some
old sucked-out lemon." She tied a knot in the belt of her
robe. "I don't know what's been troubling you lately. But
whatever it is, I'll never let you get rid of me. I'll kill myself
first." She fluffed her gold hair in place. "And that's not so
funny. I've looked death in the eye before."

His lower lip doubled on itself.

"I do hope the new preacher will arrive soon. So we can
get it over with."

He allowed himself to nod, slowly. "Yes, I suppose we
ought to get that done. Before they start talking."

"Don't the boys think we're married?"

"I was thinking for the baby's sake."

"Oh. That. Yes, of course, the baby."

He shot her a look. What? Had the thought of the coming
baby already slipped her mind so soon? By the Lord, it
actually seemed to mean less to her than it did to him.

"The last I heard, our new preacher will be here in a
couple of weeks."

The pines outside stirred in the wind.

"Shall I have announcements made then?"

He thought: "I'll probably never see Erden again. And
I've got to have at least one of my children around me."
Aloud he said, "Go ahead."

The wind pushed against the bedroom window.

He didn't deserve Erden. He was to her what Katherine
was to him.

Outside someone far up the gulch hallowed a piercing
coyote-like howl. "Oh, Joe!" The howl was picked up by
those next in line. "Oh, Joe!" It came swiftly down the gulch.

"Oh, Joe!" Louder and louder. "Oh, Joe!" As it passed by the house the gulch jangled with its echoes. "Oh, Joe!" Gradually it faded away. "Oh, Joe."

It was time to get up.

Dawn light came through the blind a dull gold. The brook below rippled over stone baffles.

He'd had a dream. It was so compelling it left him stiff. He groaned.

Katherine rolled up on an elbow to have a look at him. "What's the matter with you?"

"Nuth-ing."

She shook him. "There is too something the matter with you."

He lay staring straight up at the ceiling, eyeballs stiff.

"You're not dying on me?" She threw back the quilts for a better look.

With great effort he managed to cross his legs. It always gave him comfort of a sort to feel one leg crossed over the other. "It's nothing."

She bounced out of bed. Running, she got a bottle of brandy and a shot glass. "Here, quick, have some of this. Maybe that'll help."

He downed the brandy before he realized what it meant. "Some more?"

He stirred in his nightgown. "I mussent drink."

"As medicine it's all right."

"God."

"What's the matter with you? For a minute there I thought sure you were dying."

He drew himself up on his pillow. A great sigh heaved him up for a moment. There were low dots in his half-lidded eyes. "Just a dream."

"Must've been an awful dream the way you looked. My stars."

"No. No. It was more a kind of wonderful dream. I was all wrapped up in it. Too wrapped up in it."

She set the brandy and the shot glass on the bedstand and got back into bed with him.

He breathed deep several times. "It was about my mother."

"Your mother? I thought you said you never knew her."

"I didn't. But it was about my mother just the same." His eyes stared, set and unseeing. "I couldn't quite make her out always. But it was her. It was what she did that made me know. The way she gave me titty. And the quick way she had of walking around, like she had springs in her legs." He moved his big toe back and forth, until the edge of the sheet slid off it. "She loved me a lot, too. I could tell. She favored me over my dad even." He closed his eyes, looking within, trying again to catch sight of the face in the dream. "Funny, but I couldn't quite seem to catch it. It was just out of reach."

Katherine's brown eye first opened wide, then half-closed. "Why don't you just forget it? It's only a dream."

"No. No. Because it was more than just a dream. Because this was almost real. Man." He stirred in the sheets. "I've never before felt so drained out after. In my whole life." He shook his head. "The funny thing is, I've got the funny feeling that I knew her better than I think too." Again he shook his head. "If I could just get more of a hint of some kind. Then maybe I could find out who my ma really was."

"Your father wasn't in this dream then?"

"Oh, he was there all right. Kind of like a shadow almost. With a gun, shooting."

"What!"

"I could see my ma just as plain. Yet I can't tell you what she looked like."

A long pause. "Well, I wouldn't worry about it, if I was you. After all, it was only a dream."

"No-o. It was something about her eyes. Green, like mine."

Katherine got up abruptly. "I'll go get your breakfast."

He didn't bother to watch her go.

After a moment he reached for the brandy and had himself another shot.

The next night, before dawn, he let go with a great call in his sleep. "Maah!"

Katherine rose out of her pillow with a start.

"Maah!"

"Ransom!"

"Aaah!"

"Ransom, wake up! You're dreaming again."

"Nnnh?"

"Wake up. You're ringing wet with sweat."

"No shadows in her sheets."

"Shadows in her sheets?"

Then he rose out of his pillow with a start. "Huh?"

Katherine turned up the night lamp.

Orange illumination bloomed around them. The two of them resembled a papa and a mama bear disturbed out of their sleep by an exploding meteor.

"What's the matter?"

"Ransom, Ransom, I don't know what I'm going to do with you."

"Why?"

"That terrible dreaming. If you don't quit hitting me in your sleep, you're going to have to sleep by yourself."

"I hit you?"

"You most certainly did." She showed him her arm. A lump already showed over her bicep.

"That's funny. Because it was about my mother again. And it was another wonderful dream about her." He spoke very slowly and clearly. "I was a little baby. And I was lonesome. And then she said I could sleep warm with her."

Katherine reached for the brandy and glass. "Here. Have a shot. It settled you the last time."

"I shouldn't."

"Why not?"

"You know how bad I get when I drink."

"One shot more won't hurt a big fellow like you. And then you go to sleep."

"All right." He drank up.

"That's better."

He could feel her lying awake beside him in the dark. Well, he was plenty upset about the dreaming himself.

The next night he hit her a couple of awful ones in sleep. Her gasping woke him. He sat up. "Katherine?"

She clawed the air for breath.

He leaned across her and turned up the little lemon tongue in the night lamp.

Her face was blue. Her eyepatch had fallen off and her empty eye socket was level full with blood. He'd hit her once in the belly and once in the eye.

"Katherine?" He took her chest in both his hands and pumped the curve of it to help her breathe.

Of a sudden she filled up, and coughed. The moment strength returned to her she struck him. Blood spilled out of her eyesocket down her cheek.

He held her off. "You don't have to go into a catfit."

She felt of her face and eye socket. With a night kerchief she wiped all clean and then fitted the eyepatch back in place. "From now on you can sleep on the couch." She breathed hard. She was mad. "Alone. At least until you get over your crazy nightmares."

He glared back at her. He couldn't help the dreaming. And he rather liked the dreams. He got out of bed on his side. He pulled his nightshirt out of where it'd caught in his seat. "All right. Suits me better anyway."

"Well-l . . . you really did hurt me, you know. Ransom."

"Shouldn't've been sleeping here in the first place."

"What kind of crazy dreaming is this anyway? You got a guilty conscience or something?"

The brook outside rippled over rough stones.

"I don't suppose I dare ask if you dreamed about your mother again?"

The pine trees outside whispered in the wind.

"Was it about your darn mother again?"

"She seems to bother you more than she does me."

"Maybe she does."

"All right. I'll tell you. This time I was two people. Part of me was somebody walking into the back door of some house somewhere. The minute I got into the kitchen of this house I started shooting at my blue blanket. I don't know just how a blue blanket fits in there. But there it was. And then part of me was somebody else waiting inside this house. The minute the other somebody started shooting at my pet blanket, I shot him. All of a sudden a still somebody else let out a terrible scream. It was my mother. I could tell. Just as plain. Except that again I couldn't quite make out her face. Though I did get a glimpse of her eyes again. They're green all right. Then, snap! I woke up."

Again Katherine's brown eye first opened wide, then half-closed. And she slowly turned white.

He was instantly concerned, and started toward her. "Did I hit you that hard?"

"Get out!" she squeaked.

He jumped back. "Well! If that's the way you feel about it. . . ." With a pounce, he grabbed up all his clothes and brushed out.

The leather couch downstairs was hard. But he was glad to be sleeping alone again. Now he could think in secret about Erden without troubling his conscience too much. His heart beat fast. He wished there were some kind of heaven to look forward to with Erden.

The riffling brook and bumbling drunks kept him awake.

All of a sudden, he got up, put on his buckskin clothes and his gun and belt, and stole silently out into the night, into pale silver moonlight.

"Goddam. I really am trapped now that I've got one in Katherine's oven too."

He headed up the gulch. Some dogs who knew him came out for their customary pat on the head. When he strode past them ignoring them, they instantly set out after him, barking at him from a safe distance.

He knew the way up the gulch by heart. It was as familiar to him as stepping into his own pants.

He climbed above his holdings at the beaver dam. The smell of pine stumps bleeding rosin was sticky in the nose.

"I'll probably never see Erden again. But if I ever do, I'm going to eat a large piece of humble pie for her. About us whites piling in here like this."

He came upon the avalanche that had buried her cave. No one had disturbed it that he could see. He also checked the little park where a crow had come to sit and talk on Erden's shoulder. No sign of Erden there either. He climbed to his white-quartz claim. No sign of her there.

"I should tell Katherine about Erden. So long as I don't, I'm living a lie with her."

He sat alone in the toothy granite peaks. The whistling spirits were silent.

On the way back he found a saloon still open. It was known as No. 10.

He spotted Troy Barb at the bar. Troy Barb was wearing new store-bought clothes.

"Troy."

"Hello there, pard. What do you know for sure?"

"Not a thing."

"Out on an all-night good time, I see."

"Wish I was." Sawdust had packed up under one of Ransom's boots and he scuffed it off on the toe of the other boot.

"Have a drink?"

"All right."

"What'll it be?"

"Some good red American whiskey. A long one."

"Thought you never drank whiskey."

"Tonight I am. What the hell."

"Bence, set 'em up."

Barkeep Bence set his hands in motion. "Two smokies comin' up." Bence had the mottled face of the rachitic.

Troy Barb gave Ransom a throw of his moon eyes. "Had a fight with the wife, I see."

"What makes you say that?"

"I know the signs. I've had my dauber frosted over a couple of times myself."

"Hmm."

"Well, here's to the gals, may God bless every one of 'em. Pigs included."

Ransom took a good slug. "Where's everybody?"

"Why, pard, the night's about over."

"Guess it is at that. Though Old Wild Bill used to stay up pretty late, I hear."

"Yeh, he did."

"Too bad about him."

"Yeh. I see they still got his chair setting there where he got it."

Ransom looked toward the back of the saloon. Four empty chairs stood shoved tight against an empty table. No one was playing at the faro table beyond it either.

"Poor Bill. Getting it in the back of the head like that. And on the only night he ever sat with his back to the door."

"Yeh."

There was one girl in the saloon and she stood hovering over a game of stud poker near the fireplace.

Ransom recognized one of the poker players. Bullneck Bill. A troublemaker. Bullneck Bill hadn't found himself any gold, so spent most of his time complaining about his bad luck and other people's good luck. He made his keep by gambling, mostly with greenhorns just come to town. He had a large hump of a neck and big loose-set teeth and cold speculative blue eyes. He was always right. Dead right. The other three poker players were raw farmers fresh from Yankton. They'd struck it good only a week before.

Ransom watched them. He loved playing poker wonderfully and considered sitting in on a couple of hands. Might as well go to hell all in one bucket while he was at it. Also it would be fun to take some of Bullneck Bill's money away from him.

Troy Barb nudged Ransom. "Another Jeremiah?"

"It's my turn to cough up." Ransom turned to the barkeep. "Set 'em, Bence. Same medicine." Ransom got out his bag of gold dust and set it on the bar.

Bence obliged him, then got out his scales and poured out what dust he had coming to him.

Troy Barb downed half of his glass. "By God, pardner, when you drink this brand, you mean business." Troy Barb wiped his lips with the back of his hand. "It's burning a hole through my bladder right this minute."

Ransom drank, bottoms up. His green eyes slicked over. He pointed his empty glass at the poker players. "Who's the pig with them?"

"Rose."

"Kind of a compliment to say she's uglier than a bighorn sheep."

Troy Barb laughed.

"Though her eyes make you feel she's good people."

"Yeh."

"Probably ain't got enough brains to pour pee out of a shoe, even if you was to print the instructions on the heel."

Barkeep Bence hacked up a rattling cough. "Better not cheat on her though. She's got a voice on her like a pig under a gate."

"Ha, that's Rose all right." Troy Barb mused over his glass. "Looks like she's fell in love with that red-faced farmer. Clean through to the basement."

"You jealous, Troy?" Ransom asked.

"Maybe I am."

"You like Rose, Troy?" Ransom asked further.

"It gravels me to see what was once a nice sukey throw herself away on such trash."

"Then you do like her."

"Yeh, hell, I guess I do." Troy Barb set his glass down with a light thump. "Set 'em up again, Bence."

Bence did, and they drank up.

The third red whiskey went down like a racing flame. Ransom had the feeling that his mustache was multiplying right under his nose. Prickles came alive in his earlobes. It was just like that time in Denver when he'd gone hog wild. So Katherine couldn't stand his dreams, eh? Well, he couldn't stand Katherine in the first place. The old witch. The hell with her. The hell with everybody.

The red-faced farmer seemed to be the only one of the three farmers who knew something crooked was going on and he slowly became purple-faced. Rose hung over him like a foolish ewe.

Bence growled, "That son of a bitch Bullneck. He deserves to be dry-gulched. He ain't doing business any good in this place. Too bad Wild Bill is dead or I'd sick him onto him."

Ransom smiled a young man's whiskey smile. "Why Old Bill? What's wrong with me?"

Bence took him up on it. "Do it, by God, and you can drink on the house for the rest of the year."

"It's a whack." Ransom touched a hand to his right eye. "There's nothing I hate more than an overproud bully. But first pour us another drink."

Troy Barb didn't like it. "You ain't used to drinking much, kid."

Ransom bent hot green eyes on his partner. "You giving the orders now?"

Troy Barb backed down. "No." Then he shrugged. "If that's what you want."

"Pour, Bence."

Whiskey trickled with a sweetish smell.

Again they drank up.

Ransom's ears clicked. Who the hell was Katherine to be kicking him out of his own bed when he didn't want to sleep there in the first place? A man had a right to love his mother and dream about her if he wanted to.

Rose finally placed a hand on the shoulder of the purple-faced farmer. "Arlo, let's go home."

"No."

"C'mon, Arlo."

"No!" Arlo snapped around at her so hard his blond hair lashed out like a swath of cut wheat. "Dammit, I'm staying here till I get some of my money back. Or catch him in the act."

Bullneck's high neck bristled. "I take it you're calling me a crook, Arlo."

Arlo surged up out of his chair. "I'm standing a pat hand on what I just said."

The other two greenhorn farmers thickened in their chairs. Their ears flopped.

Ransom set down his glass. "Whoops. Maybe we better take the play away before it gets ripe." He swung his holster and gun handy. "Arlo's hotter'n a burnt boot and he's no match for Bullneck."

"I'd stay out of that," Troy Barb warned.

Bence said, "Let him go. Be good riddance if he was to plug Bullneck."

Ransom stepped slowly over to the poker players. "Some trouble here, boys?" Looking over Bullneck's shoulder, he saw that Bullneck was holding a spade flush king high.

Rose backed away, squeaking.

Bullneck lunged around. "Ha. Look who's buttin' in. A mama's boy who's struck it lucky."

"What's wrong with being a mama's boy?"

"If that's what you want, nothing, I guess."

"It's better than being born to a mule, ain't it?"

Bullneck's tan beard curled like a cat's. His sneer deepened. He backed his chair away from the table a little. "So old Kate's fancy boy is all growed up, is he?"

"Old Kate is it? What do you know about her?"

"I know all about her. I'm from Cheyenne myself, you know."

Troy Barb broke in from the bar. "Hey, Rose, why don't you favor us with a song?"

Rose quavered, "Oh, Troy."

"I'll buy you a drink if it'll help you clear your valves."

"I can't sing now."

"C'mon. Before all the horses get out."

"I can't."

Ransom said, "Let's hear more about that mama's-boy business, Bullneck."

"What about it?"

"Did you know my mother?"

"If I did've, it wouldn't be to my credit. She was probably a whore like all our mothers."

"Nobody says that about my mother. Fill your hand."

Bullneck laughed, instead spat into the spittoon at his feet.

Arlo still stood across the table from Bullneck. Gold hair hung partway down his red nose. He hadn't liked the way

Ransom had butted in. He tried to wave Ransom off. "I don't know who you are, and I appreciates your stepping in here and wanting to help. But this is my ramble, kid, so kindly stay out. I'll handle Bullneck myself."

The two other farmers suddenly broke to their feet and got the hell out of there. The swing doors slapped to several times behind them.

Ransom said, "Bullneck, fill your hand."

Arlo again tried to wave Ransom off. "Get out, kid. This is my fight."

Ransom said yet again, "Bullneck, fill your hand."

Arlo stepped between Ransom and Bullneck. Arlo had a gun tucked in his belt and his hand slowly edged toward it. "Bullneck, you bastard, I'm standing pat on what I knows."

Bullneck waved his fistful of cards at Arlo. "Sit down. And let's see you put your money where your mouth is." Bullneck eyed what was left of Arlo's sack of gold dust.

Arlo's hand touched the butt of his gun. "Bullneck, you're a crook. And, by God, you can't make a mark I won't come to."

Bullneck gradually put his cards face down. He mocked Arlo with a horse sneer. "Sit down before you get hurt, Arlo."

Then Arlo, black-faced he was so mad, made a grab for it. But the gunsight of his six-shooter caught in his belt.

Bullneck watched Arlo jerking at his gun a moment, then got to his feet and coolly drew his own gun and shot Arlo in the belly.

Arlo's eyes swam up his forehead for a second and then they slowly closed over and a suddenly lonely look spread over his face and then he slumped to the plank floor.

There was another click of a gun.

Bullneck turned, gun still leveled.

Ransom shot Bullneck from the hip without aiming.

Bullneck, shot through the temple, eyeballs suddenly hanging out, slid to the floor.

The place was full of banging echoes for a moment. The gleaming brown whiskey bottles and the glistening clear glasses shimmered with echoes.

Then Bence got out an old shammy skin and began to shine his mahogany bar. "Yep, it's like I say. Good riddance. Thanks a lot, Ransom. We could use more men like you."

6

Ransom didn't stir from the house for a week. Dogs could bark at others for a while. He sat with his feet up on the kitchen range drinking coffee.

The brook below the house ran sweetly over its stones.

Katherine swung between two poles. One moment she was in a worried fret over what he might do next; a moment later she was in a raging seethe over what she called their disgrace. When she tried to kiss him and mother him, he pushed her away; when she cursed him and called him killer, he sat sipping coffee.

"Maybe we ought to pull up stakes and take a trip somewhere," she said, standing behind him. "Get out of this awful place. I know some terrible things have been on your mind lately, the way you've been having nightmares, but really, darlin', I don't want my husband in trouble with the law. In Cheyenne I could help you. But not here."

Ransom sipped more coffee.

"Killing that Horses was bad enough, deserve it as he did." Katherine wrung her hands. "But to shoot a man down in a barroom brawl like it was no more than shooting down a jackrabbit . . . even if he had just killed poor Arlo . . . why! ohh! Because one killing doesn't deserve another. Just like that. That kind of thinking is against God Himself."

Ransom crossed his legs up on the kitchen range.

"And then the way you used to hit me in your sleep." She

paced back and forth. "Ransom! You've got to do something about yourself. You've got to have a change of heart. Or something. Because if you don't, it can only lead to one thing. That you become a habitual killer!" She raged back and forth behind him. "If they don't pick you up first and throw you in the hoosegow."

Ransom crossed his feet the other way.

"Just what are you going to do when they come knocking on our door and ask you to come along with them? Kill the law too?"

Silence. Bence had said Deadwood could use more men like him.

She stood directly behind him, her breath stirring the hair on the back of his head. "There's one thing I'm going to ask you to do. Right now. Because it's something you've got to do. Got to do."

"What's that?"

"I want you to sell your holdings. Right now."

"I'd sort of had that in mind. Provided the right offer came along."

"And when you get the money for it, I want you to put it safe in a bank in Cheyenne. We can send it over in the treasure coach."

Ransom dropped his feet to the floor. "All right. That I'll do."

"Good. Now you're being sensible. Civilized."

"And I think Troy Barb will go along with that. He's got half-share in our beaver-dam claim, you know."

"I know Troy Barb will. He told me just yesterday that he's anxious to go back home and put his wife up in style."

Long ago Ransom had decided he would never tell Katherine about that other claim, the white-quartz holding. Erden and her spirit gods were going to keep that. Untouched.

Katherine said, "Now I'm proud of you, my husband."

Ransom thought: "This is no life. Better that I should take

a bottle of poison and lay down under a bush somewhere and die. Because I'm never going to get out of this. It's all going from bad to worse."

Outside a junkman in a buckboard went rattling by, bawling, "Rags! Bottles! Sacks!"

One morning early Ransom packed a canteen of water, a bedroll, some jerky, and swung aboard Prince to have a look at Bear Butte. Bear Butte was a lonely peak standing out in the prairies apart from the Black Hills. Indians regarded it as their high holy place and often climbed it for their vigils. Ransom thought a night spent up there alone might help him.

He arrived below the butte about midafternoon. When he saw how the little mountain loomed above him like some bear asleep with its head tucked under a paw, he understood why it was called Bear Butte. There was no trail up for a horse; it was too thickly strewn with sharp volcanic rock. He found a spring in an open shelving area with some fresh buffalo grass, and put Prince out to graze. Prince would stay put until he came back. Ransom hid the saddle and bridle under a pile of black rocks.

"Oh, God, how could I have gone to bed with Katherine again so soon after that holy time with Erden?"

Ransom also decided to leave his gun and belt behind. He did it out of respect for Erden's Indian religion. One hardly went to any kind of shrine with a gun on the hip. Besides, he wanted to have a go at the peak with his bare hands.

"Something awful has got to happen to me to make up for all this."

Carefully he picked his way up a shallow gully on the south side. Good stands of pine grew on the south slope, though the steep west and east sides were mostly barren. Here and there, near trickling springs, clumps of wild plum and wild grape grew. He found several warm spots where deer had nested. Chickadees flittered across small flat slabs of weathered lava. The lava was exactly the color of their brown caps.

"I miss my little Swallow so terribly much."

A turtledove koo-kooed high above him. For a second he thought it might be one of Erden's whistling spirits, warning him off.

He paused for breath. The clear higher air had a slightly burnt savor in his nose. It felt good to be alone and high again.

"I see nothing but bad ahead."

The sloping gully ahead steepened. He veered off to the right through several clumps of spine cactus and irregular rugs of silver sage. Spalled rock lay loose at every step. He had to be careful with his footing. The soles of his boots were almost too slick for climbing.

The prairies fell away on all sides. Both he and the dark Hills behind rose into the blue skies. His breath came harsh and cleansing. He sweat. It was good to be laboring up and up.

By accident he found some black honey in a fallen pine. He scooped out a piece and ate it. The honey was very old.

"Lord, this is the best yet. None of that sticky sweetness you sometimes get. Mmm." He ate more. "More like a dark liqueur with the alcohol boiled out." He ate and ate with an almost bearish lust. It was the best he'd ever had. It was like a gift of flesh from Erden.

He stopped to sip at a spring. The water wasn't good. It had a taste like it might have come out of an old coffeepot with a burnt bottom.

He climbed upward. He wondered if Erden had ever climbed Bear Butte.

"I love her. I love her. Yet I can't have her. She's out of my reach forever."

He climbed past a pine split by lightning and torn apart by tornadic winds.

He heard the voice of a little boy in his head. The little-boy words seemed to float off before him like soap bubbles. He stopped and held his head to one side to observe them the better.

"Murderer." Pause. "You better skip the country."

He wiped sweat from his brow. He puffed.

His hand reached down for it before he was aware of what it was. What at first appeared to be a fallen willow leaf turned out to be an arrowhead. It was a beauty. Worked by a master arrowsmith. The point was more smoky glass than flint. Erden would have appreciated it. He rubbed it between thumb and forefinger until it shone. He lingered over it even as he dropped it in his pocket.

He reached a swayback between the two main humps of the peak. He paused to catch his breath. Ahead of him to the north, prairies unrolled below for miles all the way to the Belle Fourche River. Behind him the other way, prairies unrolled out all the way to Elk Creek.

The hump to the west was the highest and presently he headed for it. He leaned forward from the hips to climb the better, nose almost touching the steeping path. It was like climbing the bony spine of an enormous razorback wild hog. One wrong step either way and down he would roll.

It took him two hours to reach the summit.

He turned to take it all in. The instant view in the stark falling sunlight was so vast in all directions he forgot he was breathless. He was too high to sweat. To the east, many sleeps away, the Cheyenne River seemed to shimmer off into confluence with the Missouri. To the west, twenty miles off, the Hills resembled a herd of monster buffalo bulls kneeled in sleep.

He recognized the place as the Indian holy ground he'd been looking for. Bits of painted leather, even tattered and decorated buckskin, lay pegged to the ground in bizarre geometric design. Stones had also been placed in the crotches of pines, in some instances so long ago that lips of red bark had almost swallowed them up. The silence was still heavy with old vigils, old prayers, old visions.

"Murderer." Pause. "Better skip the country."

Just before the sun sank a last time, he found three pines so placed in a row and close together that with the help of some flat rock and forest duff he made himself a level spot on which to roll out his suggans. The spine of the summit itself came to too sharp a point to sleep on.

Not a solitary smidgen of a sign of Erden anywhere. He heard the faint dee-dee of the chickadee far below. He heard the soft sooling of the wind in the pines nearby. He heard the thumping of his own heart.

"Erden?"

Nothing.

"Swallow? Blue Swallow?"

Not even an echo.

There was no place to sit. He chewed a little on a strip of jerky; found he wasn't hungry. He sipped some water from his canteen.

Night came on swiftly. Darkness bloomed out of the east like thunderhead rain ahead of its own shadow. As the brown shadow came on, the horizon below rose to meet it.

He rode standing high on the point.

At last, when even Bear Butte went under, he turned and stooped and slid into his suggans.

He lay stretched flat on his back. The aromatic duff beneath was soft enough to make even a good bed for an invalid. He ran his hands up and down the shiny slick buckskin over his thighs. He stared up at the brittle stars above.

He recalled the story of Abraham and Isaac, of how Abraham was about to offer up Isaac at a burnt offering, when Jehovah Himself intervened and provided Abraham with a ram caught in a thicket for his sacrifice.

He longed with a great aching longing that Erden might somehow come and wake him from sleep. Like that first

time. It was almost a year ago since they'd met. By now, if
Erden were still alive, she would have borne them their
baby. A boy, he hoped. To start the new line off with. It
would be older than the one that Katherine would bear him.
And it would be the one. If he could ever find it.

He undulated once, as if to offer himself up. Then, riding
backwards willy-nilly, toes up, he drifted off, sleep coming
over him as silently as night itself.

He dreamed of Mother again. Dad was gone. When he
told Mother that he was lonesome and when he asked her if
he could sleep in Dad's place, Mom said, "Come over then, if
that's what you want." He'd just barely got in beside his
mother, between different sheets, when all of a sudden Dad
thundered him back into his own bed. And he awoke.

"Murderer!" Pause. "Better skip the country!" There was
always that pause between the two dark cries.

He returned home the next evening.

Katherine was seething white. Her occasional odd grimace had become a fixed sneer. In taut silence she set out the
supper for him: potatoes and gravy, beef, onions, dried-
apple pie, coffee.

He was hungry and so ate up.

She gathered up the dishes and carried them out to the
kitchen and washed them alone.

He went out to the front room and sat down in his easy
chair and looked out through the bay window and mused on
his miseries.

A large fern hung drooped from an iron stand in front of
the south window. A September breeze pushed in cool
through the open door. The mountain stream trickled stead-
ily over its old stones.

Katherine swept up the kitchen; and then went after him.
She began sweetly enough. "Another cup of coffee? There's
more in the pot."

"Thanks. I've had a sufficiency."

She stood behind him. "I was uptown today."

"Mmm."

"Everybody was asking where you were."

"Mmm."

She came around the chair to stand in front of him. She tried to catch his eye. "Ransom, I want to ask you something."

"Fire away."

"Ransom, you aren't some kind of road agent, are you?"

"What?"

"Tied up with that nest of outlaws near Harney's Peak? A lookout for them?"

"Good God!" He was thoroughly astounded that she should think that of him.

"Well, people have begun to wonder uptown a little. And somebody has been tipping off Curly Griffin about when the treasure coach is to run."

"Are you off your rocker, woman? Me a road agent? When I don't even drink or smoke?"

"But you do love poker. And you have shot down men."

"You don't think much of me, do you?"

"Ransom, listen to me. I've made up my mind about something. I want us to get out of here. Right now. Today. Before it's too late." She began to pace back and forth in front of him. Her long green dress flourished about her legs. Shadows moved in her gold hair as light fell on it from different angles. Torment wrinkled up her face, gave her face a very haggard look. "Oh, Ransom, I don't know, but I've got such a terrible funny feeling about all this."

"When is the baby due again?"

The question startled her. "Oh. Oh, that. Well, I haven't sat down and figured it out yet. Down to the last day, that is. I've been too busy worrying over you." She picked at the belt of her green dress. "Anyway, if this keeps up, I'll probably lose it from all the strain."

"You don't have to worry about me."

"But I have been worrying, you know."

He hardened. "Lady, I like the Hills. I'm going to stick it out here."

She rubbed her hands together until they squeaked. "Ransom, don't you love me any more?"

"Oh, for godsakes, woman."

"Don't you love me any more?"

He stared out of the green bay window. Mists of darkness were dropping down on Deadwood outside.

Then with a wonderful effort, somehow, Katherine managed to put on a sweet face, with an appealing touch of winsome petulance in it. "Aren't you ever going to wash my feet again?"

Oh God.

"Don't you really love me any more, Ransom?"

What could one say to a woman who was to bear one's child?

"Ransom?"

"Oh, shut up. If you want to leave, go ahead. But I'm going to tough it through here."

She made a strangled sound. Then suddenly with a pounce she stuck her face into his. "You son of a bitch!" Hate pulled up her mouth and eyes into a tight net of wriggling wrinkles. "You bastard!" Her single brown eye glittered bluish. Scent of puccoons wafted out of her bosom. "Mr. Earl Ransom, I spit on you." She spat. "Oh, how I wish I hadn't listened to all your sweet talk back then. Giving up my Stinging Lizard for you!" She began to yell at him, hoarse with passion. "I'd give anything to have that back again, right now, Hermie included!"

"That whorehouse full of hogs."

"Don't you dare to say anything bad about my girls! At least they were true blue. Besides being kind and tender-hearted."

"A place for cowboys to shoot off their mouths. And guns."

"Look who's talking."

"True blue? Kind and tenderhearted? Hell. What about that story I heard back in Denver last year, where, after their hog ranch'd burned down, whores were seen panning the ashes for gold fillings."

"Oh. Oh." She flounced off to the water closet. "Oh. I'll fix you for that, Mr. Ransom. After all I gave up for you."

He wished he had a drink.

Noises came from the water closet, as well as Katherine's voice. "Oh, God, what an empty house this has become!"

He longed for Erden.

Finished in the water closet, Katherine slammed the lid to with a loud bang.

The slamming set him off. A rush of savage rage hemorrhaged all through him. He came up out of the easy chair swearing like a madman. He couldn't hold it back. He swore a streak for a solid minute.

Then, grinding his teeth, and clapping on gun and belt, he in turn slammed out of the house.

"God damn her to hell forever."

Ransom went straight to No. 10, got himself a corner stool at the bar, ordered a bottle of American whiskey.

The red whiskey went down as hot as liniment. He had to swallow twice to tolerate it. Once he even rose a little on his stool to get it down.

The long bar was ringed tight with hardneck stiffs. All wore guns. All drank hard liquor. All wore broad-brimmed miner's hats. In some instances gangs of friends were lined up four deep behind their anchor man at the bar.

Talk was kindly, sometimes hilarious.

"Hey, Toby, where did our old pard Farncomb go? Hain't seen him around lately."

"He went to New York to cut a swell."

"Well, good for him. He can afford it."

"Sure wish somebody would take hold of my property and develop it like they did his."

"Yeh, but is yours any good?"

"What? Listen, when they finally get my property built up into a company, they'll have to use four lead pencils a day to keep up with the business. Why."

"Bence, another round all around."

The fresh whiskey fumes blended well with sawdust scent.

"Lafe had a pet hand of jacks full on red sevens and still lost the pot. It had to be a crooked game."

"Somebody ought to show that son of a bitch that the muzzle to a mad forty-five is the entrance to the tunnel of hell itself."

"I'll thank you for the salt, Bence."

"Salt?"

"I always dust my beer with a little salt."

"Coming up."

"Well, me, I'm thankful that out here this is still a country where a man can switch his tail in peace."

One of the men along the bar had a duskier face than usual. In the gaslight Ransom made out he was a Southerner with some Negro blood in him. He looked a little like a smoked Swede.

Ransom poured himself a second glass. He sipped slowly.

But the drinking and the jolly talk didn't help much. That sudden jolt of rage was still racing through him.

He thought: "Maybe I ought to get out of here before I get into trouble again."

He concentrated on the merry faces around him. But look and listen as he might, he couldn't help but see in the faces lives as sad as his own.

After a while, as he swung around on his stool, his eyes happened to fall on a group of men sitting immediately behind him at a big round table. Some of them Ransom

recognized: Sumner Todd, a judge, Clifford Maule, a lawyer, Carleton Ames, editor of the new Deadwood *Pioneer*,
John Clemens, another lawyer, and several members of a
mining combine just in from California.

Looking them over, it struck Ransom as unusual that for
middle-aged men there wasn't a gray hair in the bunch.
Even baldheaded Maule had completely black brows and a
heavy black beard. All were in the prime of life. Ransom had
never been East, to New York or Philadelphia, but he imagined that this was the way the Eastern bigwigs looked as
they sat around drinking at their clubs.

Newspaperman Ames was talking, one eye on the California investors. "One thing about it. Extinguishment of the
Indian title to the Black Hills is bound to make us all rich."

Maule drank up with a noisy swallow. "Ha." Maule's bald
head had the hue of a peeled egg. "At the same time that it'll
fill our lovely valley with every crazy kind of prospector in
the world." Maule had a wide mouth that was always in
motion, writhing, smiling, pouting. He also had the habit of
punctuating everything he said with a stubborn roll of his
head. "No form of lunacy can equal the damned-fool crazi-
ness of the damned-fool prospector."

Ames shook his head. His blond hair slid out of place a
little. "Oh, I wouldn't say that, Clifford. Just take a look
around here tonight. Taking them all in all, this is a pretty
good class of people. They may wear their hair a little long
maybe. A few could use a shave. Clothes are a little rough-
neck, yes. Those big leather boots and big hats might be a
little out of place in a city like Chicago. But otherwise, why,
look at 'em. A bunch of real virile characters. Proud. Fearless. And what dignity, what patience, in their faces. No
complaints. If things aren't any better today, it's because
they can't be any better. No blame on anyone."

"Then what about that shooting here the other night?
That Bullneck fellow getting gunned down?"

Ransom sat a little straighter. He wondered if the group had recognized him.

"Bullneck had it coming. He was so crooked he could spit around a corner." Ames turned to Judge Todd. "By the way, Judge, nobody's brought in a complaint on that yet, have they?"

"No."

Ames nodded. "You see, there you go. No complaints. The coward never started West, the weak died on the way."

Maule sneered. "What about those road agents hereabouts? That Curly Griffin and his gang, for instance?"

"Look, when we finally become a full-fledged state, we'll take care of the Curly Griffins in our own good time."

"Lord, let's hope so."

John Clemens had nothing to say. He drank moderately. The California investors sat smiling to themselves and waggling fat brown cigars.

Judge Todd mused aloud. "Strange case, that Curly Griffin fellow. They say he's a whale of a fellow when sober, and hell turned loose when drunk."

Ames held up his whiskey as if in toast. "Gentlemen, Deadwood has to be a great place. It just simply has to be. It is the one hope left in the Western Hemisphere that man shall erect, in time, a society in which no one individual and no one clan shall be accounted superior to the other."

Ransom spotted a gray louse wriggling on the soiled woolen shirt of the miner next to him along the bar. The louse was fat, couldn't quite make it over the prickly edge of the miner's gray shirt collar. It wriggled and struggled. It made Ransom feel delicate in the belly and he shrank from the miner. As he watched, yet another louse appeared from under the fold of the collar. It crawled as if following a well-marked route. It bumped into the rear of the first louse; stopped. It waited for the first louse to make it over the edge. The two of them were exactly like a pair of fat ewes, one waiting for the other to make it over a low spot in a prickly fence. Had there been more lice, Ransom was sure they too would have waited in line.

A thought abruptly shot through Ransom's mind: "It was terrible of me to fall into Katherine's arms the minute I got woman hungry."

Ransom poured himself another tumbler of red whiskey, drank half of it down in a single draft. His stomach reacted with a single hopping motion.

Another thought shot through his mind. "Better get rid of Katherine, somehow."

Ransom downed the rest of the whiskey. He gripped his empty glass so hard it began to scrinch in his hand.

When he looked again at the miner's soiled collar, the two lice had vanished.

There was suddenly a hell-fired commotion outside No. 10. The next thing, a man on horseback came larruping in, banging the swing doors apart.

"Speaking of the devil!" Maule exclaimed.

Ransom instantly recognized the wild horsebacker. Curly Griffin. Ransom slowly sat very erect.

People in the front part of the saloon scrambled out of the way. Chairs upset, tables tipped over. The horse craned up its head, its eyes wild opals. Foam lay sprettled over its roan coat. The rider too had wild eyes, of such a light-blue cast it was hard to see where the blue began and the white left off. Curly had been drinking.

Curly was a handsome fellow. A lash of silver-blond hair lay across his forehead, his shoulders swung wide on each toss of the horse, his clean-run legs held the horse clipped close. His clothes were flashy: a bossy felt hat, blue-serge suit, high black leather boots, silver spurs. He was armed with gun and bowie knife and wore a pair of dried human ears on his watch chain.

Curly's eyes roved savagely silver over the crowd. He gave himself a great stretch, insulting.

For a moment all sound fell away.

Curly called out loud and clear. "Bence, set me up a horse's neck." Curly gave his roan a lash over the butt with the ends of the reins. "Hup-up, Queenie, we'll take it right at the bar."

The horse moved forward in a series of restrained prancings. It couldn't rear because of the hanging gas lamps and it couldn't run even tight-stepped because of the crowd. Its shod hoofs crunched rolls of thunder into the board floor.

Bence blinked; then, equal to the occasion, set out a bottle.

Curly sneered. "Now, Bence, don't rouse me up with the sight of just one bottle. Set 'em all out. Every last one of your whiskeys. I'm particular about my firewater. I likes a chance to select."

Bence obliged him.

"Bence, friends, this is my night to howl." Curly poured himself a full glass of whiskey and downed it all in one fluid motion. "Bence, I'm a wolf on a horse tonight."

Bence nodded suavely. It was all in the course of business.

The roan kept stepping and staging about. Its never-slip caulks cut little half-moons into the wooden floor. Curly rode her with a snug rein.

Bence waited.

Curly rose in his stirrups and hurled his empty glass completely across the saloon into the fireplace. There was a crash and a tinkle of glass. "Well, Bence, friend, who shall I shoot tonight?"

"How would I know? I don't know what's your mind."

"Bence, I've decided it's gonna be you."

"Hold on, why me?"

Curly threw back his head and laughed. "C'mon, Bence, you know why."

"No, I don't. Why?"

"Or would you rather I ate you blood raw?"

"What'd I do?"

"Bence, you blowed on me and my boys. So I'm going to tongue you."

"Naw, now."

"You peached on me, Bence. Told the Army where I was hiding."

"Naw."

"Bence, where do you want to be shot? In the head or the heart?"

"The jury won't go for either one, Curly. They'll hang you as sure as shootin'."

"I'd like to see the goddam jury that'll hang Curly Griffin." Curly tipped back his bossy felt hat. "C'mon, Bence, where do you want to be shot? In the head or the heart?"

Bence could be as cool as the next man in the face of a young bully's black caprice. "I'll take the head."

"Why the head?"

"I don't like holes in my shirt."

"Goddam the shirt."

"But a hole will spoil it, Curly."

"All right, damn you, then remove it. Because I favor the heart."

Bence obliged him. Bence soon stood waiting in his red underwear.

"By God, Bence, you're the only true bullhead here. All the rest of these honyockers are yellow-bellied cowards. Terrible Turks in speech but white mice in action. Bence, maybe you didn't blow on me after all."

"You're welcome."

Everybody waited for something awful to happen.

Horse and man undulated at the bar. "But I want to tell you something though, Bence. If you ever open that big loose blab of yours again, I'm gonna shoot you down for sure at last." Again the horse reared and Curly rode it easy.

"You're welcome."

Curly sulked with his insulting smile for a moment; then,

exploding within, came up a raging cat. "Damn you, Bence, I'm gonna shoot you anyhow." There was a yellow flashing pop at Curly's side.

Suddenly Bence began to squeal his anguish as he slowly crippled down out of sight behind the bar. Bence hadn't believed Curly was going to do it.

Curly leaped off his horse onto the bar. He lay his smoking gun down. Then he jumped down behind the bar and hauled up Bence's head. Holding Bence's head viselike down on the round edge of the bar, Curly reached into the flaccid mouth and pulled out the tongue by its tip and cut it off with his bowie knife. He threw the tongue on the bar. Like a little red pepper it lay for all to see. With a cry of triumph Curly picked up his smoking gun and leaped back on his horse.

There were awful gasps.

Somebody had to do something.

Ransom found himself standing in a cleared space in front of Curly and his horse. Ransom stood quietly. A fatherly voice spoke in Ransom's mind: "Aim with the eyes, never the gun. Gut-shoot him."

Curly stared down at Ransom. "Well, and what do you want, sonny?"

Ransom touched his right hand to his right eye. "Shoot me down too."

Curly jerked erect. His horse moved under him. "Hold on. Why?"

"Go on. Smoke me." Ransom smiled full white teeth. He felt all men hang on him. His lean belly was hot. His green eyes were cold. "No risk to you."

"You better dust, kid. This ain't your play."

"Smoke me." Ransom flicked a look at Curly's smoking gun. "You already got your jack out."

"You got you some kind of ace in the hole then, I take it?"

"No, no ace. Just the king of spades maybe." Ransom's fingers hung loose.

"And that'll top my jack?"

"Let's try it."

Curly sneered elaborately. "You little doughgut you, that's the queen of hearts you're holding. Better yet, the whore of hearts. I know all about you and Kate. She's old enough to be your mother, kid."

"Whore of hearts, is it?"

"One man's trash another man's treasure."

"Smoke me."

Curly gave himself another great lazy stretch. "You're just full of barbwire whiskey, kid. You better get high behind before I irrigate your belly."

"Try it."

Curly swung his gun up and laid it between the ears of his horse. He aimed it right at Ransom's eyes. "All right, kid, take a good look at my gun. See that bullet in there all ready and set for the jump?"

Ransom could tell Curly's next move by the skim on his eyes. Ransom smiled. "Let drive, if that's your mind. I've got nothing to live for anyway."

"Pull, kid, and I'll shoot you down like a sheep."

Ransom did. He gut-shot him. Curly was quicker, but he was sitting on a stirring horse and his bullet missed. Ransom felt the bullet pass between his arm and his body. It whacked into the base of the bar behind him.

Curly leaned over his horse's neck. Blood rushed out of Curly's belly as if he were vomiting out of his navel. Then Curly fell to the floor.

There was a collective sigh. Then a roar all at once.

"Good riddance!" cried a gleeful voice.

Troy Barb quickly ran up and secured the horse.

Ransom opened his gun, picked out the empty shell with thumb and forefinger, dropped the shell in a cuspidor, clink, replaced it with a fresh cartridge from his belt.

Before men could beat him on the back and thank him for daring to stand up to the terrible Curly Griffin, Ransom ducked outdoors.

Katherine stood waiting for him in the entryway, all smiles, dressed in stunning ivory velvet. "Come in, Ransom." Before he could stop her, she stood on her toes and kissed him. "All is forgiven." Then she took him by the hand and led him to his easy chair in front of the bay window. She unbuckled his belt and gun and placed them on the table. With a slight pressure she made him sit down.

His eyes were two hells.

"How are you, Ransom?"

"Fine."

"Poor boy. Come."

She removed his boots. She lifted first his right foot up on the footstool and then his left foot. Smiling, with the air of a woman who knows she is hauntingly beautiful, she stroked his ankles and soothed his feet over the instep and massaged his calves. Then, as a final touch of wifely solicitude, with thumb and forefinger she took the tuck out of his socks between the big toe and the little toes.

His eyes became two pools of silvery green.

"What's the matter, honey?"

"I don't deserve that."

"Ransom, I want my husband happy."

His belly was full of disaster. He felt as if he had ingested a couple of plates of gray ashes soaked in moldy vinegar. He thought: "I'm never going to get out of this."

Again she reached in with thumb and forefinger, prettily, and unbuttoned his collar.

"Don't do that."

"Why not? You're my husband, aren't you?"

"I'm not worth it."

"Come now, my husband. A handsome man never needs to apologize."

"Kate, I have a soul of mud."

"Ransom."

He made a last effort to push her away. Around her it was always as if his belly was in the grip of the suck of a whirlpool drawing him over and down. "Kate, what miserable dogs we all are."

She took the pushing, and still managed to smile. "Why, Ransom, what a mean thing to say."

The hells in his eyes came back. "Kate, I just killed another man."

She shrank visibly. She seemed to wither ten years before his very eyes.

"Kate, why don't you just get an ax and cut off my right hand? At the wrist? Please?" He settled deeper into his easy chair.

She made a sound as if she'd at last lost salvation.

"Or else get the butcher knife and cut off my johnny-nods."

A withered savage grandmother, torn from her favorite pestle and mortar, looked out at him from Katherine's brown eye.

"Kate, I'm slowly getting worse and worse." He rolled his head from side to side. "Somebody had better gun me down too. And that right soon."

A violent shudder went through her body, from her eyes to her toes.

"Oh, you needn't worry that they'll come and get me. Yet. They're all too happy that I did what I did. As happy as a bunch of sheep that somebody got the wolf for them."

"Who was it this time?"

"Curly Griffin."

"Him?" She clapped hand to mouth.

"Yes. The one you wondered if I was a lookout for."

"I was wrong then."

"Did you know him?"

Her brown eye held steady.

"He said he knew you, Kate."

"Please, Ransom."

"He called you the whore of hearts, Kate." Vomit threatened to erupt in the back of his throat.

She jerked her face away. "So I am Kate to you now, Ransom?"

"Yes."

"Well!" Katherine's chin slowly set out. "Well! I've had enough at last." She snapped around, turning her back on him, and gathering up her long ivory velvet gown, slowly moved across the room and went upstairs.

"At last."

Katherine slammed the door to the bedroom upstairs. Hard. Violently. The green house rang with it.

Again the slamming set him off. A frenzy of primitive rage flashed all through him. He came up out of his easy chair moaning with it. He grabbed up his gun from the table and in three bounds was up the stairs. He kicked open the bedroom door.

She had just turned up the lamp. She whirled around. "Magnus!"

Old words burst loose in him. "You're a bad woman!" He took hold of his gun with both hands and deliberately aimed it at her belly, at where that wrinkled smiling scar would be under her dress, at their coming baby. "Better that we both should die."

"Help, help! My husband is killing me! Oh, God, God!"

He fired.

She dropped.

He stood over her and emptied the rest of his gun into her, five more shots, one of them into her good eye. "Now for sure I'm never going to get out of this."

At dawn neighbor ladies came to lay out Katherine.

Later in the morning a committee of miners came to get Ransom. The committee was led by Troy Barb.

Troy Barb said, "This time you have went too far."

Ransom handed over his gun.

"Well, I see you agree."

Ransom said nothing.

"Well, pard, I guess it's my duty to tell you that we're gonna hold court on you at the foot of Mt. Moriah." Troy Barb took Ransom firmly by the arm. "Come along."

Ransom went along quietly.

A committee member said, "We boys should've held court on him the first time."

Troy Barb said, "I thought of it personal."

"Why didn't you talk up then?"

"Because we was partners. But now he's just went too far."

Another committee member said, "I like the kid. Is this gonna be a kangaroo court?"

"This'll be a miners' court." Troy Barb's moon eyes couldn't quite hold up to the committee man. "Fair and square."

The first committee member said, "Good. Because it's high time he took the big jump, the way he's killing off people."

They tied Ransom's hands at the wrists behind his back.

A green sun shone on staggered pines. The granite peaks glistened. The October sky bloomed blue. The town brook trickled. A downhill breeze touched the cheek.

The bad news spread like a great stage whisper. Miners streamed down out of the Hills. They gathered in a black mass at the foot of Mt. Moriah. Some stood on stumps. Some climbed partway up the sides of Mt. Moriah to get a better view of the proceedings. Their dust-rimmed eyes were grim. Most were armed.

Across the brook, women in long dresses also formed lines on high ground.

A dozen men worked at setting up a gallows.

Ransom stood waiting. Troy Barb's grip on his arm was tight.

Clusters and groups of men kept coming down out of the Hills. The crowd thickened and thickened. The multitude of men was like a great thunderhead gathering weight and dimension.

At last the gallows was ready. A noose hung dangling over an upright salt barrel.

Then four well-dressed men came striding down the gulch: Sumner Todd, the judge, Clifford Maule and John Clemens, the lawyers, and Carleton Ames, the newspaperman. Their black top hats stuck out above the crowd. All four wore six-shooters under their black coats. Maule had a gimpy leg and had to hurry to keep up with the others. The black crowd made way for them. The four stepped toward Ransom solemnly.

"I got 'm!" Troy Barb cried. "He came as meek as a mouse."

Judge Todd nodded, and stood off to one side a little. Lawyer Maule glared darkly at Ransom. Newspaperman Ames watched with darting eyes.

Only John Clemens had a kind word for Ransom. "I'm sorry, son."

Ransom's lips remained silent in his black beard.

Maule hopped up on a stump. He surveyed the grim crowd.

Silence spread through the gulch. A half-fallen pine creaked where it hung caught on another pine.

Maule lifted his right arm. "Men!" His heavy voice resounded in the gulch with gravelly effect. "Men, this is a sad day for us all. As I need not remind you." He turned to all sides, limping as he did so. "But we must do our duty."

Solitary crags glistened gold in the sun.

"Men, one of us has killed his wife. This is a crime in any society." Maule stared each man in the eye. "We are still not legally a part of the United States of America, so we cannot call on the law of the States to handle this matter. Yet law we must have in this out-of-bounds territory. If we do not behave as a law-abiding people in this place, with such natural law as we already have in our hearts, we can never expect the States to accept us in time as an equal, a sister state among sister states."

Silence. Pines. Stones.

"There is no doubt that the eyes of the country, yes, the world, are upon us to see what we shall do in this matter." Maule's large lips writhed. "And in particular our attitude toward our women will determine what our sister states will think of us. All men know that the eternal feminine is needed to draw men upward." Maule's eyes seethed. "Therefore we have gathered together in a miners' court to render justice and to punish the guilty. Is this agreed?"

All the black hats nodded.

"Now in the matter as to how we shall conduct this miners' court, what is your wish?"

There were various shouts. "We got a judge here in the crowd. Let him preside. He knows the business."

"Sumner Todd?"

"That's the one."

Again Maule held up his hand. "Then it's agreeable to you that Sumner Todd shall serve as judge?"

There was a general shout of assent.

"Let's have a show of hands. Those in favor of Sumner Todd serving as judge raise their right hand."

Right hands came up like flights of arrows.

"Against."

The hands fell down.

"Carried."

Maule turned to Sumner Todd. "Judge, now it's your show." Maule stepped down off the stump.

Judge Todd looked slowly around. He spotted a light

spring wagon standing off to one side. "Somebody roll that democrat over here. We'll use that as the bench."

"Good idee. Hurray for the judge." The democrat was rolled forward.

Judge Todd climbed solemnly into the democrat and sat down on the spring seat up front. He took off his top hat and placed it carefully on the seat beside him. He had a forehead like a horse hoof. He took his gun and placed it on his top hat. "Now. As to the first order of business. We shall have to appoint a prosecutor. Anybody have any objection to Clifford Maule as prosecutor?"

There were no objections.

Judge Todd looked down with a crinkly smile as Maule, pleased, stepped up to the democrat bench. "Will the counsel for the state kindly remove his hat in respect of the law?"

There was a cheer. "Hurray for the judge. That's letting him know who's boss."

Maule obeyed the request. The sun shone gold on his bald head.

Judge Todd pursed his mouth until his upper lip touched the point of his nose. "Who'll serve as counsel for the defense?"

John Clemens removed his hat and stepped forward. "I will, Your Honor."

"Is that agreeable to all assembled here?"

It was.

"And who will serve as hangman?"

All eyes flicked from the judge to the condemned and back again.

"Anybody?"

Troy Barb raised his hand. "I will, if nobody else will."

Judge Todd stared down at Troy Barb. "I understand that you're known as the best knot-maker in town."

"I try my best."

"It is so ordered."

The second committee member spoke up. "What have you got against the kid, Troy?"

"Nothing. Just that he's starting to kill too many people."

"Now as to the jury," the judge went on. "Shall we pick twelve men good and true? Or shall we let the entire assembly serve as jury?"

There was a tangle of voices.

The judge asked for another show of hands.

Most wanted the gulch to vote on it as a whole.

"So be it." Judge Todd looked down at Ransom. "The prisoner will now climb the salt barrel. Help him up there, you."

Ransom was helped onto the barrel.

Troy Barb climbed up beside Ransom and dropped the noose around his neck. Then he jumped down.

"Poor feller," the second committee member murmured. "It's gonna be no breakfast forever for him."

A cortege came from behind Ransom's green house and headed down the street toward them. In a moment there was a commotion at the far edge of the black mob.

Judge Todd sat up. "Hold on, what's that coming?"

Maule looked. "I fear that's the body of the victim, Your Honor."

"Ah." Judge Todd stood up. "Rather an odd time to be holding a funeral. But since the fact is a fact, we'll take advantage of it." He raised his voice. "Hey you, out there. Bring the body to the bench."

The cortege hesitated; then pushed into the crowd.

"Set it down in front right there so that it may be part of the evidence. Corpus delicti."

The pine coffin was set on a couple of stumps for all to see. Although cut but an hour before, the boards of the coffin were already sweating rosin.

"Open the coffin," Judge Todd ordered.

"But judge," one of the pallbearers protested, "she ain't fit to be seen."

"Why not?"

"She's all shot up."

"All the more reason to put the body on view."

"Well, if you say so."

The coffin was opened. Katherine lay eyeless under the sun.

Ransom closed his eyes.

Judge Todd nodded down at Maule. "You may begin for the state, counsel."

Maule reascended his stump. He faced the crowd. "Friends. Fellow miners. The fate of a fellow miner is in your hands. Listen carefully to the evidence and the pleadings. Then consult your heart and your conscience and render justice according." Maule next turned to Ransom. "I too am sorry that it had to come to this." Maule paused for emphasis. "But!" Maule made a pass over his bald head with his hand. "You, Earl Ransom, you finally went too far!" Maule took a deep breath. "Yes, you did the community a favor, in a way, when you got rid of both Bullneck Bill and Curly Griffin for us. We all agree that they were no good to anyone any more and that they deserved killing." Maule paused for another big breath. "But when you killed a wife and possible mother"—Maule tolled his head—"no, no, that was going too far. No matter what the cause may have been to make you do it, that was going too far."

A far voice hallooed down the gulch. "Here comes the stage, gents!"

Everybody turned to look.

A plume of dust appeared at the far turn of the main dugway.

PART FOUR

Magnus King

1

Magnus rode up on the boot beside the driver.

As the stagecoach rounded the last curve above Dead-wood, Swifty the driver let the ribbons out some and cracked his long whip just once. The six bay horses, already scenting fresh grass below, surged into their collars like cyclones.

Swifty allowed himself a slow weathered smile. "I always likes to give my horses their head on this last stretch." The smile crinkled all the way back up under his ears. "It's a good way to jolt the cricks out of your back. My passengers always appreciates it."

Magnus didn't smile much. He had a bad back. It was the

main reason why he'd asked for a seat up on the boot. He wanted to know when the bumps were coming.

The clicking yellow wheels began to spin faster and faster, until they became the color of gold. Twenty-four hoofs beat a swiftly increasing snare-drum cadence on the pocked road.

Soon the wind of their going tugged at Magnus' black hat. His white beard flattened out against his cheeks, away from his lips. He braced himself. Dust rose above the boot. He had to slit his eyes against the exploding tan plumes. The worst dust always came right after they'd hit a puffhole.

They whirled past the first log cabin on the outskirts of Deadwood.

Then Magnus spotted a thick black crowd of people at the foot of a steep hill. He sat up. That accounted for the deserted look higher up the gulch.

He next spotted the gallows. Ah, a necktie party. "Let's hope that's not my boy, after all the hunting I've done for him."

Swifty spotted the hanging too. "Another poor bastard born to be hung," he called over the rattle of their going.

Iron knuckles of rock protruded into Main Street. Three dogs challenged the lead team.

Swifty, manipulating the lines, added, "Well, for his sake, let's hope the drop is deep and the rope tender."

The Franklin Hotel entrance hove up ahead.

Swifty hauled up on the ribbons and let go with a great "Whoa!" Knots of muscles as big as potatoes popped out on his forearms. He kicked the brakes on with his free foot.

The red stagecoach squealed to a stop precisely in front of the hotel and directly across from the Pillbox Drug Company.

For a fleeting second all the black figures below swiveled white faces toward the stagecoach; then, all seeming to blink at once, turned back to the business at hand.

"Hello," Swifty said, "nobody here to take the horses. That hanging down there has got down to where somebody's gonna need religion real soon." Swifty stared at the black mob a moment longer, then thrust the reins in Magnus' hands. "Here, hold these while I go tie the lead team to a hitching post." Swifty more fell than jumped to the ground.

A cowboy jumped out of the coach first. He let down the steps, then helped a woman and two children to the ground. The woman took one look at the gallows and then hurried the children into the hotel. The cowboy stopped to roll himself a cigarette, lit up casually, and then, with a swift look up at the blue October sky, bowlegged toward the black crowd.

Swifty came striding back. "You can tie the ribbons on the butt of the whip there, Doc, if you wanna."

Magnus did as instructed, and then climbed down.

Swifty looked down at the crowd again. "Bet there's a woman at the bottom of that."

Magnus nodded. "Some poor fellow's got over onto somebody else's range." Magnus' voice was rough and rusty. To himself Magnus thought: "By the Lord, it better not be the son I'm looking for."

"Same difference." Swifty also threw a quick look up at the October sky. "Let's amble over and get in on the drop at least."

"Lead on."

They followed the cowboy into the crowd.

Magnus walked with slim courtly grace. He combed his bush of a white beard with a quick lightly touching whip of his fingertips, almost absent-mindedly. His white hair made him stick out in the crowd. He was like a white ram in a drove of black sheep.

Magnus climbed a pine stump for a better look at the young man up on the salt barrel. Magnus winced to see that the noose was already around the young man's neck.

After a long hard look, Magnus heaved a sigh of relief. "No, thank the Lord, that's not my boy Roddy. Too old. Roddy would have been twenty this year. While this fellow is at least twenty-five." Magnus' black eyes crinkled in memory. "And this fellow is too tall. Roddy would never have got to be this big. No, thank God, it's not Roddy."

Again Magnus casually touched a hand to his beard. Magnus' beard wasn't quite smooth, suggesting that the skin beneath was rough, like deep meadow grass barely covering old pocket-gopher mounds.

The judge was speaking from his perch on the democrat. "Just a moment, counsel. I think at this point the bench should make it perfectly clear that while this may be a miners' court, that does not make it any less a court of democratic law." The judge had eyes like two curls of cigar ash. "I want it clearly understood right here and now that this man will have a fair trial. If you the jury give him this and find him not guilty, he goes scot-free. Even if I have to defend him myself." The judge touched a gun lying on his top hat. "But if, after a fair trial, you find him guilty, he shall hang, so help me God, and I'll be the first to help kick the barrel out from under him. If necessary." The judge's teeth came together for a second like the jaws of a vise. "But until you find him not guilty, or guilty, the man who touches a hair on his head will have to do so over my dead body." The judge touched his black gun again. "There shall be true buckskin justice here in Deadwood today."

A voice nearby said, "Judge Todd is a swell stiff, ain't he? It's good to know we got us a real lawman running this show."

Another voice said, "Oh, I don't know. I'm pretty much against courts myself."

The first voice said, "You don't believe in the law?"

The second voice said, "Sure I believe in the law. It's just that I'm plumb adverse to courts."

"But that's blasphemy, man."

"Oh, no it ain't. And I'll tell you why it ain't. It's because of them law wolves that gets into 'em. When them law wolves can't get you through a gate they've fixed up special to catch you, they puts up another fence and lays for you cross lots."

Judge Todd nodded down at a baldheaded man. "You may continue your opening statement for the state, Mr. Maule."

Maule went on from his stump. "Yes, you Earl Ransom, you finally went too far. Oh, we admit our indebtedness to you, that besides getting rid of two of our bad men for us, you also found our true mother lode for us. But this"— Maule pointed a long arm at an open coffin—"this murder of your own sweet wife in a crime of passion . . . no!"

A dead woman in a coffin? Magnus rose on his toes to see if he could catch a glimpse of her. But from his vantage point he couldn't quite manage it. All he could see of her was the white point of her nose.

"Told you there was a woman at the bottom of it," Swifty said.

Maule limped about where he stood. "It's not that the state is in a black passion for revenge. No. It's more that the law simply cannot tolerate the philosophy that says, 'Pistols for two and whiskey for one.' And of course the law certainly cannot tolerate the killing of a woman by a crybaby lover. This is real life and not life as lived by a character in a red-cover novelette!"

"Let's hang him and get it over with," a hard-looking stiff called from the rear. "We've got more important things to do than stand around all day listening to you, Mr. Maule."

"Don't worry," another stiff cried, "our killer is going to get it right straight along."

Judge Todd glared in the direction of the interruption. The democrat squeaked as he shifted positions.

Maule went on. "Human society has learned that the only preventative of crime is a swift and terrible retribution. To cure the killer in us, the only prescription is a stout cord and a good drop. All men finally learn that there is no place on earth so desolate and remote but what the vengeance of mankind will find him out. We, even here in this off-limits territory, simply cannot tolerate the notion that the crook, the robber, the assassin, the blood-stained murderer are nature's favorites."

Magnus grimaced to himself. Ha. That was where the fellow was clearly wrong. The robber and the murderer once were nature's favorites. In fact it could be argued that the robber and the murderer were thoroughly bred into mankind. "And that part of us, the Old Lizard, now lives in a paralyzed state in all of us. And if it wouldn't be for pain, we'd still worship blood stained winners."

Swifty spoke up, soberly, more to himself than to Magnus. "It is pitiful to see such a fine fellow, a fellow Mother Nature surely intended to be a hero, about to die like a dog with the rabies."

Words continued to issue relentlessly from Maule's wide mouth. "Earl Ransom, the state will seek to prove that you murdered your wife, that you did so most foully, that you did so most cruelly. Women are women, yes, that we all know. But we also know that for the sake of the perpetuation of the race, we've got to learn to live with them just as they are. Bless 'em, the women just can't help it if their hearts be of quicksand. Yet just because they are fickle by nature, that doesn't mean we men have the right to kill our women if they stray a little from the straight and narrow. Ha, actually, as we probably all know, most times it is just as often the fault of the man. It is he who leads her astray. It is he who is mostly the blackhearted monster, not she."

Magnus' black eyes turned somber. "Well now, here our good counsel has got a point. I'll go along with some of that."

Maule continued. "Because, truth to tell, in the man the sin of sex is as pernicious as the seed of the bull thistle, seemingly taking root sometimes even in midair."

A gruff voice behind Magnus muttered, "All we seem to get out of this Maule fellow is a lot of wind pudding."

A second heavy voice agreed. "That baldheaded fellow surely can keep himself in a fume for a long time."

Tears appeared in Maule's darting eyes. "The annals of crime have no record of a murder which more fully awakens the deepest execrations in the human heart than the murder of a sweet wife by a husband gone berserk. And especially so when this husband has killed a wife who was soon to bear him his firstborn. Lord God in heaven!" Maule wept audibly. "At the same time the annals of crime have no record of such a murder in which the guilty party was of such personable and likable nature. Look at him. Doesn't he look like a fine young man? A god among men, in fact? Friends, therefore it is that while my soul is revolted by what he did, at the same time it also is dissolved in pity for him. For this dark, lost, self-ruined life." Maule wept aloud some more. "Ah, God, look at this ruin of a man. Whom we must nevertheless hang by the neck until dead."

The young man up on the salt barrel with the knotted rope around his neck waited motionless.

Magnus' heart went out to the young man. Magnus thought: "Sure is a nice big-looking young fellow all right. Fine tower of a back. Handsome black beard and head of hair. A pity. A pity that so fine a stud of a man should have to die. With no offspring. What a waste."

Maule limped as he gyrated on his stump. "Your Honor, the state calls up as its first witness the defendant, Earl Ransom."

Judge Todd sat up. "Hold on here a minute. You have no other witness, counsel?"

"None, Your Honor."

"The defendant need not testify against himself, you know. Unless he agrees."

"That is understood, Your Honor. But he has already freely confessed."

Judge Todd peered across at Ransom. "You have no objection to testifying against yourself as a witness for the state?"

Instead of answering, Ransom tried to make room for his bearded chin inside the prickly noose.

"Did you understand the question, prisoner?"

Ransom looked up at the high hills.

Judge Todd sat very stiff. "Now we're not going to have it that you're not going to talk. That's contempt of court."

A red-bearded miner cried, "Aw, hell, judge, just give him a snort of red whiskey and swing him off."

The spring seat quivered under the judge. "You there, you with the red-hot beard, you shut up." Then to Ransom, the judge said, "Speak up, son. This is your chance."

A milky film slowly spread over Ransom's green eyes. "I have it coming."

"What?" Embers came alive in the judge's gray-ash eyes.

"I have it coming."

"You mean, you will be a witness for the state then?"

"If that's what you want."

"You're sure now that this is what you're willing to do?" The democrat rolled under the judge's motions.

"Yes."

"You're sure now?"

The red-bearded miner cried, "What the hell, judge, every man has a right to go to hell his own way. If that's what he wants, just give him a good drop and be done with it."

Judge Todd stared across at the red-bearded miner for a while.

The black crowd breathed, and waited.

Magnus knew how the young desperado felt. He'd once gone down that same path himself, that day after the shooting in Sioux City when he'd awakened to dreary daylight with one shotgun pellet in his brain and another in his throat. He'd never in all his life felt so miserably low and so utterly alone. Thank God the pellet in his brain had pricked the balloon of madness in him. While the pellet in his throat had given him, willy-nilly, the voice of iron gravity. Magnus wept. Where was poor Roddy now? "We know he got aboard the *St. Louis.* But when it docked in St. Lou, he wasn't aboard."

Judge Todd finally nodded. "You may proceed with the examination, counsel."

Maule swung in. "Your name?"

"Earl Ransom."

"Age?"

"I don't know."

"What?"

"I don't know."

"You mean you don't know when you were born?"

"No, I don't."

Maule threw a disbelieving look at Judge Todd. "Your Honor. . . ."

Ransom continued. "I can't remember anything from the time when I was a boy. I guess I was hit on the head pretty hard once."

"I see." Maule combed his bald head with deft fingertips. "Then you don't know where you were born either?"

"No."

The gruff voice behind Magnus said, "No wonder the kid always went around like a sleepwalker."

The other heavy voice said, "I noticed that too."

Maule gimped around on his stump. "Did you know your father?"

"No."

"You didn't?"

"I've never even had a dream about a father."

"But you have had a dream about a mother?"

"I think so."

"Ah, then you did know your mother?"

Again Ransom tried to make room for his bearded chin inside the noose. "Say, judge, would you have the boys grease this noose a little? It tickles so."

The red-bearded miner cried, "Good idea. The grease'll help for later on too."

Once again embers sparked in the judge's eyes. "Hangman? You there, Troy Barb, remove the noose."

Troy Barb's moon eyes opened in silvery glitter. "But, Your Honor, he'll escape. He's a dead shot."

"Not without a gun he isn't. Besides, I hereby appoint you to stand guard with a loaded shotgun trained on him. And while we're at it, free his hands too. Never let it be said that we asked a prisoner to speak the truth with the sword of Damocles hung poised over his head."

"I hears you." Troy Barb climbed up and removed both the noose and the rope binding Ransom's wrists. Troy Barb next asked for and got a loaded shotgun. Troy Barb swung the gun on Ransom's chest. "The first time you even raises so much as a little finger, you will get a quart of buckshot up your gizzard."

"Now, now," Judge Todd growled, "just stand guard. We'll do all the hard talking."

Ransom stroked his wrists to restore the circulation.

Black beards waited.

Judge Todd nodded down at Maule. "You may proceed."

Maule repeated his question. "Then you did know your mother?"

"I can't say."

A stone rattled down the side of Mt. Moriah.

Somebody called out, looking up, "What the hell you doin' up there, Larkin?"

"I prefers a high view of the operation."

Maule pushed in. "What do you mean, you can't say? You just said you've had a dream about her."

"Yes, I sometimes do dream about someone I think is my mother. But when I wake up, all memory of who this might be is gone."

Magnus touched the ends of his white beard with quick ginger fingertips.

Maule leaned back and eyed Ransom sideways. "Well then, anyway, you are a resident of Deadwood, aren't you?"

"Yes."

"You lived as man and wife with the deceased?"

"Yes."

"You had knowledge of her?"

Swifty, his eyes on Maule, swore under his breath. "Hey, you're off the scent, old man."

Magnus whispered to himself, "Why, this boy doesn't have any friends at all."

Maule continued. "Is it true that the deceased was in a family way?"

"So she said."

"In other words, two souls went to their death when you pulled the trigger?"

"Yes."

Swifty swore again. "Didn't I tell you? It's always threes with a woman."

Maule gave a little leap. "Then you admit you killed both mother and child?"

"Yes."

Swifty shook his head. "Man, man, the boy is on the steep downgrade now. Won't do him a particle of good to hit the brake block."

"You did in fact shoot your wife and child?"

Ransom touched a hand to his right eye. "Yes."

Maule turned to the crowd, a honeyed grin on his face. "Gentlemen of the jury, you have heard the prisoner confess the crime of double murder. You have seen for yourself that the prisoner has made no argument to save his life." Then Maule's face abruptly blackened over with a look of doom. "Thus the state has no other choice but to ask for the death penalty. That the prisoner die on the gallows, hanged by the neck until dead." Maule tolled his head, back and forth. "Ahh, so bad an ending argues a monstrous life. May the Lord preserve the soul of this man while we hang his body." Maule turned to Clemens with a short bow. "Your witness." Maule stepped down.

Magnus shook his white head. What a pity. "I'd surely like to know the whole story behind this thing."

A voice from a bunch of men sitting on the roof of a tin shop called out, "Get on with the hanging! We don't need any more fancy talk. Ain't he already admitted he's guilty?"

Another voice from the roof cried, "String him up! Let's go. We got gold to dig."

Still another voice called, "Seeing as how he don't like ticklish ropes none, what we ought to do is to tickle the son of a bitch to death instead."

"Yeh, it's a damned shame we're only going to hang him. I say, let's burn him to boot."

"By God, I agree. I'd go get the kindling myself even if it was three miles away."

But not all on the roof of the tin shop agreed. A shorty miner called out, "Give the man a fair shake, I says."

Instantly a fist fight broke out on the roof.

Judge Todd placed his hand on his gun where it lay on his top hat. He glared over at the fight. "Hey, you, there. You boys stay cool now. Remember, God didn't give you hands so that you could go around tearing each other's eyes out."

The fighters gradually quieted on the roof.

A black-bearded miner behind Magnus spoke out of the side of his mouth. "Think the judge can stop a real mob, if it comes to that?"

"Well, I should hope to smile he can stop a mob."

"You know, I notices that even the dogs has shut up, it's such a calamity."

"I've noticed that too."

"What I'm worried about is, maybe the kid might just make a break for it somewhere along here."

"Nah, not with old Troy Barb on the shotgun."

"Man, I'm not so sure."

"Nah, there'll be no evaporation here. Nothing like Elijah done anyway."

Just then the roof of the tin shop collapsed with a roar and a great crash. There was a hurtling explosion of dust, followed by a wild hullabaloo of cursing and groaning.

All eyes swiveled to the sudden gap in the crowd. For a few moments all sounds vanished as if sucked down a sink trap.

"Everybody all right there?" Judge Todd called out.

A dozen heads emerged from the wreckage. "Get on with the trial, judge. Tom Smith never did know how to build a roof."

Judge Todd smiled acidly. "Tom Smith hardly built it for a grandstand."

"Well, now, judge, suppose it was winter, and we was all wet snow, six feet deep?"

There was an opening laugh all around.

Judge Todd turned to Clemens. "Proceed with the witness, counsel."

Magnus shook his white head some more. "Let's hope the boy had a good reason for what he did."

Again Ransom touched a hand to his right eye.

Magnus started. "I'll be damned if that boy didn't look like he was fixing a monocle in place."

Clemens climbed up on the stump vacated by Maule. Clemens was a pink man after a summer in the sun. He had more the look of a beloved pastor than a lawyer. He had a way of looking at a man with his gentle blue eyes that not even the most hard-bitten could hold up to.

Clemens surveyed the crowd. His white fingers played with a watch chain. "Your Honor, if it please the court, before I begin my examination, I'd like to make a few introductory remarks."

"Hold on. What will be the purpose of these remarks?"

"To lay the proper foundation for the questioning."

"Ah. You may proceed. Though the court reserves the right to interrupt the remarks if counsel strays afield."

Clemens nodded. He studied the crowd some more. "Friends. Fellow miners." Clemens paused. He paused so

long it hurt. "There isn't a man here in Deadwood but what
he hasn't run away from something back in the States." A
trace of a smile touched the corners of his lips. "Now I like
to think that that's mostly because there's still a streak of the
glorious rebel left in us."

"Yes," Magnus thought, "yes, and I should have been hung
for what I did back in the States."

"We're different out here," Clemens continued. "We not
only tend to be more gloriously rebellious, but, as I think,
more courteous."

"And if I didn't hang for what I did back in the States,"
Magnus thought, "surely they shouldn't hang this fine speci-
men of manhood for what he did out here in Deadwood. If
there be any justice at all."

"Actually, rebellion and courtesy go together. Each one of
us has his peculiar past and so we're not inclined to stick our
noses into each other's affairs. The height of discourtesy out
here is for a man to ask another where he came from. To ask
that is to put oneself down as a fool."

Judge Todd and Maule listened very closely.

"And, in turn, courtesy fosters the free man. We all know
that when we are in the presence of courteous people we
feel free to be ourselves."

"This fellow Clemens means well," Magnus thought, "but
all his sweet talk isn't going to help the kid much, if I know
people at all."

"We are also different here in the West because we need
each other more. Because nature is more treacherous out
here. Because it is harder to scratch out a living out here.
Because we live farther apart from each other and are more
lonesome than usual. Thus, the loss of one good man can be
a catastrophe." Clemens paused for emphasis. "So, for all our
carrying of guns, we tend to be more sparing of life. We use
our guns, yes, and on each other sometimes, yes, but we use
them somewhat as nature uses the wolf to eliminate the weak

and the old, so that only the healthy and the strong perpetuate the race."

From out of nowhere a pair of blue swallows suddenly appeared. The blue swallows dove through the gap in the crowd where the tin shop had collapsed, then circled high overhead. Their flight was erratic, frantic, as if they had lost something priceless.

Ransom turned his head to watch them.

Clemens also eyed the swallows for a moment.

The shorty miner who had put in a word for Ransom before the tin shop had collapsed abruptly showed up beside Troy Barb. The shorty miner touched Troy Barb on the shoulder. "Troy, let me ask you something. Wasn't you once partners with the kid?"

Troy Barb let his moon eyes stray away from Ransom for a second. "Yeh, I was."

"And didn't you share the same cabin with him?"

"What about it?"

"And didn't he give you half of his strike?"

"Yeh, he did."

"A little bit ago, when you put that noose around his neck, didn't you feel for him? A little bit?"

"Yeh, I felt for him all right. I felt for his left ear." Troy Barb cackled at what he thought was a pretty good crack.

"Here, here," Judge Todd snapped. "Order in the court. You there, back away now."

The shorty miner obeyed.

Clemens picked up the thread of his thought again. "Now this is pretty strong talk for one who was once a preacher in Philadelphia, and who is at the moment an armed lawyer in Deadwood. But this is what I've come to at last."

"This fellow Clemens can't hold the crowd," Magnus thought. "Somebody else is going to have to step in and do something if the kid is to have a chance."

"My friend Carleton Ames"—Clemens paused to look at where Ames stood scribbling—"put it very well the other night when he said, referring to our local miners, 'Look at them. A bunch of virile characters. Proud. Fearless. And what dignity, what patience, in their faces. No complaints. If things aren't any better today, it's because they can't be any better. No blame on anyone.' "

Ames couldn't help but beam a little.

"Perhaps our young friend Earl Ransom here has failed in this courtesy I spoke of. Perhaps he has failed in pride. Perhaps he has failed in patience. In any case, he has killed a woman purported to be his wife, and in your eyes he is now It."

Once more Ransom touched a hand to his right eye.

"I'll be hanged," Magnus exclaimed under his breath, "but that boy did make a gesture as if he were fixing a monocle in place."

"Some of you may wonder why anyone should stand up for a prisoner who has already freely admitted his guilt. Well, let me assure you that I am not here to help free the guilty at the expense of the guiltless. Not at all. But I am here to make sure that any punishment we impose on the guilty shall be a just one. Because if the sentence we finally do impose on this man is a just one, we are that much the more courteous ourselves. And patient. And free. Even if the accused cannot be those things, we should be."

The blue swallows flittered back and forth over the black mob.

Ransom slowly wyed his black head around as he watched the wild flight of the swallows. Then, blinking, he searched through the far-off granite peaks.

"I would like it very much if we here in Western America could somehow show the world what it means to be truly civilized. And to do it without much need for busybody law. An occasional people's court, and that's it."

Ransom next looked down at the face in the coffin.

"I shall have done my duty as a citizen of Deadwood and

as an officer of the court of justice if I can help you reach a verdict in this people's court that shall enable us, every one of us, to be more courteous, more patient, more free. Such a verdict will be worth more than all the gold we find."

Ransom yet once again touched a hand to his right eye.

Magnus abruptly stepped down off his stump and began to work his way toward the front. His black eyes were suddenly smoked over and his large liberal lips worked in his white beard. Despite his bad back he moved through the crowd in a crisp courtly manner.

"Yes, we here in Deadwood, where life and gold are so much exposed, we are all miners here together in the Black Hills of the soul."

Magnus pushed past the collapsed tin shop. As he did so, he spotted a mud nest. It was stuck to a portion of the north wall of the tin shop, which was still standing. In the nest were two little baby swallows. Their little beaks rested on the edge of the hardened mud like yellow-edged arrows set out for display.

Clemens' eyes turned a dreamy blue. "It is better that ninety-nine possible guilty ones should escape than that one innocent man should suffer."

A shadow enlarged along the west wall of the gulch.

Clemens' voice turned singsong. "There were ninety-and-nine that safely lay in the shelter of the fold. But one was put on the hills away, far off from the gates of gold, away on the mountains wild and bare, away from the tender shepherd's care."

Sighs moved through the black crowd.

But Maule wasn't taken in. "Good Lord, John," he broke in, "how can you stand there reciting such sentimental drivel in behalf of a fiendish killer, a devil incarnate, who took the life of a beloved wife and a coming child? Don't you understand that out here we worship the loyal wife and the innocent child?"

Clemens had a merciful blue smile for Maule. "Clifford, your approach is always so moral. So terribly moral. Your cold sense of justice is almost enough to make one wonder."

Maule flashed Clemens a furious look, then appealed to the judge. "Objection, Your Honor."

"On what grounds?"

"I object on the grounds that the last several remarks of the defense counsel are irrelevant, immaterial, and not germane to the issue at hand."

"Objection sustained." The judge shifted positions. The democrat creaked under him. He gave Clemens a pair of narrowed eyes. "In the nature of his role as prosecutor, Mr. Maule may very well appear to have a cold sense of justice. However, the court recognizes that his notion of justice is also of value to society."

"Thank you, Your Honor."

"And proceed with the questioning, please."

Clemens nodded. He turned to address Ransom. "Did I understand you to say that you did not know your father?"

Ransom sighed. "I have it coming."

"You're not answering my question."

"Better that we both should die."

"Ah, then you did know your father?"

"I don't think I've ever even had a nightmare about him. That I can remember."

"You have never seen him then?"

"All I know for sure is that I'm never going to get out of this. Thank God."

"Then you had no father?"

"And the sooner the better because I'm of no good to anyone."

"You've never had anyone then who was like a father to you? Even like an uncle?"

"Sam Slaymaker was. He was like a father to me. He found me on the prairie out of my head and almost dead. He took me under his wing and brought me up." Ransom heaved a deep sigh. "But then Sam was killed. And the first thing I knew I found myself killing the man who killed him." Ransom heaved another deep sigh. "It was like I had to do it. Like I couldn't stop it."

"Go on."

Ransom slowly put both of his hands to his head. He spoke very softly, almost whispering it. "My whole life . . . you know, it's been a case of where when I see one fellow shooting another, I've got to step in and shoot the killer. Like I've been ordered to."

"Been ordered to by who?"

"I don't know. That's just the trouble. I can't remember."

"Try and think now. Who?"

Ransom shook his head. He was exhausted. His eyes closed. "Look. I have it coming. That should be enough for all of you. Let me die like a man."

2

Magnus stood below the judge, hat in hand. He raised his hand for attention.

Judge Todd spotted the hand. "Yes?"

"May I have a word with the prisoner?" Magnus' husky voice barely carried. "I'd like to ask him a few questions."

Judge Todd cocked a hand to his ear. "A little louder, please."

Magnus repeated his request. "If it please the court."

"By what right?"

"As a friend of the court, amicus curiae."

"Old man, this is a trial. Not a shouting bee around a cracker barrel. Life and death are at stake here."

"I know. It is to that point I speak."

"Do you know the prisoner?"

"That's what I mean to find out."

Judge Todd grunted impatience. "Look, sir, this is not a missing person's bureau. What the court wants to know is, can you shed any further light on this murder?"

"That's what I also mean to find out."

"What's that? Speak a little louder."

"I'm sorry, Your Honor, that I am in bad voice. I was shot at years ago. One pellet happened to rip into my throat. It's never been the same since."

Ransom up on the salt barrel behaved as if he hadn't heard. He went back to staring at the granite peaks.

Judge Todd glared down at Magnus. "Old man, just what is your business here with the court?"

"I am looking for my son. I found trace of him in Cheyenne. Then I heard he'd gone on to Deadwood here."

"What's that got to do with the matter here before the court?"

"Let me ask the defendant a few questions and then perhaps it will become apparent to the court."

"What do you do? What's your profession?"

"I am a physician and surgeon."

Again Ransom seemed not to have heard. Ransom watched the two blue swallows flitter over and through the black crowd.

"You have a license to practice medicine?"

"I do."

"Ah, then you didn't come here to strike it rich like the rest of us."

"Your Honor, I shall have struck it rich if I find my son." There were tears in the corners of Magnus' eyes.

"And your name?"

"Magnus King."

"Then the name of the son you're looking for should also be King? If he goes under his right name?"

"Yes, Your Honor. Alan Rodman King. Though we mostly called him Roddy."

"Well, now, but the name of this young man here is Earl Ransom."

"So it appears."

All of a sudden, Ransom broke in clearly. "You know, it's a funny thing, but if you'll look around you, you'll notice that the father is never talked about much. It's always the mother and child."

Judge Todd stared across at Ransom.

Ransom went on, still speaking very clearly. "I noticed that with Sam. He never talked about his father." Ransom's green eyes opened wider. "For everybody I guess the last person you ever get to know is your father. He is the true alien."

Judge Todd chewed his lips to himself a moment, then turned to Maule. "You have no objection to Dr. Magnus King asking the prisoner a few questions?"

"If he is a doctor, none."

Judge Todd turned to Clemens. "And you?"

"No objection. We're all here to discover the truth."

Judge Todd stared down at Magnus for a few moments, finally said, "You may proceed, as a friend of the court, amicus curiae."

Magnus cleared his throat, harshly. "Your Honor, can I first direct a question at the bench?"

Judge Todd bristled. The spring seat on the democrat bounced under him. "Why the bench?"

"May I?"

"Proceed."

"May it please the court, I should like to ask this question: Since Deadwood is still not legally a part of the United States of America, by what authority do we try this man?"

"By what authority? Why! we take it upon ourselves to do this so that we may protect ourselves. Why! the very earth itself suffers when we persist in living in sin upon it. You know that."

Magnus touched his white beard, and nodded. "All right, fair enough."

The two blue swallows continued to fleet about against the looming dark hills.

Magnus took up his stance at the foot of the salt barrel. "Son?" Magnus tried to make his voice sound like in the old days back in Sioux City. "Son?"

An awakened lizard abruptly looked out of Ransom's green eyes. "Where the carrion is there will the vulture be."

"Roddy?"

"Doctors. Lawyers. Politicians. Undertakers."

A shudder rippled up through Magnus' slight frame. Then he got a grip on himself. "Roddy, don't you remember me, your dad? Roddy?"

"High-toned tapeworms crawling around in the belly of the country."

Magnus lifted all of himself into his black eyes. "How about a great big cow pill, Roddy?"

Ransom looked across at Judge Todd. "It's hard. But fair. So go ahead."

Magnus spoke as loud as he could, breaking through the unnatural husky scratch in his voice. "Woman, if you don't admit it, here and now, before God and my son, that you're a bad woman, bad! goddam you, I'll take a club to you."

Judge Todd, and Maule and Clemens, and everyone, stiffened astounded.

Ransom's green eyes half closed. "I'd give anything never to have gone to The Stinging Lizard."

Maule interrupted. "Your Honor, isn't all this a bit far afield?"

Judge Todd studied to himself for a moment, his eyes closing.

Maule continued. "It's not pertinent to the issue that I can see."

Judge Todd's eyes slowly opened. "The court finds it

instructive. This is a hard case. The questioning may proceed."

Magnus rose on his toes and filled his voice with tender yearning. "Hi, son. Play some bad with you."

Maule almost blew up. "Play some bad with you? What kind of nonsense is that, may I ask?"

Troy Barb trained his shotgun on Magnus. "Oh, no you don't."

Judge Todd cast a wondering eye on Magnus. "Explain."

"Your Honor, by bad I mean badminton. It's what my son and I used to play together."

Maule nibbled at his large lips. "Oh."

Judge Todd glimmered down at Troy Barb. "You can go back to guarding the prisoner, Mr. Barb." Then Judge Todd said to Magnus, "You may proceed."

Once more Magnus filled his voice with utmost yearning. "Roddy, don't you really know me? Because I know you. You're my son Roddy."

No answer.

"Roddy, what do you do when you catch a man sneaking around window-peeking?"

Ransom spoke almost automatically. "Let go with both barrels."

A pinched agonized cry escaped Magnus. "But you must be careful and not hit Mother, son."

"Hit Mother?" Ransom flashed a look at the white face in the pine coffin. "Why, I shot and killed my wife."

"Roddy, don't you remember at all that your name was once Alan Rodman King?"

"Just the same, I sure learned a lot from The Stinging Lizard."

Another strangled sound of anguish broke from Magnus. "So do we all."

"Let's get it over with, judge. I have it coming." Ransom grabbed hold of the noose and dropped it around his neck again. "Somebody kick the barrel out from under me. C'mon!"

Judge Todd stared across at Ransom for a moment, then said, "Guard, remove the rope."

Troy Barb wasn't sure he should let go of his shotgun. "Ain't we almost done, judge?"

"Remove that rope!"

"All right, Your Honor."

Troy Barb climbed up on the salt barrel and removed the noose; then stepped down and resumed his position, shotgun cocked.

Ransom blinked. And again he touched thumb and forefinger to his right eye.

Magnus wept. "Roddy, don't you remember our Uncle George Worthington's picture hanging in the sitting room? And about our Grampa Worthington in England? And all the Kings? And what they meant to us? And how the old earls all used to wear a monocle?"

Eyebrows in the black crowd arched up like teetering hairy caterpillars.

Ransom held his head to one side. "Sometimes it's just like an old dream is trying to dream in me again. And then I've almost got it."

"Yes, Roddy, yes."

"What a headache I've got. By the Lord, how it hurts." Ransom again put both of his hands to his head.

"Son, son, oh my son, try and remember. Nightmares don't lie."

Ransom's eyes became sunken. "Tight papers."

"Try and remember, Roddy."

"Booted cowboys and painted ladies."

"Son, son. Don't you recognize me at all? I'm here to help you." Magnus' back cracked with pain. "Let me drink that bitter cup for you. Please, son."

"It's always so dark out."

"It's me, your dad!"

"I better skip the country."

Troy Barb lifted his shotgun an inch. "Oh, no you don't, you wife-murderer."

"Down, Mr. Barb," Judge Todd growled. "Proceed, Dr. King."

The two blue shadows still dove around the gallows, searching frantically.

Magnus girded himself up to give it one more try. He cried as a tyrant might. "What the hell is my son doing in my bed!"

A haze spread over Ransom's green eyes. "Oh, what was your name in the States? Was it Rodman or Ransom or Bates? Did you murder your wife and fly for your life? Say, what was your name in the States?"

Magnus' voice was hoarse with brutal punch. "Damnation, woman, don't you know I don't hold with sons sleeping with their mothers?"

Ransom's eyes almost closed over. "Kind friends, you must listen to my sad story. I'm an object of pity. I'm looking quite hairy. I gave up my trade freighting King's Patent Pills to go looking for gold in the dreary Black Hills."

One of the frantic swallows sailed under the judge's chin. On the next pass the judge made a snatch at it with his hand and almost caught it. At that the two mad swallows soared aloft with weeping cries.

Ransom's eyes closed. "Don't go away. Stay at home if you can. Stay away from that city they call Old Cheyenne. Through rain, cold, and snow, frozen clean through to the gills, they call me the orphan of the dreary Black Hills."

A wide blue shadow appeared at the roots of the crowd.

Ransom's eyes drifted under closed lids. "We'll build a sweet little nest far out in the West and let the rest of the world go by."

Magnus took hold of the salt barrel Ransom stood on with

both hands and gave it a shake. "Goddammit, wake the boy up and chase him back to his own bed."

Ransom frowned profoundly. "All this racket waking me up."

Magnus' eyes became circles of white with dots of black, full of yearning magnetism. "There you go, Roddy. A little more and you've got it."

"When I already should be dead."

"Roddy!" Magnus cried. "Roddy, Roddy."

Ransom spoke as if from a great distance. "I'm ready if you are, judge."

At last, seeing he was getting nowhere, a great sigh escaping him, Magnus let his shoulders drop. "Your Honor, it's no use. It didn't work." Magnus tolled his white head. "It's like singing psalms to a dead horse." Magnus let go of the salt barrel. "I'm sorry I took up so much of the court's time."

Judge Todd looked kindly upon Magnus. "What was that all about?"

"It's no use, Your Honor."

"The court found it instructive."

"The court did?"

"Are you positive that this man is your son?"

"Yes."

"How positive?"

"As sure as I am of myself standing here. My blood tells me so. My conscience shouts to me that it is so."

"Hmm."

"A King is about to be hung here."

"You are absolutely sure that you have identified him to your own satisfaction?"

"Yes. The green eyes. That look of a little boy about to jump off a tree limb onto a sack swing, of here goes nothing. That little gesture of his where he seems to be fixing a monocle to his eye."

"Monocle, eh?"

"Yes. I taught him that. Just as my poor dead mother taught me. She was the daughter of an old earl in England and she knew."

The late-afternoon shadow became a deep pool all through the gulch, whelming up to the top of the salt barrel, engulfing Magnus up to the hips.

Judge Todd leaned forward. "Then this boy is of good blood."

"If you can call it that. With both of us having murder in our hearts."

"Hmm."

"Actually, if this young man is my son Roddy, I'm really the murderer. Not him. Because I'm the one that bent him."

"Explain that."

Magnus' white lips quivered in his white beard. "I once went off my rocker too. Mentally. Went berserk. In Sioux City. I accused my wife of infidelity. When she probably wasn't guilty at all. I finally shot her. And I in turn was shot down by my son. And he did it on my instructions. Because I'd taught him to shoot anybody that might be bothering her. Even if it was me."

"Even if it was you?"

"Yes."

"My God."

"Yes. Luckily neither my wife nor I died. But by the time I'd recovered from my wounds, my wife had disappeared. I later found out that an Indian friend of hers, Gooseberry June, had spirited her away. I never found her."

"And the boy?"

"He disappeared too. And ever since I've been looking for him. Because, among other things, I wanted to tell him that everything was all right. Not just forgiven, but all right. That I didn't kill his mother after all and that he didn't kill me either."

Judge Todd studied to himself for a while. "Well now,

what I don't quite understand is this: if this boy really **is** your boy, why is it then that he pretends not to know you?"

"I don't think he's pretending. Not necessarily, anyway. He may have lost his memory. Amnesia. You must remember that he went through an awful thing back there as a boy. And the human mind can take about only so much and then it tends to blot out what it can't handle. I know that I would have gone out of my mind if it had happened to me. In fact, I went off my rocker on a lesser thing."

"Hmm."

"It's a case of where the mind itself decides to save you by the grace of silence."

"Yes, I see."

"Well, perhaps it's just as well that he doesn't know. Because suppose I did convince him, awaken his memory, that he is my son, Roddy King, what good would that do?" Magnus threw up his hands. "You'd hang him anyway, wouldn't you?"

Judge Todd brooded to himself.

Magnus wept. He tugged with little jerks at his white beard. "But, oh! I so wanted to tell him that it was me who did the wrong, not he. That I was the jealous one, of my wife's love for him and of his love for her. As so often happens between father and son and mother. When a son gets over into a father's territory, you know, sits in his armchair at the head of the table sometimes, there's bound to be a clash someday."

"Were you arrested for trying to kill your wife?"

"I should have been. But I wasn't. She didn't sign a complaint. Nor did the law. I suppose the authorities figured I'd suffered enough and so didn't bother me. It took me a long while to heal. My face was all shot up. Truth to tell, there couldn't have been a better justice. For eleven years now I've not had one happy day. Not one happy day, ever. No love at all." Magnus blinked his black eyes shut against the pain of it. "Oh! how I wanted to tell my son that he never did have a debt of blood against me. Nor I against his mother."

"Hmm."

"You wouldn't let me be hanged in his place, would you, as the one who really was the guilty one in this matter?"

Judge Todd was shaken.

"Foolish question."

Judge Todd shook his haggard face to clear it. "Perhaps we should all pray to God for divine guidance in this matter."

Magnus slowly shook his head. "I'm afraid religion has long ago played out for me."

"It has?"

"Morality, no. Christ as my Saviour, yes."

Judge Todd stared down at Magnus. "Can I ask you a question?"

"Shoot."

"Would you say you're fully recovered? Sane again?"

"Yes. I think so." Magnus coughed a sad little laugh. "For one thing, that pellet in my throat made me slow to speak. And if that wasn't enough, that pellet in my brain finally put some sense in my head. Some lead in my mental feet, you might say."

Maule's face had built up into a vast sneer at all this, and he at last broke in. "Your Honor. Hasn't this just about gone far enough? We might be tempted to show some mercy for this poor lad on the basis of what we have just heard. But the truth is, and the fact is, that in killing his wife he also killed a mother. Now I submit, sir, that that just makes it a little too thick to take."

"By the Lord," Magnus exclaimed, remembering. "That's right, I almost forgot. Reference was made earlier to the fact that he'd killed a woman who was about to bear him a son, wasn't there?" Magnus took a step toward Maule. "Wasn't there?"

"Yes. She was in a family way."

"She was! Well." Magnus snapped even more erect. "How long has she been dead?"

"Since early this morning."

Magnus turned to the judge. "It's probably already too late . . . the Lord only knows how far she was along . . . but, Your Honor, may I view the body?"

"There she lies, corpus delicti."

"The foetus is probably dead by now. Though it wouldn't be the first time I performed a Caesarean. My boy here was born that way."

"You don't say."

Magnus stepped over to the pine coffin. He leaned down to look, stiffly, as much from a bad back as out of his courtly manner.

The black crowd watched intently.

It took Magnus a moment to see the face clearly. He had expected to find a young face, even a very young girl's face. What he saw instead was a young-looking middle-aged woman with a black patch over her left eye and a bloody gaping hole where the right eye should have been.

The black crowd waited. Some of the women on the higher ground tittered.

Gradually the true face won out over the expected face in Magnus' mind. "Oh!" A start, then a terrible shudder, swept through Magnus.

Judge Todd leaned down. "Well?"

Magnus almost fell down. Just in time he grabbed hold of the edge of the pine coffin.

"Well?"

Magnus turned slowly.

"Yes?"

Magnus tolled his head. "Your Honor, this woman could not have been in a family way."

"Why not?"

"I know for a fact she couldn't." Magnus avoided looking at Ransom.

"Why not?"

"Please the court, may I examine the body further?"

"For what purpose do you wish this further examination?"

"Examination will show that this woman once underwent a Caesarean operation."

"What? How? Hey? What's this?"

"Your Honor, I know this for a fact because as a surgeon I once performed a Caesarean on her." Magnus' voice almost quit on him. "This woman is my wife Kitty. She gave birth to a boy. During this operation I accidentally spayed her."

"What? Hey? This woman was your wife once too? And you . . . ? And this is your . . . ?"

"Yes. She couldn't have had another child."

A cry broke from Ransom. "So that's what that scar was!" The black crowd whitened.

Ransom slowly turned his head and looked down at Katherine. "That funny jack-o'-lantern scar."

Judge Todd gobbled.

The black miners prickled stiffly erect. They stood like a drove of mules stunned by a bolt of lightning.

Then Judge Todd got hold of himself. He nodded once down at Magnus. "Show us."

Magnus still couldn't get himself to look at Ransom. He turned heavily back to the coffin.

Ransom seemed to rise where he stood on the salt barrel. "My God, then she lied to me!"

Magnus undid Katherine's dress. His fingers trembled like the petals of a wiggling coneflower. He opened the dress just enough to show her stomach with its puckered scar.

A shudder, almost happy, moved through the mob of men.

Judge Todd dug a knuckle into his right eye. "So you say you accidentally spayed her?"

"Yes." Magnus spoke as though exhausted from an uphill run. "You see, Your Honor, I'd never seen a Caesarean done. In fact, this was one of the first ever done in the whole country. So I wasn't too sure of what I was doing. I had to make a guess as to what was the right thing to do. But I had to do it, take a chance or she would've died. And the child would've died."

"Lord."

Ransom's green eyes slowly crossed inward. "I'll have you know that no child has ever passed these portals."

Judge Todd chewed once. "But, Dr. King, you still have not proved that this man here is in fact and in truth the child you saved from this woman's belly."

Magnus' heart almost stopped beating. His black eyes rolled ghastly. He did not want to dwell on what might happen to Ransom's mind when Ransom fully realized what the judge had just said. Magnus toppled.

Clemens caught Magnus by the shoulders and kept him from falling.

Ransom did catch what the judge had just said. Ransom shifted slightly and looked straight at Magnus. Ransom's green eyes seethed hell. "Stranger, if what you say is true, then I've slept with my own mother."

A gentle sigh escaped the crowd. A mumbling sound rose from the lines of mothers on higher ground.

Magnus still couldn't look Ransom in the eye. Magnus shook off Clemens' hands; then with professional fingers covered Katherine up again.

Judge Todd leaned forward on his spring seat. "Dr. King, then you shot at this woman too?"

"Yes." Magnus gently touched the black patch on Katherine's face. "One of my shots hit Kitty in the left eye. But I really didn't want to kill her. You see, I was a dead shot in those days and at point-blank range I should not have missed her. But I just couldn't seem to get in a good shot. I tried but my hand just would not steady in."

Ransom cried it out. "Oh my God!"

Magnus' heart beat violently, irregularly. "If only our old night watchman back in Sioux City were here. Herman Bell.

He could tell you all about it. He'd know." Pause. "Oh, God, how terrible it is to have to be saying these things."

Again Ransom cried it out. "Oh my God! Now I remember." The skin around Ransom's eyes blanched to a turnip color. "It comes back to me now like a flash of gunpowder! Herman Bell's the one that scared me into running away. He said, 'Son, my God, you didn't shoot your own mother, did you?' and I said, 'Dad did,' and he said, 'Who shot your dad?' and I said, 'I did.' Now I remember. Ohh! Ohh!"

"Pop goes the weasel," a miner in the crowd whispered.

Ransom stared down at Katherine's eyeless face. "Dad shot out one eye and I shot out the other."

A terrible cry escaped Magnus.

Ransom stared at Katherine's belly. "So I slept with my own mother."

All fell back a step. Even Judge Todd drew back on his democrat. A space opened up around Magnus and Katherine and Ransom.

Ransom gulped at the air. He quivered like a baby swallow that'd been given a curdle of indigestible alkalai to eat instead of a sweet worm.

Magnus hung onto the edge of the pine coffin. "Oh, son, how I wish now I'd never found you."

Ransom whispered, "Mother." Ransom whispered, "Wife." Ransom whispered, "Even sister at times."

All the mothers in the lines above held their bellies in their arms and moaned without knowing it.

Magnus clung to the edge of the pine coffin. "Oh, son, remember, pain makes the man. And the more pain the more love."

Ransom shuddered from head to foot as though from a poisoning. "Thank God she lied to me. Now there'll be no fruit of mine growing on my own mother's tree."

Ames the newspaperman came forward a step, leaning up from the hips, eyes bright. "Did she know?"

"She's dead now."

Ames licked his lips. "Did she ever indicate to you at any time that she knew?"

"She's dead now."

"Thank you."

"Husband to my own mother. Trying to father myself on my own mother." Ransom's lips contorted against himself. "Lusting in the lust that once conceived me."

A tear rolled down across the tips of Magnus' white beard and fell on Katherine's bosom. "It's the old story. When the father isn't respected by the wife, let alone loved, all the demons of hell are let loose."

Ransom at last fixed his eyes on his father's eyes. "This makes us brothers, doesn't it?"

"Son."

"A couple of cowbirds to each other."

Magnus wept. All had gone to smash.

"Dad."

Then Maule at last couldn't hold back any longer. "Great balls of fire!" Maule was shaking. Maule was full of revulsion at what he'd heard. "Imagine! Imagine the kind of life those two must've had togeth—"

Clemens cried, "Hold the thought! That's enough."

"Any son who has known his own mother carnally"—Maule's big lower lip curled up in loathing—"why! such a son can never be expected to love another woman ever. He's been held too close to the fire to ever feel true warmth again."

Clemens cried, "Enough, I say!"

"He who has slept with his mother has had it all."

Clemens grabbed Maule roughly by the shoulder. "God-dammit, shut up! The boy's life is ruined enough as it is."

"Learning from his own mother all the wonders and varieties of love."

"Shut up!"

"Tilling his own father's soil. Horrible delights. Ancient

animal desires satiated." Maule held his stomach. "It's enough to make one's bowels boil just thinking about it."

Judge Todd shot a finger down at Maule. "Will you shut up?"

Maule didn't hear a thing. "If we don't punish this crime of all crimes, punish it with the most terrible punishment we can possibly think of, we deserve to be hung ourselves." In his outrage Maule spat a fat gob at the rocky ground. "Why, you know as well as I do that we can't be allowed to wring our own father's neck so that we can sleep with our mother, can we?"

Ames scribbled notes furiously.

"Murder most foul and most unnatural." Froth appeared at the corners of Maule's lips. "That poor poor woman, alone with her agony and her blood." Maule balled his fist at Ransom. "Fiend in human shape! By God, come to think of it, you even have the smell of one who's going to die a most cruel horrible death. Because if I have anything to say about it, this is what we're going to do to you—we're going to boil your balls in your own blood before your very own eyes."

Judge Todd picked up his gun. "Maule, damn your soul, will you shut up?"

"But couldn't he see? Couldn't he realize? The very Devil himself must have been in him."

"Maule!"

"He must've known. He must've."

Magnus cut in. "Not necessarily."

"What! Not?"

"No. A beard almost always makes a boy look older than he is. And a long dress and face powder almost always make a woman look younger than she is."

Maule lashed a finger at Magnus. "So you've got it all figured out, have you, that we're going to let him off after all?"

"Well, sir, I do speak as a doctor who has handled many patients. Besides, in ancient times, incest wasn't always frowned upon. In some instances it was considered a mark of supernatural origin."

Maule reared up on the tips of his toes. "Why, you presumptuous dirty old bastard you, you're even more guilty than the boy is then, thinking that."

Clemens said quietly, "Let him who is without sin in this matter cast the first stone."

At that the bearded miners moved back another step. Some of the miners stood with averted eyes, some with whitened nostrils. One man wrung his ear violently.

Maule still frothed over. "Are you suggesting, John, that we've all slept with our mothers?"

Clemens gave Maule a weary smile. "The first nine months we all had to."

"Good Lord, John, you know what I mean."

"Well, you invited that, Clifford. You're such a passionate pigheaded fellow sometimes."

"Well now, I resent that."

"Who is closest to us except our mother? Unless it be a sister."

"Carnally?"

"Spiritually. And this boy knew not what he did."

"Bosh! I still say that what he did is enough to stir one's blood to madness. Absolutely horrible."

Magnus stood looking at Ransom's feet. An odd grimace worked his lips. "You know, at that, I am a presumptuous dirty old bastard."

"You admit it?"

"Because I almost wish Kitty had been with child by my son."

Everybody cried it out. "What!!" Even Ransom.

Magnus looked up at Ransom. "Because now the line dies with you."

Ransom stared down at his father. "So what?"

"You're a Worthington and a King both."

Ransom laughed a short crazy laugh. "No, it does not."

Magnus' look sharpened on Ransom. "How's that again?"

"Not that it matters."

"How's that again?"

"You couldn't find her anyway."

"You mean . . . you have a child somewhere with another woman?"

"At least I couldn't find her."

"There is a girl then somewhere who has a baby by you? Your baby?"

"What difference does it make now anyway? Yes."

"Where?"

Ransom flung his hand up toward the granite spires. "In the Hills. Where else?"

"Tell me about her."

"It's nothing."

"Tell me."

"It's nothing."

"Tell!"

"Well, when I first came to the Hills here looking for gold, I ran into a wild girl. A white girl Indian-raised." The remembering made Ransom quiver in his boots. "It was she who showed me where all the gold was. The gold that made Deadwood rich." Ransom sobbed. "Goddammit to hell anyway." Ransom sobbed. "And I betrayed her. For what? For money. For gold."

Judge Todd listened with a hand cocked to his ear. Mouths fell open in the crowd. The women fell silent.

Magnus bored in. "What was her name?"

"What do you want with that? It won't do you any good anyway. You'll never find her."

"What was her name?"

"Why do you want to know?"

"That I may know her when I find her."

There was a long long pause.

A piece of rock broke off near the top of Mt. Moriah and rattled all the way down to the bottom.

At last Ransom sighed, deep, and said, "Erden Aldridge. A sweet little slip of a girl. The darling. Like a wild swallow. Like her Indian name, Ica Psin-psin-cadan. And I betrayed her."

"Where did she live?"

"In a cave."

"Where in a cave?"

"You'll never find it, so don't bother to look for it."

"Why not?"

"Because it's gone now. Just like she's gone."

"How do you know the cave is gone?"

"I can't tell you."

"Well, where do you think she went then?"

"Who knows? Probably to some wild free mountain farther west."

"The Big Horns?"

"Erden!" Ransom danced it on his salt barrel. "Erden! Oh my God, oh my little Swallow darling, what've I done to you?"

The wide pool of the deep-blue shadow crept up to Ransom's neck.

"Oh, Erden, the worst was when I took up with this other woman the second time."

"Now, now, son. One can always use two mirrors to get a proper reflection of one's self."

"Judge, for God's sake, hang me! Hang me."

Magnus gave the salt barrel a good shake. "Now, now. Steady, steady. A real stud of a man is bound to have complex tastes when it comes to women."

"Judge, please, please order Troy Barb here to hang me. I can't stand it any longer."

Troy Barb lowered his shotgun and backed off, his moon eyes softening like a guilty dog's.

"I've had enough."

Judge Todd sat all to himself.

Ransom puffed like a cross-country runner coming down the homestretch. "Judge, you've got to get rid of me. I'm a devil supreme."

Magnus gave the salt barrel another shake. "Son, we all stand in mud. But, remember, we also have our eyes fixed on heaven."

"I'd cut myself, judge, if I thought it would do any good. End this bad line of girl-fornicators and wife-killers. Let alone mother-lovers. But little Erden's got away with some of my seed. So my stones might as well hang with me."

Judge Todd grimaced the grimace of a baffled man. "It's almost a clear case of standoff."

Ransom labored for breath. He danced crazy on his salt barrel. The sound of his boots was like the rattling of two swift snare drums. "Well, if you fellows don't know what to do with me, by the Lord, I do." Ransom once more grabbed the noose and stuck his head into it and drew it up tight around his neck.

"Wait!" Magnus cried.

Ransom yelled with a powerful voice. "Erden, I'm sorry I betrayed you!" And leaping up, and giving the salt barrel beneath him a kick away, Ransom jumped. His jump was exactly like that of a boy trying for a sack swing hopelessly out of reach.

The dull sound of the drop hurt.

Ransom's head suddenly crooked sharply at the neck. His body pendulumed back and forth a few times. His eyelashes twitched. His shoulders drew up as though for a deep breath.

"Pop goes the weasel."

A peculiar rigidity set in around Ransom's half-closed eyes. His hands turned purple.

The two blue swallows made another swoop past the gallows.

Ransom's body hung motionless.

Ames folded up his notes. "Well, back to the cases." Ames started walking toward the print shop up the street.

The next day Magnus borrowed a spade, and alone, despite a bad back, dug two graves on the upper slopes of Mt. Moriah.

Magnus first covered the body of his wife Kitty. "Sex plus pain plus love."

Magnus next covered the body of his son Roddy. "Sex is yes and pain is no and love is triumph. The smiling lips. The wincing eyes. The sweet acid in the skull."

Magnus whittled two names on a common board and nailed the board on a nearby pine tree. "All too soon no one will remember what these names stood for. Well, that's America for you. Better to carry the blood than the name."

Later Magnus went up the gulch going west. "Erden should make the perfect mother. A white girl Indian-raised."

When a son's blood is finally spilled, which mother weeps most?

The stallions.

January 6, 1966
Blue Mound
Luverne, Minnesota

ABOUT THE AUTHOR

Frederick Feikema Manfred was born January 6, 1912, on a Siouxland farm north of Doon, Iowa, in Rock township, just a few miles from the Minnesota and South Dakota borders. Mr. Manfred is the oldest of six brothers. His mother died in 1929; his father now lives in California.

He was educated in northwest Iowa until he attended Calvin College, Grand Rapids, Michigan, from which he graduated in 1934. From then until 1937 he wandered back and forth across America, from New York to Los Angeles, stopping off now and then to fill jobs which ran the entire gamut of temporary employment. In May, 1937, he became a reporter for the *Minneapolis Journal*. In 1939 he did social work and opinion polls. In 1942 he married Maryanna Shorba; they now have three children, Freya, Marya, and Frederick.

In 1943, Mr. Manfred, concluding that it was now or never, devoted full time and energy to writing. Since then he has published seventeen books, including the novels *Lord Grizzly, Riders of Judgment, Conquering Horse, Scarlet Plume, Morning Red*, and the trilogy *Wanderlust*. He has received many grants and writing fellowships, from such sponsors as the American Academy of Arts and Letters and the Huntington Hartford Foundation. Until 1951 he wrote under the pen name of Feike Feikema, an old Frisian family name, of which Frederick Manfred is a translation. In Frisian genealogy his full name is Feike Feikes Feikema VII.

Mr. Manfred has lived in the Upper Midlands, mostly in Siouxland, all his life. He likes gardening, fixing fence, and chopping wood; and enjoys taking long rambling walks alone through the countryside.

The Buckskin Man Tales
by Frederick Manfred

Conquering Horse
Lord Grizzly
Scarlet Plume
King of Spades
Riders of Judgment

All available in Gregg Press editions.